END ZONE

THE DEEP STATE SERIES: BOOK 3

DC ALDEN

GLOSSARY

AAR: After Action Review
AFB: Air Force Base
APC: Armoured Personnel Carrier
BSO: Basic Security Option
CDC: Centres for Disease Control and Prevention
CentCom: Central Command
CIA: Central Intelligence Agency
CQB: Close Quarter Battle
DDO: Deputy Director of Operations (CIA)
DEVGRU: The Naval Special Warfare Development Group/SEAL Team Six
DOD: Department Of Defence
EOD: Explosive Ordinance Disposal
GAT: General Aviation Terminal (private)
GDP: Gross Domestic Product
HAHO: High Altitude High Opening
HVT: High Value Target
JDAM: Joint Direct Attack Munition
Jefe: (*Spanish*) A boss or leader
JSOC: Joint Special Operations Command
JSOTF: Joint Special Operations Task Force

JSOTF HQ: Joint Special Operations Task Force Headquarters

Langley: CIA Headquarters, Langley, Virginia

LZ: Landing Zone

M4 CQBR: Close Quarter Battle Receiver (Colt M4 infantry rifle variant)

MI5: Military Intelligence 5 - UK Domestic Intelligence Service

MRE: Meals Ready to Eat

NSA: National Security Agency

NVD: Night Vision Device

NVG: Night Vision Goggles

Op: Operation (Military)

OTC: Operator Training Course (Delta Force)

PNG: Persona Non Grata

ROE: Rules Of Engagement

Rucks: Rucksack

SAD: Special Activities Division (CIA)

SATCOM: Satellite Communications (equipment)

SecDef: Secretary of Defence

SecState: Secretary of State

SITREP: Report on current military situation

SOCOM: United States Special Operations Command

"Just because you do not take an interest in politics doesn't mean politics won't take an interest in you."

Pericles

LAB RAT

Dave Piper squeezed the knife a little tighter as the footsteps drew closer.

He had no idea who it was. The shop doorway was deep and dark, and he lay still, curled up inside his sleeping bag with his back to the street. Out there the rain still hammered down. Tactically he was at a disadvantage, but clutching the small knife gave him some comfort. If he kept still, whoever it was might just piss off.

It was after midnight, and Dave was on the verge of slipping into an exhausted sleep when he'd heard the vehicle pull into the kerb. He'd listened to the idling engine, the drum of windscreen wipers, the clunk of an opening door. Then came the footsteps.

It wouldn't be the police, he knew that much. Central London was virtually overrun with rough sleepers and the police had long given up trying to move them on. Trespass, shoplifting, drug use; Old Bill turned a blind eye to most things these days.

So that left two options.

The first would be the outreach do-gooders, who sniffed around alleyways and basements, trying to coax the homeless into drop-in centres or hostels, but Dave wasn't interested. They asked too many questions and stuck their noses in where they didn't belong. Even when the temperature plummeted, and the ice was thick on the pavements, Dave knew of a hundred warm air vents and underground car parks where he could bed down in relative comfort. So if the footsteps belonged to a Good Samaritan, Dave Piper would politely but firmly tell them to get lost.

Then again, it might be the second option; trouble.

The footsteps stopped close by. Dave heard quiet breathing in the dark and wondered what was coming. Maybe a stream of hot piss, or several sharp kicks to the ribs, accompanied by vicious encouragement and hoots of laughter. If it came to that, Dave was ready. He gripped the knife tighter and lay like a stone.

'Hello? Is anyone in there?'

A woman. Dave wrestled his upper body out of the sleeping bag. The knife was still in his hand, out of sight. Women couldn't be trusted either. A bitter, vengeful bitch was the reason Dave Piper had lost everything and dropped off the grid in the first place.

He stared at the figure standing over him, saw the ponytail at the back of her head, though her face remained in shadow.

'What d'you want?'

'My name's Marion. It's okay, I'm not with the police or anything.'

A do-gooder. 'I don't need help. I just want to be left alone.'

Marion crouched down next to him, but not too close, Dave noticed. He knew he smelled rank.

'I'm looking for volunteers, for a health initiative that's being run by Westminster Council.' She held up an ID card. 'We're studying the long-term effects of street living, poor diet, hygiene, that sort of thing.'

Dave reached between his legs and scratched at the lice. 'I told you, I'm not interested.'

'You'll be paid for your participation.'

Dave's eyes narrowed. 'How much?'

Marion reached inside her jacket and pulled out a roll of notes. She peeled one off and held it out.

Dave snatched it from her fingers and held it up. *A fifty-pound note.* He felt the crispness of the paper, held it under his nose. Cash had a certain smell and texture, and in another life Dave's addiction had been money. He ran his tongue over cracked lips, his mouth suddenly dry.

'What's this for?'

'A sign of good faith. There's another four-hundred and fifty if you join the program. And you'll be paid cash, no questions asked.'

Dave dropped the knife and sat upright. Hot, fetid air escaped from the folds of his sleeping bag. Marion stood up to avoid the stench.

'What's the catch?'

'No catch. What's your name?'

'Dave.'

'Well, Dave, it would mean accompanying me and the other volunteers to our facility outside London. You'll be served hot meals and snacks and you'll be assigned your own room, complete with en-suite facilities and Sky TV. All we want in return is your permission to conduct a medical. Nothing intrusive; blood pressure, lung capacity, a few samples, urine, blood, stool, etcetera. We'll also be measuring your sleep patterns.'

'That's it? Because I don't want anyone's finger up my arse.'

Marion grinned. 'No, it's nothing like that. You'll be well looked after, and when it's over you'll get some new clothes and a brand new sleeping bag. How does that sound?'

'And the cash, right? The four-fifty?'

'Of course.'

Dave threw back the sleeping bag and scrambled to his feet. 'Fuck it, I'm in.'

HE WOKE WITH A START, JOLTING FORWARD AS THE DRIVER pumped the minibus brakes.

He rubbed his eyes, then shoved a hand down his filthy jeans, his fingers probing for the fifty-pound note. It was still there, tucked deep inside his rotten underpants, and he relaxed a little.

He watched the vehicle's wipers sweep back and forth, beating off the rain. He felt the vehicle turn as the headlights swept over tall brick pillars and large black gates. One of them was open, and Dave glimpsed a figure in a hooded rain-coat waving as the van drove past. He twisted in his seat to get a better look but the rear window was steamed up with condensation. It didn't matter. Wherever they were going, Dave figured they'd arrived.

He sat a little straighter, watching the road ahead as it wound through dark woods. Classical music played quietly on the radio and green digits glowed in the dark; almost three in the morning. Dave saw Marion lean over and mumble something to the driver, a hulking, bearded silhouette who wore latex gloves, just like Marion. The driver grinned and nodded, and Dave wondered what she'd said to him. Dave got the impression it was about their cargo, and that wasn't very polite. *Bitch.*

He clocked the faces of the other volunteers around him and saw a mixture of apprehension and excitement as dirty hands swiped at the foggy windows. As the minibus slowed, Dave was distracted by the building ahead. He knew a thing or two about property. Back in the day he was Charlie Big Bollocks, king of the East Sussex developers. Well, maybe *king* was an exaggeration, but life had been good once, and the money had poured in. Then came the parties, the cocaine, the affairs, the terrible investments, the slags at Customs and Excise, the divorce, the bloodsucking lawyers. That life was ancient fucking history, but Dave still recognised quality real estate when he saw it.

The minibus crunched to a halt on a wide gravel drive. Marion climbed out and yanked the side door open. Cold air snatched away the warm, comforting stench.

'This is it. Follow me, please.'

Dave ducked out into the pouring rain and stood off to one side. Cold rain streamed down his face as he squinted up at the darkened building, at the tall windows and chimney stacks, the chipped and weather-beaten portico. No lights, anywhere. Odd.

'Come on, pal.'

The big lump with the beard was waving at him. Dave followed the others, their feet crunching on wet gravel as they followed a high stone wall to a heavy-looking wooden gate. Dave funnelled through with the others, expecting to see manicured rear gardens. What he wasn't expecting was a concrete staircase. Dave reached out for the cold, wet handrail and followed the others down into a gloomy corridor. A couple of naked yellow bulbs hung from the low ceiling, throwing everything else into shadow. He smelled cold earth and rain, and his breath fogged on the dank air. Marion held open another door and waved them through.

'Inside, please.'

Dave was the last to enter the room; another low-ceilinged basement. Marion followed him inside, slamming the door behind her. A row of trestle tables stretched across the room, each with a large brown wheelie bin next to it. Dave counted twelve. One for each of them.

'Choose a station and put any valuables into the plastic tray provided,' Marion told them. 'Once you've done that, take off your clothes and put them in the bins. That includes hats, blankets, sleeping bags, anything you brought with you.'

'You want us to strip off here?' Dave asked.

Marion smiled and nodded. 'It's hygiene protocol. You'll also notice a small EpiPen on each table. That's a tetanus shot, which one of my team will administer. Once you've had that, I'll take you through to the shower area. Fresh clothes will be issued afterwards, and a hot breakfast served in the canteen.'

Dave headed towards a table. He dug into his crotch and unfolded the fifty-pound note, smoothing it out and laying it carefully in the tray while he glanced at the others. They were already getting undressed, kicking off their filthy shoes and clothes. Dave did the same, scooping up his garments and dropping them into the bin.

'How much did they promise you?'

Dave turned to his left. She had a shaved head, and her loose, naked flesh was heavily tattooed and dotted with sores. Most of her teeth were missing and her eyes were bloodshot. Mid-thirties, Dave figured. Life on the street often added at least ten years.

'Five hundred quid,' he whispered from the corner of his mouth.

'Yeah, me too. My name's Lem. As in lemon.'

'Dave.'

'I saw you get in the van. Any idea where we are?'

'None, and I don't give a fuck as long as I get that money.'

Lem offered a toothless grin and leaned closer. 'I've got a rock of crack tucked up my fanny. We can hit it later if you like.'

'Sounds good,' Dave said, giving her a wink. He'd probably fuck her too, which would be a bonus. She wasn't a looker, not by any standard, but beggars were definitely not choosers. He sniggered at his own joke.

'Stand still, please.'

A man in a surgical mask with a long grey ponytail picked

up the EpiPen on Lem's table. He wiped her upper arm with a swab and jabbed her with the small needle. Lem didn't flinch, Dave noticed. She was used to needles.

Ponytail placed the used EpiPen back on the table and stood in front of Dave. 'Arm, please.'

Dave twisted his shoulder. Ponytail wiped his upper arm clean. 'Why's mine blue?'

Ponytail's eyes narrowed. 'Excuse me?'

Dave cocked his head towards Lem. 'Her needle had a white label. Mine's blue.'

Ponytail shrugged. 'Different batch, probably. Stand still.'

He jabbed Dave's arm. Dave winced, and Ponytail moved on to the next table. Dave watched him, and at one point the man glanced back at him. *You're a wrong 'un*, Dave thought.

Marion addressed the room. 'Is everyone ready?'

Dave cupped his privates, shivering in the cold. Others stood brazenly, tits and cocks on display. Dave wasn't that shameless, nor that well-endowed for that matter. He kept his eyes front as Marion pointed across the room.

'Let's get you through the showers. Then you can all eat and relax.'

Dave hadn't noticed it before; a big green door, with a thick handle and ringed with rusty rivets. The bearded driver held it open, and its thickness reminded Dave of the door on a bank vault. He felt uneasy, and not for the first time. There was Marion's quiet joke with the driver, then the odd look from Ponytail. Something wasn't right. As the others filed into the darkness beyond, Dave hesitated.

Marion appeared next to him. 'In you go. Nothing to be nervous about.'

'Yeah, come on.' Lem patted Dave's bony arse and winked. He remembered the rock and followed her inside.

The floor was cold beneath his feet. The door swung closed behind him with a heavy thump, shutting out the light. Dave's heart began to race. He swallowed to clear his ears.

'Soundproofing,' a voice muttered from somewhere in the inky blackness. 'I used to be a session musician back in the day. Worked a lot of studios.'

'Worked a lot of gear too,' cackled a woman in a thick Scottish accent. Nervous laughter filled the dead air.

Then the lights snapped on, just four small yellow bulbs sunk into the ceiling. Dave blinked. The room was much bigger than he'd imagined, and he saw they'd formed a tight, naked group near the door. As people began to spread out, Dave ran his hand along the wall, feeling the smoothness of the yellowed tiles. The same tiles covered the floor and ceiling, where a dozen deflated black balloons dangled from brass nozzles.

Balloons?

Lem jumped up, her dog-eared boobs flapping as she tried to grab one.

'*Do not touch the apparatus,*' crackled a disembodied voice.

'Put the fucking water on!' the Scottish woman snapped back. She was short and dumpy, with a bird's nest of wild red hair. 'We're freezing our tits off in here!'

Dave searched for the source of the voice. There were no windows, just muffled air and thick walls. A sudden wave of claustrophobia washed over him. He swallowed hard. He wasn't used to being confined, especially below ground. The smell of fresh, wet earth had followed them into the chamber. Panic bubbled. Dave wanted out.

He marched towards the door. There was no handle, so he banged it with a bony fist. 'Hey, open the door! I've changed my mind!'

'It's alright,' Lem said, scrambling to his side. 'The water will come on any second, you'll see.'

'*Stand by,*' said the voice, and Lem gummed a smile at Dave. She took his hand and led him beneath one of the brass nozzles. '*The rubber seals are part of the hygiene protocol,*'

8

explained the voice. *'Momentarily they will fill with air and then the showers will begin. Thank you for your patience.'*

'Get tae fuck!' snarled the Scottish woman, then she bellowed with laughter.

Pipes clunked and groaned somewhere above them, then the balloons began to inflate. Dave found himself watching the black orb grow larger, saw the liquid sloshing about inside, heard the creak of the expanding rubber. They were going to burst, and Dave stepped back, as did a couple of others.

'Come on!' another voice shouted. 'Get on with it!'

The balloons swelled. Pops rippled around the room, and the air was suddenly filled with a fine mist.

'What the fuck is this?' Dave whispered. The mist settled on his skin. He wiped his arm, leaving a long thin streak of dirt. He watched Lem do the same. She looked up at Dave. Her eyes were bloodshot, and he saw a pattern of blue veins snake across her neck and chest. She stepped closer, then jammed a filthy finger deep into Dave's eye socket.

Dave screamed and staggered backwards. 'You fucking bitch!'

Lem came after him, raking her filthy nails against his face and chest. Dave swung his fist, catching Lem on the jaw and knocking her to the tiles. More screams filled the dead air as the room erupted into sudden, savage violence. Dave staggered to the door.

'Help me! Let me out!' he screamed, but his cries were lost in the furious roar that filled the chamber. He spun around, a hand cupped over his left eye, the blood running through his fingers and down his arm. He saw the Scottish woman leap onto the back of a man with long dark hair who tried desperately to throw her off. She vomited all over him, then slipped to the floor, her screams unintelligible. Everyone was fighting, clawing, biting. Dave shrunk into a corner, his skin crawling with terror. Then, almost as quickly as it had started, the violence stopped. The terrible screaming suddenly faded to nothing. Even the wounded barely uttered a sound.

Dave whimpered. They were looking at him, all of them, a blood-soaked mob of stark naked lunatics. They moved slowly towards him, eyes wide, their hands like bloody claws as they closed in like a tightening noose.

'No!' Dave screamed. 'Please!'

And then they charged. He tried to fight them off, kicking out and swinging his fists, but they swarmed all over him, yanking the hair from his head in bloody clumps, gouging out his other eye. Hot vomit splashed over his face and chest. He felt an arm wrenched from its socket, and screamed as his balls were ripped from between his legs. He felt teeth sinking deep into his flesh, felt fingers in his mouth, pulling, clawing, tearing.

Dave stopped struggling. He wanted it over.

The others ripped him to pieces.

'SAFE TO SAY THAT THE FIELD TRIALS ARE A SUCCESS,' MARION announced, watching the CCTV monitor.

'When do we do this for real?' asked Ponytail. His name was Terry, and the greasy rat tail that hung from the back of his skull was the only hair he had left. The other twelve members of the newly formed *Global Liberation Front* were a mixed group of men and women of various ages, all of whom had been convicted of violence against the state in the name of animal liberation or the survival of the planet. They were extremists in every sense of the word, but Marion could tell by their faces that the last few weeks had taken a heavy toll. It was time to say something.

'You've all worked very hard, and at considerable risk. You've witnessed some very strange, and at times disturbing events here, but it hasn't been for nothing. Mother Nature is in trouble, we all know that. She needs someone to fight for her, and if the governments of the world refuse to take up that challenge, then it's up to us. Am I right?'

'Too bloody right,' Terry said, looking at the others.

Marion pointed to the CCTV monitor. 'This is the game changer. This will focus the world's attention and steer us away from the precipice.'

No one spoke for a moment. The only noise in the room was coming from the chamber below, the sounds of feet slapping against tiles, the grunts and snarls of the infected as they marched in a circle around the room.

'When do we get to tell our families?'

It was Olivia, a twenty-something in jeans and a combat jacket. Her face was pale, her blond dreadlocks tied in a thick knot behind her head. 'After all, they'll need time to adjust, right? Prepare themselves for what's coming.'

'Livvy's right,' said a silver-haired academic type in glasses and a thick cardigan. 'The spread of infection is almost immediate. Things will collapse pretty quickly. We need to tell our loved ones about the Refuge, how to get there, what to bring — '

'You can tell them soon, once we leave this place.' Marion explained. 'Of course, some will be resistant to our plans, which is why only Terry will be given the location. After we leave here, you'll liaise directly with him.'

'And use your common sense,' Terry warned them, tapping a finger against the side of his head. 'After the collapse of society we'll need individuals who'll be able to adjust quickly to a pastoral world. We'll need strong people, both physically and mentally, and women of child-bearing age. We can't afford to carry any dead weight, so no cripples or coffin-dodgers. Right, Marion?'

Marion nodded. 'Terry's right. We're building a new world from the ground up. It's going to be difficult enough without adding unnecessary burdens.' She looked around the room. 'Any other questions?'

'What do we do about that lot?'

Terry pointed at the CCTV feed, where the infected were still circumnavigating the room.

'Dispose of them, same as the others. I'm sure this will be the last batch.'

Marion saw relief on their faces. They'd gassed and incinerated at least a hundred people in the last two months. They needed to know there was light at the end of the tunnel. After all, this wasn't Auschwitz.

'Thank you, Marion.' Terry turned to the others and clapped his hands. 'Right, let's get to work.'

Just before she left the room, Marion paused in the doorway. Everyone stopped to listen as she looked back at them and smiled.

'Stay focused, and stay positive, everyone. The new world is almost upon us.'

BUNKER MENTALITY

'TWO OF THE MORE SIGNIFICANT QUESTIONS ABOUT THIS phenomena concern the levels of sexual activity and the capacity for non-vocalised language, which can be an indicator of reproductive strategy and group dynamics. Language is arguably the hallmark human trait, and from the limited footage I've seen, it's clear that some kind of proto-language is being employed.'

Coffman glared across the conference table at Curtis Stringer, the ageing Nobel Prize-winning Paleoanthropologist. 'In English, please professor.'

Stringer scratched at his straggly grey beard. 'My apologies, Madam President. Let me put it another way...'

As Stringer continued, Coffman's mind began to drift. Her National Security Council had occupied the secure conference room for almost two hours now and the President hated being below ground. She wasn't claustrophobic, but the more time she spent inside the bunker located beneath the north lawn, the more she craved fresh air and sunlight.

She'd been President for less than six months, and according to the latest polls she'd dealt admirably with the fallout from Baghdad. Medals had been pinned to American

13

chests and much praise heaped upon the Iraqi people. The Aswad government had been duly rewarded with billions of dollars of clean-up money and infrastructure development. Coffman had attended more memorials than the five previous presidents combined, and in doing so had ingratiated herself with the American people. They were actually using the word *love,* according to the latest focus group data, a bizarre concept for any politician, but if the soccer-moms of America had her back, she was going to exploit that approval to the full. Because with love came trust, and once she had that, Amy Coffman could pretty much get away with anything.

And then came the video, just as the political waters were losing their chop. It was the reason she was meeting with her NSC below ground, why Coffman had the world's foremost Paleoanthropologist smuggled in under a blanket of total secrecy.

Baghdad was coming back to haunt her.

She refocussed her attention on the ageing academic.

'…violent tendencies, so in conclusion, this phenomenon is proving to be both fascinating and deeply troubling. The virus has the ability to strip away hundreds of thousands of years of human evolution, resulting in something that resembles pre-Neanderthal behaviour and cognitive function, as found in the sub-species *Homo heidelbergensis,* hence the reference to the *H-1 virus* in my report. As for the group circular movement behaviour, that's still a mystery. There's nothing in human history that can explain such a regression and associated behaviour.'

Coffman waved a hand. 'Thank you, Curtis. Someone will show you out.'

The President looked around the room. Stringer's now-vacated seat aside, every other chair was occupied. Flanking Coffman were Karen Baranski, her former head of State Department Operations and now her National Security Advisor, and Erik Mulholland, her ever-loyal Chief of Staff. To

Erik's right was another ally, Admiral Charlie Schultz, Chairman of the Joint Chiefs, and Drew Clark, Coffman's Secretary of Defence. The others were all National Security Council principal committee members; the Secretaries of State, Treasury, Energy, Homeland Security, the Attorney General, the Director of National Intelligence, the Director of the Central Intelligence Agency, and the United States Ambassador to the United Nations. A security full-house.

Before anyone could talk, Coffman pushed back her chair and walked around the table, stopping in front of the TV on the wall. An image from the Baghdad drone footage was frozen on the screen, the infected circling an indiscriminate structure in the embassy compound like a giant human doughnut. Coffman could feel the anger building. She assumed all this was behind her. She assumed, wrongly, that she could control something like this. She had underestimated Mother Nature, like so many before her.

'Play the video again,' she ordered.

Coffman remained standing, her arms folded across her chest, as she watched the man in the black ski mask and sunglasses appear on another screen. He represented a group called the *Global Liberation Front,* and the email was the second one they'd received via a now-obsolete email address bounced from a chain of dark-web servers that no longer existed. The first email, received almost eight weeks after the destruction of the Baghdad embassy, had been shocking enough; a video of Marine Lance Corporal Hector Nunez, locked inside some sort of fish tank as he vomited blood and fluids and vented unholy screams. A living, breathing, fast-moving bio-weapon, now in the hands of terrorists.

The second email had arrived just a few hours ago, and it contained a list of demands; the immediate shutdown of all fossil fuel industries, an end to deforestation, mineral mining, chemical and industrial dye manufacturing, a total ban on commercial air travel, the internal combustion engine, and most bizarre of all, the artificial inducement of a meat allergy into the general populations of the western world in order to curb the impact of intensive meat farming. Coffman had almost laughed out loud at that one; try selling that to the hamburger-loving American public. According to the eco nut-jobs, the implementation of those demands would ensure an end to rising temperatures and man-made climate change. They would also ensure the death of the global economy.

Three months, that's all they had. Three months to dismantle western civilisation.

'Who the hell are these people?' Coffman asked.

All heads turned to CIA director James Buchanan. 'We have no intelligence on the group at all, Madam President. They're clearly the new kids on the eco-terrorism block. Video analysis confirms that this Philip character is not an Arab; he's European, either a German or Austrian, possibly Swiss or Dutch. All of those countries have very strong environmental movements whose fringe elements have employed direct action in the past.'

'So, how does a homicidal Swiss tree-hugger find himself standing in the rubble of the US embassy in Baghdad? And more crucially, how does he smuggle an infected and highly contagious Marine out of the country without anyone noticing?'

It was a rhetorical question, Coffman knew. The intelligence apparatus of the United States had been trying to unravel that ball of string since video number one, with little success.

'The window of opportunity was extremely tight,' Admiral Schultz reminded the room.

Like the others he was dressed in civilian clothes, a demand made by Coffman. They had to keep this off the radar, which was why they were meeting on a Sunday morning. The last thing anyone needed was for this to go public.

'We had boots on the ground four hours after the blast,' Schultz said. 'Whoever took him had to move quickly.'

'And the drone footage gave us nothing?' Coffman asked.

'Afraid not, ma'am. The Green Zone was hidden beneath a cloud of dust for much of the day.'

'There *has* to be some Iraqi involvement in this,' insisted Secretary of State Jayne Pascoe. 'This is their back yard after all.'

Coffman shook her head. 'This has nothing to do with the Aswad Administration.'

Pascoe frowned. 'With all due respect, Madam President, how can you be so sure?'

Because the Aswads were in on the whole thing, she thought but didn't say. 'We've earmarked billions in compensation and reconstruction over there, Jayne. The Iraqi government wouldn't jeopardise that.'

Pascoe didn't look convinced. 'A rogue element, then. Hard-liners unaligned to the Aswads, perhaps?'

'That's a more probable scenario,' Coffman admitted. She walked around the table and retook her seat. 'We'll get to *how* in due course. Our priority now is to find Nunez.'

Drew Clark spoke next. She was the first female Secretary of Defence in US history, an appointment that boosted Coffman's progressive credentials, but the president cared little for political correctness except when it suited her. She chose people for their skills, their ability to take orders, and their loyalty to her cause. Clark was such a creature, a graduate of the University of Notre Dame with a masters in political science. A former diplomat in Coffman's State Department, Clark's twenty-one years of service in the US Army made her a shoe-in for her role as the nation's military attack dog. Physically she was tall, almost six feet, and she wore thick-framed glasses and a bob haircut. She habitually wore grey trouser suits — a colour that matched Clark's demeanour — over a figure that was devoid of any womanly curves. And when she spoke, her Minnesotan accent was buried beneath a career shaped by international travel and diplomatic service.

'From a military perspective we've got Iraq under the microscope,' Clark told them. 'Global Hawks are providing aerial reconnaissance twenty-four-seven, and right now the Iraqis are living under an invisible dome of surveillance. We also have a JSOC element embedded with the Fifth Fleet in the Gulf, ready to deploy if we need them.'

'Every intelligence asset we have over there is working the problem,' Buchanan added, 'but without a detailed brief I doubt they'll make much progress.'

'If it were me, I would've got Nunez out that same day,' Schultz told the room. 'My opinion? He's being held else-where, the Middle East, possibly Europe or North Africa.'

'What about here?' Mulholland speculated. 'Maybe they put him on a boat, shipped him across the pond. It's possible, right?'

Coffman glanced at her Chief of Staff. She could see the uncertainty in his face, the flicker of fear in his eyes. Despite his assurances, Coffman believed Erik was still troubled by the event. After all, he'd witnessed the horror in real time.

Across the table, Homeland Security chief Diane Grady waved Erik's concern away. 'Highly unlikely. Port of entry checks are very robust.'

'Would you stake your career on it?' Schultz countered. 'Last time I looked, our southern border is still leaking like a tin roof in a monsoon.' Schultz turned to the President. 'As this asshole in the video said, they're prepared for the *End Times*. They're ready to pull the trigger, Madam President, and the clock is ticking.'

'Then we'd better start preparations. At the very least we need a plan in place, to give the impression that we're cooper-ating with their demands. A plan that'll buy us time to continue the hunt for Nunez.'

'Do they even need Nunez?' Mulholland asked the room.

'You heard the man; *Nunez's body fluids will find their way into the human food chain.* They could take a syringe filled with Nunez's blood and inject it into food, like a coffee pot in a diner somewhere. People will still get infected, right?'

Coffman looked at the faces around the table and saw them all imagining that very thing. No one answered the question.

'What happens when we find them? Do we have a plan?' Grady asked.

'Depends where they are,' Buchanan answered, 'but we'll need a team on point, preferably from CIA's Special Operations Group. SOCOM can provide additional support and logistics. That okay with you, Drew?'

Clark nodded. 'Absolutely. Anything you need.'

'Set it up,' Coffman ordered.

They debated the subject for another thirty minutes before the President called a halt to the meeting. When the door finally closed, only Coffman, Mulholland, Baranski, Schultz and Clark remained.

'We have three months,' Coffman reiterated, 'or witness a pandemic the like of which we've never seen before.'

'Unless we find the bastards first,' Schultz growled. 'Ma'am, you've just ordered the biggest and most intrusive surveillance operation the world has ever seen. Finding these GLF assholes is the priority now. It's just a matter of time.'

'A commodity we don't have,' Coffman reminded the Admiral.

'And when we do?' It was Clark this time. 'Find them, I mean. What if it's a foreign country whose government will not cooperate? What's the plan for that?'

Schultz shrugged. 'We drop a Tomahawk on them anyway.'

'That's an act of war, Charlie.' Behind her glasses, Clark's brown eyes switched to Coffman. 'And what about Nunez?'

The President sighed. 'Charlie's right, we need to eliminate the threat instantaneously. The Nunez family believe he died in Baghdad anyway, and rescuing a highly infectious casualty in a combat situation seems like a pretty stupid thing to do.'

'What about the fallout?' Baranski asked. 'Is there a chance a missile strike could spread the infection?'

'It didn't in Baghdad. Maybe extreme heat kills this thing.'

'What if we can't use a missile?' Mulholland asked. 'What if they're hiding Nunez in a city? What happens if they cut him loose on the New York subway? How could we even combat that kind of threat?'

'We nuke the city.'

All eyes turned to the white-haired Schultz. Coffman broke the stunned silence. 'First Tomahawks and now nukes, Charlie? Come on.'

'An out-of-control bio-weapon is something that's been gamed many times by the war planners, ma'am. And Erik has raised a valid point; imagine Nunez spraying his shit all over a carload of rush hour commuters. How many could he infect before he was stopped? Fifty? A hundred? Next thing you know there's a thousand homicidal maniacs pouring out of the subway into Times Square. The only way to stop it cold would be to use tactical nukes. Or fuel air ordinance.'

Erik looked like he was going to throw up. Baranski and Clark had paled significantly. As far as Coffman was concerned, the solution made perfect sense.

'You're telling me that plans exist for such a scenario?'

Schultz nodded. 'Back in the day, an outbreak situation would be managed by containment and isolation, but advances in bio-weaponry, delivery systems and contemporary culture has influenced the war planners' thinking to a significant degree.' The admiral smiled and said, 'they call it the Zombie Protocol.'

Clark was the first to speak. 'You can't be serious. The Pentagon has war-gamed *zombie* scenarios?'

'Forget the word and its flippant connotations for a moment,' Schultz cautioned, turning to the SecDef. 'You and I faced off against the Russians during the Cold War, remember? Chemical weapons were a frightening scenario back then, all those blood, blister and nerve agents the Soviet Union had stockpiled in massive quantities, ready to use against us.' Schultz tapped his finger on the table. 'What we're dealing with here is not so different. This H-1 virus is nothing more than a commutable bio-weapon that turns the host into a highly-infectious, prehistoric killer. And what do you do when ten thousand of those maniacs pour across the Brooklyn Bridge towards the most densely populated borough in New York?'

'You blow the goddamn bridge.'

Schultz turned and smiled. 'See? Erik gets it.'

Coffman raised a surprised eyebrow at her Chief of Staff. He shrugged and said, 'We can't afford to take any chances, right?'

'And what if H-1 is released in a dozen different cities?' Coffman countered. 'What do we do then, Erik? Nuke them all? Do we nuke the Canadians and Mexicans if our borders are threatened? Where does it end?'

Mulholland ran a hand through his thick grey hair. 'I'm thinking aloud, that's all.'

Coffman turned back to Schultz. 'Did they game-plan a multiple-target scenario, Charlie?'

'They did. A two-city attack, one on each coast.'

'And the nuclear option was used both times?'

'Only in the Manhattan scenario. The tall buildings, they helped to contain the fallout. California was different, a lot of real estate with a widely dispersed population. Artillery and fuel-air explosives were deployed successfully but there was some leakage. Ultimately the attack succeeded.'

Once again, Coffman cursed her luck. How many newly-elected presidents were forced to consider the prospect of nuking their own people in the first six months of their presidency? Then again, she thanked her lucky stars that she was on the inside, the ultimate decision-maker. The buck stopped with her, and she was glad of it. *This is what you wanted*, she reminded herself. And then there was another question, one that Coffman knew the others would also want the answer to.

'This *zombie* scenario, Charlie. What happens if it can't be controlled? If it becomes so widespread that society disintegrates and everything goes to hell. Like in the movies. Have we got a plan for that?'

Schultz nodded his head and smiled. 'Believe it or not, yes we do. And it doesn't involve living underground either.'

For the first time in almost three hours, Amy Coffman finally had some good news.

PHILIP STOOD BENEATH HIS UMBRELLA AS HE WATCHED A COLD rain front sweep across the Sachsenhausen Forest. The low clouds were keeping the dawn at bay, and impenetrable shadows lingered between the surrounding trees where men with guns stood guard. This was to be a private ceremony after all.

He watched the forklift truck bounce and sway through the trees towards the rectangular hole in the ground. The clearing was several hundred yards from the main house and far enough from any of the paths that criss-crossed the estate. It was as remote as the conditions and terrain would allow, and Philip was confident their activities would pass unnoticed.

The forklift rocked to a halt by the hole in the ground. Ten of Philip's people stepped forward and manhandled the containment unit off the forks and onto the muddy ground, threading thick ropes through the unit's strongpoints. On a signal from Philip, they dragged the containment unit to the edge of the hole and lowered it into the ground. The ropes followed it, and Philip stepped forward. They surrounded the grave, their faces unseen, the rain running off their dark hooded slickers, and Philip was reminded of other times and other rituals. Perhaps those days would return, he mused. Perhaps.

He looked down. Fifteen feet below his mud-caked boots, Lance Corporal Hector Nunez stared back at him through the reinforced glass panel of the containment unit, his toothless mouth opening and closing like a dying fish, his fingers brushing against the safety glass. His body squirmed a little, but the thrashing intensity Nunez had once possessed was gone, along with a lung, a kidney, both his legs and one arm.

As the rain drummed against Philip's umbrella he felt a twinge of sadness for the American, but it lasted for just a moment. He gave the order. He stepped back as the thick pipe that dangled into the grave shuddered. He watched Nunez bare his toothless gums in a final gesture of defiance before the containment unit disappeared beneath a steady stream of liquid concrete. After twenty-four cubic metres of wet slurry had been pumped into the hole, the hose was retracted and the digger moved in, piling the freshly-dug earth back into the unmarked grave. Philip waited, until the ground had been flattened, until the new saplings had been planted across the clearing and the earth returned to its original state. He waited until the vehicles had wound their way back to the Schloss, until his people had trudged out of sight. And then Philip waited a little longer, until the gentle rhythms of the forest had returned, the sigh of the wind through the firs, the steady drip of rainwater, the musical chorus of wild birds as they greeted the new day.

Order had been restored, and as a proud Pole of German descent, Philip respected order above all things.

As he followed the path back to the distant Schloss, he thought about the days ahead. There was much work to do; the house had to be cleaned and mothballed, all traces of their recent habitation erased before the property could be vacated and secured. Then they would head south, to the compound on the outskirts of Vienna.

Where all the sacrificial lambs had gathered in one convenient location.

CRASH TEST DUMMIES

Marion came down the stairs, a large rucksack slung over her shoulder, head-counting the members of the Global Liberation Front's UK branch as they waited in the dark-panelled lobby of Scotton Manor. All there, she saw, all twelve of them. Good.

She'd spent the last hour packing her things and scrubbing the bathroom and door handles with bleach. She'd worn latex gloves for much of her time at the Manor, as had Lucas, but one couldn't be too careful.

'Good, you're all here.'

'Ready to go,' Terry confirmed. He was surrounded by the others, all huddled together in winter coats and hats, bags piled at their feet. Lucas entered the lobby via the heavy front door and a blast of cold wind.

'The minibus is all topped up,' he told Marion.

'I hope you gave it a good clean,' Terry said. 'Those tramps were ripe. I don't fancy sitting in there for an hour wrapped in their stink.'

'She's fresh as a daisy,' Lucas told him.

Marion stood by the front door. 'Right, let's make a move then, shall we?'

The dreadlocked Olivia was the last to leave. 'How can we get in touch, Marion? You know, before it starts?'

The quiet one, Marion observed. Olivia Paige was a recent recruit, and Marion's background checks revealed that the reserved, diminutive Olivia had a considerable police record, including criminal damage, harassment and violent assault. *Never judge a book,* Marion reminded herself. She'd also formed a relationship with Lucas, and Marion hoped for his sake it wasn't serious. Marion smiled.

'Terry will know how to contact me. If you have any questions or concerns, speak to him.'

Olivia looked down at her trainers.

Marion frowned. 'What's the matter?'

'Terry's been a bit weird lately. It's making me feel a little uncomfortable. I'd rather talk directly to you, Marion. Have you got a number I can call you on? I won't tell anyone else.'

'Really, Olivia? Tough little thing like you, worried about old Terry? You'll be fine,' she said, opening the door a little wider. 'I'll speak to him, when we all meet at the Refuge.'

'Where is the Refuge exactly?'

'You'll find out soon enough. Now, drop your bags by the minibus. Lucas will load them.'

Olivia offered a fleeting smile. *Unconvinced,* Marion realised. She watched Olivia trudge towards the vehicle, then she pulled the door closed. She helped Lucas load the last of the luggage then climbed aboard. Five minutes later they'd left Scotton Manor behind them and were heading north.

'You're going the wrong way,' Terry said from behind her. 'Kettering's south.'

Marion twisted around in her seat. 'I thought we'd drop you at Peterborough. It's a bit further but the trains to London run every thirty minutes.'

Terry shrugged. 'Makes sense.'

Marion smiled and turned back around. Daylight still lingered over the horizon and a cloak of mist hung over the surrounding countryside. They drove for another fifteen minutes, the mood subdued, the passengers lulled by the warmth and motion of the minibus, then Lucas turned off the main road onto a narrow country lane. After a while, open fields gave way to thick woods.

'What's this now, a bloody shortcut?'

Terry again. Marion wanted to tell him to shut his mouth. 'We have a storage facility up ahead. There's something I need to pick up. It won't take a minute.'

A smaller gravel track disappeared at a right angle into the trees. Lucas pumped the brakes and turned onto it. Trees crowded the minibus, and the shadows ran deep on either side. Branches scraped against the windows. Lucas hit the brakes again and the minibus stopped in front of a chain-link fence.

Marion jumped out, removed a heavy padlock and swung the gate open. Lucas drove through and Marion climbed aboard once more. They drove for another minute, the track twisting and turning through the woods. Up ahead, the trees thinned and a patch of grey sky appeared.

Lucas brought the minibus to a halt.

'I'll only be a minute,' Marion announced, climbing out.

She slammed the door behind her.

OLIVIA PAIGE'S HEART WAS BEATING LIKE A JACK-HAMMER.

She reached behind her head and re-tied the thick knot of dreadlocks with shaking hands. What she'd heard these last few weeks, what she'd seen, had scarred her deeply. The training she'd undergone was designed to prepare her for most things. When she'd joined the group she'd expected to see some rough stuff; violence, intimidation, criminal damage. She was prepared to get her hands dirty. She'd attended enough marches and demos in her time, had seen plenty of blood and broken bones, but this was a different world entirely. Nothing had prepared her for Scotton Manor.

Terry had been the target, and like most men he'd been easy to manipulate. She'd met him at the Boomtown festival in Hampshire, back in the summer when her uniform of choice had been cut-off denim shorts, biker boots and a series of brightly-coloured crop tops that barely contained her generous, bra-less boobs. They'd smoked dope and talked politics. She'd even tugged him off one mad, ecstasy-fuelled night, and after that she was in, but the middle-aged activist had never returned for more. Olivia discovered that there was only one thing that gave Terry a real hard-on, and that was the death of industrialisation and the modern world.

At first she thought it was all talk, but then he'd introduced her to Marion and Lucas. It wasn't long before Olivia knew she was involved in something far darker than blockading shale gas sites.

It was the hulking giant Lucas who'd told her the whole story. To her surprise and frustration it had taken three weeks to bed him, and while the sex had been a disappointment, the post-coital pillow talk had revealed a story so horrific that Olivia had welcomed the dark of her bedroom if only to hide the revulsion on her face.

The training had seen her through. Were it not for that, Olivia knew her body language would've screamed the type of signals Marion would surely have detected.

Despite some very subtle probing, Olivia knew nothing about the woman. She was a blank canvas, a forgettable individual of indeterminate age and origin. All electronic devices were banned at the Manor, and Marion had worn latex gloves all the time, even during the late-night drinking sessions that gave them all a chance to decompress after killing and cremating another batch of homeless people. No phones, no pictures, no fingerprints. Even Lucas had remained silent about Marion, despite Olivia riding him like a bucking bronco night after night.

As she watched them talking by the side of the track, Olivia remembered her first time in the control room, when she'd witnessed the infections and carbon monoxide gassings. She'd choked back the bile as she'd helped stretcher the bodies to the incinerator at the back of the house. Terry and the others had taken it all in their stride, committed as they were to a cause that Olivia could not have imagined. The moment she was clear of them, she'd make contact with her handler. The priority then would be to stop them.

Impatient grumbles rippled around the minibus and Olivia blocked it out. She was focussed on Marion and Lucas, their body language. Marion's arms were folded, her head cocked to one side. Lucas was tight-lipped, nodding his head as Marion appeared to lecture him about something. Whatever it was, Lucas didn't like it. Then Marion put a hand on his arm, smiled, and walked into the trees.

Olivia shifted in her seat, her heart beating fast. She watched Lucas take a bunch of keys out of his pocket and walk towards the vehicle.

'About bloody time,' Terry grumbled.

Olivia tracked Lucas as he walked around the back of the minibus. She heard a key in the lock and saw him check it with a huge paw. He did the same with the side door, then he climbed behind the wheel.

'Come on big 'un, we've got a train to catch.'

Lucas ignored him. Instead, he fired up the engine then reached down beneath the seat. Olivia couldn't see what he was doing but she was filled with a sudden dread.

'Lucas?' She watched his big shoulders wrestling beneath his coat, his hands working earnestly out of sight. 'Lucas!' she yelled.

Terry spun around in his seat. 'Jesus, Livvy, what the hell's wrong with you?'

The van's engine roared. Lucas turned around. He looked directly at Olivia and said, 'I'm sorry.'

And then he was scrambling out of the minibus as it lurched forward and accelerated along the gravel path. Terry and the others were shouting and swearing, but not yet terrified. Olivia was already there. She could see the plastic ties locking the steering wheel in place, imagined the length of timber jammed onto the pedal. Her hands scrabbled for the seatbelt, dragging it across her chest and snapping it home as the minibus hurtled towards the clearing ahead.

Not a clearing, Olivia realised.

Trees flashed by on either side and then the ground opened up. She saw the wide canyon ahead, the distant trees that crowded its impossibly steep flanks.

One of the girls screamed. Terry joined her, then the others. Olivia's stomach lurched as the ground fell away and the minibus hurtled into the quarry. She glimpsed the steep walls rushing by, heard the scream of the engine as it competed with the death cries of the people around her.

Black water rushed up to meet them.

Olivia took a lungful of air and squeezed her eyes shut.

GRAVE DECISION

THE SERVICE WAS HELD AT THE WESTHAMPTON MEMORIAL PARK, a quiet, well-tended cemetery located five miles north-west of downtown Richmond, Virginia.

By the time Ray Wilson had parked his car and marched to the graveside, Kelly Novak was being lowered into her final resting place. Ray stood behind the large crowd of mourners as the rain drummed against his umbrella. *Hell of a day for it,* he observed. More often than not, nature seemed to conspire against memorial services. Ray had attended several over the fifty-three years of his life, and he couldn't remember one where it hadn't rained. Or maybe he just *misremembered,* as the folks up on the Hill often said.

Memorials were supposed to be a celebration of a life well lived, but for the most part they were depressing affairs, all black clothes, whispered conversations and a lot of tears. Fond memories and smiles came later, and occasionally laughter, once the alcohol began to flow. But not today, Ray knew.

Kelly Novak, citizen journalist turned investigative reporter, had been cut down in the prime of her life. Not even thirty years old. Beyond tragic. Through the tangle of umbrel-

31

las, Ray watched a middle-aged guy in a black suit help a similarly clad woman out of her chair. Kelly's mother, Ray assumed. Her shoulders shook as she grabbed a handful of dirt and tossed it into the hole in the ground. Then she broke down, her knees buckling beneath her. Family members sprang out of their chairs, steering the woman back into her seat. A ripple of thunder accompanied the moment, and Ray glanced up to the heavy grey sky; Mother Nature, adding her own accompaniment to the drama.

After the final prayer the gathering broke up, the mourners hurrying towards their cars to escape the rain. Ray stepped forward to Kelly's grave. The polished grey casket was spattered with muddy tributes, and Ray reached over to the pile of dirt and made his own contribution. He wasn't a religious man but he respected the tenets of Christianity, the message of peace and goodwill, the fight for good over evil. As Assistant Managing Editor at the Washington Times, Ray knew all about that fight, a conflict waged on many levels both in DC and across the world. Kelly Novak had joined that fight, and had started to make a name for herself. It was tragic that she'd never get to fulfil her potential.

'Mister Wilson?'

Ray turned around. It was the woman from the graveside, Kelly's mother. Kelly had been an only child, her father losing his life to sepsis when she was a teenager. The woman who stood before him had experienced more than her fair share of tragedy. Ray shook her hand.

'I thought that was you,' she said, trying to control her emotions. 'Thank you so much for coming.'

'Missus Novak, I can't tell you how sorry I am. Kelly was an exceptional — '

'Please, Mister Wilson. I don't think I can take another platitude, well-meaning as they are.' Beneath the wide brim of her black hat, the grieving mother's blue eyes were moist and expectant. 'You'll join us back at the house, yes?'

'Thank you, ma'am. I will.'

'Good, because there's something I'd like to discuss with you. About Kelly.'

Ray could smell more than cut grass and damp earth.

'I'll follow you in my car.'

WHERE SHE SUMMONED THE STRENGTH FROM, SHE DID NOT know.

Her fingernails were cracked and bleeding, her hands caked with freezing mud, and they were the only things keeping her out of the flooded pit beneath her. Her body shook violently, the twin assaults of cold and shock, and a voice in her head pleaded with her to release the terrible pressure on her fingers, to slide back into the black waters below, to succumb to its cold, eternal embrace.

But Olivia was determined to cling to the muddy wall, because help was coming. She also knew they would have to move fast. Despite her determination to survive, her strength was failing.

Her body shook again as the terrifying event flickered through her mind. The minibus had tumbled through the air, landing roof-first on the water. The disorientation, the shock of the freezing black water, had almost stopped her heart. Then she'd felt the minibus sinking and she'd opened her eyes, catching glimpses of pale hands and faces in the darkness, bodies thrashing and spinning around like clothes in a washing machine. Her fingers had worked furiously to release her seatbelt, and she'd managed to grip the side of a broken window and haul herself out. As she'd clawed for the surface she'd glimpsed the minibus beneath her, sinking into blackness.

Salvation sparkled above her, fractured light on a distant surface. She'd kicked upwards, struggling against the weight of her coat. She'd shrugged it off, her lungs screaming for air, and then gasped and choked as she broke the surface. She'd swam for the side, tried to haul herself out of the water, but the quarry walls were steep and slippery. She'd managed to find a handhold, but clumps of wet clay broke off beneath her bloodied fingers. She'd kept moving sideways, the water chilling her blood and bones. Finally she'd found a root embedded in the mud wall and managed to lift her upper body out of the water. She'd called for help, her voice echoing feebly around the quarry walls. Only the birds answered, oblivious to her plight.

Time stood still. She'd watched an airliner pass high over-head, its occupants oblivious to the struggle taking place below them. Olivia's choices were limited; hold on, or join the others at the bottom of the quarry. Delirium assaulted her mind. Terry had whispered to her from below the water. She'd heard the buzz of an approaching insect. It sounded huge, and she imagined it hovering behind her, its antenna brushing her wet hair. She thought she might grab its legs, have it lift her to safety. She'd twisted her head...

And saw the drone, riding the air behind her.

Terry's whispers were drowned out by its rotors. She'd heard shouting somewhere above her. *Hold on*, that's all she had to do, all that mattered. Time passed. She'd heard another roar, thunderous, the clatter of rotor blades. Brightly coloured ropes had tumbled past her. Something hit the water beside her and Olivia saw it was a bright orange life-preserver. But letting go would mean certain death, so she'd clung on while the helicopter roared somewhere above, while men in red flight suits had abseiled down to her. They'd prised her fingers from the muddy root, and finally she'd given in.

Everything after that was a blur; the open sky, the stretcher, the downdraught of the rotor blades. She drifted in and out of consciousness. Lights were shone into her eyes. She heard concerned voices, urging her to stay with them, to not give up. They needn't have worried, because Olivia had stopped listening to the seductive whisper of death. He'd called her many times that morning, from inside the minibus, as she'd clawed her way up through the black waters, as she'd clung to life against the quarry wall.

Death had tried, and death had failed. Death could go fuck itself.

Because Olivia had a story to tell.

THE HOUSE WAS LOCATED IN THE COLONIAL PLACE DISTRICT IN the west end of the city, a quiet suburb dotted with expensive properties set back from tree-lined roads. The Novak house was a sprawling, thirties-built dwelling that had been impressively renovated, and they were greeted at the front door by a Hispanic housemaid who took their coats. As Kelly's mother - *Barbara*, she insisted - led him through the house, he learned that she'd taken control of her husband's fledgling property portfolio after his death and turned it into a profitable business. Ray was starting to get a better sense of Kelly's own drive and ambition.

They passed a large reception room filled with mourners, most of them attending their first funeral, Ray guessed, and he found that fleeting image of so many young people gathered together in mourning desperately sad.

Barbara's private office was at the back of the house. The room was all dark mahogany and lit with brass lamps. Tall windows overlooked the wide patio and the manicured lawn beyond. It was a quiet room, and all Ray could hear was the rain against the windows as the storm rumbled across the city. They sat on couches opposite each other and Ray accepted a glass of Scotch. Barbara poured herself a larger measure and settled in, crossing her thick legs.

'I knew this day would be tough. I just didn't realise how much.'

'I can't imagine,' Ray offered.

'Do you have children?'

'Two, both in college. I don't see them as much as I should.'

'Are they likely to follow in their father's footsteps?'

Ray shook his head. 'They have first-hand experience of the damage a busy newsroom can do to a marriage.'

Barbara's eyes drifted over to her desk where there were several framed images of her daughter. 'Being a reporter was all Kelly wanted to be. She was deeply indebted to you for taking her on at the Times.'

Ray recalled the first time he'd met Kelly, the bright young intern with dark curly hair and an infectious smile, who'd taken his hand with a confident grip and made eye contact when she spoke. Intelligent, hard working, popular around the newsroom, confident beyond her years; Ray was sorry to see her go.

'We were lucky to have her. When she turned down my job offer, it was one of the major disappointments of my career.'

Barbara smiled and looked away, and for a moment Ray thought she might break down again, but she held it together.

'She held you in the highest regard. The Times itself, not so much. But you know that, of course.'

Ray did, because Kelly had told him to his face. She'd lost faith in the mainstream media and their ability to report the truth, a contagion that had swept the nation and much of the western world since Nine Eleven. *Kelly Novak is a truth seeker*, she'd told him with that wide smile of hers. She wasn't going to be controlled by Big Media. Ray had wished her well and they'd promised to keep in touch.

That was a year ago. Kelly had taken the alt-media path, much to Ray's disappointment. Established media groups like the Times had a long tradition of reliable news-gathering built on credible sources and verifiable data. The alt-media was speculation built on wild theories and rumour.

Why Kelly had been drawn to that world, Ray didn't understand.

'You said you wanted to discuss something. About Kelly.'

Barbara swallowed the rest of her drink and set her glass down on the table between them. She leaned forward, elbows on her knees, her fingers interlocked. Steeling herself, Ray realised.

'Are you familiar with the circumstances of Kelly's death?'

'Only what I read.'

'The truck was stolen in Baltimore the day before it hit her car in Fredericksburg. Kelly was waiting at an intersection when it rolled over the top of her Honda Civic and just kept going. They found the truck abandoned in a wood several miles away. The driver is still on the loose.'

'The police will run down leads,' Ray assured her. 'They'll get the guy.'

'The truck's cab had been doused in bleach, which means no fingerprints or DNA. There's no CCTV out on that high- way, and there were no witnesses. Hardly surprising, given the remote location.'

'What was Kelly doing out there?'

'She got a call, about the story she was working on, that's all I know. I think she was lured out there.'

'Lured?'

'That stretch of road is very quiet, rural. And it was late when it happened.' Barbara looked at him and said, 'You want to hear the best part? The Fredericksburg PD has lost the file.'

'What d'you mean, *lost*?'

'Exactly that. A week ago they had some sort of data breach. Kelly's case file was wiped, along with dozens of others. Backups are gone too. Allegedly,' she concluded.

Ray raised an eyebrow. 'That's it? That's all they told you?'

'They apologised and promised to continue the investigation, but I don't hold out any hope.' She paused for a moment. When she spoke again, her voice trembled with emotion. 'I went out there, to the place where she died. I got out of my car and stood at that intersection. It was ten-thirty at night and there wasn't a single vehicle in any direction. There were no rubber marks on the road either. That truck driver, he didn't hit his brakes at all. It was no accident.'

Ray watched mascara tears roll down Barbara's face. It was not an unusual reaction to an unexplained and untimely death; there would be doubt, suspicion, a blatant refusal to accept the possibility of a freak accident, but Ray's antenna was quivering like Barbara's bottom lip. If everything she'd told him panned out, it might lead somewhere.

Barbara went to her desk, rummaged around a bit then sat back on the couch. She placed a small USB thumb drive on the coffee table between them.

'Occasionally Kelly would send me one of these for safe-keeping. I received this one about a month ago.' Barbara fixed Ray with her piercing blue eyes. 'She called me, not long after she sent this. She made me promise that if anything happened to her, I'd get this to you. Boy, was I mad at her for saying that.' She dabbed at her eyes with a tissue and forced a smile. 'Kelly laughed, blew it all off, but she made me promise none-theless. Twelve days later she was dead.'

Ray shook his head. 'Why me? We hadn't spoken for a year.'

'Respect. Trust. She never said.'

'What was she working on?'

'Kelly never discussed her work with me. We clashed, politically I mean.'

Ray picked up the small data drive and held it in the palm of his hand. 'Ma'am, with all due respect, the possibility still exists that what happened to Kelly was nothing more than a terrible accident. You shouldn't get your hopes up.'

Barbara stood. 'I've neglected my daughter's friends for

too long. Some of them have travelled a long way to be here.'

Ray took the hint and pocketed the drive. 'I can't promise anything, that's all I'm saying.'

'I understand. And one more thing, the drive, it's password protected.'

'What's the password?'

'*Wilson*. With a *one* and a *zero*.'

IT TOOK RAY JUST OVER TWO HOURS TO DRIVE BACK TO HIS apartment in Arlington.

He took a shower, made a pot of coffee, then flipped open his MacBook. He plugged in Kelly's USB drive.It contained five gigs of data, all of it neatly catalogued. Nothing jumped out at him immediately so he started going through the folders one at a time. Much of it was political; Federal Library papers, Congressional records, C-SPAN transcripts, and reams of official, non-sensitive documents relating to a variety of subjects that were already out in the public domain.

Nothing to get the juices flowing.

After an hour he took a break. He made himself another coffee and stood at the window. Night had fallen, and across the Potomac River his nation's capital shimmered. He sipped his coffee, watching planes turning in the sky over Dulles, and wondered why Kelly Novak feared for her life and who might've wanted her dead. And if both of those things were true, why? Ray knew there was only one way to find out.

It was after two a.m. when he found his first clue. The subfolder was buried several layers deep. It was labelled *State* and it contained documents related to the incident in Baghdad earlier that year. Beneath it there was another folder called *Bragg,* containing just one file, a Microsoft Word document. Ray opened it and began reading. A minute later he was snatching pages out of the printer.

As he crossed the room he picked up his reading glasses

and a yellow highlighter. He flopped onto the couch, slipped his glasses on and kicked his feet up. He re-read the document several times, highlighting important sections and making copious notes on a legal pad. By the time the sun had risen, Ray Wilson had a good idea why Kelly believed her life might be in danger. Sure, she'd made some assumptions in her research, but taken as a whole the document that lay on the couch next to Ray contained just enough fact and testimony to warrant a little more digging. He also knew the Times wouldn't sanction it, not in the current climate.

For almost a year, the political world had witnessed a series of seismic upheavals. Every G8 country had suffered to various degrees, the United States especially, so Kelly's work, if it ever saw the light of day, would once again plunge the country into political and economic uncertainty. And that was the upside.

It had been a long time since Ray Wilson had worn out the shoe leather chasing down a story, a long time since he'd knocked on doors, waited in empty parking lots and sat drinking in bars until the sun came up. Ray had made a name for himself by putting in the time and effort, and never leaving a stone unturned. The thought of getting out of the office, of becoming a real reporter again, excited him. He welcomed the idea, embraced it, because for the last few hours all he'd felt was a growing anxiety that bordered on —

What exactly?

Fear, he realised.

Kelly had started to piece together a story. In death, she'd passed the baton to Ray. She was challenging him to turn his back on journalistic orthodoxy, to venture out into the shadowlands of fake news, rumour and conspiracy. To become a *truth seeker.*

Ray couldn't promise her that. What he would do was follow up a couple of leads, see where it took him.

And he would start with the sniper.

SAVAGE KINGDOM

Mike Savage was unshaven, filthy, and exhausted to the bone.

For the last three days he'd managed only six hours of sleep, and his clothes were caked in dirt and dust. The darker patches were blood, but thankfully not Mike's. The mission was over, that was the good news. The bad news sat and glared at Mike from the seat across the aisle.

Mike stared right back at the forty-three-year-old Libyan in the torn suit and bloodied shirt. The man had lost his shoes, and his socks were shredded and caked with blood. His hands were zip tied behind his back, though it didn't appear to bother him. He slouched in his window seat, occasionally glancing at the world outside the SAAB 340B turbo-prop, but mostly he stared at Mike, his pockmarked face a mask of defiance. It was a look that said, *you've fucked up, and now you're going to pay.*

In normal circumstances the prisoner would be hooded, but that was pointless now. Mike watched him sneer and was struck by the similarity to his cousin; the thick moustache flecked with grey, the tailored suits, the habitual wave of the left hand when smoking a cigarette, the guttural Arabic he used to berate his lackeys. It was an understandable mistake. Unforgivable too, Mike wagered.

For the last seventy-two hours, Mike Savage and four of his best men from the CIA's Special Activities Division, Special Operations Group, had staked out a smallholding in the green, fertile lands to the south of the city of Al Bayda, Libya. It was one of many farms in a sparsely populated area dotted with crop fields, woods and orchards, and Mike and his team had moved into position under cover of darkness, establishing their observation post in a drainage ditch less than fifty yards from the main building.

The sunrise saw the arrival of a fleet of dusty Mercedes, and the occupants had been photographed extensively, especially the well-dressed, forty-something man who barked orders at the others, who took evening tea alone on the veranda at sundown, who swore drunkenly into his phone late at night. The team's long-distance audio equipment had recorded the man's voice and the subsequent intelligence package had been squirted back to Langley for analysis via their portable SATCOM gear.

Then they'd waited, barely sleeping, their minds and bodies locked in a constant, nerve-jangling state of alert. When the encrypted message came back it was in the affirmative. The target was ID'ed as Walid al-Khatib, one of the most influential and dangerous men in Libya.

On the surface, al-Khatib was a reclusive businessman and major exporter of wheat, barely, olives, dates, livestock and other commodities, transporting his goods all over Europe and the Middle East. In reality he was a smuggler of fuel, weapons and people. The secretive Libyan was responsible for the deaths of thousands as they paid to clamber aboard his fleet of ramshackle boats and dinghies and make the perilous crossing to the promised land of Europe. And lately, not just migrants.

For the past few months, ISIS and Al-Qaeda fighters had

quietly joined the ranks of the desperate and had disappeared into Europe. Langley had gotten wind of an operation from an asset in Tripoli; a terror strike was being planned, against unknown targets by unknown personnel. The intel suggested the strike would be on a scale not seen before. They also knew that nothing moved out of Libyan waters without al-Khatib knowing who it was and where they were going. Now Uncle Sam was going to make him talk.

That was the original plan.

Mike clambered out of his seat and stretched his body. Every muscle ached, and his eyes were tired and gritty. He yawned as he slung the short-barrelled M4 CQBR over his back. The Libyan watched him and smiled. Mike ignored him. He walked up to the cockpit of the aircraft and stood between the two CIA pilots. Beneath the nose of the plane, the vast, blue expanse of the Mediterranean Sea stretched towards a hazy horizon.

'How long?' Mike asked.

'Forty minutes until we hit the outer marker. Altitude is set. You're good to go.'

'Roger that.'

He stepped back into the passenger cabin. His team was spread out in the seats around al-Khatib, all of them physically strung out but thankfully in one piece. They'd taken a risk but it had been unavoidable; what self-respecting man could hide in a ditch while a child was getting raped a few yards away? Not Mike Savage, as it turned out.

The plan was to wait until pre-dawn, but the little girl's pitiful screams had put an end to that. Instead, at just after three a.m. local time, Mike shoved his combat knife into the windpipe of the nearest sentry and opened him up without a sound. Then he led Miller and Flynn through the kitchen door while Tapper and Boswell stayed in the trees and covered their entry point. The Rules of Engagement were simple; drop anyone who posed a threat.

Mike's second kill was in the hall outside the kitchen, a guy who'd just stepped out of a bathroom and was hitching up his trousers. Mike shot him twice in the chest at close range, but even suppressed rounds and falling brass can make a lot of noise at three in the morning.

Bare feet slapped around the building. There were shouts in Arabic and screams of terrified young girls. Mike and his guys spread out in the hallway and waited. Tactically, the enemy were no match for the Americans, and five of them lay dead before they figured out that someone should probably loop around the building and assault from the rear. When they did, Tapper and Boswell's lethal arcs of fire took care of them.

By the time the shooting stopped, all twelve of al-Khatib's security people were dead. They found the man himself hiding in the master bedroom wearing only his underwear. They also found the naked, violated and strangled body of a ten year-old girl in his bed. Mike wanted to shoot him on the spot. Instead he let him get dressed and had him escorted outside.

The six kids locked in another bedroom were traumatised but okay. All of them were African, trafficked up from the sub-Saharan countries. The oldest was a seventeen-year-old Rwandan who told Mike she could drive a car, so he gave her the keys to one of al-Khatib's Mercedes and a bag stuffed with US dollars they'd found in his bedroom. Mike told her to head east, to the Egyptian border. The girl thanked him and corralled the other youngsters into the car. Mike watched them drive away into the night, praying they'd make it but knowing they'd probably be robbed and abandoned long before they reached safety. If they were lucky. The world, he knew from much experience, was a severely fucked-up place.

The domestic staff took off into the night and the CIA operators policed up all the discoverable intelligence they could find. After al-Khatib had been bundled into the trunk of the remaining Mercedes saloon, the team headed south along a dusty back road. Pat Flynn, a former Delta Force operator from south Boston, drove with the lights off and his Enhanced NVGs on.

The extraction point was eleven miles south of al-Khatib's compound and the SAAB 340B appeared on time and low on the horizon, just as the sky was paling to the east. The aircraft landed on an empty road, spun around in a cloud of rust-coloured dust thrown up by its powerful twin turbo-props, and rocked to a stop. Mike torched the Mercedes as the others bundled the prisoner aboard. Less than sixty seconds after it had touched down, the aircraft lifted off again, heading fast and low across the hills towards the Libyan coast. The SAAB 340B was a CIA plane and its jammers went to work, masking its passage as it headed out to sea. As the plane climbed higher, Mike's spirits began to sink.

His hood and gag removed, the prisoner began protesting his innocence and issuing threats. And then the encrypted message had come through.

You've got the wrong guy.

The real Walid al-Khatib had just been positively ID'ed by a Libyan government official who, at that very moment, was loitering outside the Minister of Interior's office in Tripoli. Behind the office's thick mahogany doors, al-Khatib was having a private meeting. The government official had even covertly photographed al-Khatib and his entourage.

You've got the wrong guy —
So who have we got?
Omar al-Khatib, Walid's first cousin and occasional doppel-gänger, missing presumed dead after the Akakus Oil transport plane he was travelling on crashed in the desert over a year ago. Walid uses him to throw others off his scent…

Now Mike had new orders.

He stood in the aisle and cocked his chin at the two guys

sat behind al-Khatib, Jake Boswell and Ty Miller, the big red-head from Saint Paul, Minnesota.

'Get him up.'

The former Black Knights linebacker and army Ranger yanked the Libyan out of his seat.

'You make big mistake,' al-Khatib protested in broken English. 'Maybe I tell TV people Americans kidnap Libyan citizen. Or maybe America pay me money to keep my mouth shut, huh?'

Mike took a step forward until he was toe-to-toe with the man. His breath reeked of cigarettes and garlic, and Mike's stomach churned, but it wasn't the smell. It was the memory of that frail, broken body in al-Khatib's bed, the sightless eyes that had no doubt witnessed more than her fair share of pain during her short, miserable life. The last face she'd seen before she'd died was the man standing in front of him. Mike was so disgusted he had to turn away.

'Crack it,' he ordered.

Boswell looped his Sig Sauer SBR over his back and dropped to his knees in the cargo area behind the seating. Flynn helped him as their hands went to work, flipping latches and lifting out a section of the floor. The roar of rushing air and the thunder of turboprop engines filled the cabin.

'Get him prepped,' Mike yelled.

Miller spun the Libyan around and marched him to the back of the plane. When al-Khatib saw the hole in the floor, the man's socks began to slide on the carpet as he pushed back against his captor. Miller grabbed him by the collar and forced him to his knees.

Mike stepped around the hatch and squatted down to face the prisoner. There was still some defiance there but it was leaking away fast as al-Khatib's wide eyes drilled into Mike's.

'You trying to scare me? You in big trouble, my friend! I have human rights!'

'Untie him,' Mike ordered.

Don Tapper, Mike's XO, stepped up, yanked a black-bladed Spyderco from his chest rig and sliced through the zip ties behind al-Khatib's back. The Libyan rubbed his wrists, still refusing to look down. There was real fear in his eyes now, the severing of his bonds an almost symbolic gesture, and one that al-Khatib understood immediately.

It said, *You're free to leave.*

Mike stood. Any resistance that al-Khatib still possessed, left him. He looked up at the CIA officer, his hands clasped together as if in prayer, his voice piercing above the roar of the engines.

'Wait! You cannot do this!'

Mike had seen a lot of people die in a lot of different ways. It was unavoidable in his profession, but it was dead children that triggered the nightmares he occasionally suffered. Like the little African girl, now wrapped in a rug beneath a Libyan olive tree.

'My brother, I can give him to you! Please!'

Mike held up a finger and shouted above the thundering turboprops. 'If you want to live, tell me where Walid is right now.'

He saw the hesitation in the man's eyes. 'He is in Morocco! A hotel in Rabat! I swear!'

Mike shook his head. 'I gave you a chance, pal.'

He stepped back from the hatch. The plane was starting to lose height but they were still several thousand feet above the waves. It would be a long fall. An opportunity for al-Khatib to reflect on his crimes.

'Do it,' he told Miller.

The former Ranger lifted a big leg and stamped on al-Khatib's back, sending him flying forward into the hatch. The Libyan screamed, his hand slapping desperately at the metal edge, and then he was gone, the scream snatched away by the roar of wind and engines.

Mike caught a final glimpse of him, a tiny black figure tumbling into nothing against the deep blue expanse of the Mediterranean Sea.

'Seal it up.'

THE AIRCRAFT LANDED TWENTY-FOUR MINUTES LATER AT THE US Naval Support Facility at Souda Bay on the rugged Greek island of Crete. Before they disembarked, Mike and his team packed all their gear and guns into holdalls and loaded them into a waiting minivan.

The debriefing was carried out in a grey-walled classroom beneath the facility's training building. Stan Lando, a Special Operations Group Field Supervisor, reinforced the point that no one was to blame; the voice print and photo analysis were a positive match. It was regrettable, but reminded them that *shit happens*. On the plus side, the phones and laptops might offer up an intel bonus, and the team managed to free a few young trafficking victims, but Mike didn't take much comfort from any of it.

Lando wrapped up the debrief and cut the guys loose. As they filed out of the room he asked Mike to wait.

The door closed and they were alone. Lando sat next to Mike. He had sweat patches under his arms and his tie was pulled loose from his shirt collar. It had been a tough few days for all of them.

'Hey, the guy had us all fooled,' Lando said. 'Look on the bright side, cousin Omar might've been clean. Now *that* would've been embarrassing.'

Mike gave him a dark look. 'He wasn't.'

'And he'll never hurt anyone again, right?'

'True. Would've been nice to bag the big guy though. It'll take a while to work up another opportunity. Walid will go to ground. It's going to be tough to reacquire him.'

'Forget about al-Khatib. He's officially on the back-burner.'

Mike raised an eyebrow. 'What's up, Stan?'

'Something else has come up. It's a *drop-whatever-the-fuck-you're-doing* type of deal. Highest priority, supersedes everything on the slate right now, including al-Khatib. And it stays that way, until the situation is resolved.'

Mike cracked a weak smile. 'You wanna let my guys catch their breath?'

'This is no joke, Mike.'

'What's so goddamn important?'

Lando's eyes narrowed, his skin wrinkling as he frowned. 'It's related to Baghdad. To the outbreak.'

Mike's smile faded. CIA Head of Station Bill Jacobs had been killed during the incident. Bill had been a friend and mentor of Mike's, and the news had hit him pretty hard. He'd also seen some of the recovered footage, plus the stuff on LiveLeak and YouTube. The scale and speed of the outbreak had been truly terrifying. Guns and grenades Mike could deal with; WMDs were something else. A filthy, nasty business.

'So, what's the deal, Stan?'

Lando grabbed his laptop and sat back down. 'Take a look at this.' He tapped a play icon and turned the screen so Mike could see the man in the black turtleneck, the ski mask and sunglasses who sat in front of a tarpaulin and spoke in heavily-accented English.

'President Coffman, for many years I have been a great admirer of your country, especially your armed forces...'

Then the tarpaulin dropped.

Mike swallowed hard.

SHE CRACKED OPEN A TIRED EYE AND SAW A MAN STANDING OVER her bed. Despite the closed blinds and minimal lighting she could see he had short fair hair and wore a suit and tie. A winter coat was draped over one arm.

'Who are you?'

'My name is Bradshaw. I'm from the Security Services. We spoke on the phone.'

'Show me your ID, please.' Her paranoia was way off the charts but she didn't care. When she closed her eyes all she saw were dead people, naked, gassed and drowned. They pointed at her and whispered her name. They terrified her.

Bradshaw flipped open a small black wallet and Olivia clocked the pyramid badge of Britain's domestic security service and Bradshaw's stern-faced mugshot.

'Okay if I sit?' asked the MI5 officer.

Olivia shook her head, mindful of the thin oxygen tubes snaking up her nose. Bradshaw hung his coat on a stand and pulled a chair close to the bed.

'Thank you for coming,' she told him. Her voice was weak, croaky.

'Olivia or *Mizz* Paige, which do you prefer?'

'That's not my real name.'

Bradshaw smiled. 'Likewise. We'll keep it simple for now, okay?' Olivia nodded. 'So tell me, why won't you talk to your own chain of command?'

Olivia took a tired breath. 'I was delirious when they brought me in. I must've said some things because I heard them talking about me.'

'Who?'

'Uniforms. Senior bods from the Met. They stood right there.' She pointed to the end of the bed. 'They thought I was sleeping. They think I've gone crazy. I've been working them for some time, you see.'

'The environmentalists?'

Olivia nodded her shaved head. Without her trademark dreads, her head felt as light as a balloon. 'I went deep for weeks, no contact with my handler, no phone calls or emails, no dead-drops, nothing. They were paranoid about security. We were practically prisoners.'

'And you've spoken to no one about this?'

She shook her head, the tubes brushing against her pale cheeks. 'Only you.'

Bradshaw reached inside his pocket and pulled out a small device. 'Do you mind if I record this?' She didn't, and Bradshaw set the device down on Olivia's bedside table. 'I want you to start from the beginning. I want you to tell me the whole story; names, places, events, everything. As much as you can remember.'

And so she did. Olivia talked for just over an hour, in which time Bradshaw uttered not a single word. As she recounted her experiences she felt her heart rate rising, echoed by the beeping of the ECG monitor beside her bed. By the time she was finished, Olivia was exhausted.

Bradshaw retrieved his recording device, briefly checked the audio, then pocketed it.

'I'm going to have you moved to a private hospital in London. Say nothing to anyone, doctors, nurses, and especially your fellow officers.'

'Okay.'

Olivia felt wiped. The session had drained her more than she realised and sedatives lingered in her bloodstream. She felt her eyelids getting heavier by the second. 'You have to find Marion and Lucas. Especially her. She's the brains. I got the impression there were others too.'

She coughed several times, a deep wet hack that threatened to develop into something serious.

'It'll take a couple of hours to get organised,' Bradshaw told her. 'In the meantime get some rest. I'm going to stay here with you, wait for the transport, make sure you're taken care of.'

'Thank you,' Olivia mumbled, watching him get to his feet and dial a number on his phone.

Oblivion beckoned like a warm duvet slipping across her body. She finally gave into it, let it wrap itself around her in its comforting embrace. Two words followed her into the darkness, two words uttered by the man from MI5 who stood in the shadows at the end of her bed.

National emergency.

FUNKY COLD

The city of Medina, a suburb of King County, Washington, is one of the most exclusive neighbourhoods in the whole of the United States.

Its residents are an eclectic mix of tech billionaires, financiers, rock stars and entrepreneurs, most of whom value their privacy above all else, which explains why Medina is also one of the country's most densely surveilled neighbour-hoods. At the southern end of that immaculately-groomed peninsular stands the modern, glass and steel residence of Robert Blake, co-owner of defence giant Kroll Industries.

Bob and his wife Celine loved to entertain, and were studiously selective about the guests they chose to invite to their frequent soirees. For their party that night, one guest had flown in from Washington DC, despite the troubling development from London. Her trip was a private one, and her car avoided the brightly-lit main entrance and stopped around the side of the house where the external lights had been switched off, and where Bob Blake waited for her in the doorway of the staff entrance. He wore a black tuxedo with a silk cummerbund, and his thick dark hair had been combed back off his forehead. Even his beard had been neatly trimmed, Coffman noticed. The man had smartened up his act.

She swung her legs out of the armoured Chevy Suburban and took Blake's outstretched hands.

'Madam President, a pleasure as always,' he gushed, pecking her cheeks.

'It's good to see you, Bob.'

Blake looked past her to the suited Secret Service detail who crowded the doorway behind her. 'Guys, I've got you set up in the staff lounge. Brian will take care of you.' He pointed to a hovering flunkey.

Coffman waved the detail away and followed Blake along the basement corridor, feeling a little uneasy. Her detail consisted of four agents; Blake had at least a dozen armed contractors patrolling the house and grounds, all of them former Special Forces. Despite her long association with the industrialist, despite the fact he'd helped her secure the White House, being in Bob's lair made Coffman nervous.

They continued beneath the house, passing the kitchens where Coffman caught a noisy glimpse of frantic chefs, clouds of steam and blue-flamed hobs. In truth, Coffman wasn't ecstatic about making the trip to Washington, but Bob had insisted. He had news, he'd told her. Good news. Exciting news. It would be worth the trip. Coffman had relented. Bob was a lot of things, but a time waster he was not.

'How's Matt?' she asked.

'The cancer has spread to his lungs.'

'I'm sorry.'

Blake shrugged. 'He's lived a good life. No regrets.'

Matt Sorenson had founded Kroll Industries alongside Blake. They'd built the company up from nothing, becoming one of the biggest and most innovative defence companies in the world with an annual turnover of thirty-nine billion dollars. Like Blake, Sorenson had been instrumental in the destruction of Baghdad and Coffman's rise to power, so the fact he'd be dead soon brought Coffman some comfort. One less witness to the crime, so to speak.

They climbed a short flight of stairs into the main house. Coffman had to admit that Bob Blake's home was magnificent, with its vaulted ceilings, its hardwood and marble floors, the glass walls, the expensive antiques and chic furniture. As they strolled towards the main reception room Blake boasted about his seven bedroom suites, his two acres of prime waterfront real estate, the Romanesque swimming pool, his private dock on Lake Washington, and the Sea Ray L650 power cruiser that was tied to it. It wasn't the biggest he could afford, he told her, but if he needed to impress people he'd have one of his military drones photograph their house. Once again, Coffman felt a flutter of apprehension as Blake escorted her into the main reception room.

She was greeted with wide smiles and a smattering of applause from the thirty or so well-heeled guests scattered around the white-walled, modernist space. Coffman recognised many of the guests, all of them close friends of Blake, including the heads of Amazon and Twitter, the CEO of Lockheed Martin, the owners of three of the world's biggest hedge funds and various other luminaries, all of them accompanied by wives, husbands and significant others. Flesh was pressed, health and business briefly discussed, and then Coffman was veering towards Erik Mulholland and Charlie Schultz. Her Chief of Staff and the Chairman of the Joint Chiefs had also made the trip to Washington, even though Blake had insisted they speak alone. That wasn't going to happen.

'Quite the gathering,' Schultz opened.

'This is Bob's version of informal,' Coffman smiled.

All the men were wearing tuxedos, the women designer dresses and shoes. Coffman's own outfit was a power-red Dolce and Gabbana that accentuated her trim figure.

'Did he give you any hints about his good news?'

Erik was also wearing a tux, though unlike Charlie and

the older men in the room, he was clad in a blue satin Tom Ford. Good looking *and* impeccable taste, Coffman had to admit, which accounted for the discreet surveillance he was under from the other women in the room.

'He'll wait until after dinner,' Coffman told him. 'Bob likes to fatten you up before he fires the bolt through your skull.'

They mingled for another twenty minutes, then the dinner gong sounded and Blake ushered his guests into an ornate dining room, the centrepiece of which was a huge, beautifully-decorated glass table. The fine art on the walls had been relegated to the shadows by the steel and smoked glass pendant lights strung above the full length of the table. It was impressive, Coffman had to admit, and for the next ninety minutes Coffman actually forgot about the threat facing them. Instead she listened with great interest to the techies and the financiers who had the world at their fingertips. Yes, they had amassed great fortunes and were the catalysts for global change, but they sure as hell couldn't order the launch of a cruise missile or have a SEAL team assassinate their enemies. Coffman could, and the assembled Lords of the Universe would be wise to remember that.

After dinner they retired to a vaulted sitting room with giant glass walls that overlooked the black waters of Lake Washington and the distant, gleaming towers of downtown Seattle. More drinks were served, but Coffman was finding it increasingly difficult to make small talk. She looked across the room and caught Erik's eye. He read her look, paused his conversation with the inebriated wife of a Microsoft executive, and walked around the room to where Coffman sat in a white lounge chair. He leaned into her ear and she caught the scent of his cologne.

'Everything okay?' he whispered.

'Bob and his goddamn parties,' she griped, glancing at the gold Cartier on her wrist. 'Tell him to take a shit or get off the pot.'

'I'll speak to him.'

She watched her Chief of Staff circle back around the room and take Blake to one side. A moment later the industrialist was headed towards her.

'Forgive me, Madam President. Calvin is trying to persuade me to pump ten mil into one of his experimental funds. He's a goddamn snake charmer, I swear.' He smiled, a heavy crystal tumbler of something dark grasped in his big hand.

'I don't give a rat's ass about Calvin's fund, and I certainly didn't fly all the way out here for the filet mignon, exquisite as it was. You said you had news.'

'Of course. Let's talk.'

Coffman got to her feet and followed Blake towards the door, her arm linked through Erik's, more to piss off the ladies than to appear casual.

Schultz broke away from his own conversation and intercepted them. 'About goddamn time,' he growled, the smile as hard as granite on his craggy face.

Blake turned to Coffman. 'I was hoping we could speak alone.'

'You know I don't keep secrets from my team.'

The industrialist relented, escorting them through the house and down into a secure basement that resembled a hotel corridor. They passed a wine cellar, a large cinema room and a well-equipped gymnasium. The head-turner was the glass-walled indoor firing range. The paper targets were cartoon zombies, Coffman noticed. Blake stopped outside an open door and invited them to step inside.

'Welcome to my private den. Please, make yourselves comfortable.'

It was the most intimate room so far, Coffman observed, stepping down towards four large, comfortable sofas arranged around a marble centre table and lit by an overhead panel. Around the walls, bathed in recessed lights, Coffman saw a Van Gogh, a spectacular Monet, and something modern that she failed to recognise. *The real deal*, she imagined, and that surprised her. Bob had never expressed an interest in art. She thought she knew him, but she was starting to doubt that now. Bob Blake had changed, she realised. He'd grown confident in the wake of Baghdad, emboldened by his proximity to the American throne and his hand in Coffman's ascendancy. His company had since been awarded hundreds of millions of dollars in defence contracts. He was rich and powerful beyond his wildest dreams. Did he now believe he could summon the President of the United States to his home on the other side of the country *and* keep her waiting?

Think again, Bob.

Coffman watched him hovering by the drinks cabinet, refilling his glass with bourbon and icing it with a couple of cubes. 'Drink, anyone? Amy? Guys?'

Coffman glared at his back. 'Sit down, Bob.'

Blake obeyed, unbuttoning his jacket as he flopped onto the couch. Coffman sat opposite, while Mulholland and Schultz took up flanking positions on either side. Coffman folded one leg over the other.

'How are we doing, Charlie?'

Schultz set a small grey electronic device on the table. 'You can speak freely.'

Blake looked crestfallen. 'C'mon, Amy. You really think I would bug a private conversation?'

'Don't take it personally, Bob. So, why don't you tell me why I'm here?'

'Sure.' Blake took a sip of his bourbon and said, 'It's about Lance Corporal Hector Nunez.'

For a moment Coffman was unable to speak. Erik and Charlie were equally dumbstruck.

'On second thoughts I'll take that drink,' she said. She didn't want one especially, but it bought her a little time to think.

Blake handed her a generous shot of bourbon and sat back down. She took a sip and smiled sweetly. 'Do you have an asset on my National Security Council, Bob?'

'No ma'am.'

'Another *Gatekeeper*?'

'Negative.'

'So how can you possibly know about Nunez?'

Blake swilled a mouthful of bourbon and smacked his lips. 'The idea came to me at Rock Creek. I saw an opportunity and made a phone call. When the embassy blew, it flattened the Green Zone and killed a lot of my guys, but not the team who'd taken cover below ground. They suited up, dug around the rubble and found Nunez unconscious but alive. They sealed him in a crate and drove him to the Northridge office at Baghdad International. He was out of the country before the Marines showed up.'

Coffman took several moments to process what Blake was telling her. There could only be one conclusion. 'You're the *Global Liberation Front*, right Bob?'

Blake smiled and spread his hands. 'Live and in person.'

Schultz's jaw dropped. 'You're what?'

'Did you send the videos too?' Coffman pressed.

'Yes.'

Schultz leapt to his feet. 'You goddamn lunatic! D'you realise the shit storm you've caused?'

Blake gave the older man an icy stare. 'Sit down, Charlie. You'll give yourself a coronary.'

Schultz took a step towards him. 'You fucking maniac — '

'Enough,' barked Coffman.

She swallowed a generous mouthful of bourbon as Schultz retook his seat. The dark, fiery liquid burned a path down her throat. The threat of the H-1 virus sweeping the nation had been hanging over their heads for months, like some goddamn Sword of Damocles. Coffman had lost a lot of sleep, as had most of her security council. The NSA was practically glowing in the dark trying to find Nunez. Her emotions swirled; shock, relief, then a rumbling anger.

'How many homeless people did you kill in England, Bob?'

Blake's jaw dropped as he stared at Coffman. 'How could you possibly know that?'

'Because you fucked up,' Schultz told him. 'One of your tree-huggers was an undercover cop. She survived your clean-up operation.'

'Wait, that…that's not possible,' Blake stuttered.

Schultz turned to Mulholland. 'What were those names, Erik?'

'Lucas and Marion,' the Chief of Staff confirmed, showing Blake the images on his phone. 'No last names but good photofits. That's straight from British intelligence.'

'The UK government has raised their threat level to Critical,' Schultz told him. 'It's only a matter of time before your people are caught, and then they'll point the finger at you, Robert Blake, close personal friend of President Coffman. You goddamn idiot.'

Blake stared at him, his mouth twisted into a sneer. 'D'you think we're stupid, Charlie? Kroll has been running black projects for over a decade. Our people know how to keep secrets, unlike some in the federal government.' He turned back to Coffman. 'Only four people know the whole picture. Everyone else thinks they're saving the planet.'

'Four people,' Coffman echoed. 'That's you, this Philip character and the woman from the UK. Who's the fourth?'

Blake smiled. 'It's Matt.'

Coffman's glass froze halfway to her mouth. 'Sorenson? You said he was dying.'

'Being a billionaire can buy you a lot of time. He resigned his position at Kroll months ago. He's running this whole thing from his ranch in Arizona. It's his parting gift to humanity.'

'Mighty generous of him,' Schultz mocked.

'What about Corporal Nunez? Where is he?'

'Dead,' Blake told her. 'Buried in a forest outside Berlin.'

'How the hell did you get him there?'

'He was flown from Baghdad to a facility in Qatar, shipped to Turkey, then driven overland to Berlin. Once we got him there he was effectively dismantled. We amputated his limbs, harvested his organs, analysed his blood, his DNA, broke it all down to a cellular level, until we were able to synthetically reproduce the infection.'

'Then threatened us with it,' Coffman reminded him. 'Why, Bob?'

'To give you political cover,' Blake explained, as if to a child. 'There's a lot of eyeballs on you right now, Amy, especially after the collapse of Stein's administration. Your initial shock, the reactions and decisions of the National Security Council, they all had to be completely genuine. People had to be convinced that the threat was real. Including you,' he told her, pointing across the table.

'Scarily, it makes sense,' Erik admitted.

'And you also have the perfect scapegoat,' Blake continued. 'A bunch of crazy Europeans with a fucked up manifesto and a devastating bioweapon.'

'Right now the only suspects are the Iraqis and your own goddamn company,' Schultz growled. 'No one's buying European involvement.'

Blake wagged a finger at him. 'But everyone will buy an Iraqi corruption narrative, right Charlie?'

Coffman simmered. 'Do I need to remind you that the Aswad's helped get us here?'

'No ma'am, but we can point the finger elsewhere. The Aswads have a lot of enemies. Throw in a disgruntled military or religious faction, a history of dubious weapons sales, a vengeful Caliphate with links to Europe, and you've got more than enough to muddy the waters. People will buy anything we goddamn tell them if the dossier has a presidential seal on it. Besides, we invaded Iraq on a bunch of bullshit. This is no different.'

Coffman teased the bourbon around her glass as she watched Blake. Truth was, she wanted to throw it at him, but she had questions, lots of them. The first three would decide how the rest of the meeting went.

'Tell me something, Bob. Do you have a mental health issue?'

Blake frowned. 'Excuse me?'

'What possessed you to go rogue and cut me out of the loop?'

'I really don't — '

'Is this a shakedown? Have you dragged me across the country to tell me that *you're* calling the shots now?'

Blake put his glass down on the table. 'Amy, I — '

'*Madam fucking President!*' Coffman screamed at him.

Her hands shook as she watched Blake's face drain of blood. Erik and Charlie stared at her, speechless. She got to her feet. She needed air but she wasn't going to storm out of the room like some menopausal woman. Instead she wandered over to the Monet, allowed herself to be distracted by its beauty. She wasn't an art expert but she knew this piece; *Nymphéas en fleur,* worth tens of millions of dollars. Bob was a wealthy man before Baghdad but that wealth had increased significantly, thanks to Amy Coffman. Why would he risk going to war with the President of the United States when —

No, she realised. Bob wasn't trying to blackmail her. He was trying to tell her something.

She stood in front of the painting for another minute or so, controlling her heart rate, daring any of the men behind her to open their mouths. They didn't. Power restored, she sat down again.

'Talk to me, Bob.'

'Madam President, if I've offended — '

She silenced him with a raised hand. 'You and Matt have gone to a lot of trouble. The question is, why? What's the end game here?'

'To finish what they started,' Blake said, setting his empty glass on the table.

'Who's *they*?' the admiral asked.

Blake stared at Coffman, as if he were willing her to make the connection —

And then it all made sense.

'You're referring to The Committee,' Coffman said.

Blake gave her a single nod. 'Yes, ma'am.'

'You and Matt were part of that?'

Blake pinched his thumb and forefinger together. 'No, but we came this close.'

Coffman's pulse quickened. 'Who made the approach?'

'Former Defence Secretary Scranton. He figured Kroll Industries would be a key player in their global security force. He told us about the Angola virus, the dismantling of the UN, NATO, everything. Gave us the whole playbook. That was a week before they took out the hotel in Switzerland. Me and Matt were not on anyone's radar at that point, so no one came looking for us.'

'Sweet Jesus,' Schultz muttered.

Blake ignored him and focussed on Coffman. 'Did The Committee approach you too, ma'am?'

The President forced herself to look indignant. 'What makes you think I would be party to such a ruthless conspiracy?'

Blake shrugged. 'Baghdad, of course.'

'What about it?'

'The brutal audacity of it. Your willingness to sacrifice American lives for personal ambition. It got Matt and I thinking. We concluded that you must've been involved with The Committee somehow.'

Coffman shook her head. 'Sorry to disappoint you, Bob.'

Blake looked disappointed. 'Really? They never approached you?'

'They did not,' she admitted, suppressing a stab of jealousy. She let the denial hang in the air as Blake shifted in his seat. He'd gone all in, and now he was waiting for Coffman to flip her cards. She decided to let him sweat a little longer.

'So, when they asked you and Matt to join their conspiracy, what was your answer?'

Blake didn't blink. 'We said *yes.*'

'Why?' Coffman asked, knowing she would've said the same.

'Scranton gave us the data. The timescales are a little off, but there's no doubt that global population is increasing faster than expected. Factor in climate change and rising sea levels, not to mention increased nuclear, biological and chemical weapons proliferation across the Third World, and a few years down the line we'll be staring into the abyss. We're talking about unprecedented population migrations, collapsing economies, social unrest, resource wars — '

'All that chaos and uncertainty translates into bigger defence budgets,' Coffman pointed out. 'That's good business for Kroll, no?'

'What's good for Kroll are localised conflicts, like Iraq, Afghanistan, Syria. Continental wars with unstable nuclear powers are bad for everyone.'

'That's a bunch of baloney,' Schultz snapped. 'No one can predict the future.'

Blake stared back at the white-haired admiral. 'You got grandkids, right Charlie? You wanna gamble with their lives?'

'Humanity will adapt,' Schultz countered.

'And if we don't? Or can't?'

Schultz switched focus to Coffman. 'Don't tell me you're buying this, Amy.'

Coffman ignored him and addressed her Chief of Staff. 'What do you think, Erik?'

She watched him swallow a mouthful of bourbon before he spoke. 'I think we should hear Bob out before we rush to judgement.'

'Agreed.' Coffman turned back to the industrialist. 'So the world is slowly spiralling out of control. I take it you have a plan, Bob?'

Blake got to his feet, retrieved a fresh bottle of bourbon and returned to the couch. No one objected as he refilled everyone's glass.

'Not a plan,' he began, 'but what Matt and I want to give you, Madam President, are options. You now have an unstoppable weapon at your disposal, one that's deployable in any number of undetectable ways. A strategic solution, to stop the world from going to shit.' Blake shrugged. 'Or I can call Matt and shut the whole operation down, right now. Just say the word, ma'am.'

Coffman liked options, and Presidents could never have enough of them. 'Let's not be too hasty, Bob. Why don't we explore this a little further?'

Blake spread his hands. 'Happy to, ma'am.'

'If this thing were released, what's to stop the rest of us from turning into bloodthirsty maniacs?'

'A vaccine, fully tested and one hundred percent effective. Our pharmaceutical facility in Kansas has been working round the clock to produce enough for the general population.' He looked at each of them in turn. 'I have a batches for all of you. And your loved ones,' he added, glancing at Schultz.

'What about the eco-terrorists?' Schultz asked. 'What's the story there?'

'Marion and Philip recruited two cells,' Blake told him, 'one in the UK, one in Berlin, all of them with criminal records and all connected to fringe environmental groups.

Aside from the witness you mentioned, the UK team are all dead. The Berlin team number around thirty, and they're all holed up in a warehouse in Vienna right now, waiting for you to cave into their demands. And that's your terror cell right there, ma'am. They're yours to drop the hammer on. I would recommend none of them live to tell the tale.'

'And then what?' Coffman asked him.

'That's your decision.' Blake loosened his collar and leaned back on the couch. 'H-1 can cripple any city on the planet within hours, or a whole country in days. The possibilities are endless.'

Coffman suddenly realised where the conversation was headed. 'Including depopulation, right Bob?'

Blake smiled. 'Exactly, Madam President. Which brings me to the reason for this meeting…'

THE SIKORSKY S-92 HELICOPTER PICKED THEM UP FROM THE practice ground of the Overlake Golf and Country Club and flew them seven and a half miles to Boeing Field, where Air Force One was waiting. In this case the presidential jet was a Dassault Falcon 8X which would deliver the presidential party back to Andrews AFB in just over four hours, time enough for Coffman to process her conversation with Bob.

As the aircraft lifted into the night sky and turned east towards the Montana border, she caught Erik looking at her from across the luxuriously-appointed cabin. He wore a worried frown, his tanned temple creased, his jaw tense. Coffman knew that look well. It was the same one he'd worn during the Baghdad operation and for about a month afterwards. She thought she'd seen the last of those looks. Like her, Erik had been looking forward to an easing of tensions, for her presidency to sail into calmer waters. Instead, thanks to Bob, it had become more complex, and far riskier. But

Coffman also saw the opportunity that Bob has presented to them. Clearly it didn't trouble her as much as it did Erik.

She glanced at Charlie, sitting in his chair with a drink and a magazine, like he was going on vacation. Charlie certainly had a ruthless streak, but did it match her own? And how far was he prepared to go? She'd find out soon enough.

As the Falcon levelled out at fifty thousand feet, Coffman decided to head for her private cabin and get some rest. There was much to do in the days ahead, and if events unfolded as they'd discussed, the lives lost in Baghdad would pale into insignificance.

That was fine with Amy Coffman. After all, she had the blood of thousands on her hands already.

A couple of billion more didn't matter that much at all.

THE CABIN IN THE WOODS

RAY WILSON WAITED IN A QUIET CORNER BOOTH OF THE BLACK
Bear Diner and watched the passing traffic out on Route 19.

The converted railroad car was located just outside Bryson
City, North Carolina, and Ray's booth offered a perfect view
of the gravel parking lot and the highway beyond. *Your guy's
a no-show,* his inner voice told him again. Ray ignored it, and
decided to wait a little longer.

There were at least a dozen cars and trucks scattered
across the lot when he'd first arrived. Now there were two,
and one of those was Ray's rental, a black Chevy Impala. He
presumed the other belonged to the owners, a fifty-something
couple cashing up the days' takings at the end of the counter.
Ray checked his watch again; the diner was closing in ten
minutes. When it did, it would mark the fourth hour of his
vigil.

He flew in to Asheville regional airport that afternoon and
drove south for seventy miles along the Smoky Mountains
Expressway to Bryson City, a quiet little town of less than two
thousand citizens. He'd found the diner easily enough and
enjoyed a late lunch of surprisingly tasty hotdogs and freshly
made coleslaw, his eyes flicking between the parking lot and

the entrance door, whenever its musical chimes announced a new arrival.

Those hotdogs were now a distant memory. The sun had dipped behind the foothills of the Smoky Mountains and the *closed* sign had been flipped for some time. The only people left inside were Ray and the owners. She was a big lady with a ready smile and a slash of red lipstick. Her husband was more guarded, a small, wiry guy in stained chef's whites who glanced at Ray with suspicious eyes every thirty seconds. The kind of guy who probably had a short-barrelled weapon in easy reach beneath the counter.

When Ray had risen that morning he'd felt energised by his impending road trip and what it might bring, but as the hours ticked by he was reminded of past experiences, of wasted days and unreliable sources. Today was turning out to be one of those days.

He's a no-show.

Ray watched the waitress waddling towards his booth. She wrote up his check and slapped it on the table.

'Closing in two minutes, hon. You need a refill for the road?'

Ray smiled. 'I'm all good, thanks.' He got to his feet and flipped open his wallet, peeling off a couple of bills and leaving them on the table. 'Appreciate the hospitality.'

The waitress scooped up the notes and acknowledged the generous tip. She glanced over her shoulder and took a half step closer to Ray. 'Whoever stood you up, she's a fool. Good looking man like you don't need to be waiting in diners.'

She gave Ray a wink and sashayed back to the counter. Ray smiled and shook his head. Last time he checked he was a pale, balding, middle-aged man who could afford to lose at least twenty pounds. Still, he was flattered.

He stepped outside into the fresh air. The sun had set, and the clear blue sky was darkening by the minute. Overhead, the first stars glittered and dark, wooded hills stretched away in every direction. Ray had a choice to make; take a room at the local hotel and come back tomorrow or drive straight to Asheville and catch a flight to DC. Going home felt preferable. He was too old to play the waiting game.

He hit the *unlock* button on his car key and orange blinkers flashed in the gloom. He pulled off his raincoat and climbed into the Chevy. He started the engine and reached up to adjust the rear view mirror —

'Jesus Christ!'

'Be quiet and listen,' hissed the bearded, paint-streaked face in the mirror. 'Did you tell anyone you were coming here? Anyone at all?'

Ray shook his head. 'Not a soul.'

'If you're setting me up, you'll die first, do I make myself clear?'

Ray felt it then, the tip of something cold and sharp against the skin on the back of his neck. 'Crystal.'

'Give me your phone and get out.'

Ray obeyed. The man climbed out too. He wore dark, military-style clothing and a baseball cap pulled low over his brow.

'Put your hands on top of the car and don't move.'

Ray complied and the man frisked him thoroughly. He even checked Ray's raincoat on the front seat. Then the world went dark as a hood was pulled over his head.

'Wait a minute —'

'Don't talk.'

Ray felt his wrists bound with plastic ties and he was forced to lie down on the back seat. The engine purred into life, and a jazz tune played on the radio. A sudden, terrible thought crossed Ray's mind.

'Wait, you're Sergeant Kenny Chase, right?'

'No, I'm Ted fucking Bundy, now keep your mouth shut.'

Ray felt the Chevy bump up onto Route 19 and turn left.

'Where are we going?'

'No talking. Last chance.'

They drove for twenty minutes or so, and Chase had made several turns, both left and right, and at one point had even reversed a short distance before spinning the car around and heading off in another direction. Jazz music filled the car. *Disorientation techniques,* Ray guessed, and they were working. He had no clue where they were.

After a while the car slowed and turned. They left the asphalt and continued along a rougher surface, bumping along a well-worn track or something. Ray felt his body pressed against the back seat and realised they were heading up a steep incline that seemed to twist and turn for some time. Ray was on the verge of asking for a restroom break when the car levelled out and rolled to a stop. His abductor shut off the engine and the jazz quartet was replaced by an ominous silence.

Ray's heart beat loud in his ears. He could hear the man breathing slowly, steadily. He imagined him sitting behind the wheel, contemplating how best to deal with his victim and dispose of his body. *He's not a serial killer,* Ray tried to convince himself. *It's Chase, and he's being careful, that's all. He's on the run, paranoid, probably more scared that you.*

He heard the man get out. The rear door opened and Ray felt a rush of cold air as strong hands dragged him out of the Chevy. He stood Ray up, spun him around and held him against the car. He heard a snip, and then the plastic ties fell away from his wrists.

'You can take off the hood.'

Ray did as he was told, and found himself face-to-face with Sergeant Kenny Chase, erstwhile member of 1st Special Forces Operational Detachment, Delta. At least, Ray assumed it was Chase because the man had yet to identify himself. Kelly's file didn't contain a photograph but it did mention that Chase was a native of Tennessee. Ray was no expert, but the man who'd kidnapped him certainly had a twang.

'You're Kenny, right?'

The man nodded, and Ray took a deep, grateful breath. As his eyes adjusted to the dark, he saw he was standing on a thinly-wooded plateau high above a rocky valley. Behind Chase was a single-story log cabin set back beneath the trees, and a pale ribbon of track twisted across the plateau and down into darkness. Night had fallen, he was far from human habitation, and he was being held prisoner by a man whose business was killing. *Is this exciting enough for you, Ray?*

Chase threw Ray's raincoat at him and pointed towards the cabin with his knife. 'Inside.'

The building looked pretty rustic; a low-pitched timber roof, a wide porch, thick log walls and shuttered windows. Stepping inside, it was larger than Ray imagined and lit by a couple of storm lamps. There were rugs on the stone floor, two battered couches, a bookcase and a basic kitchen. Beyond that was a corridor cloaked in darkness. Bedrooms, Ray assumed.

'Take a seat.'

Ray obeyed as Chase took off his jacket and cap and tended to a dying fire in the wood burner. The Delta soldier was a big guy, with messy red hair and a beard to match. He wore dark green camouflage trousers and a black t-shirt, and it was clear that he'd spent most of his adult life performing strenuous exercise. *Ripped*, that was the term used in popular culture. He also noticed the knife was back on Chase's belt. It was black and ugly, and Ray figured Chase was as skilled in its use as any surgeon.

The Delta man crossed to the small open kitchen. He never spoke as he made coffee, didn't ask Ray if he needed cream or sugar. Instead he handed him a milky brew and sat on the opposite couch.

'Be under no illusion, if you attempt to fuck with me in any way, I'll kill you, understand?'

Ray nodded, his mouth suddenly dry. He took a sip of coffee, desperate to change the subject. 'Is this your place?'

The former Delta operator shook his head. 'I broke in. Lot of empty vacation cabins in these hills.'

That didn't make Ray feel any better. 'I was sorry to hear about Kelly,' he said, eager to get the conversation started.

'She was a brave lady.'

'How did you two meet?'

'The internet. She'd written a piece on Baghdad so I reached out, hinted that I knew something. She said I'd done the right thing. That I couldn't trust you guys.'

Here it comes, another sermon about the evils of the mainstream media. Ray had been cornered many times by friends and acquaintances, and occasionally strangers, all eager to explain to him he was working for a corrupt industry that had issues with the truth.

'Trust in the media has certainly eroded, I'll grant you that. The problem is, the resulting void is filled by unsubstantiated rumours and wild conspiracy masquerading as news.'

Chase snorted. 'Bullshit. You mainstream guys hate losing control of the message, that's why you're scared of people like Kelly.'

'I don't agree.'

'Sure you don't. There's what, five or six giant corporations that own every media outlet in the country? That's pretty much a monopoly, right? You're telling me they don't have agendas or try to influence public opinion? The whole thing's a fucking scam, man.'

'With respect, that's a very simplistic view. The truth is much more nuanced.'

'The truth can get you killed,' Chase countered.

Ray let it slide. A political debate was counterproductive. 'I was hoping we could talk about Kelly. Why someone would want to kill her.'

Chase took a sip of coffee and leaned back on the couch. 'I killed her,' he said.

Ray's blood ran cold. His heart beat rapidly, and he thought about making a run for it. His chances were zero, he knew that. Chase was twenty years younger, an elite soldier. He'd be dead before he reached the door. Ray swallowed hard as he imagined bolting across the room, fumbling for the lock, as Chase caught him and stabbed him several times, skewering his organs —

'You okay?'

Chase was staring at him from the other couch. Ray shook the image from his mind. 'Sorry, you were saying?'

'I got Kelly killed. I told her what I knew, pressured her to investigate the story. She started fact-checking, making calls, sniffing around the swamp. She suspected she was being followed, that her phone was tapped — '

'Wait, I need to make notes.' Ray pulled a notebook from his raincoat. He settled into the couch, clicked his pen, scribbled the date and time on a fresh page. Then his eyes settled on Chase.

'Before we begin, I need to say something.'

'Go ahead.'

Ray cleared his throat. 'It was Kelly's wish that I follow up her story in the event that something happened to her. It's a responsibility I never wanted. She was a good kid, and I have no doubt she would've made her mark in journalism. She was all about truth and honesty, Sergeant Chase, and I expect the same from you. No theories, no rumours. Just the facts.'

Chase glared at him from the opposite couch. 'It's Kenny. And you'll get the truth. The question is, what you gonna do with it?'

'That depends on what you tell me.'

Ray flipped to a page of questions he'd compiled over the last couple of days. It was a long list, but Ray wasn't going anywhere. Now that his nerves had settled he felt that familiar rush of excitement. Kelly's source was sat in front of him, a man intimate with the world of black ops and government deniability. 'Kelly left copious notes, but I'd really like to hear the whole story, from the horse's mouth so to speak.'

The soldier draped his big arms along the back of the couch. 'Where d'you want me to start?'

Ray shrugged. 'Where every story starts. At the beginning.'

It took two more pots of coffee and a round of sandwiches before Ray felt he had a thorough understanding of why Kelly Novak had been murdered, and why Kenny Chase, a decorated Special Forces soldier, had driven out of Fort Bragg in the middle of the night, never to return. Much of it was hearsay and would require verification. That would be tough, Ray knew.

Throughout Chase's narrative Ray had made numerous notes. Now he flicked back through them, his eyes skimming the pages of old-school shorthand.

'Just to confirm, the rest of the Delta survivors from Baghdad are all deceased?'

'Every single one of them.'

'And they all died on the chopper in Alaska?'

'Official story is a bird strike. '

'From which you got pulled at the last minute?'

'About an hour before they boarded. My dad had a stroke, so I jumped a flight from Elmendorf back to Bragg. When I got there I heard about the crash. That's when I realised I was the last man standing.'

'Except for Costello, right?' Ray referred back to his notes. 'Sergeant-Major Nick Costello. You said he handed in his papers, left the service.'

'That's correct. After we got back to Kuwait, a couple of suits from DC made us all sign hush papers. Nick refused, so they threatened him with thirty years in Leavenworth. Nick had a real hard-on for the President. He said she'd played all of us, that she'd deliberately sacrificed everyone in that embassy for political gain.'

'And you agreed?'

'Someone was fucking with us in Baghdad, that's for sure. Major Roth and RSO Bosco were convinced that State was playing us off against each other. Bosco was told we were part of a coup that was happening in DC — '

'A coup?'

'That's right. Look, someone had the juice to cut that embassy off from the outside world, probably the same person who triggered *Grand Slam*. How many people in DC have the power to do that *and* cover it up? A handful at best, right?'

Ray said nothing as Chase cleared his throat and shifted on the couch. Dredging up memories of Baghdad was clearly upsetting him.

'The debriefings took almost a month,' he continued. 'They grilled us all one by one, day in, day out, tell us about this, tell us about that, how did you feel about such and such. It was relentless. Baghdad was the worst kind of hell, and we had to relive it for weeks afterwards. By the time we got back home most of the guys were pretty strung out, especially the family guys. So we got together, made a pact; we'd put it all behind us and move on. Nick was pretty mad about that. He called us all traitors. Turned out he was right.'

Ray's pen scribbled across the page. 'Are you still in contact with him?'

Chase shook his head. 'Not since he left service.'

'Any way of getting in touch?'

'I can give you his contact details, but my guess? He's dead.'

Ray's pen froze. 'Why would you think that?'

'When I landed at Bragg and found out about the chopper

crash, I knew I wasn't going to make it. I was the last one, the sole survivor, so I grabbed some gear, drove to Fayetteville and dumped my car. I kept moving, stayed off-grid, until I ended up here.'

Ray wrote for another minute or so, then looked up. 'How's your dad?'

Chase shrugged. 'He didn't make it either.'

'I'm sorry.'

He meant it too. The guy had lost pretty much everything; his father, his *brothers,* as he referred to his Delta buddies, and a career that he loved. He'd lost Kelly too. Chase had every reason to feel that the gods were conspiring against him, but his story resonated with Ray. Kelly had trusted him, believed in him. Ray would take it one step further.

'Before I came down here I tried contacting RSO Bosco. Seems he's out of the country on State Department business. They wouldn't tell me where.'

Chase shook his head. 'You won't get to any of the survivors, and even if you did, they won't talk. They've bought off everyone they can and killed the rest.'

'And you believe all this was sanctioned by President Coffman?'

'Probably others too.'

Ray thumbed through his notebook. 'You said the reason you went to Iraq in the first place was a classified mission. Can you tell me about that?'

Chase picked up his mug and drained the last of his coffee. 'The job was to neutralise a bio-weapon facility. It was hidden beneath a disused oil rig, a series of very sophisticated labs. It's where Jackson got sick.'

'Why were US forces involved?'

'They were manufacturing the Angola virus there. For global dispersal. The plan was to kill half the world's population.'

Ray's eyes widened. 'Excuse me?'

Chase got to his feet. 'I'll make some more coffee.'

IT WAS AFTER TWO A.M. WHEN RAY FINALLY CALLED A HALT TO the interview. Chase offered him the spare room and Ray left the former Special Forces soldier sitting on the couch, a black rifle lying within easy reach.

The next morning, after coffee and eggs, Chase drove Ray back to the edge of town. When the Chevy stopped and the blindfold came off, Ray saw they were parked in a dirt cutaway on an empty, wooded road. The soldier got out and Ray climbed behind the wheel. He powered down the window and Chase handed back his phone.

'I've got a burner,' he told Ray. 'I programmed the number into your phone, under Kelly's name. I'll turn it on for five minutes, every day at midday. In case we need to talk.'

'Good to know.'

Chase handed him a Wells Fargo ATM card. 'The PIN code is written on the back. There's a couple of hundred bucks in there. Do like I say and it'll confirm what I've told you.'

Ray took it. It was a standard *EasyPay* visa card with Chase's name embossed in the corner. 'What will you do now?'

'I got plans,' he said, his eyes watching the road, the trees. 'Nick Costello was right about one thing; we betrayed the guys we left behind, not to mention the twelve hundred people who died in that embassy. I couldn't see it back then, but I see it now. Not sure I can live with that.'

Ray was suddenly afraid for the man standing by an empty roadside. 'Don't do anything stupid, Kenny. If you need help, I can arrange it.'

The soldier's bearded face cracked a smile. 'Forget about me. You just focus on blowing this thing wide open.'

'That could take years.'

'So don't let me keep you.' He slapped the roof of the car. 'And try not to disappoint Kelly, okay?'

'I'll do my best.'

'Do better than that.'

Chase turned around and disappeared into the trees. Ray sat for a moment, the engine idling quietly. He had a story, that was for sure. Where it would lead him was another matter. If Chase's account panned out, this might just turn out to be the most dangerous assignment Ray had ever undertaken. His fingers hovered over the radio button, then he decided against the distraction. He needed to think, percolate the information, let it brew. Then make a decision.

He slipped the visa card in his wallet, the car into gear, and headed east towards the expressway.

CASH POINT

THEY WOULD COME FOR HIM, HE KNEW THAT.

The moment Ray Wilson started asking about Alaskan helicopter crashes, the reporter would be put under surveillance. His emails would be intercepted, his phones tapped, his home watched, his vehicles tracked. They would know that someone had spoken to Wilson about Baghdad and they'd know it was Kenny Chase.

He'd warned Wilson they would say bad shit about him, that he had PTSD, drug and alcohol problems, that he was a threat to himself and others. They would provide medical reports, witness accounts, maybe even grainy CCTV footage of a Kenny Chase lookalike waving a gun around. They would try and convince the reporter that Chase had gone loco and had to be locked up or put down. Either way, he was well and truly screwed.

Wilson himself would be pretty safe, the Delta man figured. After all he was an important guy, a senior editor at a well-known DC publication. Wilson was chummy with Congressmen and Senators, and had White House press credentials. He was a face around town, an experienced guy who knew how shit worked. Chase felt pretty sure Ray Wilson would be okay.

But not him. That's why he had to move fast. Wilson had promised to hold off his inquiries until nine a.m. the following morning, which gave Chase a twenty-four hour head start. After that, all bets would be off. While they gave the reporter the runaround, others would trace Wilson's movements, track his phone to a diner outside of Bryson city. They would send men with guns to talk to the locals, sniff around, but Chase had been careful. No one knew about the cabin.

He stepped outside into the cold November air. The sun's rays carved through the forest, burning off the blanket of pre dawn mist that clung to the wooded slopes. He made his way around the back of the cabin, to where his midnight blue Toyota Land Cruiser was parked beneath a camouflage net strung between the trees. It was registered to his father's elderly neighbour, recently serviced and juiced to the max. It had power and traction, plenty of storage room, and enough space to make a bunk if he needed to.

He fired up the engine and loaded his gear. He didn't have much, just a large waterproof holdall with clothes and toiletries, a couple of tactical rucks and his weapons cases The first contained an M4 carbine that was smuggled out of Iraq several years ago. Nestled in the second was his favoured weapon, a Heckler and Koch G28 Designated Marksman Rifle. Chase was more than proficient in its use, something he'd proved many times during the course of his active duty deployments.

With the vehicle loaded and ready to go, he returned to the cabin and gave it a final once over. He'd broken in without causing damage, and he was pretty sure the owners would be unaware someone had stayed there. He climbed behind the wheel of the Toyota, dropped it into gear and drove back down the track towards the valley floor. It took ten minutes to get there, another fifteen until he'd cleared the Bryson city limits, and then he headed north-east towards the Ohio border. He would drive slowly and carefully, because right now no one was looking for a midnight blue Toyota with a former Delta Force operator behind the wheel.

The moment Ray Wilson picked up his phone in Washington DC, all that would change.

As Kenny Chase headed for the Ohio state line, Ray Wilson was hiding in a beat-up GMC cargo van in the parking lot of the Rhode Island mall in Brentwood, Washington DC.

Not hiding, he reminded himself. He was *surveilling,* just like a cop. Sat next to him in the rear of the vehicle was the Times' chief sports photographer Chris Farmer, who had his telephoto Canon camera set up against the rear window. Farmer was clearly getting a buzz out of his new-found surveillance role, and admitted to Ray — with a wink and a wry grin — that it was almost on a par with shooting the Philadelphia Eagles cheerleading squad. Ray had laughed; that was the kind of joke a guy just couldn't crack in the office anymore.

Twenty minutes earlier Ray had handed Kenny Chase's ATM card to a homeless dude on Tenth Street with strict instructions to use it in one of the ATMs just outside the mall's main entrance. Ray had given Pablo Vasquez fifty bucks, and the promise of fifty more on completion of the task. He could also keep everything he took from the ATM. The rake-thin, fifty-something addict had agreed without question.

The minutes ticked by. Ray looked at his watch for the tenth time in as many minutes. Next to him, Farmer was squinting through his viewfinder. Then he twisted the optical ring of his Canon. 'Here he comes.'

Ray picked up a pair of binoculars and zeroed in on the mall. He saw Vasquez strolling towards the ATM, his long, greasy mullet spilling out from beneath a Redskins beanie, his body wrapped in a thick winter coat.

'Are you getting this?' Ray asked the photographer.

'Uh-huh.'

Ray didn't know what to expect as he watched Vasquez insert Chase's card into the ATM. He felt a little guilty coercing the guy, but Vasquez had assured him he'd done far worse things for money. Ray studied him through binoculars as he tapped in the PIN; he could almost feel Vasquez's excitement as he stabbed at the buttons before whipping the cash out of the dispenser and stuffing it in his pocket. Then he loitered, pacing up and down outside the entrance. Farmer tracked him with the camera. After a few minutes, he turned to Ray.

'You want me to keep filming?'

Ray was about to answer when he saw two dark coloured Dodge Chargers turn in off the street and speed towards the mall entrance, red and blue grill strobes flashing. Vasquez turned and hurried away in the opposite direction. Doors flew open and the fleeing man was quickly surrounded by a group of men in civilian clothes and dark glasses. Ray caught a glimpse of guns, then Vasquez was cuffed and bundled into one of the cars and they took off at speed, leaving a crowd of bemused onlookers in their wake.

'Holy shit, did you see that?' Farmer asked him.

'Tell me you got the license plates.'

Farmer scrolled back through the footage. 'Got 'em.'

'Good. Let's get out of here,' Ray said.

So, Chase was right. The Delta operator was being hunted, and the speed with which his pursuers had reacted was chilling. Ray felt a cold stab of fear; he was getting involved in something very dangerous here. *Or not,* he thought. He could drop the whole thing right now, make a call to Kelly's mother and tell her that her daughter's investigation had led nowhere. But that went against everything Ray Wilson believed in.

Even so, he was pretty relieved when Farmer steered the Chevy into the Times' parking lot on New York Avenue. Thirty minutes later the photographer had emailed the edited footage to Ray who called a meeting with his Managing Editor. He took a seat in Tammy Lindberg's glass-walled office overlooking the busy newsroom. Lindberg sat behind a desk piled with messy stacks of newspapers, cuttings and printouts. Like her father before her, Lindberg lived and breathed news. It was said that ink flowed through her veins. Ray was about to put that cliché to the test.

'Thanks for seeing me.'

'Make it quick, Ray. I'm on my way out.'

So he did, speeding through the story of Kelly Novak, her fledgling investigation, her suspicious death. He told Lindberg about a *government employee* who had intimate knowledge of the events leading up to — and during — the Baghdad disaster, a man who was now on the run for his life. And he told her about the recent incident at the mall.

'I called around. No one's been booked for any alleged crime outside that mall. It's like the guy just disappeared.'

'Maybe your friend Vasquez is waiting to be processed.' Lindberg leaned back in her chair and folded one trouser leg over the other. 'Who's the *government employee* you're referring to?'

'I can't give you a name. Not yet.'

'And he's intimate with Baghdad?'

'*He* could be a *she*,' Ray countered. 'And yes, that person has first-hand knowledge of the events leading up to the disaster, including why US Special Forces were in Iraq in the first place.' Ray leaned forward in his chair and lowered his voice. 'Tammy, if this thing pans out we could be looking at the biggest political conspiracy in living memory. The word *explosive* just doesn't do it justice.'

Lindberg hesitated.

'Maybe we should take a breath here, Ray. You're talking about the potential collapse of another presidency. I'm not sure the country could stomach that so soon after Stein's incarceration. And Coffman's approval ratings are the highest I've seen for *any* president. She's built up a lot of trust.'

Ray opened his mouth to reply. He was about to tell her about the lab in Iraq, about the Angola virus, the planned decimation of the human race — the missing pieces of the puzzle that had seen an American president dragged out of the Oval Office in chains...

But he stopped himself. 'Okay, so how should we play this?'

Lindberg toyed with the platinum wedding band on her finger. 'For now, write it up and send it to me. I'll need context and background, and I'll need the name of your source.'

Ray shook his head. 'I can't do that, Tammy. I made a promise. His life is in danger.'

'You don't know that for certain. Besides, legal will insist on it. I'll need to speak to the board too.'

Ray leaned back in his chair. 'I'm sensing a little reluctance here, Tammy.'

Lindberg got up and approached the glass wall. She looked out over the newsroom, arms folded, silent, thoughtful. Then she turned around.

'We have to tread very carefully, Ray. This can't look like a witch hunt — '

'With all the bodies piling up? C'mon, Tammy.'

'Be that as it may, we have to be sure about everything. *Before* we publish.'

Ray nodded, tight-lipped. Tammy was right, they couldn't take a chance with this one. They had to be sure. And then a thought occurred to him. 'I have an idea,' he said. 'An opportunity to test the story's credibility.'

Lindberg crossed the thick carpet and sat in the chair next to Ray.

'I'm listening.'

SNOWCAT

'PLEASE PLACE YOUR HAND ON THE SCREEN, MADAM PRESIDENT.'

The palm print scanner was recessed into the granite wall and Coffman rested her hand against it, watching the light bar sweep up and down. The mahogany double doors parted with a quiet hiss of air.

'Like something out of *Star Trek*,' she observed with a smile.

Coffman stepped inside. Directly facing the door was another granite wall, this one decorated with the Seal of the President of the United States. She followed Schultz around the wall and the apartment opened up before them. The admiral, dressed casually in corduroy trousers and a roll neck sweater, had been at the mountain retreat for the last two days, and he gave Coffman the grand tour of the master suite. She had to admit, it was pretty goddamn impressive; a luxuri-ously-appointed bedroom, a vast dining and relaxation area that overlooked the snow-dusted plateau below, a private gymnasium, steam and sauna facilities, a library and even a private cinema room. It was an apartment built for a man who'd intended to rule the world. Unfortunately for him, he'd been forced to downsize into a narrow concrete box.

Schultz pointed across the marbled lobby. 'That's a private elevator. It'll take you down to the lobby, the conference floor, and the parking lot below. It also has direct access to the emergency shelter. Would you like to see it, ma'am?'

Coffman shook her head. She'd had enough of underground facilities.

'There's another fifty apartments on the levels below us,' Schultz continued, 'which means we can accommodate the Cabinet and National Security Council.' He shook his head. 'This place really is something else, isn't it?'

Coffman had to agree. The Eyrie was a remote redoubt built to accommodate The Committee's most senior members so that they may escape the chaos and death in the wake of the Angola virus, and Coffman was again stung by the decision to exclude her from their ranks. Except now they were all dead or in jail, and Amy Coffman was the one enjoying the fruits of their labour. *Every cloud*, she mused.

Trailing her around the room, Schultz continued his running commentary. 'Everything's in perfect working order; power, climate control, water and sewage systems, communications, everything. As for security, well, it's certainly on a par with Camp David. We're talking about a highly-sophisticated surveillance system that covers the whole mountain. Right now we have a company of Marine infantry providing physical security, but we can scale that up to a full battalion if the situation demands it.'

'And all this now belongs to the federal government?' Coffman asked.

'You signed the Executive Order yourself, when you first took office. That gave us the power to seize all of The Committee's real estate. We've also used *eminent domain* statutes to extend the security envelope into the surrounding valleys and erect additional fencing. Blue Grouse Peak is now a federal facility, codenamed *Snowcat*.'

Coffman turned to look across the room. Erik was

standing at the glass wall, staring into the plateau below. She was starting to worry about Erik. By his own admission he was more than a little disturbed by Bob's plan. For the first time since she'd known him, Coffman had doubts about her consiglieri.

'What d'you think, Erik?'

Mulholland stopped chewing his fingernail. 'This place? Yeah, impressive.'

'Think we can sit out the end of the world up here?'

His eyes twitched. 'Excuse me?'

'I'm kidding,' Coffman quipped. She switched her gaze to Schultz. 'We need to talk. Dinner is at seven. Just the three of us.'

'Yes, ma'am.'

COFFMAN SETTLED IN FOR THE EVENING. WITH BAGS UNPACKED and the pressing business of government dealt with via tele-conference, she returned to the privacy of the Presidential Suite where she pounded the treadmill for thirty minutes. Afterwards, she hit the steam room for another thirty. By the time dinner was served, the President of the United States was feeling pretty good.

Beyond the glass wall, night had fallen across the plateau. The blinds were lowered and coffee was served. Throughout the meal, Charlie had gushed about *Snowcat* while Erik ate in relative silence. After the white-jacketed stewards had retired for the evening, Coffman invited them both to join her on the couches arranged around the glowing granite fireplace. It was decision time. The clock was ticking and the ball was already in play.

'We've all had plenty of opportunity to digest Bob's plan,' Coffman opened. 'The question is, what do we do next?'

'The concept has merit,' Schultz replied, 'at least from a geopolitical standpoint. Theoretically, an immunised America would find itself in a position of unrivalled power and influence in the wake of a global H-1 pandemic. International tensions could go either way in the short term; an increase is probable in unstable regions, while an overall de-escalation is likely as the pandemic spreads and countries topple like dominoes. So Bob's plan is workable. Theoretically,' he reiterated.

'It's mass murder,' Mulholland stated bluntly. 'Baghdad was bad enough, but this is a whole other level.'

Coffman smiled. 'Correct. This time we're in control.'

'How do you figure? At least Angola was clean. H-1 is ugly and murderous. How do we control something like that?'

'With the appropriate munitions,' Schultz told him. 'Lighten up, Erik. This won't be happening on our shores, remember?'

Mulholland ignored him. 'We're talking about a lot of deaths, Amy. Millions.'

Coffman put down her coffee cup and sat forward on the couch. 'Tell me, Erik, how many people die of starvation every year? Ballpark.'

Mulholland shrugged his shoulders. 'I have no idea.'

'Then let me educate you. The figure is at least forty million, and it's rising. You think that's acceptable in the twenty-first century?'

'I didn't realise you gave a damn.'

Coffman's eyes narrowed. 'I'm making a point. Take our southern border for example. It's practically under siege by people who've been driven to our doorstep by food insecurity, political instability and economic opportunity. I promised to do something about it during my campaign, remember? I'm being pressured to open that border. If I do, we'll never be able to close it again. In a decade, maybe less, Texas, New Mexico, Arizona and California will all fold, leading to further instability.'

Her Chief of Staff frowned. 'What has any of that got to do with Bob's plan?'

Coffman didn't answer straight away. Instead she finished her coffee and put her cup down. When she spoke again, the flames of the fire danced in her eyes.

'It's about control, Erik, and we're losing it. Rich and poor, black and white, red and blue, we're all at each others' throats, and those divisions are slowly tearing the fabric of this country apart. And when the public learns the truth about The Committee, any faith in government and its institutions will disappear overnight. Legislative business in DC will grind to a halt. Rumours, suspicion and accusations will tear both Houses apart. On the streets there'll be outrage, anger and fear. Violence will swiftly follow. Society will fracture and people will be forced to pick a side. At that point, we'll be staring down the barrel of another civil war.'

The fire spat and crackled. In her mind's eye, Coffman saw the flames of rebellion engulfing the White House.

'It'll happen faster than we anticipate,' Schultz said, underpinning the President's bleak vision. 'The financial scandal cover story is taking on water, and Moody's widow is still pissed that her husband got the blame for Baghdad. She's started making noises about his role in stopping, quote, *a global disaster*. My guess is, she knows about the Angola virus.'

Coffman snorted. 'Of course she does, and the Delta guy Chase is still out there in the wind. Christ knows who else he's talking to, but you can bet your ass he's talking. Either way, one of them is going to light a match under this whole goddamn powder keg, and when it blows, well…'

Coffman left the statement hanging in the air as she stared into the flames. 'The old order is dying, and not just here in the United States; Europe, Africa, the Middle East, Korea, they're all political pressure cookers. Bob's right, factor in increased WMD proliferation, a deepening climate crisis and rising starvation, and you've got a cocktail for global disaster. Whichever way you cut it, people are going to die in huge numbers.'

Coffman got to her feet. She dimmed the lights and pushed the button to raise the blinds. Beyond the glass wall, the plateau glowed white beneath a new moon and a light dusting of winter snow. Stars glittered in the clear night sky. She heard footsteps as the men crossed the room to join her.

'It's beautiful, isn't it?'

'Yes, ma'am.'

Coffman waited for some time before she spoke again. 'Bob has handed us a blueprint for global control. I say we run with it.'

Mulholland turned away from the glass. 'And inherit what, Amy? Deserted cities, billions of rotting corpses, disease, failing infrastructure, environmental damage — '

'All of that,' Coffman shot back. 'You're right, Erik. It won't be easy. The clean up may take decades, but the United States will be insulated from it all. *We* decide which countries are saved and which ones get rebooted. We'll control it all.'

Mulholland bit his lip. 'I don't know — '

'It's the right thing to do. And the moment the virus breaks, our first priority will be to protect this country, keep us all safe. Tell him, Charlie.'

Schultz turned to face Mulholland. 'We're going to close the southern border and seal it tight. And I mean seal it, with a *real* wall. Then we'll offer Canada our protection. Eventually we'll take over, annexe the country, increase our land mass and create a huge, natural buffer zone.'

'In other words, we will prevail, Erik.' Coffman stared out at the frozen wilderness. 'And somewhere in that future, Bob has to go.'

Schultz shared a look with Mulholland. 'Ma'am?'

Coffman turned away from the glass. 'He developed a bioweapon, then threatened us with it. He had us fly all the way to Seattle so we could gasp at the size of his balls. Good intentions aside, I can't accept that. Matt will be dead in six months, tops. Bob's a loose cannon. He needs to go too.'

'It's a prudent move,' Schultz agreed.

Coffman turned to Mulholland. 'Erik?'

'We've discussed this before, Amy. A guy like Bob will have the goods on you. Remember that first meeting with Aswad? Bob set it all up. Probably recorded it too. Then there's the slush funds, the donations — '

'I don't mean now, Erik. I mean sometime in the future, after we've consolidated our power. Bob will want a seat at that table. In fact, he's probably got his eye on the throne itself. Men like Bob Blake are never satisfied.'

'He's vile,' Mulholland said. 'The world will be better off without him.'

'So, we're agreed then.' Coffman stared out of the window, at the untamed beauty below her. 'I get goosebumps just thinking about what lies ahead.'

Mulholland stepped closer, a warning note in his voice. 'This is Pandora's box, Amy. Once we open it we might never get the lid back on.'

Coffman laid a hand on Mulholland's cheek. 'I'm worried about you, Erik. You've not been yourself since Baghdad.'

The Chief of Staff swallowed. 'It shook me up, I won't deny it, but the scale of what we're contemplating frightens me, Amy.'

'We don't have much choice,' Schultz told him. 'The way things are going, this may be the last chance we have before the country starts coming apart.'

Mulholland shrugged. 'Then maybe we should let it. Maybe the whole system needs to come down so we can build it up again — '

'No,' Coffman snapped. 'I can't allow that. Not after everything I've sacrificed to get here.' She stood in front of

Mulholland, her arms folded across her chest. 'I need to know, Erik. Are you in or out? It's your choice.'

Mulholland held her expectant gaze. 'I'm scared, Amy, sure I am, but you know what *really* scares me?' He tapped a finger on the glass. 'Being out there, just another citizen, a nobody, cowering in the dark, not knowing what's coming. This is where I need to be, right here, on the inside. The alternative is something I can't contemplate.'

Coffman smiled then turned to Schultz. 'Are you ready for this, Charlie?'

'We had the grandkids over last weekend,' he told her. 'Watching them gave me pause, forced me to think about the world they'd grow up in. Everything you've said tonight is true, ma'am. The way I see it, what we're about to do is painful but necessary.'

'Your descendants will thank you for it.'

'What about Karen?' Mulholland asked. 'She's your National Security Advisor. And she knows all about Baghdad.'

Coffman smiled. 'Karen's already on board. So, we're decided then?'

The men shared a look, then nodded. Coffman crossed to the drinks cabinet and poured each of them a couple of fingers of scotch. She handed out the glasses and raised her own.

'To us. And to the future.'

'The future.'

Cut crystal echoed off the granite walls. Coffman emptied her glass and set it down.

'So, let's get to work.'

THE C-17 GLOBEMASTER IDLED AT THE END OF RUNWAY ZERO-Nine at Ramstein AFB, its grey fuselage slick with rain, its anti-collision lights pulsing.

Mike Savage and Stan Lando were stood a short distance away as they watched Mike's guys board the aircraft, hefting their black gear bags up the loading ramp. They wore civilian clothing, as did the four other men who clambered out of an air force minivan and followed them up into the aircraft. Stan had to shout to make himself heard above the engine noise.

'I got you four guys from Red Squadron, Seal Team Six. Guy in charge is Senior Chief Billy Finch. They'll provide security and tactical support, should you need it.'

'Roger that.'

'If and when you liberate Nunez, the CBRN team will oversee his evac to the Regional Medical Center at Landstuhl.' He pointed to the Transport Isolation System mounted inside the aircraft. Specialists from the US Army's 1st Area Medical Lab fussed over its clear Trexlar flanks, connecting hoses and data lines. 'They'll stay onboard until you call them up. Embassy transport will meet your team in Vienna and get you to the location. You'll liaise with their counter-terror guy, name of Unger. And Mike…' Lando stepped closer, leaned into Mike's ear. 'This is their turf. They're running point on this one, so let the locals do all the heavy lifting. Your job is to ID Nunez then evac his ass, nothing more. Debrief will be at the embassy. I'll fly in later tonight.'

He gave Mike a good luck slap on the arm and hurried through the rain to a waiting Ford Explorer. Mike jogged up into the belly of the Globemaster and the ramp doors closed behind him with a loud, hydraulic whine. A big guy with short dark hair and a few days' growth on his face was waiting to greet him. He held out his hand.

'Billy Finch.'

'Mike Savage. Good to have you aboard. Take a seat and we'll talk once we're in the air.'

Mike shook hands with the other SEAL operators and headed up to the cockpit. It was lit only by its instrumentation as the pilots went through their pre-flight checklist.

'We're good to go,' he told them.

The captain nodded. 'Three minutes to departure.'

Mike took a seat in the rear cabin, belted up, then started flipping through the intel package. A couple of minutes later he felt the engines wind up and the fuselage shudder. The brakes were released and then they were moving, thundering down the runway and lifting up into the skies of southern Germany.

STAND TO

PHILIP WAS PACKING CLOTHES INTO A SMALL WHEELED SUITCASE when Marion entered the room and closed the door behind her. She beckoned him to follow her into the bathroom. She pulled him close and whispered in his ear.

'Did you see the text?'

'What text?'

'From Arizona. We have thirty minutes to get clear.'

Philip marched out of the bathroom and picked up his phone. He read the message, swore under his breath. 'Meet me in the lobby in ten minutes.'

Marion hurried from the room as Philip threw the rest of his things into the case and snapped it shut. The text was expected, but Philip assumed it would come later. It reminded him of the other message he'd received, back in the Northridge ops room in Baghdad. That one had also been brief, a sudden and explicit warning. He'd led his best men down into the basement, cringing as the blast swept away the building above their heads. They'd survived — just — and then they'd dug Lance Corporal Nunez out of the rubble. As Philip lifted his case off the camp bed and wheeled it across the room, he felt a fleeting stab of sympathy for the sad, limbless creature they'd buried alive beneath that distant German forest.

He checked his documentation; two passports, several credit cards and eight thousand dollars in cash. He placed the items into various pockets, pulled on a thick North Face parka and left the room.

Marion was waiting downstairs. The lobby was in darkness, the reception desk empty, the building long since abandoned by its previous tenants. Steel shutters covered the doors and windows. Men and women passed to and fro, hard-core anarchists and environmentalists who'd been recruited along the way. Like their British counterparts they were committed to the cause, fanatical to the point of extreme violence, violence that was necessary in order to save the planet. Unlike their British counterparts, they were still alive, but that wouldn't last long.

'Ready?' he asked Marion.

She nodded.

A voice barked. 'Where d'you think you're going?'

Philip turned and saw Gunter Warburg walking towards them. Warburg was the money man, a Bavarian businessman and former politician whom Philip had duped into leasing the Schloss outside of Berlin, a man possessed of a streak as cold as any Nazi death camp guard. Warburg had also leased their current accommodations, and he'd personally overseen preparations for the coming storm; food, water, power generators, fuel, weapons, ammunition, medical supplies. Warburg and his people had it all. Except the full picture.

His deep, booming voice drew others out of the surrounding rooms, all keen to break the monotony of waiting for Armageddon.

Philip forced a smile as Warburg blocked their path to the main door. Physically he wasn't a big man; below average height, with a bald head and a rotund belly that strained at his shirt buttons, but like all leaders he had presence. When

Gunter Warburg spoke, people listened. It was why he'd run as a Green candidate in the Euro elections, but the cut and thrust of political life had exposed Warburg as a man short on patience, a bully with a quick temper and a penchant for trouble. And those were his good points, Philip knew, recalling the man's wild enthusiasm for the lethal testing they'd carried out on Berlin's unfortunates.

Warburg's eyes flicked towards Marion and the overnight bag at her feet. 'What's this?'

Marion held up her phone. 'My contact at the European Space Agency has finally come through on those freeze-dried food packs. I'm going to Munich to finalise the shipment. It will supplement what we've already stockpiled by at least a year.'

'We have enough supplies,' Warburg told her. 'This is an unnecessary risk. For you *and* us.'

'It's an overnight stay,' Marion assured him, 'and besides, the shipment will guarantee our survival should anything happen to our existing supplies.'

'It's a prudent move,' Philip added, 'which is why I'm going along. To provide support and security.'

Warburg shook his head. 'No, no, no, I won't allow it. Lucas!' he bellowed over his shoulder.

The lumbering Englishman stepped out of the recreation room, a table tennis paddle in his hand.

'Yes, boss?'

'Pack a bag. You're going to Munich with Marion.'

Lucas scratched at his thick beard. 'Now?'

'Now,' growled Warburg. 'You!' he barked, pointing at a thin young man with long, lank hair. 'Take Philip's bag up to his room.'

'I just —'

'It's decided, Philip. Meet me in my office in five minutes. There's a few things I want to go over.'

Philip nodded. 'Of course, Gunter.'

Warburg marched away. Philip watched the boy dragging his roller up the stairs. Marion spoke loud enough for the onlookers to hear. 'Walk me to the taxi, Philip?'

'Sure.'

Philip escorted Marion to the main doors. A shaven-headed German girl, Greta, inserted a key into a wall panel and the shutters rattled upwards. Daylight stretched across the lobby. Greta unlocked the glass front doors and held one open. A cold wind swirled around the lobby and rain lashed the parking lot outside.

'Let me take that,' Philip said, clutching Marion's roller. He grabbed a large black umbrella from the stand by the door and popped it open. Marion took cover beneath it and together they crossed the courtyard. Rain drummed on the brolly, on the cars and trucks in the parking lot.

'Your luggage,' Marion whispered.

'Replaceable,' he told her. 'Keep walking.'

'D'you think he knows?'

'How could he?' Philip replied. 'It's paranoia. After all, he believes Europe is about to be ravaged by the virus.'

'Wait up!'

Philip glanced over his shoulder. Lucas and Karl were jogging through the rain towards them. Lucas wore a hooded parka and had a rucksack slung over his shoulder. Karl was one of Warburg's security team, a former Politzei officer. A noisy ring of keys jangled in his hand.

'Gunter wants you back inside,' Karl said to Philip, jerking a thumb over his shoulder.

Marion smiled, slipping her arm through Philip's. 'He's walking me to the taxi. Be a *liebling* and open the gate, would you Karl?'

Karl hesitated, then unlocked the heavy steel door set into the high concrete wall. He swung it inwards and Philip glimpsed the yellow Mercedes taxi parked by the kerb outside, its lights glowing in the gathering darkness. He took a step towards the steel door. Karl blocked his path.

'The boss was insistent. Inside.'

Lucas took the case from Philip's hand and stepped out onto the street. He rapped his knuckles on the taxi roof and the trunk popped open. Marion gave Philip a hesitant smile.

'Well, I'll see you in twenty-four hours.'

'Have a safe trip,' Philip said smiling, and holding the brolly aloft.

'Let's go,' Lucas shouted, climbing into the taxi.

'Wait, I have something for you,' Philip told Marion, patting his pockets. He turned to Karl. 'Hold this, would you?'

Karl tutted and took the umbrella. As he did so, Philip grabbed the back of Karl's neck and plunged a knife deep into his throat, jamming it to the hilt and working it side to side. Karl gasped, his windpipe already severed, the air escaping from his lungs. Marion moved quickly, snatching the umbrella from his hand. Watery blood ran freely down Karl's exposed neck as he stared into Philip's eyes, a familiar expression of surprise and pain on his face. Philip lowered him to the ground as Karl began choking on his own blood. Anyone watching from the warehouse would surely sound the alarm.

'The taxi, quickly!' Philip ordered.

Marion ran to the vehicle and climbed in. Philip was seconds behind her. He yanked open the other door.

'Lucas, something's wrong with Karl! Come quickly!'

Lucas frowned and clambered out of the car. Philip pointed to the steel door.

'Get something under his head! I'll call an ambulance!'

Lucas lumbered across the pavement. Philip slipped into the taxi and eased the door shut.

'Go,' he ordered the driver.

The Mercedes pulled away from the kerb. Philip twisted around, saw Lucas disappear behind the steel door.

'Nicely done,' Marion said. She spoke in Polish because the driver was a middle-aged Turk whose radio was tuned into a Turkish talk show.

'I had no choice,' Philip replied in the same tongue.

The taxi slowed for a corner and the warehouse disappeared from sight.

'Poor Lucas,' Marion said, turning around in her seat.

'He'd served his purpose. They all have.'

Philip watched the street ahead. The traffic was moderate, the grey skies darkening by the minute. He saw a sign for the train station and settled back into his seat.

'Gunter will lose his mind,' Marion observed.

Philip smiled and looked at his watch. 'The stage is set. It's up to us now.' He reached out and squeezed Marion's hand. 'Are you ready?'

'I'm ready,' she said, and smiled.

'WHAT DO YOU MEAN, HE'S DEAD?'

'Philip cut his throat open,' Lucas said, panting.

'Philip?'

'He jumped in the cab with Marion. They've gone.'

Warburg frowned. 'Gone where?'

'No idea. I dragged Karl inside and locked the gate.'

Warburg ran a hand over his dome. 'I knew something wasn't right. I knew it! Marion too. That bitch.'

He headed across the lobby and out into the rain, flanked by half a dozen security guys. Lucas didn't know many of them, and he couldn't speak the language either. He felt abandoned. Alone.

Karl's body was behind the door where Lucas had left him. He lay on his back, eyes and throat wide open. Water dripped from Lucas's thick beard as he stared down at the body. Warburg stood next to him, his shirt plastered to his skin.

'Philip did this,' he told them all. There was a murmur of disbelief. Warburg silenced them with his next words. 'He's probably police, or a government agent, something like that. Marion too.'

Lucas shook his head. 'That's impossible.'

Warburg looked up at him, blinking away the rain. 'Why d'you say that?'

'I've worked with Marion for months. She did away with the other team in England.'

'What d'you mean,' Warburg spluttered. 'They're at the Refuge.'

Lucas shook his head. 'That's what they thought. There is no Refuge. We drowned them in a quarry. All of them.'

Warburg's mouth dropped open. 'You did what?'

'Marion ordered me to do it. She said we couldn't take the risk of anyone talking. No copper would ever do that, don't matter how deep they are.'

The rain trickled down Warburg's wrinkled face as he stared at Lucas. Then he went to the steel door, yanked it open, stepped out onto the street. Lucas followed, the others spilling out onto the wet pavement behind them.

'Not a single car,' Warburg told them, head swivelling left to right. 'No traffic, no people, nothing.'

Warburg was right, Lucas realised, there wasn't a single living soul to be seen. The normally-busy street was empty, the buildings around them dark and lifeless. The only sound was the rain and the quiet hum of cars on the distant overpass.

'They're watching us, right now.'

'Who is?' Lucas's wide eyes searched the windows of the buildings across the street.

Warburg pushed him backwards. 'Everyone inside, quick!'

The door slammed shut. Heavy bolts clanged home. Lucas's heart pounded as Warburg gathered them close.

'We've been set up. Just like the British team.'

103

'Set up?' Lucas echoed.

Warburg tapped the side of his head. 'Don't you see it, *Dummkopf*? Marion had you do her dirty work for her. Now look at us, all gathered together in one place, and not a single drop of the virus to our name. Philip and Marion have used us. Now they're going to sacrifice us.'

The rain swept across the compound as reality sunk in.

'Fuck the police,' snarled one of the security team. 'I'm never going back to prison. I say we go out fighting.'

Warburg slapped the man on the shoulder. 'That's the spirit! Break out the guns and ammunition. Let's get ready!'

Lucas's mind raced as they splashed across the compound and back inside the main building. He was confused. He was also frightened and angry. He was scared because he didn't know what was about to happen. He was also angry at Philip and Marion, because they'd fooled him and escaped. He imagined them sitting in the back of the taxi, laughing.

The glass doors were closed and locked, and the steel shutters rattled back down. Everyone had gathered in the lobby, their faces confused, scared.

'We've been betrayed!' Warburg yelled. 'Everyone prepare to fight!'

BREACHER UP

MIKE SAVAGE BROUGHT THE SPOTTER SCOPE BACK TO HIS EYE AS cold sheets of rain swept across the roof of the clothing factory.

He was huddled beneath an extractor vent alongside Billy Finch, watching the target building across the street. To the untrained eye, it was an unremarkable structure, a grey, two-storey industrial unit surrounded by high concrete walls topped with rusted barbed wire. Mike and Billy's observation skills saw something else; an easily defended compound, a main building constructed of steel and cinderblock and ringed by open ground which offered overlapping fields of fire from its many windows.

'What d'you think?' Mike asked Finch.

'Well, dropping a JDAM through the roof isn't an option, so I guess we'll have to see how the locals want to play it.'

As if on cue, a man in black assault gear scuttled across the roof and crouched down next to them. 'Drone feed is online,' he said. 'Take a look,' His name was Unger and he was the commander of the *Einsatzkommando Cobra* federal tactical unit that was leading the operation. Mike took the military-grade tablet and watched the thermal imaging footage. The drone was lost in the low cloud, moving in slow circles above the target building.

'Is that a body?' Finch asked, wiping the rain from the screen with a gloved hand.

'*Ja,*' Unger confirmed, 'and judging by the low heat signature I'd say he's been dead for less than thirty minutes.'

Mike and Finch studied the feed. They saw ghostly figures appearing and disappearing behind the upper windows. Their movements were frantic; there was a lot of running, waving and pointing.

'Guns,' Finch warned.

Mike saw them too, the clear silhouette of a weapon in almost every figure's hands.

'Weapons seen, affirmative,' Unger repeated, taking back the tablet and passing it to a subordinate. He looked at his watch. 'We breach in eight minutes.'

'Roger that.'

Mike and Finch followed Unger and his men downstairs. They moved quickly through the factory and out onto *Salamongasse,* a road that ran parallel to the *Kollarzgasse* where the target building was located. Unlike the empty *Kollarzgasse,* this road was thick with Austrian police vehicles and personnel. There was little noise and no flashing lights, just a quiet air of professional urgency. Mike and Finch peeled away and headed towards the two unmarked black Mercedes Transporter vans that had ferried them from the airport to this northern suburb of Vienna. One was a mobile comms unit manned by a couple of CIA operators from the US Embassy. He approached the other one and yanked open the side door.

Inside, the guys were sat waiting, CIA operators and SEAL assaulters, ready to deploy. Everyone wore green NBC coveralls, ballistic vests, combat rigs, tactical goggles and helmets. No one wore insignia of any kind, not even a velcro Stars and Stripes, and all of them cradled short-barrelled HK 416 A5's mounted with Vortex Razor holographic battle sights. All except Pat Flynn, who favoured his Benelli M4 semi-auto shotgun.

'They know we're coming,' Mike told them.

His XO, Don Tapper, frowned behind his goggles. 'How so?'

'Doesn't matter at this point. Intel suggests a head count of approximately thirty men and women scattered across both floors, some of whom have military or law enforcement training.'

'What kind of hardware are we facing?' one of the SEALs asked.

'Handguns and hunting rifles,' Finch told him. 'Nothing military-spec as far as I can tell.'

'What about the virus?' Ty Miller asked. 'How exposed are we going to be in there?'

'There's no evidence the hostiles are taking any NBC precautions, but that doesn't mean the threat doesn't exist, which is why the locals have a team of chemical troops embedded with them. They'll take the lead as and when.'

'Hey, if I go nuts, someone shoot me,' Flynn quipped.

Everyone grinned except Mike.

'Pat's got a point. Let's keep Baghdad in mind, okay?' He studied the faces around him. 'We're here to evac Nunez, nothing more. This is their turf, and these are serious troops, so we take their lead.'

There was a sharp knock on the van's door. One of Unger's men, heavily-armed and dressed head-to-toe in black tactical gear, pointed down the road.

'Transport's waiting. You follow, okay?'

Mike led the Americans out into the rain. It was coming down harder now, and the light was fading fast. They jogged behind the Austrian commando, weaving through a cluster of police and military vehicles. Lined up along the road were four, eight-wheeled Pandur 2 armoured personnel carriers, dark green monsters glistening in the rain. The commando pointed Mike towards the nearest one, and they piled into its compact interior, slamming the doors shut. The rumbling of the turbo-charged diesel engine filled the metal compartment.

Mike looked at each of them in turn. 'Remember, this is their operation. We're observers, unless we're called upon.'

The engine roared and the APC lurched forward.

'Here we go.'

LUCAS HAD NEVER BEEN SO SCARED IN ALL OF HIS FORTY-ONE years.

He'd never fired a gun before either, and his fingers were slippery with sweat as he tried to plug rounds into the revolver's chamber. *Wrong size*, he realised. The canteen table was filled with boxes of ammunition, and surrounded by men and women desperately loading their weapons. Bullets spilled across the table and scattered on the floor. Lucas realised Warburg was yelling at him.

'It's the thirty-eight calibre ammunition!' He picked up a cardboard box and jammed it into Lucas's chest. 'There! Hurry!'

'I hear engines!' someone shouted. 'They're coming!'

Everybody around the table stopped to listen. Then Lucas heard it, a low rumble somewhere in the distance. He prayed it was thunder but knew it wasn't. The overhead lights went out and the room was plunged into darkness. Warburg began shouting again.

'Everybody to their positions, now!'

Lucas stared at him. He usually wore slacks and a shirt, but now Warburg was dressed like a revolutionary, his camouflage trousers tucked into high-legged boots, a bullet-proof vest strapped over a black polo neck. He wore a pistol on a holster around his waist and Lucas watched him pull it out and cock it. The thunder outside got louder.

'This is it!' Warburg roared. 'Kill them all! Kill the pigs!'

Lucas bolted from the room with the others. With the power cut and the windows boarded up it was difficult to see. Torches bounced in the darkness. Lucas made for the staircase and clambered up to the second floor, praying no one would notice. His assigned defensive position was downstairs in the main corridor, behind the hastily-constructed barricade, but Lucas didn't fancy his chances behind an overturned canteen table. He'd seen enough TV to know that when the authorities mounted raids they did it tactically, with helmets and machine guns. Lucas didn't have the stomach to stare down the barrel of a machine-gun.

I should've run, he berated himself. But he didn't. Instead he'd sounded the alarm, and now he had a gun in his hand and his back against the wall of the upstairs landing. He crept along it and peered through a window overlooking the street. The rumbling got much louder, and with it, the beating of Lucas's heart.

The pistol felt greasy in his hand, and then he remembered it was still empty. He dug into his pocket and pulled out the box that Warburg had given him, spilling the rounds onto the floor. Greta was standing at the next window and cursed him viciously, and then her head exploded in a puff of red mist. She folded to the ground, her side-by-side shot gun skittering across the tiles. People began shouting and screaming as glass exploded and more people were hit, their blood leaking across the hallway. Lucas finally managed to load his revolver. He flipped the chamber closed and held it in his sweaty palm. The roar of vehicles filled the air and drowned out the screaming and shouting around him. Lucas risked a look and saw a line of tanks thundering along the road towards them.

Holy fuck!

The first one turned, crashed through the vehicle gate below and disappeared into the compound. The others followed, their huge tyres screeching. Lucas dropped to the floor as more bullets shattered the windows. He stared into Greta's lifeless eyes as her blood leaked across the tiles. *So much blood.* Running feet pounded past him and down the stairs towards certain death. Lucas wasn't interested in dying.

When the last person had passed him, he threw the revolver away and began crawling over Greta's dead body towards the other end of the building.

MIKE AND HIS TEAM TOOK COVER BEHIND THE HEAVY STEEL doors of the APC, weapons trained on the building. Inside, gunfire lit up the walls and ceilings. Shouts and screams competed with the shooting and concussive thump of stun grenades. Mike's eyes scanned the windows as he listened to the calm, measured voices on the radio net they were dialled into. Much of it was in German. But not all of it.

'Charlie Team, receiving.'

It was Unger. 'Send it.'

'Need you in here, asap.'

Mike whistled over to Finch. 'We're moving.'

Finch nodded, his SEALs taking point. Mike led his guys after them, weaving amongst the APCs. They squeezed past the lead vehicle, it's nose buried in the lobby and covered in chunks of cinderblock. Mike saw a body crushed beneath the huge front tyres and kept moving. Unger and several of his men waited on the other side, spread around the walls of the lobby. The sound of gunfire was deafening.

'What's the deal?'

'This place is a rat's nest,' Unger told him. 'They've erected barricades and strong points all over the ground floor. We're taking casualties.'

'Any sign of Nunez?'

Unger shook his head, then pointed to the ceiling. 'Need you to clear the top floor.'

Mike nodded. 'Roger that. Stand your snipers down.'

'Already done. And don't take any chances; these people are fanatics.'

Mike conferenced with Finch and the SEALs double-timed up the staircase, leapfrogging the two Austrians providing cover on the landing. Mike and his guys followed, watching the SEALs bracket the long, shadowy hallway, gun barrels sweeping for targets. Wind and rain lashed through the shattered windows, and bodies littered the blood-stained floor.

'A goddamn turkey shoot,' Tapper whispered over the net.

Mike's boots crunched glass as he approached the nearest window and signalled with his torch. He saw a flickering red response, then keyed his mic.

'Objective is to secure this floor. Billy, take point, clear as we go, and watch your background. Nunez may be up here.'

Finch gave him a brief nod. 'Roger. Moving…'

Mike left Boswell and Tapper to cover their rear and followed the SEALs down the hallway. His guys had a ton of CQB experience but the SEALs did this kind of thing in their sleep.

The hallway stretched away, shattered windows on the right, doors on the left, bodies in between them on the blood-soaked floor. The first three rooms were empty. The fourth was not. Bullets cracked through the door as Finch tested the handle, punching concrete chips out of the opposite wall. Finch turned and pointed along the line to Pat Flynn and his combat shotgun.

'Breacher up.'

Ray leapfrogged the SEALs and studied the door. It had a cheap lock, so he covered it with his barrel. Finch counted him down with silent, gloved fingers.

Three, two, one…

The shotgun round blew out the lock, followed a half-second later by two flash-bang grenades that detonated inside the room with a blinding crack. The SEALs charged into the room, splitting left and right, firing as they moved. Mike followed them inside. He saw a young girl sprawled lifeless on the floor. Lying next to her was a grey-haired, middle-aged woman. She rolled around in pain, her knees drawn up, her arms wrapped around her bloody stomach.

'Hands! Hands!' Finch yelled as he advanced towards her. Red dot lasers swarmed across her body. Her hands came up, one of them holding a revolver. Suppressed weapons chattered. Brass casings sang as they bounced across the floor. The woman died instantly, her eyes wide in death, the holes in her sweater bloodied and smoking.

'Clear!' Finch called.

'Coming out!' Mike yelled as they backed out of the room.

By the time they'd reached the end of the hallway they'd dropped another three targets. That left only one room to clear, behind a narrow door that looked like it might be a storeroom. Finch reached out and tried the handle. He shook his head. Flynn stepped up again and held the barrel of his shotgun an inch from the lock. *Boom!* The slug took a huge chunk out of the door and it swung inwards, shedding splintered wood.

'Don't shoot! Please! I'm unarmed!'

The room was small, not much more than a narrow space crammed with buckets and mops and a few shelves. And a large bearded man lying on the floor. A man with empty, bloodied hands and fear in his eyes. A man who spoke English.

Finch jammed his gun in the man's face. 'Do as I say and you'll live.'

The man nodded several times, hands shaking.

'Are you armed?'

The big beard shook violently from side to side.

'Got a live one,' Finch shouted over his shoulder. 'Coming out.'

The SEAL commander backed out of the cramped space and ordered the man to crawl towards him. As soon as he was clear of the room, Mike and Flynn moved in. The prisoner's hands and ankles were secured with plastic ties. He was searched, then hooded.

Mike hit the transmit button and spoke to Unger. 'Upper floor is secure.' He squatted down in front of the prisoner. 'What's your name?'

'Lucas,' the hood said, twitching left and right.

Mike's eyes narrowed behind his tactical goggles. 'Are you British?'

'Yes.'

He yanked the prisoner's hood off. Mike gestured to Tapper who swiped open a military-grade tablet. He pulled up the photofits, studied Lucas's face.

'Positive ID,' Tapper confirmed.

Mike handed back the tablet and grabbed the collar of the man's coat. 'Where's the hostage, Lucas?'

'What hostage?'

Mike pulled his pistol and jammed it in Lucas's chest. 'Last chance.'

'What fucking hostage!' Lucas wailed. 'I don't know what you're talking about!'

Mike had seen fear before. The Brit was telling the truth. 'What about the virus? Where's it kept? Tell me, right now!'

'I don't know, I swear! Marion and Philip, they'll know. They're in charge — '

Mike pulled the hood back down over Lucas's face. 'Don't move, don't speak.'

The shooting downstairs had intensified, and Mike recognised the sound for what it was, a final, desperate, defensive action. Gunfire and flash-bangs shook the walls, and then several louder, heavier concussions.

'Grenades,' Finch observed.

Mike swore as he listened to the sounds of battle, registering the different weapon reports, trying and failing to count the rounds. He radioed Unger several times without success.

Finch shook his head. 'Who the hell are they engaging down there? The goddamn Taliban?'

'Fanatics,' Mike told him.

Finch nodded to the prisoner at their feet. 'Could've fooled me.'

'Clear down. Ground floor is secure.' It was Unger, breathless over the radio.

Mike gathered his team and escorted the prisoner downstairs. He left them in the lobby and went looking for the Austrian commander. He found him in a canteen at the far end of the building. Or what used to be the canteen.

Mike ignored his own rule and flipped up his goggles. He waved his torch around; the carnage in the room was incredible. Charred furniture lay in a messy pile, a pointless barricade of tables, chairs, overturned cupboards, all of it turned into Swiss cheese by hundreds of bullet holes. The walls were pockmarked and blackened by multiple explosions, the windows blown out, the rain now falling across the blood-streaked floor. And the bodies lay everywhere, some piled on top of each other, many of them limbless and mangled beyond recognition. Mike couldn't even tell what sex they were. He saw Unger walking towards him.

'What the fuck happened?'

'Let's step outside,' the Austrian said, steering Mike towards the hallway.

'Fine by me. It's a goddamn abattoir in here.'

'Like I said, fanatics.'

Out in the hallway the Austrian troops were picking through the debris. 'Call the NBC teams up,' ordered Unger.

Mike flipped his goggles back down. 'You find Nunez?'

Unger shook his head.

'How many live ones have you got?'

'They're all KIA.'

'All of them?'

Unger shrugged. 'Prisoners were not a mission objective.'

Mike glanced over the Austrian's shoulder, at the slaughterhouse behind him. Unger wasn't kidding. It wasn't just blood and cordite making Mike's nose wrinkle.

'We bagged one.'

Beneath the rim of his black helmet, Unger raised an eyebrow. 'You did? Okay, we'll take custody.'

Black uniforms gathered in the gloom, watching the exchange. They were still keyed up, gun barrels hot, trigger fingers still twitchy.

'He's American,' Mike lied. 'I've already called it in. We'll take it from here.'

'Wait a minute — '

But Mike was already moving, striding back to the lobby where his guys had gathered behind the beached APC. Miller and Boswell had a hooded Lucas between them. Mike grabbed Tapper's arm.

'Call up the vans and get them to meet us out on the street.'

'Already done,' his XO told him.

'Nice. Move the prisoner right now. Keep his head down and his mouth shut.' Tapper obeyed immediately. Mike turned to the SEAL commander and said in a low voice. 'We're moving to the street. Cover our six, okay? The atmosphere's getting a little frosty in here.'

'Affirmative.'

Mike followed his team outside. The rain had stopped and night had fallen. The compound was a shadowy no-mans-land and Mike imagined crosshairs on his back all the way across the wet tarmac. He clambered over the rubble of the wall and out onto the darkened street where the two Mercedes vans idled by the kerb, lights off. Tapper had already bundled the Brit inside the team vehicle. Mike waited for the SEALs to board and slammed the door shut.

'Airport, now,' he ordered the driver. 'Don't stop for anything.'

He held on tight as the van took off at speed, followed by the comms van. Finch's SEALs had already safed their weapons and were stripping off their gear. Mike leaned across and shook Finch's hand.

'Thanks, Billy. Good job.'

'No problemo. What was the deal back there?'

Mike started pulling off his coveralls, mindful of the silent, hooded prisoner in their midst. 'Let's just say that the quicker we're wheels up, the safer I'll feel.'

'Understood.'

They lapsed into a calm, professional silence as the two Mercedes Transporters threaded through the police cordons and headed east towards Vienna International Airport.

DOUBLE DOWN

'LADIES AND GENTLEMEN, THE PRESIDENT OF THE UNITED States.'

The James S Brady press briefing room was packed, as she'd expected it to be. Every seat was taken, the aisles jammed, the cameras broadcasting live. As she stepped up to the podium and arranged her notes, the White House Press Corps retook their seats and settled in. Coffman slipped on a pair of red-framed designer glasses, cleared her throat and began.

'Good afternoon.'

A chorus of respectful responses greeted her. She glanced around the faces in the room, saw the Coffman acolytes seated in the front rows, the sympathetic others seated in the chairs behind, all fervent admirers who'd sipped the Coffman Kool-aid and decided they liked the taste. This was a long way from a tough crowd. It would make the sell that much easier, but everything was in the wind right now, and although Coffman felt nervous about the future and what it might bring, she also felt a great deal of excitement. In fact, with the fate of billions in her hands and the pieces already in play, she realised she'd never felt happier.

'As most of you know, fourteen US personnel serving in Afghanistan recently contracted a rare form of typhoid and are currently undergoing treatment at an undisclosed military installation outside of that country. None of the affected personnel are in any immediate danger and the families have been informed.'

Coffman raised her eyes. Everyone was staring at her, pens poised over notepads.

'Some personnel who'd been exposed to the outbreak recently returned to their units here in the United States. These men and women have since been located, checked and cleared, however, the incident has highlighted the need to provide better screening and preventative measures for our brave men and women serving overseas. To that effect, the US Army Medical Research Institute of Infectious Diseases, in conjunction with the CDC and its corporate sponsors, has begun an extensive immunisation program to protect our troops and DOD workers both here and abroad. This will be an ongoing program, and will be incorporated into the US military's existing health systems, to ensure our troops are protected and remain able to defend our nation.'

Coffman sipped from a glass of chilled water as hands went up around the room. She ignored them and continued.

'Moving on, the terrible tragedy of Baghdad just a few short months ago will live long in our memories, and the courage of those who made the ultimate sacrifice should always be remembered. Good prevailed that terrible day and night, but the forces of darkness are never far away.'

She stole another glance around the room, noting the inquisitive frowns, the shared looks. They could smell it, because reporters had that kind of nose. Something big was coming. One didn't use phrases like *forces of darkness* without good reason.

'A short time ago, US and Austrian counter-terrorism

forces successfully neutralised a terrorist plot in the city of Vienna, a plot devised by a previously unknown group of environmental terrorists. The group threatened to release the H-1 virus in an unnamed city somewhere in the world if their demands were not met — '

The room erupted. Hands shot up in the air as reporters clamoured to ask questions. Coffman waited until the furore had died before she continued.

'The plot only came to light after a series of videos were sent to the State Department, confirming the retrieval of infected materials from the wreckage of the embassy in Baghdad by a rogue element in the Iraqi security forces. The materials were subsequently sold on the black market to an environmental terrorist group known as the Global Liberation Front...'

For the next few minutes Coffman filled in most of the blanks, then finished her statement by assuring the assembled media that the international intelligence community remained vigilant to all such threats. She kept it brief, and light on detail. She took another sip of water and prepared herself for the inevitable barrage.

'Okay, I'll take a couple of questions, then I'll hand off to Paula Bustamante from Homeland Security. Jon?' She pointed to the MSNBC reporter in the front row.

'Thank you, Madam President. What form did these infected materials take and how have the Iraqis dealt with the security breach?'

'Paula will get into the detail, Jon, but I'd like to take this opportunity to thank the Aswad administration for their cooperation in this matter. Rebecca?'

Rebecca Adams, CNN, a gushing sycophant.

'Madam President, can you give us any background on the terrorists?'

'The investigation is still ongoing, however we know that

119

they were a well-organised group of environmental extremists from a mixture of European countries, most with long histories of violence. Again, Paula will give you more detail.' She pointed to the smart-suited hack from Al-Jazeera. 'Kim?'

'Has the H-1 virus been recovered?'

'The clean-up operation is still underway. The suburb of Vienna in which the cell was operating has been cordoned off and specialist teams are combing the site for contamination. So far nothing has been found.'

'Was Vienna the target?' the reporter persisted.

'It's too early to speculate,' Coffman told her, 'but international security agencies will continue to remain vigilant to all threats. Rachel?'

Rachel Phelps, BBC. A Coffman fangirl.

'Madam President, there are unconfirmed reports that the UK government has recently raised its threat level to Critical in response to an unspecified WMD incident. Is this related in any way to the events in Vienna?'

'I can't confirm or deny that at this time,' Coffman told her. She glanced at her watch; it was time to wrap things up, and the waters had been sufficiently muddied. 'Okay, I'll take one more question.'

She looked around the room, seeking an unrecognisable face. It wouldn't hurt to mix it up. Then she saw him, a balding, middle-aged man in the centre row with his hand in the air. She pointed directly at him.

'Thank you Madam President, Ray Wilson, Washington Times.'

Coffman noticed a few heads turn. She wasn't familiar with the name, but she knew the paper's owner, Tammy Lindberg. Not an ardent support during Coffman's presidential campaign but pretty positive overall. She smiled in anticipation of another softball question.

'Ma'am, with regard to the recent events in Baghdad, can

you confirm that US Special Forces were in Iraq to neutralise a bioweapon facility. One that was manufacturing the Angola virus for global dispersal?'

Definitely not softball.

Coffman kept her expression neutral as a jolt of electricity passed through the room. 'I'm afraid I can't talk about that, Mister Wilson.'

'Can I ask why not?'

Coffman glanced at her notes, knowing the answer wasn't there. 'It's classified,' she told him.

'Ma'am, was the success of that mission directly linked to the collapse of President Stein's administration?'

Coffman faked a smile as she struggled for an answer. Wilson didn't wait.

'Ma'am, when will the American people be told the truth about President Stein and his administration?'

'The truth?' Coffman echoed. Wilson hit her again.

'Yes, ma'am. Many of those indicted alongside the former president have yet to be charged with specific crimes. Has *habeas corpus* been suspended for these individuals?'

Coffman shifted behind the podium. 'The Attorney General will be making a statement on the issue in the near future,' she lied.

'Ma'am, on the night of the Baghdad disaster, the North-ridge security contractors abandoned the embassy walls after the power was cut. Can you tell us where that order originated from?'

Coffman's brain reeled as cameras stuttered manically. She stared at Wilson, as did the rest of the press corps. They were electrified, hanging on his every word. Coffman knew she'd lost the room.

'My administration has worked incredibly hard to steer this country through its recent problems,' she said, struggling to control her temper. 'Right now, what ordinary Americans need is a strong and stable government. *That* is the priority of my administration.'

Coffman took a moment to sip her water, buying herself a little more time. She knew syrupy platitudes just wouldn't cut it.

'And yet you've asked some important questions, Mister Wilson, questions that demand answers, and to that effect I will be establishing a Select Committee that intends to fully investigate the events leading up to, and during, the Baghdad disaster. It is my absolute determination that no stone be left unturned, so we may find out the truth of what really happened both here in our nation's capital, and in Iraq — '

'You called them true American heroes, ma'am; I'm referring of course to the Delta Force soldiers who survived Baghdad. You awarded each of them the Distinguished Service Cross for extraordinary heroism.'

Coffman seethed. *Where the fuck was her Press Secretary Jim Magee?* Why wasn't he stepping in, deflecting? He was stood to her right, but he might've been a thousand miles away for all the good he was doing.

'That's correct, Mister Wilson. It was an honour to meet them.'

'And yet there was no statement from the White House when they were all killed in a helicopter crash two months ago.'

Another buzz rippled around the room. Reporters twisted in their chairs. Coffman boiled, her knuckles whitening as she gripped the podium. Every eyeball in the room was fixed on her, hers on Wilson's.

'Why was the Alaska crash kept secret, ma'am?'

Coffman's throat was drying fast. She soothed it with a sip of water.

'Losing so many heroes was very difficult for me to deal with, especially so soon after Baghdad. I know many others felt the same, so it was decided to spare the American people more heartache, in the short term at least. Naturally the families were informed.'

'But they didn't all die in that helicopter crash, did they?'

The statement hung in the air like a rancid fart. Coffman wrinkled her nose, adjusted her glasses.

'I'm afraid I — '

'Two of the Baghdad survivors were not on that aircraft. In fact, they're missing. Isn't that the case, ma'am?'

Curious murmurs hummed around the room. Coffman saw pens and pencils scratching furiously across notepads.

'Their names are Nick Costello and Kenny Chase,' Wilson announced for the scribblers. 'Costello was discharged not long after Baghdad and hasn't been seen since. Chase drove out of Fort Bragg and vanished.'

'Well, I'm sure that the relevant agencies — '

'They're not on any missing persons database, ma'am. I've checked. Likewise Pablo Vasquez, a homeless man from right here in the city. Vasquez was abducted from outside the Rhode Island mall three days ago after he used Kenny Chase's ATM card. I've checked with every police department in the city; Vasquez was never booked in anywhere. He's disappeared.'

Coffman felt her eyebrow twitch, and cursed silently. Every reaction, every expression, every physical tic and change of skin tone would be analysed and debated by an insatiable media. *Was President Coffman telling the truth? What did she know? What was she hiding?* She was a deer caught in the headlights, transfixed, unable to move. Wilson was still driving, foot down hard, heading right for her.

'A reporter named Kelly Novak was killed in a hit-and-run on an empty highway a few weeks ago. At the time of her death, Novak was investigating rumours of a conspiracy swirling around Baghdad, of State Department interference and deliberate mismanagement during the crisis. Hers is just one of many deaths that have occurred in the wake of the Baghdad disaster. Can you shed any light on these matters, ma'am?'

Coffman opened her mouth to speak. Magee beat her to it, springing up onto the stage and leaning into the microphone.

'That's all the President has time for, thank you. Paula will now answer any questions about troop vaccinations or the operation in Vienna. Paula?'

Magee waved the smart-suited Latino up onto the stage. Coffman stepped down, white anger pinching her face. She felt Magee's hand on her arm, heard his voice in her ear.

'Ma'am, walk away, right now. I'll deal with this.'

She allowed herself to be guided towards the corridor where Mulholland and Baranski waited. She stormed past them as the Briefing Room erupted in her wake. Thirty seconds later she was in the Oval Office. She waited until her Chief of Staff and National Security Advisor had closed the door behind them before giving vent to her fury.

'I want that asshole's credentials pulled, right now! I want him, and anyone else from that fucking paper of his, barred from this building!'

Mulholland held up his hands. 'That would be a mistake, ma'am.'

'And Magee, that fucking idiot! He should've yanked me off that stage!'

'That would've looked worse for you,' Baranski told her.

'Really, Karen?' Coffman stabbed a finger at the door. 'D'you think that was a solid performance? He grilled me like a fucking prosecutor!'

Coffman cleared her desk with a furious sweep of her hand. Papers fluttered to the carpet. She dropped into her chair and spun it towards the window. She closed her eyes, took a deep breath and held it. She let it out slowly, allowing her fury to dissipate. Anger was bad for her, cancerous to critical thinking. She needed a clear head. One fact, however, was indisputable. She turned back to face the room.

'Wilson knows.'

Mulholland nodded. 'Has to be Chase who's talking. I did a little digging while you were up there. Novak interned at the Times, under this Wilson guy.'

'Who is he?'

'Assistant Managing Editor. He stood in for the Times' regular staffer.'

'Goddam him.' Coffman's nostrils flared, the fury still smouldering. She began chewing an exquisitely painted thumbnail, something she hadn't done in years.

'I warned you, Amy. Silencing Novak was a mistake.'

'No, Erik. The mistake was allowing Chase to live.'

'That was bad luck.'

She rapped her knuckles on the antique desk. 'How does a DC bum end up with Chase's ATM card? What are the odds, for Chrissakes?'

'Chase must've given it to Wilson, to use as bait,' Baranski reasoned. 'The whole thing smells like a set up. Wilson probably has footage.'

'Where's Vasquez now?'

'Bob's people dumped him in North Philly with a roll of cash and a pocketful of grade-A smack. I doubt he'll make it to the holidays.'

Coffman got to her feet, crossed the room and sat down on the couch. She swung one leg over the other and massaged the growing throb behind her temples. Mulholland and Baranski took seats opposite.

'Don't let it rattle you,' Mulholland advised. 'Pretty soon the press will have bigger things to write about.'

Coffman glared at him. 'Is there something wrong with your hearing, Erik? Wilson just told the whole world about the Angola conspiracy and linked it to my predecessor. He practically accused me of involvement in the Baghdad thing, and now he's talking about cover-ups and body counts.' She pointed at the Oval Office door. 'Did you see them in there? They were salivating over Wilson's every word, like he was shovelling chum to a school of sharks. Every media outlet in the country will start digging. They'll be talking about nothing else.'

She bit her tongue as Coffman's private secretary tapped and entered.

'Madam President, Admiral Schultz would like to see you. It's not in your diary.'

'Show him in,' Coffman ordered.

The Chairman of the Joint Chiefs entered the room, resplendent in his black naval uniform, a white service cap tucked beneath his arm. He took a seat and waited until the thick door had closed before speaking.

'I caught the whole thing on C-SPAN. Who the fuck does that guy Wilson think he is?'

'A crusader,' Coffman told him.

'It's breaking news on every channel.'

'No shit.'

'Well, the financial scandal cover story is toast,' Schultz declared. 'Angola will break sooner than we anticipated. A couple of weeks and the whole world will know about The Committee.'

'Exactly.' Coffman wrung her hands, her mind whirling. 'Where do we stand? With Bob's people?'

'They're in transit,' Schultz told her. 'Bob will let us know when they're ready.'

'They need to move faster. Are we prepared? Domestically?'

'Drew's on top of it. We're up to speed on military preparedness, fuel and food supply chains, health care, infrastructure security, border defences — '

'What about the anti-viral?'

'Using the typhoid scare as cover, Kroll has shipped

consignments to over four-hundred strategically important military bases in the continental United States, so the bulk of our armed forces should be immune over the next week or so. That includes our Coast Guard too. National Guard units and big city police departments are also on the distribution list, though reaching those folks may take some time.'

Coffman glanced at her watch. 'We need something to keep the press off our backs. Erik, talk to Jimmy, tell him to prepare a statement, one that reinforces the White House's commitment to a full Senate investigation into Baghdad. And let's get Moody's widow over here for the announcement, give her the full West Wing treatment. Take the sting out of that bitch's tail.'

She turned to Schultz.

'Charlie, I want you to speak to Bob, get surveillance up on Wilson, see if we can locate Chase. And explore some options.'

Schultz raised a white eyebrow. 'Options?'

'For Wilson. He needs to go.'

'Yes, ma'am.'

Coffman got to her feet, restless. She waved the others back into their seats and crossed to the window, her eyes seeing nothing, her mind running through scenarios and outcomes. Everything was coming to a head. Her reputation had been dealt a blow by Wilson. Doubts had been raised. Her approval rating would start to plummet as rumours began to swirl around DC. There would be talk of investigations, her relationship with Stein exploited by her political opponents, and when the truth about Angola hit the streets, civil disorder would follow. That's when it would happen, she knew.

...Madam President, for the good of the country you'll need to stand down...

No.

She crossed the room and retook her seat. 'We're going to release H-1 here at home,' Coffman told them.

Her inner circle stared back at her in stunned silence. Schultz was the first to recover. 'Are you serious?'

'Do I sound like I'm joking, Charlie? We need a crisis on our own soil, one that will make people forget about embassies and helicopter crashes. One that will allow us to pass emergency legislation. A crisis that will scare the living shit out of the American public.'

'Ma'am, with every respect — '

'Get Bob to send a threat to State, from the GLF. They're running out of time, patience, that sort of thing. They're going to give us a display of their power.'

'A display?'

'Yes, Charlie. Are you going to keep repeating everything I say?' Schultz shook his head. 'Good. Now, I need you to pick a city, one of little strategic or economic importance. One where the virus can be easily contained. I want the visceral, undiluted horror of H-1 beamed into every home in this country. And then we'll come riding to the rescue. We'll stop it dead and we'll employ the full power of the US military to do it. It'll be broadcast live on TV, like a Hollywood movie, and the people of this country will drop to their knees and thank us for stopping the spread and saving them. They will know that the President of the United States will do anything to protect her people.'

Mulholland shook his head. 'You can't do that, Amy.'

'Of course we can. And we're going to, Erik, because who nows how long it will take for the world to fall apart. And in the meantime, this White House will be put under the microscope. I will not risk that, so revisit the emergency powers enactments. Make sure we're prepared, from a constitutional standpoint. Am I making myself clear, Erik?'

'Honestly? I don't know if — '

Coffman swiped a newspaper off the coffee table and

hurled it at him. Mulholland flinched as the broadsheet hit his chest and came apart in his lap.

'Enough,' she barked. 'I'm not asking for permission, Erik. We've spoken about this, remember? It's all been gamed out in the Pentagon's *Zombie Protocol,* am I right Charlie?'

Schultz nodded. 'Absolutely, ma'am.'

'Then let's get on it.' All three advisors got up to leave. 'Erik, a word, please.'

Schultz and Baranski left the room. Coffman stood up and took Mulholland's hands in hers. 'I'm sorry, Erik. That was unacceptable. Please accept my apology.'

'You're under pressure, I get it, but releasing the virus here? That's just crazy.'

Coffman squeezed his hands. 'Think about it, Erik. People will be so frightened they'll expect us to do everything in our power to protect them. And we will, I promise. We're talking about a very limited outbreak, a few hundred casualties. It's drama, Erik, pure theatre. And when it breaks around the world, on the scale that Bob has predicted, our path will be clear.'

Mulholland nodded. 'I see the logic Amy, but what if it spreads?'

'It won't.'

'But if it does — '

Coffman let go of his hands. 'Enough, Erik. Deal with it and move on. A year from now and all this will be ancient history.'

Mulholland took a deep breath and let it out slowly. 'You're right. I'm sorry.'

'I can't do this without you,' she admitted, laying a gentle hand on his cheek. 'You're my rock. I need you.'

'I won't let you down,' he told her.

Coffman smiled and nodded. 'I know. Now, go see the Attorney General, get a legal handle on those emergency powers. Everyone needs to be ready.'

'Yes, ma'am.'

She watched him leave the room, then her eye caught the newspaper on the carpet, the headline that warned of a simmering trade war with China.

Coffman smiled.

Trade would soon be the very least of Beijing's problems.

BLACK DOLPHIN

PHILIP WHEELED HIS NEW CARRY-ON ACROSS THE CONCOURSE. Marion was waiting for him in the seating area, and she smiled as he approached. He sat down next to her, casually scanning the crowds for anything unusual. The glass-domed departure lounge at Munich International Airport was bustling with travellers, holidaymakers and business people, all jetting off to a hundred different locations across the globe, but Philip saw nothing to alert him, not on the train from Vienna nor here in Munich. They were safe, he decided.

For now.

'What did you get?'

'The essentials.'

'No present?' Marion teased. She linked her arm through his as she leaned against his shoulder. They'd used this ruse before, two lovers entwined, oblivious to the world around them, all smiles and whispers. Yet this time the emotions were real, the words sincere.

'How long until you board?'

Marion looked up at the wide bank of departure monitors. 'The gate's open. I should go.'

Philip pulled her close and pressed his lips to her cheek.

'This is real-world, now. It will spread much faster than either of us anticipate. Make sure you recon your escape route, allow enough time to get out before things escalate.'

Marion smiled and patted his hand. 'Thank you for reminding me. It might've slipped my mind.'

'I'm sorry. I'm being overcautious.'

'It's sweet,' she told him. Her smile faded as she searched his eyes. 'I can take that to my grave. In case this is our last assignment.'

Philip brushed her hair back over her ear. 'This is the life we chose, *kochanie*. How many have we ourselves betrayed over the years?'

'You think Blake and Sorenson might cut us loose?'

Philip shook his head. 'I don't, because we've always delivered for them. This time will be no different.'

'You're wrong, my love. This is completely different.'

Philip pressed his lips against her ear. 'Banish the thought and focus only on the mission. That's your priority now.'

Marion nodded, kissed him on the cheek and stood. Philip got to his feet and held her close.

'Send word when you get to Norway. Let me know you're safe.'

'Of course.' She disengaged and smoothed her hair. 'Take care, Philip.'

He watched her head towards the departure gate, wondering if he would ever see her again. They'd worked together for several years now, and were occasional lovers when circumstances allowed, and Philip had felt a certain attachment towards his former military intelligence colleague. They'd been through much together, but nothing could compare to the mission they were now embarked on, and it wasn't only their employers who were relying on them - the future of humanity was at stake, and the responsibility for lighting the fuse had been passed to them both. Philip believed that this might be the proudest moment of his life.

He looked up at the monitors, then settled back into his seat, filled with a restless energy. Another few days and he would be in position, waiting for the signal, ready to deploy.

No, he corrected himself.

Ready to make history.

THE C-17 TOUCHED DOWN IN A CLOUD OF SPRAY AT RAMSTEIN Air Base, a little under two hours after lifting off from Vienna International Airport.

The aircraft avoided the bright cluster of terminal lights and taxied towards the southern perimeter of the airfield where personnel wearing rain slickers and waving orange wands guided the Globemaster towards an unlit and rarely used concrete apron. There, the engines were shut down, and it waited silently beneath a fine drizzle. Two dark coloured minivans glided to a stop a short distance away. The ramp was lowered and Mike Savage led his team off the plane, leaving the frustrated medical personnel and their isolation equipment behind. Wearing civilian clothes, they bundled their gear and the still-hooded Lucas into the waiting minivans.

It took two minutes to travel from the apron to the dark building partially hidden by the thick woods that surrounded the airbase. Stan Lando was waiting for them in the lobby. He shook hands with Finch and his SEALs. Mike's team followed behind. Lando watched them escort the prisoner down the hallway.

'Jeez, he's a big fucker.'

'Curled up like a baby when we found him.' Mike stepped a little closer. 'He's lucky to be alive, Stan. Those Austrian troops were operating on a shoot-to-kill policy.'

'No Nunez or WMD's either,' Lando added. 'The intel was off.'

'Where did it come from?'

'Let's save it for the debrief.' Lando pointed down the hallway. 'We're in room fourteen. You guys grab a coffee and some chow and we'll get into it in thirty minutes.'

It was well after midnight when Mike had Lucas escorted to the interview room.

Miller handcuffed his right wrist to a steel loop set into the table. The walls were covered with soundproof tiles and the dead air inside the room smelled of cigarettes and sweat.

Tapper set up the audio equipment and gave Mike a nod. Miller whipped the hood off Lucas's head and left the room. The bearded Brit blinked several times as his eyes grew accustomed to the bright overheads.

'Where am I?' he asked, his voice croaky, his head swivelling around the confined space.

Mike and Lando were sat across the table. Mike was the first to speak. 'You hungry? Thirsty?' Mike knew he would be; Lucas hadn't been fed or watered since his capture.

Tapper came off the wall and popped open a tin of soda. Lucas snatched it up and tipped it into his mouth, gulping noisily. He devoured the offered candy bar just as quickly. Mike waited until the big man had finished.

'You're a lucky guy,' he told Lucas.

The Brit rattled his handcuffs. 'I don't feel so lucky.'

'All your tree-hugging buddies are dead,' Lando explained. He cocked a thumb at Mike. 'If it wasn't for my colleague here, you'd be lying toes-up in a Vienna morgue. Take a moment to think about that.'

Lucas stared at the two men sat in front of him, at Tapper leaning against the wall. 'I want to speak to a lawyer. A British one.'

Lando looked confused. He turned to Mike. 'You pass any British lawyers out in the hallway?'

Mike shook his head. 'Can't say I did.' He turned around. 'What about you?'

Tapper glared at Lucas. 'I doubt there's a Brit lawyer anywhere within a five hundred mile radius.'

Lucas's shoulders slumped. 'I've got rights,' he muttered, unconvinced.

'Not anymore.'

Lucas swallowed, his free hand stroking his thick beard. 'Who are you people? I mean, I know you're Americans.'

'He's a quick study,' Lando smirked.

There was a knock at the door and one of Lando's team entered. She handed over a note and left the room without a word. Lando read it, then nudged Mike.

'Let's talk.'

Mike followed him out into the hallway, closing the door behind him. 'What's up?'

Lando handed him the message. 'DDO wants this guy returned to Vienna, asap.'

Mike raised an eyebrow. He read the message, saw the name of the CIA's Deputy Director of Operations. Authority didn't come much higher than that.

'Why?'

'Must be a political angle here.'

'The Austrian op was total overkill. I've seen less carnage after a Paveway hit.' Mike lowered his voice. 'You know what I think? I think if Lucas goes back to Vienna, he'll be dead by morning.'

'I agree, something stinks.' Lando looked at his watch. 'I'll give you one hour, Mike, so squeeze the guy hard and fast. And lay off the heavy stuff, okay? He goes back to Vienna in one piece.'

'Can I hold on to this?' He waved the message slip.

Lando nodded and Mike stepped back inside the interview room. He gave Tapper a covert wink as he re-read the message in his hand. He sighed dramatically, then looked at Lucas and shook his head.

'Wow, you guys fucked up big time.'

Lucas frowned. 'What d'you mean?'

'One of your people in Vienna; turns out she was a Russian intelligence agent. Moscow is going apeshit. They've called dibs on you, so you're heading east. Sorry, buddy.'

Lucas bolted out of his chair, the chain around his wrist snapping tight.

'Wait a minute. What Russian?'

Mike ignored him, turned to Tapper. 'Let's get him prepped for travel. And make sure he gets a decent meal before we hand him over. I doubt the Russians will care too much about feeding him.'

'Hey! I told you, I don't know anything!' Lucas yelled, his voice pitching up a notch. 'I was in Vienna for less than a week. I didn't know anyone, and definitely no Russians.'

Mike stared at him. 'Not interested, buddy.' He headed for the door.

'You can't do this! I'm a British citizen!'

Mike stopped and turned around. 'Let me tell you what you are; you're a major player in an international conspiracy, which, by law, renders you legally stateless. That means the security apparatus of any country on this planet can claim you if they have an interest.'

'In your case it's the Russians,' Tapper added, 'and stateless individuals rarely make it back from the motherland.'

Lucas's head swivelled between the CIA men. 'What the fuck does that mean?'

'You ever hear of *Black Dolphin*?' Tapper asked him.

Lucas's face had paled. 'No.'

'It's a lifers prison near the Kazakhstan border, filled with Russia's most dangerous criminals; serial killers, child rapists, cannibals, terrorists — you get the picture. Once they've squeezed you dry they'll probably dump you in there.

There'll be no file, no paperwork. You'll just disappear.' Tapper shrugged. 'That's how they roll. You should prepare yourself.'

Lucas stared at them open mouthed, his eyes wide. When he spoke, his words trembled. 'I've done some bad shit, I admit it, but I don't know anything about a Russian agent, I swear. Please, don't let them take me.'

Mike stood in front of the table, his arms folded. 'Moscow has claimed you, so deal with it. Besides, you've told us jack shit. We don't even know your last name, and quite frankly it's better for us if we don't.'

'Lucas Wynn,' he blurted. He rattled off his place and date of birth, his address in the UK, the names of his parents and siblings.

'That's nice,' Mike told him. 'The Russians are real big on family. I'm sure your roomies will find all that fascinating.'

'I'll tell you everything,' Lucas jabbered. 'I'll tell you about the tramps, the virus, the incinerator, everything.'

Mike frowned. 'Tramps?'

'You know, homeless people. We killed loads of 'em. With the virus. It worked too. Fucking lethal that stuff.'

Mike raised an eyebrow. 'You mean your operation in England? Yeah, we know all about that.'

Lucas stared open-mouthed. 'How?'

'One of your people was an undercover cop. She survived your hit job.'

'She?'

'A young woman. She gave a very detailed brief about her time with the Global Liberation Front. In fact, she mentioned you by name.'

Lucas dropped back into his chair. 'Olivia,' he whispered. His body deflated like a balloon, his forehead resting on the table. Then he bolted upright. 'Can I see her? It wasn't my fault, see? Marion ordered me to do it.'

Mike picked up a tablet and swiped it open. He showed

Lucas the photofits. 'That's you. This woman is Marion, right?'

Lucas nodded, made scissor fingers. 'She's cut her hair since. Dyed it too.'

'Was she at the warehouse in Vienna?'

'Yeah, but she left with Philip, just before you lot showed up.'

'Who's Philip?'

'A friend of Marion's. She ran the UK operation and Philip looked after Berlin.'

'What's in Berlin?'

'That's where they made the virus. Where they kept your bloke. Nunez.'

Mike took a second or two to digest what he'd just heard. 'Are you talking about Lance Corporal Hector Nunez?'

Lucas nodded. 'They dug him out of the rubble in Baghdad, kept him in some kind of steel box thing. Scared the living shit out of me when I saw him. That was the first one I'd ever seen.'

'And this was in Berlin?'

'That's right. At some old hotel, just outside the city. Me and Marion went there once, to pick up the first batches for testing. After that I'd drive over to France to collect them. They were disguised as mixers, you know, for gin, vodka, so I could smuggle them through customs. Clever stuff.'

'Who was making it?'

Lucas shrugged. 'No idea. Scientists I suppose. I never saw 'em.'

Mike's fingers worked the tablet. He browsed to the *Wall of the Fallen* website, the one that listed everyone killed in Baghdad. He enlarged the picture of a fresh-faced Latino Marine with a dark buzzcut. *Lance Corporal Hector Nunez, USMC.* He flipped it around, shoved it under Lucas's nose.

'Is that the man you saw?'

Lucas nodded. 'That's him. He doesn't look like that anymore, though.'

'Is he there now? In this hotel?'

Lucas bit a nail, spat out the clipping. 'I doubt it. They chopped him up.'

Tapper's face twisted in disgust. 'They *what*?'

'That's what Marion told me. It's how they made the virus.'

Mike leaned closer. 'Tell us about Philip. Age, height, hair colour, anything you can.'

Lucas frowned and stared at the table. 'Same age as Marion I guess, early forties, thin, going a bit bald on top. He was German, I think. Then again, I heard him and Marion speaking some other funny language. I can't say for sure. I only met him once.'

'To clarify, Philip and Marion were in charge?'

'And Gunter Warburg. He bankrolled everything. Used to be a politician or something. Google him.'

'Where's Warburg now?'

'At the factory, in Vienna.'

Mike and Tapper shared a look. The guy was probably being scraped off the walls at that very moment.

'To clarify, Philip and Marion were in charge?'

'Yes,' Lucas nodded. Then he snapped his fingers. 'Wait, there was someone else, an American. I heard Marion talking to him a few times, on that satellite phone of hers. I had my earbuds in, you know, listening to music, but sometimes I'd switch it off and listen to her.' He tapped the side of his head. 'I can be smart too, you know.'

'An American? You're sure?'

'Definitely. He was loud too. A typical Ya — ' Lucas bit the word off and cleared his throat. 'Anyway, Marion did a lot of nodding and listening, like he was giving her orders. And he coughed a lot too. I could hear him hacking away down the phone. A smoker, probably.'

'You hear anything else? Names, places, dates, anything?'

'Nope.'

'And Philip and Marion left before we arrived?'

'That's right.' Lucas spent a minute or two explaining their escape.

'So let me understand this,' Mike said, leaning over the table and fixing Lucas with a hard stare. 'Marion had you clean up the UK operation, making sure you left no witnesses behind. You then accompany her to Vienna, where the Berlin team have gathered, at which point the police show up and kill everyone in sight. Except Philip and Marion.'

'And me,' Lucas told him.

'That's right, and you.'

The Brit frowned, and Mike thought he could hear the man's cogs grinding. Then his eyes widened, and he slapped a big hand on the table.

'They knew you lot were coming, didn't they? That's why they were in such a hurry.' His head drooped, his thick beard brushing against his chest. 'I worked with Marion for a long time. We got on, y'know? I thought we were friends.'

'She sacrificed you, Lucas.'

'I did all her dirty work, killed all them smelly bastards, and for what?' He looked up at Mike, his eyes wide, almost childlike. 'I thought we were doing the right thing, saving the planet. She told us it was the only way. I believed her. We all did.'

'Where were they going?' Mike asked.

Lucas frowned. 'Who?'

Mike clapped his hands in front of the Brit's nose. 'Wake up, goddammit! Philip and Marion; when they left the factory, where were they going?'

'Munich.'

'Which is probably bullshit. So where else would they go?'

'No idea,' Lucas said, and shrugged. 'Somewhere with a lot of people I suppose.'

'To do what? Lie low? Hide?'

Lucas stared at Mike. 'Haven't you been listening? They're going to release the virus.'

HE TOOK THE STAIRS TWO AT A TIME AND HEADED STRAIGHT TO Lando's temporary office, knocking once before marching inside. The field supervisor was busy eating a sandwich as he tapped away on his laptop.

'He give you anything?' Lando mumbled through his food.

'We've got a problem,' Mike told him. 'We've got two targets in the wind. One of them is Marion, the UK intel subject. The other is a guy called Philip. They got out of the factory in Vienna just before the locals threw up the cordon. Like they'd been tipped off.'

Lando put down his sandwich and wiped his mouth with a napkin. 'The DDO will need more than that, Mike.'

'He saw Nunez some months ago, at a location outside of Berlin. They had a lab there, tested H-1 on vagrants kidnapped from the city, just like the Brit operation. He said they chopped Nunez up to reproduce the infection.'

Outside, a C-130 barrelled down the runway in a cloud of spray, the roar of its engines rolling across the airbase. Lando pushed his plate to one side.

'Say that again?'

'Whoever's running this operation has already tied up the loose ends. The UK and Berlin sites have been shut down. Vienna took care of the hired help. Now Philip and Marion are in the wind and they're going to release H-1.'

Lando paled. 'Have we any idea where?'

Mike shook his head. 'Negative.'

'You believe this Lucas guy?'

'I gave him the Black Dolphin line. He's cooperating, believe me.' Mike placed his hands on Lando's desk. 'We have to find these people, Stan. And we'll need every resource available. That'll mean Oval Office approval.'

Lando reached for his phone. He punched a number and leaned back in his chair.

'There's something else,' Mike warned. 'There's another player, a ringmaster, someone calling the shots. An American.'

Lando stared at him for a moment, then the call connected. 'I need to speak to the DDO,' the field supervisor said. 'Right now.'

BOWEL MOVEMENT

MUMBAI, OR BOMBAY AS IT WAS KNOWN BEFORE 1995, IS THE
capital city of the Indian state of Maharashtra. It is the wealth-
iest city in India, and home to the highest number of billionaires and millionaires across the country. It is also the
financial, commercial and entertainment capital of India, and
one of the world's top centres of commerce in financial flow,
generating over six percent of India's GDP. It houses the
Reserve Bank of India, the Bombay stock exchange, the
National Stock Exchange of India, and numerous Indian and
multinational corporations. Its wealth and economic opportunities attract migrants from all over India, creating a melting
pot of cultures and communities.

Philip knew much of this information about Mumbai long
before his plane landed at the city's international airport, but
there was really only one fact that he was interested in, and
that was the size of the city's population. At the last count,
Mumbai's metropolitan area was home to over twenty-four
million people, and even that figure was a conservative one.
For a man who grew up in the remote, fertile countryside of
western Poland, the number was staggering, as was the
potential for chaos. Despite the mild claustrophobia Philip felt

143

at being at the epicentre of such a vast human nest, he was excited by the prospect of unleashing the H-1 virus. He was genuinely interested to see how fast it would spread to the outlying regions of the city and beyond, and perhaps even to the Pakistan border, which would add its own incendiary ingredient to an already volatile mix of Indo-Pak politics.

Philip had entered the country using a Dutch passport, and had passed through customs without incident. A taxi had taken him across the city's appallingly chaotic road network to the Hotel Manama, a pretentious two-star hotel frequented by international travellers on tight budgets, an establishment where Philip would blend in easily, and one where the duty manager was more than happy to take cash for Philip's three day visit. The room was perfunctory, bordering on spartan, and his fifth floor window had a restricted and uninspiring view of the docks. But Philip had no interest in views, only in the hotel's location. He unpacked, turned the air conditioner up and climbed into bed. He woke at seven the next morning feeling reasonably refreshed and ready to work.

After a shower and a cup of coffee, Philip removed a white business shirt from the wardrobe. It was a high quality garment, with double-stitched lining, a stiff collar and double cuffs. He sat down at the small writing desk and took a pair of scissors to it, cutting off the collar and cuffs. It took him another hour to pick out the stitching and extract the wafer-thin plastic sachets that had been ingeniously inserted into the garment. The eviscerated shirt went back into Philip's suitcase. The sachets were held up to the light for inspection. Thankfully they were unmolested and intact, and Philip locked the sachets in the closet safe. He picked up his key card from the sideboard and headed for the door. It was time to go shopping.

Less than five hundred yards to the west of Philip's hotel was Chhatrapati Shivaji Terminus, one of India's busiest railway commuter hubs. Every day over twelve hundred long-distance and local trains pull in and out of its eighteen platforms, carrying over three million passengers on its main and suburban lines. It was another staggering figure, and Philip bore witness to it as he wandered through the station, skirting the rivers of people that swept past, wary of being sucked into the fast-flowing torrent. The heat, the noise and stench assaulted him; if Philip needed reassurance that he was doing the right thing he found it here, where businessmen hurried past emaciated child beggars, where desperate men competed to survive by shining shoes and cutting hair for sums of money that most Europeans wouldn't bother to pick up off the ground. And that was just inside the station.

Philip was relieved to step inside the electronics kiosk and extricate himself from the swirling mass of humanity. The shop sold a wide variety of telecoms and computer accessories, and Philip purchased a mobile phone and a SIM card with plenty of credit. He paid the man an extra two thousand rupees to insert the SIM and test the device by making a call, which the man duly did. Satisfied, Philip left the chaos of the station and strolled back to his hotel along the tree-lined St George Road, admiring the European and Asian architecture of nearby buildings.

And it was on this shaded avenue that Philip made his first mistake.

He caught the scent of spiced food and suddenly Philip realised he'd not eaten since the in-flight meal the day before. There was a food stall ahead that appeared to be particularly popular with the locals, and Philip ordered a styrofoam carton ladled with chicken hakimi and white biryani rice. He found a bench in the shade. He had several hours to kill before he made the call, so he took his time over lunch, spooning spiced chicken and rice into his mouth as he watched the world pass by. On the road, cars, buses, taxis, trucks and bicycles competed dangerously for real estate and the air was alive with blaring horns. It was both fascinating and increasingly claustrophobic, a suffocating mix of heat and noise, and Philip soon tired of it.

He found an overstuffed rubbish bin that was under siege from a mixed flock of sparrows and pigeons, all hopping and fluttering amongst the rubbish. Philip decided their existence was no different from the daily battle their human neighbours endured, and once again he felt justified by his decision. Trash would be the least of Mumbai's problems in the next few days.

He walked back to the hotel, his lightweight shirt soaked with sweat. It wasn't that hot, probably around thirty degrees, but Philip was certainly feeling the heat. Even the air-conditioned lobby did little to stem his discomfort.

Back in his room, Philip's started to feel unwell. He turned up the air-con and laid down on the bed. Then his stomach began to churn, gurgling like a drain. He thought back to the spiced chicken, the greasy mess of meat and rice, and he lurched off the bed and staggered to the bathroom. He only just made it, vomiting into the toilet. His bowels gave way at the same time, and Philip cursed his stupidity, his weakness that had well and truly poisoned him. He knew from past experience that this was just the beginning.

As the nausea receded, Philip stripped off his soiled clothes in the shower cubicle, knowing he had to make two urgent communications. The first one would be a phone call to the hotel manager, to secure the immediate services of a doctor. The second would be an email, an encrypted one that would bounce across several dark web servers until it reached its destination in Flagstaff, Arizona. There the recipient would print out the message, place it in an envelope and transport it to the luxury ranch to the north of the city, located in the Kaibab National Forest.

There, the man with incurable cancer and a burning desire to leave his mark on the world would open the message, knowing who it came from and what it meant. It would contain only one word.

Delayed.

AT THE SAME TIME PHILIP WAS SUCCUMBING TO FOOD POISONING, Marion was conducting her second reconnaissance mission since arriving in China.

The former intelligence officer had carried out her first recon after checking into the Ritz Carlton hotel in Shanghai, where she'd settled into her room on the forty-eighth floor, one that offered impressive views of the city across the Huangpu River. After a shower and a change of clothes, Marion stepped out of the high-rise building into the chilly mid-morning air, walking the short distance to Lujiazui Metro Station. She'd worn a dark navy coat, a high neck sweater and large sunglasses, even applying a little makeup in an effort to look like the western businesswoman she was pretending to be. She'd pre-purchased a travel pass that allowed her unlimited use of Shanghai's transport network, and she'd used it to travel one stop to the Metro station at East Nanjing Road. There she'd alighted, and made her way up the stairs onto the busiest shopping street in the world.

Nanjing Road was the commercial heart of Shanghai, a pedestrianised avenue packed with every fashion, sport and luxury goods store a shopper could desire. It was a spectacular, three-mile-long strip of noise, light and colour. Nanjing Road also boasted over one million visitors a day, a fact that put Shanghai at the top of Marion's target package.

Now night had fallen, Marion returned once more, only to discover the street was even busier than earlier. She craned her neck and was staggered by the sheer volume of people packed between the high buildings, an undulating, shifting mass of humanity that stretched into the far distance. Neon lights and digitised signs bathed the crowds in a kaleidoscope of changing colours, adding to the almost carnival-like atmosphere of unbridled consumer joy. Shopping had never been Marion's thing, but even she felt an unfamiliar lure to what resembled the biggest Aladdin's cave in the world.

But Marion wasn't there to partake in a naked orgy of consumerism.

She bought a burner phone with international credit and wandered the street, noting the CCTV security poles, the black-clad, stern faced policemen and women watching the crowds with suspicious eyes. Thankfully they were few and far between, and Marion was confident their presence wouldn't pose a problem. No, Marion had only two issues to resolve; where to trigger the outbreak, and how to make good her escape before Nanjing Road went to hell.

She'd decided on two targets, just to be certain. The first was the Number One Department Store, a luxury goods emporium built in the nineteen-thirties that had undergone a recent and highly impressive transformation. Marion took the elevator to the ninth floor where the coffee shop and book-store were located. There was also a public toilet facility. Marion stepped inside, impressed by the subtle lighting and gleaming black-tiled floors and walls. And most of all the cleanliness. It made her think of Philip and she smiled, knowing he would be suffering through the heat and filth of Mumbai.

There were four empty stalls to her left, four mirrored sinks to her right. She would target the far stall, she decided. She stepped inside and locked the door. She twisted her wrist and started the stopwatch function on her black military G Shock. She mimicked the physical actions, taking the infected wipe from the pouch and swiping the clear solution over the flush button, the seat, the inside door lock. She flushed the toilet and stepped outside, pretending to wipe the door handle on the way out. One drop of H-1 would be enough. Marion would be spreading over two hundred millilitres of the pathogen. Mass infection was guaranteed.

She left the toilet and crossed to the bank of glass elevators, riding one to the ground floor. Shoppers thronged the main hall. Marion swerved and smiled her way across the impressive atrium and exited the building.

She headed south along Xizang Road towards the People's Square Metro Station where she stopped at a ticket machine. She faked another swipe of the virus across the buttons and then used her own pass to access the barrier.

She took the stairs to the platform below. The next train that was due in less than two minutes, and even though she was performing a dry run, Marion still felt nervous. Perhaps targeting the ticket hall was a mistake. Perhaps it was too close.

The Metro train thundered into the station in a rush of air and a squeal of brakes. Marion boarded, the doors thumping close behind her, and then they were moving. She stopped her stopwatch. Eighteen minutes from first dispersal to evacuation. It would be enough time, she decided. There was a risk to every mission, however she was confident she'd chosen well. The virus would spread down through the department store and out onto the street, likewise the Metro ticket hall. The the virus would spread organically.

The train decelerated, pulling to a stop across the river at Lujiazui. She left the station and strolled back to the hotel. In her room, she made a coffee and stood at the window, looking out across a true twenty-first century city and knowing that her batch of H-1 would send it back to the Dark Ages.

She thought of Philip again, and wondered how his preparations were proceeding. She wanted to call him, to hear his voice, but that was simply not possible. Besides, she had work to do.

She went to the wardrobe and removed a shirt from its hangar, a business shirt, with thick cuffs and a stiff collar.

Marion sat down on her bed and with a needle from her small sewing kit, began to pick away at the collar's stitching, thread by tiny thread.

RAY WILSON SAW THEM AS THE TAXI TOOK HIM FROM THE airport to downtown Lubbock.

He counted four of them, Apache attack helicopters, clattering low over the flat Texas plain.

'They've been buzzing around for the last couple of days,' said the driver, glancing at Ray in his rear view mirror. 'A buddy of mine saw a huge convoy out on Route Eighty-Four last night, heading towards the city. Must be on manoeuvres or something.'

'Right.'

Ray watched the helicopters veer away and disappear into the distance. The sky was grey, the temperature outside pretty damn cold. Ray settled back in his seat. It wasn't the best time of year to be visiting Texas, but Ray was excited nonetheless.

After the White House press conference, Ray's phone line at work had been jammed. Much of it was personal abuse from Coffman fans who'd somehow managed to obtain his direct number. A disgruntled employee had probably leaked it on the Internet, Tammy had told him. She wasn't very happy either. The paper's owner had been confronted several times since Ray's grilling of the president, and it was clear that people were upset.

That had Ray confused. There was the possibility of a cover-up, of serious political wrongdoing, of sudden, unexplained deaths, yet people appeared to be more concerned about the reputation of the president. Ray was starting to believe Americans had lost the ability to know right from wrong. It was all about Blue versus Red now. It made him feel thoroughly depressed.

'Let me ask you a question,' he said to the driver.

'Sure, go ahead.' His name was Raul, or so his dashboard ID badge said. He had dark, slick hair and a white smile. A set of wooden rosary beads dangled from the mirror.

'What d'you think about the President? You think she's doing a good job overall?'

Raul shrugged his shoulders. 'I got a sister and three nieces being held in the detention centre down at McAllen. President talked about an amnesty for undocumented migrants during the debate, right? What's she gonna do about that, man?'

'Fair enough,' Ray said, unwilling to be drawn on such a contentious issue. The truth was, everybody had their own agenda and Washington was a world away from west Texas. People cared about local issues, not what happened months ago in an embassy six thousand miles away.

Raul dropped him off at the Overton hotel, a three star high-rise that was clearly one of the more upmarket establishments that Lubbock had to offer. Ray's room was on the eleventh floor and had a distinctly uninspiring view of the freeway that dissected the city. Beyond the freeway the landscape lay flat and grey, the horizon dotted with clusters of distant wind turbines turning lazily in a cold breeze.

Ray had never been to the South Plains. He'd been to Texas before, to Dallas and Houston, but never this far west. There were no other cities for a hundred miles in any direction. It felt remote, isolated, but Ray was convinced the trip would be worth it.

He took the elevator down to the lobby and snagged a seat in the coffee shop. He flipped open his laptop and caught up on his mail and social media. More abuse, he noticed, including a few imaginative memes that depicted Ray having intimate relations with a variety of farmyard animals. Some people definitely had too much time on their hands.

He scrolled to the email that had brought him to Texas, the one that had followed the mystery phone call and had

DC ALDEN

provided confirmation of the whistleblower's veracity. Ray took a look around the coffee shop. There were a few other guests dotted around, tourists, business people, but no one was taking any notice of Ray. He slipped his ear buds in and played the video file. He'd watched it several times, but the sense of horror and revulsion never dimmed.

It was drone footage, recorded from above the embassy in Baghdad. Like most people he'd seen the online content, the footage shot by Iraqis, but much of that was just light and noise. What Ray was looking at now was a recording of what went on *inside* that facility, a series of edits that showed people being hunted down and torn apart, or becoming infected themselves. It showed uniformed personnel opening fire, it showed flames engulfing the Chancery building, people running, falling, dying. And it came with audio too, gunfire, explosions, and the terrible screaming that made the hair stand up on the back of Ray's neck.

There's more, the anonymous email had promised. *Meet me in Lubbock, Texas. Email me when you're there. I can be with you in six hours.*

Ray tapped his reply and hit *send*, giving the mystery man or woman his location and room number. He'd done the math too; Fort Hood was five and a half hours away by car, and home to almost seventy thousand troops. Fort Bliss was roughly the same distance and another significant installation. His contact was military, Ray was almost sure of it. Whoever it was, they would help him put the pieces together.

As he sipped his coffee he heard the sound again, and looked out of the window. Shadows flashed across the parking lot outside, and Ray glimpsed a couple of helicopters, Black Hawks this time, thundering low over the city.

For some odd reason, the sight made Ray feel distinctly unnerved.

HORROR SHOW

THE C 17 GLOBEMASTER BUMPED AND DIPPED THROUGH THE cold night air on its final approach into Munich International Airport. Mike Savage, sitting in the jump seat behind the co-pilot, was winding up his radio call with Lando when he heard the low, morse-like beeping of the outer marker.

'Wheels down in seven minutes,' the captain said, his hands busy with the controls.

'Roger.'

Mike ended his call and headed back to the cargo bay. He took the seat next to Tapper and strapped in. Lucas was seated in the middle, surrounded by CIA operators and SEALs. Everyone wore civilian clothes, and everyone was armed, their scaled-down rigs hidden beneath their coats. Mike gestured for Finch to come and join them.

'We've got a green light,' Mike told them both, raising his voice above the low roar of the aircraft's jet engines. 'Lando's confirmed diplomatic status for the whole team, including the Brit. We've been designated callsign Task Force Zero, and JSOC has given us a blank cheque.'

'What's the deal with the Austrians?' Tapper asked.

'One fatality, three serious. They're justifying the level of force and the White House is backing them.'

'That's some bullshit,' Finch said.

'They traced the taxi driver. He confirms he dropped the targets off at Vienna's main station. He claims he heard the word *Munchen* twice. Could be a red herring, then again it's all we've got.'

'CCTV?' Tapper asked.

'The Austrians don't have facial recognition, and Marion has allegedly changed her appearance, so that's needle and haystack country. Same for the Germans, but their CCTV systems are fully integrated, which might give us an edge. They're all set up and waiting.'

The aircraft vibrated as the landing gear was lowered. Tapper raised his voice.

'How d'you want to play this?'

Mike glanced over his shoulder at Lucas. The thick beard was gone, his face now smooth, his unkempt hair neatly trimmed. He wore dark trousers and trainers, and an Air Force parka. He could have been one of them, except for the rigid handcuffs that locked his hands in front of him.

Mike felt the aircraft sink lower, and saw the lights of the terminal buildings through the aircraft window. 'We have to pray that the Brit can ID either of these assholes quickly. To that end, German security services have a room all set up with feeds into their transport network, including this here airport. Don, I'll need you to interface their network with our facial recognition hardware. Billy, I want you guys watching and listening. Don't be afraid to holler if you feel the need. We're a team now, so if you've got something to contribute, speak out.'

'Aye, aye,' the Navy assaulter said.

The C-17s wheels slammed into the runway and the airframe shuddered as the aircraft slowed. Mike snapped off his seat belt. Everyone was already on their feet, prepping to deplane. Everyone except Lucas. Mike shimmied along the aisle in front of him and leaned over the seat. Lucas was staring through the window as the aircraft bumped along the taxiway. Mike snapped his fingers.

'Hey!'

Lucas turned, his eyes wide, his expression uncertain. Exactly how Mike wanted him to be.

'That's Munich out there,' he told the Englishman. 'Where you go next depends on you. If you give us false intel or send us on a wild goose chase, you'll be in a Russian hellhole by sunrise, I absolutely guarantee that. If you ID Philip and Marion, you have a chance to walk away.'

That was a lie of course. Lucas was a mass murderer, as heartless as any pathological serial killer. He was going down, he just didn't know it yet.

Lucas nodded. 'I'll do my best.'

'Good boy.' Miller and Boswell flanked the prisoner. 'Get him on his feet,' Mike told them

He led everyone to the port door near the rear of the aircraft. A helmeted airman cracked it open and cold air rushed inside. A fleet of dark vans waited for them. Mike led them down the steps, and he shook the hand of a waiting German intelligence agent. As he took a seat inside the van his stomach suddenly churned. *What if we don't find them? What if we fail and millions die?* He banished the thought from his mind.

There was no *if*.

And failure was not an option.

COFFMAN TRUDGED THROUGH THE WOODS, HER BREATH FOGGING on the frigid air.

She was wrapped in a thick winter coat and presidential beanie, and as she followed the path up towards the distant ridge, she remembered another time, when the creature had charged down through the trees towards her, when she'd come close to death. Back then she'd deliberately foregone the protection of her security detail, and her would-be assassin, Costello, was now buried somewhere down in the dark gorge below her. She'd believed his death had marked the beginning of a new era, a future filled with promise. Then the first of Bob's videos had arrived, and that changed everything. When Bob had dangled the carrot of global dominance she'd taken the bait. After the events in Baghdad, what else would she do?

But the world had turned and things were starting to run out of control. She'd expected that, had steeled herself for some degree of chaos and unpredictability, but awkward questions were now being asked about Baghdad, Alaska and missing soldiers. Wilson's phone was ringing off the hook with invitations to every political talk show imaginable. So far he hadn't accepted any — at least that's what Bob's surveillance was telling them — but that wouldn't last.

Erik walked beside her, wearing thick boots and a quilted parka. He stared ahead, his hands thrust into his pockets, his bearded face like a stone mask. The new look suited him, Coffman decided, though she thought the reason for its growth might be psychological, something to do with telling lies and the subconscious desire to cover his mouth. *Not lies*, she corrected herself, *disinformation*. They'd barely spoken since they'd left the complex, and Coffman could feel her Chief of Staff's anxiety radiating off him.

Up ahead, the lead Secret Service agent had disappeared over the rise. She glanced over her shoulder, saw the other agent further down the hill. Around her, scattered through the trees, the others were too far away to hear anything that passed between them. She slipped an arm through Mulholland's and kept her voice low.

'You seem preoccupied.'

Mulholland offered a strained smile. 'I'm thinking about all those spinning plates.'

'So, what's the word from Bob?'

'One of the deployment team has gone down with food poisoning. It's not a problem, just a delay.'

'Jesus Christ,' Coffman cursed, 'You're telling me that our plan to reshape the world has been put on hold because somebody shit their pants? Has Bob never heard of a backup plan?'

'It's frustrating, I agree. And to make matters worse, the UN Security Council has started making noises. They believe we've been holding out on them since Baghdad.'

Coffman snorted. 'You mean the same Security Council who okayed the plan to nuke the city? They've got a goddamn nerve.'

'We still need allies, Amy.'

'Agreed. Pencil some face time with the ambassador.'

'Will do.'

'What else?'

'Wilson's down in Lubbock as we speak,' Mulholland told her.

Coffman snorted. 'Guess he's not so smart after all.' They walked in silence until they crested the ridge, where they stopped to take in the view. The sparsely wooded slope fell away towards the valley below, rising up again like a dark wave to form another ridge, and another beyond that. Above their heads, a slab of grey cloud moved low and slow across the sky. Coffman turned to face Mulholland. His hands were buried in his pockets as his eyes watched the trees and the distant men who loitered between them.

'They're too far away to hear anything,' Coffman reassured him.

'Can't help being paranoid.' He held her gaze and said, 'The pressure's building. Jim's getting bombarded daily with requests for interviews. Even Metro PD is inquiring about

Vasquez. Unless we move soon, the tide might just turn against us and — '

'They'll bury us both. I get it, Erik. So, we light the fuse ourselves until Bob's guy can peel his ass off the can. Is everything ready in Texas?'

Mulholland scanned the trees as he spoke. 'Reserve units have been mobilised across the country, and Charlie has ordered field deployments in a handful of key states, including Texas. Forts Bliss and Hood have surged men and equipment into the field, which gives us political cover, but it's raised a few eyebrows. Jim's preparing statements for when the time comes. There'll be an outcry, Amy. You'll be burned in effigy for not passing on the warning to the public.'

'And start a national panic? Besides, we'll stop the outbreak dead in its tracks.'

Mulholland held up his hands. 'You know my feelings on that.'

'Only too well,' she said. She took a deep, cold breath and let it out slowly. 'So we're ready?'

'As we'll ever be.'

Coffman pulled her beanie down a little lower as the first flakes of snow began to spiral down from the sky. 'Get word to Bob. Tell him to start the party.'

CHESTER STOKES HAD TWO SIMPLE JOBS TO DO.

The first was to deliver a letter to the concierge desk at the Overton hotel, and the second was to drive across town to the South Plains Mall and go watch a movie. *Easy, peasy, Japanesey.*

He parked his beat-up Impala in the parking lot and strolled into the mall. He'd been told to buy a ticket for the evening movie at the IMAX cinema. He had to take an end-of-row seat and wait to be joined by a fifty-something guy who would identify himself as *Ray.* Chester would then hand over the padded envelope and leave the cinema. For his troubles, he'd be paid one thousand dollars, in cash. He'd already received five hundred in advance, thrust in his hand by a big guy in a cowboy hat and sunglasses who'd propositioned Chester in the parking lot of the Lubbock County Probation Office behind Main Street. He'd climbed inside the man's pickup truck, listened to the terms of the deal, and readily accepted. He'd pocketed the cash, with the promise of doubling his windfall after he'd completed the mission. As an added bonus, if the guy didn't show, Chester could keep whatever was in the envelope. It was an easy gig by any standards, and the Lord knew Stokes needed some good luck.

A career criminal for half of his forty-two years, Chester had long ago reached the conclusion that crime didn't pay. The big job he'd always dreamed of had never materialised, and Chester, despite being a born and bred Texan of poor white stock, had an unlikely aversion to firearms, so liquor stores and banks were not an option. Instead his trade of choice was burglary, domestic as opposed to commercial, and small-time frauds. He'd had a couple of decent scores in his time, had burgled a couple of houses where he'd hit pay dirt, but success, like his ill-gotten gains, had never lasted long. Truth be told, Chester Stokes was a loser.

He'd said as much to the suit in the probation office. After all, eighteen months ago he'd sunk low enough to attempt to rob an old lady of her life savings while posing as a telephone repairman. Her son had arrived unannounced at the old lady's home in Fort Worth, and to compound Chester's bad luck, the man, a former prize fighter, had beaten Chester very badly. After a stay in hospital he'd spent fourteen months in county jail, where he'd reflected on life and the growing futility of it. However, release had come early and Chester decided it was time for a fresh start. And it was outside the parole office when the cowboy had approached him. Maybe his luck had finally turned a corner.

Now, with five crisp Benjamin's in his jeans pocket — and the promise of five more — Chester wandered through the South Plains Mall to the IMAX cinema where he purchased a ticket, a bucket of popcorn and a mega-soda before making his way into the movie theatre. They were showing some kind of superhero crap, but Chester didn't care. He was juiced by the thought of a thousand easy bucks, and as he settled into his seat and tipped a handful of popcorn into his mouth, Chester Stokes wondered what other work the cowboy might have for him.

RAY WILSON CLIMBED OUT OF A CAB AND HEADED THROUGH THE doors of the mall, chased inside by a cold north-easterly wind. Inside, shops and restaurants were busy with the Friday night crowds, and as Ray passed a Tex-Mex restaurant his stomach grumbled with hunger. A freshly-grilled steak would certainly hit the spot. His doctor had advised him to lay off the red meat, but he was in Texas, goddammit. Sometimes exceptions had to be made, so the plan was to persuade his mystery contact to talk over steak and fries. Meeting inside a cinema was an odd thing to do, especially on a busy Friday night. Ray had questions, and tonight he hoped to get some answers.

The letter had promised as much. It had been dropped off at the hotel and hinted at unedited video footage from the Baghdad embassy, of as-yet-undocumented testimony from a civilian eyewitness who'd survived that terrible day and night and wanted to go on the record. Ray was as excited as he was intrigued; all the other testimony had come from military or State Department sources, which naturally would be heavily redacted. This unknown, courageous soul — whoever he or she was — wanted to give an unvarnished account of events. It was Ray's job to get as much out of the witness as possible.

But Ray had to be careful too. Powerful individuals would do anything to cling to power, and that involved making problems go away. It was why somebody had run a truck over Kelly Novak's car, why a military helicopter that just happened to be carrying all but one of the Delta survivors had crashed. And why that man had dropped off the grid to save his own life.

All of these thoughts crossed Ray's mind as he hurried through the mall to the IMAX cinema. He purchased a ticket and made his way inside the dark auditorium. Light flickered across a sea of faces watching the giant screen behind him. Ray scanned the aisle seats in the centre block and saw the guy with the white Dallas Cowboys cap a few rows above him. The man was eating popcorn and watching the screen. Ray gestured to the adjacent seat.

'Do you mind?'

The man looked up. 'Are you Ray?'

Ray nodded and the man got up and moved along a seat. Ray sat down next to him. 'Is there somewhere we can talk?' he whispered.

'About what?'

'Baghdad.'

The man stared at him a moment longer, then reached into his coat pocket. 'I got an envelope is all.'

Ray took the offered package and felt it in the dark of the theatre. It was padded envelope, and the contents were rectangular and malleable. Ray's first thought was money.

'What's this?'

'No clue,' the man shrugged, taking a long slurp of his drink.

'Hey, you wanna keep the noise down?'

Ray twisted in his seat, saw a young guy behind him, a college-age kid with a square jaw and a pretty girl sat beside him. 'Sorry,' he whispered. 'He leaned in closer to popcorn man. 'We can't talk in here. Can we step outside?'

'You don't want it?' the man asked, spitting popcorn crumbs.

'What's in it?'

'The fuck should I know?'

'I said, shut the hell up. Don't make me tell you again.'

The kid behind was getting riled. Courtship rituals for the benefit of the girl, Ray figured. He heard her giggle in the darkness.

'It's not that simple,' Ray persisted. 'I have questions.'

The man snatched the envelope out of Ray's hand. 'You don't want it, fine. Your choice.'

'Look, this isn't how it's done. Whoever's paying you — '

'I'm just the messenger,' the man hissed. 'You want the package? It'll cost you fifty bucks.'

'Excuse me?'

The man grabbed another handful of popcorn and tipped it into his mouth. 'You heard me,' he munched, 'you want the package, it's fifty bucks.'

Ray's heart sank. The mystery phone call and email that had brought him to Texas were genuine, he was convinced of it. The letter delivered to the hotel was also genuine, or so he believed, but the dark and quiet location, plus popcorn guy's bizarre attitude were ringing serious alarm bells. Ray decided there was only one way to find out if this whole setup was on the level.

'I think we're done here.'

'Whatever,' the man replied, watching the screen.

Ray hesitated for just a moment, then he stood up and headed for the exit. He lingered out in the foyer for a couple of minutes, just in case the guy took the bait and came after him, but he didn't show. Ray swore under his breath and walked away.

He decided to go back to the Overton and send an email to his mystery contact, but it felt a little hopeless. Lubbock could be a dead end, he decided. He was no closer to discovering the truth of Baghdad than he was before he'd left DC. He'd been lured to Texas, that much was obvious, so that left only one question that needed an answer.

Why?

CHESTER'S HEART POUNDED IN HIS CHEST AS HE WATCHED THE guy get up and leave the theatre. He'd walked away empty-handed too, unwilling to take the package that Chester had most certainly offered him. Instead of a simple hand-off, the guy had complicated matters by asking stupid questions. And who the fuck did he think he was giving Chester Stokes orders? *I ain't in county jail any more, no sir.*

He congratulated himself on his quick thinking; the fifty bucks thing was genius, and it had scared the guy off, a stupid move on his part. Because Chester was convinced the envelope contained a brick of money.

His stomach churned with excitement. The cowboy told him he could keep whatever was in it if the guy was a no-show. Well, he'd showed, and he'd also walked away empty-handed. Asshole.

Chester put the empty popcorn container on the floor and slapped his hands clean. He reached inside his coat for the envelope, checking his watch at the same time. It had been almost ten minutes since the guy had left. Long enough.

He kept his eyes on the movie, waiting for the sound to crank up so he could rip open the envelope. He also didn't want to piss off the kid behind him. He was a big guy, probably some kind of football hero, and the memory of his beating at the hands of a younger, fitter man still lingered.

Up on the giant screen a car barrelled along a city street before flipping over in a crescendo of light, noise and flame. Chester ripped open the package and put his hand inside.

He pulled out another bag, this one smaller and made of thick, clear plastic. There was something dark and rectangular inside. Chester took his door key out of his pocket and sliced open the plastic. He reached inside for the object then yanked his fingers back. They were wet. *Motherfucker.* He brought his fingers to his nose and sniffed.

It was the last rational thought Chester Stokes would ever have.

He jumped to his feet, his consciousness shutting down as a terrible rage coursed through him. And then the smell hit him, the stench of so many vile creatures all packed together in one —

'Sit the fuck down, asshole!'

Chester spun around and vomited a stream of barely-digested popcorn across the kid's face and chest. The thing next to him screamed and Chester grabbed her hair, dragging her over the seat towards him. He ripped fistfuls from her scalp and she screamed in agony, collapsing into the aisle. Chester lifted a foot and crunched his shoe into her mouth before being knocked off his feet by a screaming stinker. Chester scrambled upright and launched himself onto the next row, filled with an insatiable urge to spill blood. There were others behind him now, just like him. He could sense them in the darkness, hear their cries, and was comforted by their proximity, by their rage.

He leapt into the stairwell as hundreds of people stampeded towards the exits, pushing, pulling, crushing the weak and vulnerable. He leapt on backs and ripped faces open with his bare hands. He vomited, bit and screamed.

They didn't know it, but the violence now being meted out by Chester Stokes and dozens of others far exceeded anything that was being played out on the screen above them.

'THAT'S HER! AND THAT'S HIM, THAT'S PHILIP!'

'You're sure?'

'Hundred percent. She's cut her hair, dyed it too, but that's definitely Marion.'

Mike stared at the screen, at the couple entwined in the departure lounge. The positive ID had taken over three hours. Tapper had interfaced the proprietary facial recognition software into Munich airport's CCTV system and reran the video feed from the predicted time-frame window. Marion's photofit had been matched with forty-one potential targets, using identifiers such as skull shape, facial bone structure, measurements between eyes, ears, noses and chins, and a dozen other permutations. The data had been crunched, and the forty-one targets had been whittled down to a dozen, then four, then one.

None of them had been Marion.

Mike had cursed the technology. It still wasn't fit for purpose.

The security suite was located three levels beneath the airport's main terminal. It was past two in the morning and Mike and his team occupied a large, windowless conference room alongside a couple of dozen of Munich's finest and a team of German intelligence agents. Cooperation was a necessity, and Mike was conferencing with his German counterparts when Lucas's voice barked across the room.

'There she is! Look!'

Lucas was sat in front of a bank of monitors, working a mouse as he trawled through hours of footage. One of his legs was handcuffed to the table, and he was being shadowed by Pat Flynn and Ty Miller. Now he bounced excitedly in his chair, his finger jabbing at the screen.

'Look!'

Everybody in the room gathered around Lucas's desk. Mike leaned in closer. On the main screen, frozen in time, a couple sat side-by-side on a bank of seats. They were a nondescript couple, dark clothing, standard roll-on hand luggage, magazine and newspapers on the seats beside them.

She was leaning on his shoulder, her hair cut fashionably short, her arm linked through his. He looked like a librarian, or a low-level civil servant. He wore round glasses and a dark polo neck top. He sat straight-backed, one leg folded over the other, a mobile phone in his hand. There was nothing notable about either of them, which made them serious players.

'I've never seen him wear glasses,' Lucas observed, his finger tapping the screen. 'He's trying to look all serious, you know, like a businessman or something.'

'You're absolutely sure it's them?'

Lucas nodded like an excited child. 'Absolutely. I'd stake my life on it.'

'You just did,' Mike told him. He straightened up and spoke to the senior German intelligence officer. 'I need to know their cover names, passport numbers, destination, flight numbers, departure, arrival times, potential transfers, the works. Everything you can give me.'

The German intelligence officer, a thin, austere agent in a dark suit and tie, offered Mike a curt nod. Then he turned and barked several orders in rapid-fire German. His troops scattered like mice, some settling back in front of their computers while others headed for the door.

It was a waiting game now. The footage was thirty-six hours old. Philip and Marion could be anywhere in the world, and that frightened Mike. He felt the satellite phone in his pocket vibrating and he walked to a quiet corner of the room.

'Go ahead.'

'Mike, it's Stan. I've got a company Citation inbound to your location, ETA two-seven minutes. Fastest wings I could get you at short notice. It'll be waiting for you at the General Aviation Terminal — '

'Stan, we found them. Lucas made a positive ID in the departure lounge. They've got a thirty-six hour jump on us. The locals are nailing down the flight information now.'

'Get it to me asap,' Lando ordered. 'I'll kick it up to the Director, get the diplomatic wheels spinning.'

'Roger that. We'll head to the GAT now, wait for the transport. What about the Brit?'

'I've got a team inbound from the consulate in Munich. They'll meet you at the GAT and take custody.'

'Roger that.' Mike ended the call and pocketed the phone. As he crossed the room, he gave Billy Finch a nod. The SEALs got to their feet and Mike pointed at Lucas.

'Get him up. We're moving.' He turned to the German agent. 'We have transport inbound to the GAT. Call me the moment you have anything.'

'Of course,' the German answered. He shook Mike's hand and then the Americans were moving.

BUG ZAPPER

PHILIP CRACKED OPEN AN EYELID AND SAW THE RISING SUN streaming through his hotel window.

He felt exhausted, empty, but at least he wasn't throwing up any more. The diarrhoea appeared to have stopped but his stomach still cramped and gurgled. He cursed his stupidity for the hundredth time. What idiot buys food from a street vendor in Mumbai? *You're getting old*, he chided himself, *and this the most important mission of your life*.

The room spun as he sat up and swung his legs off the bed. His sheets were soaked in sweat but he felt the fever had passed. Maybe it was the vitamin shot. The hotel doctor had administered it before relieving Philip of five hundred dollars in cash from his wallet. It was tantamount to theft but Philip didn't care. All that mattered was getting the mission back on track.

He tottered to the bathroom on weak legs, bracing himself for a tableau of squalor. He wasn't disappointed. His waste was splattered on the floor and around the toilet, and Philip reeled with nausea. He stepped into the shower and let the warm water run down his body as he held onto the wall. He soaped himself clean several times, then used the flexible head to wash down the toilet, sink and floor.

After a liberal use of spray bleach around the whole room, Philip stripped his bed and lay back on the bare mattress.

The virus —

He hurried across the room to the small refrigerator. He yanked it open and saw the clear plastic container with the viral pouches within. He breathed a sigh of relief and flopped onto the bed. The light-fingered doctor could've taken those too, and then where would he be? Philip imagined being trapped in a city gone to hell and unable to escape. Immune he may be, but an infected person could easily kill, such was the level of rage.

He propped a pillow behind his head and reached for his phone. He dialled the number and waited.

'Hello?'

'I'd like to book a trip to the elephant caves,' Philip said.

There followed a few moments of silence on the line, then a heavily-accented male voice said, 'Your name?'

'Visser,' Philip told him, giving the name on his Dutch passport.

'I've been waiting for your call, Mister Visser.'

'I've not been well. I'll need to push back another twenty-four hours at least. I'll call tomorrow to confirm.'

'Tomorrow, then,' the man echoed, clearly disappointed.

'I'm obliged to you.'

Philip ended the call, then sent an update via text message to Arizona. He apologised for the delay, assuring his employers things were back on track.

He picked up the hotel telephone and ordered bottled mineral water and two packs of plain crackers. He needed to eat, but it was all he could stomach right now. The experience reminded Philip how much he hated the Third World, the abject poverty, the virulent diseases, the mortality rate, and the stench of decay that permeated the developing world. He despised the widespread corruption, the slavish and backward devotion to barbaric religions and animal gods, and their sheer inability to drag themselves out of their self-inflicted mess. They were children, and like all children they needed discipline and supervision.

Philip was looking forward to the realignment of power, to the culling of humanity, knowing it was necessary and longing for the day when he would wake up to a world that was run by a single, civilised government, one no longer bound by the shackles of international diplomacy, political correctness and historical guilt. A brave new world, orderly, prosperous, obedient. As it should be.

He stared up at the ceiling, soothed by the rhythmic ticking of the air-conditioner. He would wait for room service, drink more water and attempt to eat a couple of crackers. Then he would sleep.

When he rose the next day, he would be ready for the Pakistani.

THE DOOR WAS BOLTED FROM INSIDE AND BARRICADED WITH A heavy glass-fronted fridge. The lights were switched off and the bug-zapper threw a cold blue wash over the restaurant kitchen.

Ray, along with several other staff and diners, were pressed together beneath a couple of stainless steel preparation tables. His knees were drawn up to his chest, his body squeezed against the others. There were two kids amongst their number, and their terrified whimpers drew frightened looks and whispered warnings from their parents.

Ray didn't blame them. The noise outside the barricaded kitchen doors would make anyone's blood run cold. He checked his watch — less than thirty minutes since he'd walked out of the IMAX. Everything had happened so fast Ray barely had time to catch his breath.

After his odd and frustrating encounter in the IMAX he'd headed back through the mall, deciding to console himself with a decent steak and a beer. He'd veered towards the Tex-Mex restaurant he'd passed earlier and took a table inside. He was sipping a cold beer when he'd heard the commotion. He turned towards the IMAX entrance and saw people spilling through the doors and scattering across the concourse. Some were hurrying away, looking over their shoulders, tugging at the arms of their frightened children. Others were running fast, pounding past the restaurant, pumping arms, colliding with others. Then he'd heard screaming, a mixture of fear, pain and anger, echoing across the mall. They kept coming, streaming past the restaurant, pushing, shoving, like a herd of frightened deer.

Then he saw the woman.

She was twenty yards away, a young woman, blond, pretty — and covered in blood. She stood still, her head snapping left and right, then she looked right at Ray. Her eyes were cold and dead, and Ray swallowed a frightened yelp. Then she was running towards him, a scream of rage tearing from her throat. Ray's limbs were frozen. The woman had almost reached the restaurant when a fleeing group of shoppers cut across her path and she crashed into them, knocking them to the ground like bowling pins.

Deafening gunfire echoed through the mall, snapping Ray out of his inertia. He backed away, deeper inside the restaurant. People around him were scrambling in every direction, knocking over chairs and tables. Food squelched under his shoes. *This was Baghdad*, Ray realised. *This is what it must have been like.*

He heard glass breaking and more gunshots. The noise was incredible, and terrifying. He heard more screams. No, not screams, more like the howls and screeches of wild animals. A pack of bloodied and infected people scrambled past the restaurant, knocking over tables and chairs, chasing down their victims. Any moment now one of them would spot him.

He turned and ran for the kitchens, and collided with a young family. He tried to steer them towards the double doors nearby but the man shoved him away, his face confused, frightened. Ray grabbed the kids' arms and dragged them into the kitchen. Mom and dad were right behind him, screaming, clawing at Ray's shirt. A huddle of chefs and waiting staff looked at them with wide eyes as they barged through the door. One of them, a Latino in his thirties, dragged them in and dropped the door bolts. Then he'd hit the lights.

'Help me, quick!' he gasped, wrestling with a tall, glass-fronted refrigerator. Ray and a couple of others helped him move it in front of the doors. 'Everyone, out of sight, now!'

They scurried beneath the food preparation tables. Ray's chest was heaving, his throat raw. He was badly out of shape.

'What the hell's going on?' She was crouched underneath the adjacent table, a young lady in chef's whites, her face almost the same colour as her tunic.

'Quiet!' hissed the Latino. He had a gold name badge above his left breast pocket.

'Felipe, right?'

The man shifted around and looked at Ray. Beads of sweat dotted his smooth face, but he looked pretty much together. He certainly had smarts enough to seal the room and knock the lights off.

'I know what this is,' Ray told him. Now everyone was listening, staring at Ray, hanging on his next words. 'Remember that thing in Baghdad? The virus?'

Felipe's mouth dropped open. 'You think that's what this is?'

Ray nodded his head. The noise spiked as people cursed and whimpered. The two kids he'd dragged inside were

172

crying, their mother clutching them together, her own sobs competing with theirs.

'We have to be very quiet,' Ray warned, raising a finger to his lips. 'We're safe as long as we're quiet.'

'Not if they get in here,' said the kids' dad.

Ray turned back to Felipe. 'Is there another way out of — '

The kitchen doors shook with considerable force. The refrigerator wobbled.

'Open the fucking doors!'

The voice boomed around the kitchen, a man's voice, obviously terrified.

'What do we do?' The girl again.

'Leave the motherfucker out there!' It was the guy next to Felipe, a skinny African-American in soiled chef's whites and a red bandanna wrapped around his head.

The doors shook again. Something fell to the ground and smashed.

'Let him in, for god's sake,' pleaded a middle-aged lady, black streaks of mascara painted down her face.

'We let him in, those crazy fuckers could get in here too. Is that what you want?' Leon snapped at her.

'Pipe down, all of you!' Ray crawled out from under the table and very slowly peered over the edge. The refrigerator had blocked out the doors' round windows, except for a half-moon of glass. The man was peering inside. His eyes widened.

'I fucking see you, man! Let me in! Please!' He pummelled the door with his fists.

Ray ducked back down. 'We have to help him,' he told Felipe. The restaurant manager shook his head.

'No chance, man.'

'That's right,' agreed Leon. 'No one's doin' nuthin.'

Ray opened his mouth to answer when an ear-splitting scream filled the kitchen. Ray risked another look and saw a melee' of arms and bloodied faces. The man was still screaming, in pain, in desperation. The doors buckled. The refrigerator wobbled violently, the door swinging open. Chilled goods spilled to the ground. Wild, bloodshot eyes filled the half-moon. Ray ducked back down.

'We need to get out of here,' he told them. They were all looking at him now. They needed reassurance, leadership. Ray was unsure whether he was up for the job or not, but right now he didn't have much choice. 'Is there another way out?'

'There's a service corridor out back,' Felipe told him, pointing across the kitchen. 'It leads to the loading bay.'

'There's a security booth out there too,' Leon added. 'We can hide in there. They got guns and radios — '

'To hell with that!' blurted the kids' dad. 'I say we get as far away from this place as possible.'

Mascara woman gasped. 'Dragging those poor babies with you? Are you insane?'

Then a thought hit Ray. He jammed his hand in his pocket, pulled out his phone. No signal. 'Somebody call nine-one-one,' he told them.

Everyone tried. No one else had a signal either.

The doors shook again, and more hands pummelled the wood like a deafening, discordant drum beat. Maybe it was because they'd seen Ray, or maybe it was the smell of food. Either way they had to get out of there. It was Leon who stated the obvious.

'Those doors ain't gonna hold. Let's get the fuck out of here while we can.'

Ray nodded. 'He's right, but we should try and shore up that barricade. Once they see us they'll go nuts. They're clever too. They work stuff out.'

'How the fuck d'you know?' Leon asked, his eyes narrowing.

'It doesn't matter. The fact is we have to buy ourselves

time. I suggest we try and shore them up with something, give the others a chance to get to the security post.'

Felipe nodded. 'Sounds like a plan.'

Ray took a headcount. There were fourteen of them, five guys, seven ladies and the two kids. This was no time for an equality debate. The guys were all bigger, stronger. It might just keep them alive. They thrashed out a rudimentary plan beneath the table, but the kids' dad wasn't buying it. He was getting his family out, and that was final. No one argued.

Ray looked around the shadowy faces and forced a confident smile. 'Ready?' He was met with silent nods and wide eyes. 'Okay, let's do this.'

Slowly and quietly they eased themselves out from their hiding place. There was no cover between the tables and the entrance to the service corridor. When they moved, the infected would see them.

Everyone crouched, like sprinters waiting for the gun.

'On the count of three; one, two…three!'

Ray scrambled to his feet and the group split, the guys scrambling towards the freezer chest, the others to the back of the restaurant. The infected howled and the doors rocked beneath the onslaught. Bloody fingers squeezed through the gap as they manhandled a long freezer chest and jammed it against the glass-fronted refrigerator, adding significant weight to the barricade.

'Let's go,' Ray commanded.

The howls of the infected chased them through the staff area towards another door plastered with security signs. Felipe threw it open, disappearing to his right. Ray was the last man out and followed the others down a long corridor with cinderblock walls. Ray's lungs started to burn. Screaming echoed along the corridor and suddenly Ray cannoned into Leon.

They'd stopped.

Ray saw they were twenty yards short of another set of

double doors, solid ones with hazard signs and metal kick plates. A CCTV camera pointed down towards it, and beyond that door, the screaming intensified.

'Oh shit,' he heard Felipe whisper.

And then the doors flew open.

Ray saw the father, his neck soaked with blood, his family no longer by his side. The young girl in chef's whites pushed past him, snarling, crimson blood soaking her tunic.

Ray put a hand to his mouth. 'Jesus Christ — '

The boy squeezed past his father's legs. He wailed an awful, animal scream, then he ran towards them on chubby, bloodied legs.

Leon turned and shoved Ray against the wall.

'Move!' he roared, then they were all running back the way they'd come.

Ray's shoes pounded the concrete, their stampede echoing off the cinder block walls. He passed the door to the restaurant and glimpsed arms and legs squeezing through the failing barricade. He heard snarls and grunts behind him, and the rumble of chasing feet. The only thing that would keep him alive now, and stop him turning into one of those monsters, was speed. Ray couldn't remember the last time he'd run for anything.

He looked over his shoulder. The corridor behind him was filled with infected, the girls from the kitchen, now joined by at least a dozen others, some of them security guards, others in civilian clothes, all of them enraged and howling for blood. They pushed and shoved, and one of them fell, bringing down several others. The charge faltered, but only for a moment. Ray realised he wasn't going to make it.

He ducked around the corner and then Felipe was stood right in front of him. He grabbed Ray and shoved him sideways through a door. Ray stumbled and fell against a flight of steps, cracking a shin. Then he saw Felipe closing the door, fast and silent.

Ray used the banister rail to pull himself up. Everyone was leaning against the door, hands spread, bodies at forty-five degrees. Ray rubbed his shin and gulped air like a beached fish. Outside the snarling and grunting reached a crescendo, but there was no pounding against the door, no bloodied fingers squeezing through the gap. The pack kept moving.

Death, or something worse, had passed them by.

The others straightened up. Felipe was pointing to the ceiling, urging the others up the stairs with hand gestures, leaving the door behind them unlocked. Ray looked around, realising they were in a grey concrete stairwell. *A fire escape.*

Which meant no locked doors.

As they climbed the stairs, Ray had never felt more exposed in his life. With every step he expected the door below to crash open, for a swarm of infected to charge up towards them. They passed several landings but no one was interested in going back inside the mall.

They kept climbing until they reached another door, this one made of grey steel and secured with heavy bolts top and bottom. Felipe eased the bolts back and stepped inside. Bringing up the rear, Ray followed the others into a short corridor. Pipes ran across the ceiling and there was a work-bench against one wall. They found some lengths of timber and braced the door handle behind them. Ahead of them was another grey steel door, and Leon pressed down on the bar, pushing it open. A cold wind swirled around them, and Ray followed the others outside, grateful for the fresh, frigid breeze, before it started cutting through his thin shirt. That's when he realised his overcoat was folded on a chair in the diner downstairs.

Everyone walked towards the roof's edge that overlooked the main parking lot, drawn by the terrible screaming. And there was gunfire now, volleys of shots that sounded like hollow pops on the night air.

They reached the edge of the roof and looked down into hell.

There were bodies everywhere, some dead, some injured and some crawling. People ran in all directions as packs of infected hunted them down. Men, women, children, no one was safe or spared. A short distance away a gas station burned, the red flames licking up over the apron as black smoke boiled up into the night sky.

Ray watched in horror as a large pickup truck accelerated away from the mall, swerving wildly, clipping bodies, bouncing over others, dragging them beneath the chassis, leaving a trail of blood and broken humanity in its wake. He looked away, sickened.

The he heard something else, a low, rising tone that turned into a wailing, screeching blast. The tornado warning system had been activated, its doom-laden scream reaching across the city. Ray's eyes were drawn back to the terrible scene below, and he was jarred by the similarity to the drone footage from Baghdad.

But this time it was different.

This time there were no walls to keep the infection in.

BOMBAY BLUES

THE CESSNA CITATION X LANDED IN THE STEAMY MID-afternoon heat at Mumbai International Airport. As the aircraft taxied to the private jet terminal, Mike took a call from Stan Lando on his sat phone.

'The locals aren't being as cooperative as we'd like,' the field supervisor told him. 'They wanna know everything before they green light any op.'

Mike winced. 'Are you kidding me? Don't they realise what's at stake?' The line crackled as the signal bounced across the globe.

'The White House is on the case,' Lando responded, 'but in the meantime, the carrying of weapons has not been authorised. Gordon Kappes will pick up that slack. He's Head of Station at the Consulate.'

'This is turning into a shit-show, Stan.'

'Agreed, but the NSA is quietly crawling all over the Indian networks. We've got Philip on CCTV all the way through the terminal, including the licence plate of the taxicab he got into. The bad news is, we lost the vehicle in the traffic. They're tracing the driver as we speak.'

'What about Marion?'

179

'Whereabouts are still unknown. Stay focused on this Philip character, Mike. As soon as we have a location, we need him lifted and squeezed.'

'What if the locals don't play ball?'

'We go anyway.'

'Good enough.' Mike ended the call and walked to the cockpit. The pilots had shut down the engines, and through the windows, Mumbai's airport rippled in waves beneath the afternoon sun. Two dark blue Nissan Pathfinders emerged out of the shimmer and swung around the side of the aircraft.

'Fuel up and standby,' Mike told the pilots. 'We may have to leave in a hurry.'

The pilot nodded behind his Ray Bans. 'Roger that.'

Back in the cabin, Mike briefed his Task Force. 'The locals are being problematic, which means no operational jurisdiction. We leave weapons on the plane, but take your personal rigs. Replacement hardware will be made available at the Consulate. Let's move.'

With an Indian police escort on blue lights, it took twenty-two minutes to get to the consulate, a collection of sand-coloured rectangular buildings ringed by high perimeter walls. Like most US embassies located in Third World countries, they were a target, and security was tight. The Nissans passed through the checkpoints and skirted the main building, stopping inside a large vehicle shed near the perimeter wall. The heat beneath the corrugated metal roof was oppressive, but they were invisible to anyone either inside or outside the embassy. And there was always someone watching.

As Mike climbed out of the Nissan, an imposing figure approached and held out his hand. 'Gordon Kappes, Station Chief.'

'Mike Savage, SOG. This is my XO, Don Tapper, and Senior Chief Billy Finch, DEVGRU.'

Hands were shaken all round. Kappes was a big guy, over

six feet, with red hair and pale, freckled skin. The sweltering Indian city was probably not his favourite posting.

'This way,' Kappes said, leading them down a flight of steps into an underground tunnel. The narrow passage led to a sub-level of the main building. He took them straight to the consulate armoury where they were met by a Gunnery Sergeant from the Marine Security Guard.

'Gunny Warren will take care of you,' Kappes told them. 'I need to hit the phones. Get back to you soon.'

As Kappes headed out, Warren escorted Mike and his team into a well-stocked armoury. Warren had a nose that looked like it'd been broken several times, and wore a dark green combat utility uniform. He invited his guests to peruse his well-stocked gun racks.

'Best I have are Sig sidearms and M27 rifles,' Warren told them as they inspected the hardware. 'Optics and suppressors are standard issue. You need any specialised gear?'

'Combat shot gun for Flynn here.'

'Ah, a connoisseur,' Warren said, smiling. He lifted a black Benelli M4 off the rack and cleared the action, handing it to Flynn.

The Bostonian turned it over in his hands. 'That'll work. Ammunition?'

'Double-oh buckshot and breaching rounds.'

'Nice,' Flynn said.

'We'll need flash-bangs and smoke,' Mike told the Gunny.

'I got M84 stun grenades and M18 smoke. You need any HE?'

Mike shook his head. 'Not expecting that kind of trouble. This is supposed to be friendly territory.'

'So you'd think,' the Gunny said, and winked.

Mike cocked a thumb over his shoulder. 'This is Senior Chief Billy Finch, DEVGRU. His guys might have additional requirements.'

The Gunny grinned. 'Welcome aboard, Chief. Not often we see you guys in these parts.'

Finch shook his hand and they talked weapons, with Finch making a couple of tactical hardware changes. Gunny Warren escorted them into an empty training room next door where Mike and his Task Force geared up. As they discussed comms and scenarios with the CIA team and Defence Attache, Kappes entered the room.

'The taxi driver's been picked up.'

Mike raised an eyebrow. 'Is he cooperating?'

'He wants ten grand, plus Green Cards for him and his family, so put him to work, Mike. Make sure he delivers.'

'Roger that.'

'ETA five minutes. Take the tunnel back to the vehicle shed and wait for him there. You got comms?'

'We're set,' Mike told him, tapping the earpiece in his left ear.

'Good luck.'

As Kappes turned to leave, Mike called after him. 'What's the plan? If the virus is released before we can get to him?'

Kappes shrugged. 'If it all goes to hell we hunker down, ride it out. Too many people here for an orderly evac. I doubt most of us would make it.' The CIA man smiled and wagged a finger at them. 'Hey, I've spent too goddamn long in this sweatbox, so don't let me down, got it?'

Kappes left the room. Mike followed a minute later, leading the Task Force through the tunnel and up into the vehicle shed.

Two battered-looking Toyota HiAce minivans with local plates and authentic dents and scratches waited for them. Kappes had also organised a similarly banged-up Isuzu pickup with two Latino Marines aboard. They wore civvies and passed for locals at a glance, aside from the M4 carbines at their feet.

A female CIA liaison waited with the vehicles. She shook Mike's hand as his team climbed aboard the Toyotas.

'The drivers know the roads. They'll get you where you need to go to.'

'We may need to move fast.'

'Can't guarantee speed unless you use the local cops, and that might spook your target,' she told him. 'Best we can do, given the circumstances.'

'Understood.'

A moment later a small Ford saloon swept into the shed. A bemused-looking Indian climbed out, escorted by a couple of embassy personnel. Mike threw open the side door of the Toyota and gestured the guy inside. He shook the Indian's hand.

'My name's Mike,' he said, sliding the door closed. The man was in his thirties, had a well-trimmed beard and sported thick glasses. He wore a baggy cotton shirt and pants, and his taxi ID badge was still clipped to his breast pocket.

'It's Sanjay, right?'

The man wobbled his head in that way that Indians do. 'Yes, sir.'

'You got kids, right?'

'Two,' the taxi driver told him, stroking his beard nervously.

'That's good, because I want you to think about them while you're working with us, okay? If you do everything we ask, help us catch this guy, this might just work out for your family. Am I clear?'

Mike saw it in his eyes, the glimmer of hope, a sudden vision of a better life on the other side of the world. Sanjay pointed off into the distance.

'I took him to the Hotel Manama. To the south of the city.'

'That was almost three days ago,' Finch warned. 'He might've flown the nest by now.'

Sanjay shook his head several times. 'No, no, no,' he said.

183

'I called the hotel before your people picked me up. Mister Visser has been very sick. Food poisoning. He is still there, still in his room.'

Mike shared a hopeful look with Finch. He slapped the back of the driver's seat. 'Let's go.'

The convoy swung around the shed and headed for the main gate.

PHILIP SAT ON THE BED, HIS EYES GLUED TO THE TELEVISION.

The images coming out of Texas were truly remarkable. Much of it was phone footage, grainy and shaky for the most part, but the violence and the noise bordered on the cinematic. The viewpoints were varied and riveting, some taken from high-rise buildings, some from inside people's homes, others from swerving, speeding vehicles, and in one hair-raising instance, from the lobby of a hotel, which captured a screaming pack of infected charging across the parking lot towards the entrance. CNN was clearly being careful, plastering *graphic content* warnings everywhere. But for Philip the conclusion was obvious.

H-1 had been released.

He was confused. He'd not been made aware of any operation targeting the United States. He'd been present throughout the planning stages, with Blake, Sorensen, their people, and many countries had been discussed, but never the United States. Was this something organic, or deliberate? Philip googled the town of Lubbock. It was an unremarkable place, known principally for its tech university and for cotton harvesting. He checked its location on the map and saw that it was isolated, with only seven major roads leading in and out of the city. Even the interstate terminated in Lubbock. It was literally in the middle of nowhere.

So, it was planned.

The TV footage was mesmerising. Fires raged in several

downtown buildings, and thousands of people ran through the streets, fleeing or infected, it was difficult to tell. The police were swamped, and gunfire could be heard across the city. The talking heads were discussing the outbreak, the shots cutting between the CNN studio, Lubbock and the White House. Philip wanted to continue watching. The footage excited him, and also made him a little apprehensive. Mumbai would go the same way, although that outbreak would be far larger and impossible to control.

He checked his watch and swung his legs off the bed. He stood up slowly, mindful of his weakened state. He'd slept on and off for over twelve hours and yet he still felt groggy. His enforced diet of bottled water and crackers hadn't triggered any further sickness, but it wasn't going to sustain him for much longer. He was glad the operation would soon be underway and he would be able to leave this godforsaken place. Then could he relax, eat decent food again and regain his strength.

He took a shower, scrubbing his hands like a man with a disorder. He dressed in lightweight trousers and a cotton T-shirt. He packed his clothes and emptied the safe, putting his passport and money in his pockets. He was ready to leave. The only thing he hadn't packed were the three pouches of H-1 that were still in the refrigerator.

He walked to the window and looked out over the busy port a couple of hundred yards away. He saw a cruise ship, a few large tankers and half a dozen smaller cargo ships tied against the dock. Other vessels navigated the turquoise waters beyond. He couldn't see the MV *Sea Star*, but her captain had acknowledged Philip's text message and confirmed the ship's safe arrival in Mumbai. Philip had the necessary papers clipped inside his passport and he was expected aboard soon. The ship would then weigh anchor, sailing with the evening tide as Mumbai descended into hell behind them.

He sat back on the bed and decided to watch the news for a little longer. He'd barely settled when he heard a quiet tap on the door. He got up and peered through the spy viewer, recognising the distorted face. He opened the door.

He was expecting Jamal, but not the two men who hurried into the room behind him. *Fool,* Philip cursed himself. His illness had weakened him both physically *and* mentally. One of the men went to the window and pulled the drapes closed, while the other checked the bathroom, sweeping the shower curtain against the wall. Both of them nodded to the third man who stood in the middle of the room.

'How are you, Philip?'

'Jamal,' Philip nodded. 'I wasn't expecting company.'

Jamal cocked his head towards the TV. 'I wasn't expecting to see that.'

Philip said nothing, unwilling to admit his own ignorance.

'I think we should talk,' Jamal said.

Philip sensed the borderline belligerence, a precursor to confrontation, something he wasn't prepared for. Jamal Bashir was a former agent in Pakistan's premiere intelligence agency, the ISI, but now he was a contractor, just like Philip. Jamal had carried out many assignments for Northridge over the years, in both Pakistan and across the border in Afghanistan. He'd always been a trusted professional, but more than that, Jamal harboured a passionate hatred for India, something he'd discussed with Philip many times over the course of their relationship. It was why he was stood here, in Philip's Mumbai hotel room. Technically, this was Jamal's dream job, a chance to deal a terrible blow to his sworn enemy *and* get rich in the bargain.

But things had changed, Philip could sense it. Jamal stood in the middle of the room, his thick, muscular forearms crossed defensively across his barrel chest. He wore a baggy shirt, tracksuit pants and Nike trainers, and he reminded Philip of a stereotypical bad guy from a Bollywood movie.

His two friends were similarly dressed. One had a shaved head and a religious beard, while the other had collar-length hair and kept his sunglasses on. And they were all armed, Philip's experienced eye noticed. He also saw the outline of a concealed holster beneath Jamal's shirt, a tell-tale bulge just above the waistline of the Beard's jeans. Sunglasses wasn't giving much away, only that he was an amateur. No serious professional wore shades inside a hotel room.

Philip didn't deal with amateurs. They were a liability. Jamal was a serious player, always professional, discreet, so why bring these two with him? This was beginning to feel more like a drug deal.

'You want to talk? Fine, we can do that. Alone,' he added for emphasis.

Jamal shook his head. 'No, my friend. We'll talk now.'

Philip knew he was at a serious disadvantage. In his weakened state, unarmed and physically outnumbered, it was Jamal who held all the cards. 'Talk about what exactly?'

Jamal tipped his head towards the TV. 'Mumbai will go pretty much the same way, no? It wasn't something we discussed.'

'Yes it was,' Philip insisted. 'I've briefed you on the mission, proscribed the antiviral, advised on your escape route out of the city. What were you expecting?'

The antiviral that Jamal had been issued was a placebo, nothing more than a course of aspirin. Like most involved with the H-1 program, the man was expendable.

'I wasn't expecting that rate of infection, nor the level of violence,' Jamal countered. 'It changes things. Including my fee.'

So, this was a renegotiation, nothing more. Philip was relieved. He could deal with that. Money was unimportant, nothing more than a number, and Philip was interested to know exactly how much Jamal wanted on top of the quarter of a million dollars he'd already been paid.

'Have you a figure in mind? One that will ease your concerns?'

Jamal didn't blink. 'Two million, plus five-hundred thousand for each of my partners here.'

Philip knew that Jamal's twitchy associates would never see a single dollar. The money would be for him, and him alone. How short-sighted.

'I'll need to run it by my people,' Philip told him. 'I can tell you now, they won't be very happy.'

'Maybe not, but given this thing is on every channel across the world, I'm guessing the money won't be a problem. And besides, this is my last op. I'm getting out, so consider it a pension dividend.'

Philip raised an eyebrow. 'I'm sorry to hear that, Jamal. Perhaps I can negotiate something extra? For your loyal service?'

'Sure. See what you can do.'

Philip motioned to the door. 'Give me an hour. You can wait in the lobby.'

Jamal pulled up a chair and sat down. 'If it's all the same to you, we'll wait here. As soon as the transfer is confirmed, we'll execute the mission.' He unbuttoned his shirt, revealing a dirty white vest and the covert holster beneath his left armpit.

'Of course,' Philip said, forcing a smile.

It was another reason he hated the Third World. Everything was always about money. And that greed had just cost Jamal his life.

CIA Director Jim Buchanan leaned in close and spoke quietly into Coffman's ear.

'Northridge is sending us the files of everyone who was stationed in Baghdad during the crisis, Madam President. It's only a matter of time before we ID this Philip character.'

Coffman acknowledged the information with a curt nod. She knew that would be a fruitless task. Bob Blake had assured her there were no files on either Marion *or* Philip, no photographs, no personal information, nothing. They were ghosts.

'What about this Marion character? Do we know where she is yet?'

Buchanan winced. 'We do not. The Germans believe she changed her clothes in a restroom before she boarded her flight. They're still fine-combing the CCTV footage.'

'And Mumbai?'

'It's a fluid situation.'

'Thank you, Jim. Keep me posted.'

She was back in the secure conference room, five storeys beneath the north lawn of the White House. She'd been there for the last six hours, and hadn't once considered the sixty feet of earth between her and the cold night air above ground.

The room was solid with people, and the air hummed with tension. Her National Security Council occupied every seat around the conference table, and White House staffers hurried back and forth with paper messages and whispered words. The bank of high-definition monitors on the wall gave Coffman direct contact with the Pentagon, Langley and Fort Meade. Other screens were broadcasting thermal and infra-red feeds from the military drones that criss-crossed the sky over Lubbock. A couple of local TV crews who'd managed to survive were also providing live footage, ensuring a constant and inescapable tableau of horror, savagery and destruction for everyone in the room.

Coffman could see it on their faces, even as she maintained her own furrowed brow. The mood had shifted dramatically. What was thought to be a public disturbance had quickly escalated into something far worse, a biological terror attack, the blame quickly laid at the feet of the Global Liberation Front. Now her National Security Council were panicked by the very real potential for the virus to escape across the West Texas plain and beyond. That's when her National Security Advisor Karen Baranski had significantly upped the ante and dropped the threat of *Reverse Zoonoses* into everyone's lap; the potential for the virus to pass from humans to animals. That one had certainly caused a few assholes to pucker. The horrific scenario of infected animals attacking humans and spreading the virus — especially birds — focussed minds like never before. It couldn't happen, Coffman knew. Blake had assured her of that, but Baranski's sombre delivery was enough to tip the scales in their favour.

No one was thinking about saving the good people of Lubbock any longer. They were thinking about the possibility of attacks in other cities, of millions becoming infected, of society crumbling around them. Of their own survival.

'Oh my God!' a voice cried.

Up on the thermal imaging screen, ghostly white figures tumbled off a hotel roof as a sizeable mob of infected swarmed after them. The spectacle was too much for Homeland Security chief Diane Grady. She sprung out of her chair and pointed at the screen.

'Madam President, we must do something!' she shrilled. 'For God's sake, this thing could spread across the whole of Texas!'

'Diane's right,' SecState Jayne Pascoe added. 'We have to act now.'

Grady snatched a message slip off the table and waved it dramatically. 'The governors of Arizona and Oklahoma are demanding you declare a State of Emergency. They've mobilised the National Guard. They're going to seal their state borders with or without federal authority.'

'The media isn't helping,' said the NSA representative up on the monitor wall. 'They're stoking the panic. We could be looking at major civil unrest.'

'I'm already seeing reports of looting across the country,'

Grady piled in, 'even in states as far away as Oregon and Minnesota. Ma'am, it's getting out of control.'

All eyes turned towards the President. Her own were fixed on the message slips in front of her, all urgent and doom-laden, as she'd anticipated. She lifted her head and looked around the room.

'I agree, the virus cannot be allowed to escape the city.' She turned to Secretary of Defence Drew Clark. 'Is everything ready, Drew?'

Clark's face was chalk white. 'Not quite. A ten-mile exclusion zone has been established around the Lubbock metropolitan area, and another thirty thousand troops have been mobilised, but there are still a lot of gaps to be plugged in terms of routes out of the city. In the meantime state troopers are turning back escapees, but I'm afraid there have been some shootings. People are desperate.'

'What about screening? Can't we let the healthy ones through?' asked a voice at the other end of the table.

Clark shook her head. 'We simply do not have the time or the infrastructure to screen a quarter of a million people, and nor can we risk the infection breaching the exclusion zone.'

Coffman cleared her throat, her voice dripping with faux compassion. 'Have we done enough to warn people?'

Beside Clark, Grady nodded. 'Ma'am, we've been broadcasting an emergency message for the last two hours, on every local TV, radio and cell network. People have been ordered to get off the streets and seek shelter below ground. The hospitals have barricaded their doors and windows, and are running on generators. First responders have spread the word as much as they can. Ma'am, we simply can't wait any longer.'

No one spoke. Coffman strung the moment out for as long as she could, building the tension. Finally she said, 'You all understand what this entails? Innocent American lives will be lost, potentially thousands of them. This is a decision that we must make together, as an administration. And more importantly, take responsibility for.'

'What choice do we have?' Grady asked rhetorically. The room nodded in agreement.

Up on the wall, the Chairman of the Joint Chiefs underpinned Coffman's carefully crafted strategy in the gravest of tones.

'Madam President, if the virus is not contained quickly and decisively, it will reach Dallas within days. If that happens, we will not be able to contain the spread. Oklahoma City will fall, as will Albuquerque and San Antonio to the south. If it reaches El Paso, Mexico will be directly threatened, and that is simply unacceptable. We have a responsibility, Madam President, not only to our fellow Americans but to the international community. For their sakes we have to act, and act decisively, because this may be the first and only chance we have of stopping this terrible outbreak. The American people will expect nothing less.'

Well said, Charlie. Coffman looked around the silent room, making eye contact with as many people as possible. There were no more dissenting voices, no more half-hearted pleas for restraint. Lubbock had become a fast-mutating cancer that needed cutting out fast.

Coffman got to her feet, and the table rose around her. The record would show that President Coffman had been reluctant to take such drastic action, and that ultimately she'd had no choice. If America was to be saved, someone had to make the final decision, and the buck stopped with her.

She turned to face the Pentagon feed. Charlie stared back at her, surrounded by silent uniforms, her dogs of war straining at the leash.

'Do what needs to be done, Admiral Schultz. And God help us all.'

THROWBACK

T͟H͟E͟Y͟'͟D͟ ͟T͟H͟R͟A͟S͟H͟E͟D͟ ͟O͟U͟T͟ ͟T͟H͟E͟ ͟P͟L͟A͟N͟ ͟O͟N͟ ͟T͟H͟E͟ ͟W͟A͟Y͟ ͟T͟O͟ ͟T͟H͟E͟ Hotel Manama.

First job was to secure the building, which would be simple enough; there were four entry points in total and the hotel was fairly small. The second was speed — from the moment they seized control, they'd be on the clock. If everything went as planned, Philip would be in their custody within the hour. Or in a body bag, if they were unlucky.

Mike had nothing on Philip, no history at all. Was he military? Former special forces? Langley was running down the Northridge angle, but Mike's mind was already made up; *he's military, and he'll have a plan.*

He watched the Isuzu up ahead swerving through the evening traffic as the convoy headed south towards the Eastern docks. The lady back at the consulate had been right about her drivers; all three vehicles weaved through the traffic as if they were tied together. Mike found himself bracing every few seconds, expecting the crunch of metal and broken glass, but all he heard was the blare of horns and the roar of traffic around him.

'It's just ahead, a couple of hundred yards,' Sanjay said, pointing through the windscreen.

Mike hit the transmit button on his radio. 'All call-signs, target is two-hundred yards and closing. Standby.'

All three vehicles swerved into the nearside lane and slowed. The sidewalks were packed with people, a constant, chaotic crush of noise and colour. He saw the hotel sign ahead. The convoy stopped fifty yards short of the entrance. Mike keyed his radio once more.

'Eyeball-One, this is Task Force Leader, we are thirty seconds out.'

The CIA operative seated inside the lobby of the Hotel Manama answered immediately and quietly. 'Target in situ. Clear to deploy.'

Mike yanked open the side door and headed towards the hotel entrance. Sanjay walked ahead of him, while Flynn covered their rear. Flynn's shotgun was held low on a sling beneath his thin rain jacket. Mike sweated beneath his own coat. He knew they might attract a little attention as they crossed the pavement, but the risk of trying to stop Philip unarmed was too great.

Sanjay pushed open the glass door and stepped inside the air-conditioned lobby. Mike followed him, seeing a concierge desk to the left, a lounge area to his right. There was only one person there, a dark, overweight lady reading a USA Today. She got out of her chair and nodded at Mike.

All clear.

There were two people behind the concierge desk, a smart-suited man in his forties and a young Indian girl with a long ponytail and wearing hotel livery. The man, clearly a managerial type, had his nose buried in paperwork. The girl looked up and smiled as Sanjay approached her and asked something in Urdu. The smile slipped from her face as Flynn went behind the desk and pulled the Benelli from under his coat. He held it low by his leg and the girl stared at it, speechless, her bottom lip trembling. The suited man looked up, irritation on his face. Then fear, as he clocked the deadly black weapon.

'Inside, now.'

Flynn backed them into the adjacent office and made them sit. Mike came around the desk, advising them to stay calm and not try anything stupid. Hotels in Mumbai were no strangers to men with guns, and the look on their faces told Mike that the manager and his receptionist would offer no trouble.

Mike got to work, disabling the hotel phone system and the elevators. Flynn locked the main entrance doors and cracked open the rear service door for the rest of the team. There was no time to secure the whole building, and as the team gathered in the lobby, hotel staff could be heard scrambling for the rear exits.

'No doubt someone has already dropped a dime on us,' Mike told them, 'so we're on the clock. Our target is on the fifth floor, room twelve. Seems he has company, three local males, identity unknown. You can all ID Philip from the airport CCTV, so let's keep him alive. Watch your corners and clear your sectors.'

Forced entries were always risky, and even though Mike and his team had a lot of real-world experience, having enough time to breach *and* stop a potential virus release was going to be difficult.

He turned to his XO. 'Don, take two SEALs and secure the ground floor. Keep the route to the parking lot clear, and put the manager behind the front doors. The story is a gas leak.' He looked at each of them in turn. 'Are we all good? Okay, let's go.'

JAMAL WAS GETTING IMPATIENT, HUFFING AND FIDGETING IN HIS chair every few seconds. And he wasn't the only one. Philip noticed his two companions were also feeding off their employer's agitation, pacing the room, flicking TV channels. They were making Philip nervous.

The money wasn't an issue — Jamal could've asked for anything he wanted. No, the issue was authority. Philip had some, but not enough to transfer millions of dollars. The okay would have to come from Sorensen himself. Blake could do it, but he was too high-profile now, and he didn't want any involvement in the operational side of things.

Philip checked his watch. The sun had yet to rise in Arizona, and Sorensen was still sleeping. The cancer had made a resurgence, and his medical team were refusing to wake him.

Jamal huffed and got out of his chair. 'Look, if you want us to hit the station during rush-hour, you'd better get a move on.'

Philip forced himself to remain calm. 'Have we ever let you down, Jamal? You've always been paid well, and always on time. Just do the job, please. We can work this out later.'

'D'you think I'm stupid? Mumbai will go to hell, along with half of India. There's a chance none of us will make it, but if we do, the world will be in chaos. Our money might be easily forgotten in the confusion.'

'Nonsense, Jamal. Look, I can double your money right now, but that's the best I can do. Just take it, for God's sake!'

Jamal's eyes narrowed. 'Don't ever raise your voice at me again.'

'My apologies,' Philip said, swallowing his anger.

Jamal stared at him for several moments. 'Fine, pay me what you have. But I want the rest, Philip. Understand?'

'You have my word. Give me fifteen minutes to transfer the funds.'

'I'm hungry,' moaned Sunglasses. He was sat on the bed watching TV, the sunglasses now perched on top of his head.

'Me too,' the Beard added.

Jamal waved a hand at the phone. 'Order room service. And make it quick.'

Philip flipped open his laptop and sat by the window. The last thing he needed now was the WI-FI signal to drop during the transfer. He opened up a secure browser window and typed in the Belgian bank's web address…

'The line's dead.'

Philip turned around. Sunglasses was sprawled on the bed, the phone held to his ear. He shook the handset and listened. 'Definitely dead.'

Philip crossed the room, snatching the phone from Sunglasses and tapping the cradle button several times. Nothing. He crossed to the writing bureau and plucked a hotel brochure from the small wooden stand. He flipped it over and used his mobile to call the main number. Nothing.

'Hotel switchboard is busy.' He shared a look with Jamal, one born from years of operational experience.

Jamal hurried to the window and cracked the blind. Philip went to the door. He peered through the spyglass out into the corridor. Visibility was limited, and all he could see was the opposite door. He gave Jamal a quick head shake.

The former intelligence agent snapped his fingers and motioned Sunglasses to his feet. 'Go downstairs, have a poke around for anything unusual, then call me, understood?'

Sunglasses swaggered from the room, and Jamal switched his attention back to Philip. 'What about that money?'

Philip sat back down and rested his laptop on his knees. The bank's window was open. He typed in his username, password and seven-digit code. He thought about relieving Jamal of the gun in his fist, about shooting him and the Beard and doing the job himself, but he still felt weakened by his sickness. He transferred another quarter of a million dollars into Jamal's account, consoling himself with the knowledge that somewhere down the line, the infection would find him.

'There,' Philip announced, flipping the laptop around. 'The money's in your account.'

Jamal pulled out his smart phone, eager to check the transaction. As he did, Philip's phone beeped with an incoming message.

He thumbed open his phone, read the text.

His heart rate skyrocketed.

You're blown. Get out now.

SUNGLASSES STABBED THE ELEVATOR BUTTON AGAIN, CONVINCED his repeated pushing would result in the arrival of a lift. The former Pakistani soldier waited another minute before cursing under his breath and heading for the fire escape.

He barged the door open and stepped into the stairwell. Something hit him hard in the face and strong hands slammed him against the wall. His head smacked off the concrete as someone yanked the gun from his waistband. He blinked tears from his watery eyes and blood ran from his nose. The gloved hand around his throat was pinching his windpipe and he wheezed noisily. His eyes refocussed. He was surrounded by armed white men. The one that choked him, a well-built, fair-haired man with a stubbled face, relaxed his fingers a little and allowed him to breathe.

'You speak English?'

Sunglasses nodded, coughing.

'Is Philip in the room?' Mike showed him a CCTV still from Munich Airport.

Another nod.

'How many guns?'

'Two,' Sunglasses said, gasping.

'Bag him.'

Mike stripped off his raincoat, revealing his M27 and combat rig beneath. Around him the others pulled on safety goggles and checked weapons. They moved out into the fifth-floor hallway, leaving Sunglasses bound, gagged and hooded on the landing.

The hallway was empty, but Mike knew that wouldn't last. He led them down the carpeted corridor, his weapon up and ready. There was barely a footfall or a rattle of equipment as they passed rooms six, eight, then ten. He heard music playing, a TV maybe, and the murmur of voices behind doors.

He held up a fist. The operators crowded the doorway around him, ready to breach. Mike produced a master keycard and held it up for the team to see. Pins were eased from stun grenades as Mike slipped the key card into the door.

The beep was deafening.

The green light blinked —

He threw open the door and took cover as the stun grenades detonated inside. Mike was first into the room, with Billy Finch right on his shoulder. Through the smoke, a bearded figured staggered, hands clasped over his ears. Finch's double tap dropped him like a rag doll. Mike registered a flash and then the punch to his chest knocked him to the ground. Flynn stepped over him and opened up with the Benelli, the *boom* deafening in the confined space. Mike reached beneath his chest plate — his hand came up dry. *Lucky bastard.* He dragged himself to his feet as Flynn and Miller threw another guy face down onto the bed and cuffed him.

'Room clear,' yelled one of Finch's SEALs.

'All good?' Finch asked, eyes flicking to the scorched impact hole in Mike's rig.

The Team Leader nodded. 'Lucky for me the guy was a good shot. Secure the floor, Billy. No one in or out.'

As Finch double-timed from the room, Mike inspected the body lying by the bathroom door. Half his face had been shredded by Flynn's M4, as well as his shoulder, neck and

199

right arm. He saw the gun lying at the man's feet. He picked it up, dismantled it, and dropped the parts back on the carpet.

'Nice try, buddy.'

He turned his attention to the man on the bed. He sat stiff-backed, flanked by Flynn and Miller. His appearance hadn't changed since Munich.

'Where's the virus, Philip?'

The prisoner gave Mike nothing but a defiant smile. Mike whipped his hand back and slapped it off his face. Philip's eyes drilled into Mike's.

'Got something to say, asshole? I know you speak English, so answer me now. Where's the virus?'

'Not here,' Philip responded, spitting blood on the carpet.

'What's the inventory?' he asked Miller.

'Passports, cash, credit cards. Found a power lead but no laptop. No phone either.'

'Bingo!'

Boswell was bent over the small refrigerator across the room. Carefully he removed a small plastic container and showed it to Mike. Inside were three pouches of clear liquid.

'Is this it?'

Philip smiled. 'Why don't you try it and see?'

'Where's Marion?'

Philip's smile melted momentarily. 'Who?'

'You'll talk,' Mike promised him. 'It's just a matter of time.'

Philip grinned, his teeth red with blood. 'A commodity you do not have.'

'Agreed, which means we'll have to forgo your human rights to get the information we need. Bag him, get him outside,' he ordered.

Mike keyed his microphone. 'All call-signs, this is Task Force Leader. Package is secure and in transit. Clear a path to the vehicles.'

There was a burst of static in Mike's ear and then he heard

Tapper's voice, almost drowned out by a thundering storm.

'We've got a situation here. The local cops showed up, and there's a crowd, a couple of hundred maybe, right outside the hotel. Transport had to bug out, and we've got hostiles covering the rear of the building.'

Mike went to the window and looked down into the street. The crowd had spilled out into the road and he saw blue and red lights crawling through the traffic, converging on their location. Sirens wailed across the city.

He tugged out his sat phone and dialled the consulate. Seconds later he was talking to Kappes.

'Be advised, we have the package and the WMD but we are unable to exfil. Local cops have surrounded the hotel and there's a pretty lively mob with them.'

'You're all over social media,' the station chief told him. 'The word is, a group of foreigners are trying to seize the hotel and take hostages. The ambassador is on the horn to New Delhi as we speak. How long can you hold out for?'

Down in the street, traffic had been brought to a standstill as hundreds of people poured across the road and joined the mob outside the hotel. 'Not long enough.'

'Find a safe haven and barricade yourselves in as best you can. We're pulling out all the stops here.'

'Roger that.' Mike called down to Tapper on his radio. 'Get everyone up to the fifth floor, right now. Tell Sanjay to lose himself in the crowd. Do it now.'

Mike hurried out into the hallway. He glimpsed frightened eyes as room doors slammed and locked around him. Finch's SEALs had the fire escape door wedged open. Multiple footsteps pounded the stairs below.

'Friendlies incoming,' the senior chief told him.

Mike pulled a small rechargeable screwdriver from his kit. He removed the elevator control plate and cut all the wires inside. He had no idea if it would disable the lift but when the cops gained entry they would try that first.

Tapper and the rest of the team spilled out into the hallway. 'We've secured the door on the ground floor but it won't hold for long. What's the plan?'

'The plan is, we wait,' the SOG leader told him.

Tapper's face told him that was a bad idea. 'Mike, that's one angry mob down there, and the cops aren't in control. If they get to us, we won't be able to stop them. There must be another way.'

'Kappes is working the problem. Until then, we find somewhere to hide and barricade ourselves in. Take a couple of guys and go room to room, clear the whole floor. After that, we block the stairwell.'

He walked over to Philip. Flynn had him stood facing the wall. Mike saw his head twitch under the hood as he stood next to him. 'If he tries anything, break an arm.'

'Roger that,' Flynn said.

The rest of the team pounded doors, then began kicking them in. They cleared the floor in less than a minute, then they went room to room, closest ones first, and started clearing them of furniture — tables, chairs, mattresses, anything they could carry was hauled into the stairwell and tossed onto the landing below. Before long they'd managed to create a very respectable blockade that would be difficult to negotiate. But not impossible.

The thundering from down below reached a crescendo and then they heard glass shattering and a huge roar.

'The main doors just gave way,' Tapper said.

Mike ducked into one of the empty rooms and looked down onto the street. The mob was funnelling into the hotel like water down a drain. They were fired up as only Third World mobs could be, and hundreds of them waved sticks and other weapons. There would be no reasoning with anyone here today, no bargaining or pleading. And if it came to it, they didn't have enough ammunition to stop them all.

He hurried back out to the hallway. Everyone was waiting

for Mike's next order. They were calm and assured, the ultimate professionals, a special breed who would normally be
able to extricate themselves from pretty much any kind of
trouble. But not here, not today. If the mob got to them, this
would be their Little Big Horn.

The phone in his rig warbled. *Kappes. Finally.* He glanced
at the display.

Not Kappes.

'Stan, I can't talk right now. We've got a situation and I
need to keep this line clear.'

'Got an eye in the sky right above you,' Lando told him.
'The whole street is under siege.'

'I'm ending this call, Stan. Kappes is working the phones,
trying to get us out of here.'

Mike was about to thumb the *End* button when Lando
said, 'You're out of time, Mike. I've got an alternate exfil, an
inbound Seahawk, ETA fourteen minutes. Can you hold off
until then?'

Mike did the math. 'There're ten of us, Stan.'

'She's stripped down, but she can't land, just in case the
roof doesn't hold. Move your team, Mike. I'll call you back.'

'We've got an inbound Seahawk,' Mike told the others. He
pointed to the hooded prisoner. 'Get him to the roof, right
now. The rest of you, we need to reinforce that barricade, buy
ourselves fourteen minutes.'

The guys needed no incentive. They went to the closest
rooms, dragging out beds, mattresses, wardrobes, and
anything that could be prised off the floor or walls. All of it
went down into the narrow stairwell. As Mike manhandled a
thick mattress through the door, he heard a *boom* from below.

The roar that followed was terrifying, a vengeful
crescendo of noise. Mike looked over the rail. Five floors
below, the mob filled the fire escape, a solid crush of
humanity rushing up the stairs. He held out his hand. 'Flash
bang.'

Finch handed him a stun grenade. Mike pulled the pin and dropped it down the shaft.

'Grenade,' he warned, covering his ears. The detonation rocked the stairwell like a thunderclap. A collective scream followed. Mike looked over the rail and saw panic. 'Get some smoke down there, and more flash-bangs. Do it!'

Munitions were dropped over the rail. Repeated detonations shook the building, and purple smoke rolled up towards them. Then they were moving, up through the smoke to the roof. Mike held them one floor below and pointed at Finch.

'When they close in on that barricade, put some rounds down there. Try not to hit anyone, okay? I'll call when the helo is here.'

'Roger that.'

Mike took the stairs two at a time. Up on the roof, Tapper, Flynn, Miller and Boswell were all crouched behind an air-conditioning unit. Between them, Philip was on his knees, a hood over his head. Mike hurried over and crouched down next to them. He checked his watch.

'The chopper should be here in five minutes. It can't set down, so toss that motherfucker inside as soon as he's low enough. Where's the WMD?' he asked Boswell.

The CIA operator jerked a thumb over his shoulder. 'Sealed in a dry bag in my rucksack. We're all good.'

Mike did a quick circumnavigation of the roof. There was plenty of airspace for a Seahawk to approach, but there were also lots of faces at the windows of the surrounding buildings. Mike prayed none of them were armed, and minded to take down a helicopter. His sat phone warbled and Mike snatched it out, crouching low behind some aluminium ducting.

'Talk to me, Stan.'

'We've got the chopper on visual, Mike. He's a click to the south-east, coming in low and fast.'

'Popping smoke now,' Mike told him. He yelled across to

the others. 'Someone toss a smoke grenade. Helo needs a visual.'

Boswell sprinted across the roof and set down a canister. Yellow smoke billowed into the warm evening air.

'Pilot sees yellow smoke,' Lando relayed down the phone. 'Thirty seconds out.'

Mike pressed the transmit switch of his radio. 'All call-signs, fall back on my position right now.'

Two of Finch's SEALs burst out of the fire escape door. Behind them, Mike heard the rattle of suppressed rounds and raced inside. Finch and one of his guys were shooting chunks out of a wall a couple of floors down. Mike looked over the rail. The mob were crawling all over the barricade, dismantling it as they went. The front runners were already past it and heading upwards.

Mike tossed the last of the smoke and flash-bangs down into the stairwell. He raised his weapon and squinted through the optics, sizing up a sliver of wall below. He fired, chopping chunks out of the concrete below. He heard rounds cracking off the walls and pinging off the metal handrail, praying they wouldn't find a human target.

And then there was another roar, one that drowned out the screeching mob.

Mike slapped Finch on the shoulder. 'We're moving!'

He ran back up to the roof, the SEALs right behind him. They slammed the door closed and then the Seahawk rose up from behind the hotel and thundered over their heads in a steep circle, its rotors chopping the air. Mike ran to his men and helped lift Philip to his feet.

The Seahawk circled once then flared over the rooftop, its grey body settling into a hover a few feet above the asphalt. The noise was tremendous, and the downdraught battered them as they scrambled aboard. Mike squatted next to the crewman manning the M134 mini-gun.

'Watch that door!' Mike yelled in his ear. 'Anyone comes

through, fire a warning burst! No casualties!'

The crewman nodded behind his black visor. The aircraft bounced on the hot air as Mike helped get the others aboard. The Seahawk had a passenger capacity of five. Philip was strapped into a seat. Those without one just held on.

Mike gave the thumbs up to the crew chief, who relayed the order to the pilot. The engines wound up and the nose of the aircraft dipped as it cleared the edge of the roof. Then the chopper was falling like a stone between the surrounding buildings before the engines screamed again and the thundering rotors clawed for altitude. The docks slipped by beneath them and then they were feet wet, banking to the south-east.

Finch reached over and slapped Mike on the arm, pointing behind them. Mike turned, looking out beyond the tail of the aircraft, and saw a human wave spilling across that now distant roof. It had been a close-run thing, but Stan had come through.

Mike motioned to the crew chief, tapping his ear. The airman handed him a headset that was pre-dialled in. He hit the transmit switch.

'Appreciate the pickup,' Mike told him. 'Where're we headed?'

'*USS Independence*,' the crew chief told him. 'It's a thirty minute ride, so sit back and relax.'

Mike wanted to tell him that none of them could relax. He wanted to tell him that they'd just averted a disaster that would make Texas pale into insignificance. But he didn't. Truth was, they were all grateful to be out of that hotel. But it wasn't over, not by a long shot.

He stared at the hooded man sitting opposite, his hands and ankles bound with plastic ties, the warm wind whipping at his clothing. They had averted one disaster. Philip was the key to preventing another.

And that meant finding Marion.

DRY RUN

THEY WERE SOLDIERS OF THE THIRD BRIGADE COMBAT TEAM, First Cavalry Division, and their two armoured Joint Light Tactical Vehicles straddled either side of a muddy track twenty yards into the trees. Each vehicle was manned by a driver and a turret gunner, and both crews sat in silence, watching and listening.

The other six guys in the deployment were spread out along the nearby tree line, looking out over the flat Texas plain. They scanned the darkness with their magnified, low-light optics, partially comforted by the fact that their careful surveillance was further augmented by the unseen drones somewhere overhead, monitoring the terrain with their own thermal imaging systems. Yet despite the layers of technical sophistication, the reports coming out of Lubbock did little to steady the soldiers' nerves.

They all knew about Baghdad. It was no secret what had happened to the Americans out there, and how they'd made the ultimate sacrifice in order to spare the city from the death plague that had cost the lives of twelve hundred America souls. None of them imagined that same virus would raise its vile head on US soil. And yet it had.

They'd been assigned a grid reference, which placed them twelve miles south of the hot zone and far from human habitation. Those people who lived close to the edge of the exclusion zone had fled to one of dozens of relocation centres. The only people left in Lubbock were either hiding, dead or infected.

The detail commander, a Staff Sergeant of considerable operational experience, had gathered his men together and explained that, like most of them, he had a family, and it was his intention to return to that family after the crisis was over. His men, who put great trust in their Staff Sergeant, agreed. So, in the darkness of that Texas wood a pact was made; if their position was threatened in any way, they would shoot first and to hell with the Rules of Engagement. They were a team, and they would stick together no matter what.

So they waited in the trees, silent beneath that cold Texas sky, watching the fields for movement, for the infected. That's when they heard a familiar rumbling to the south, one that peaked and faded across the flat terrain; low flying aircraft. The rumbling intensified and the unseen flight of aircraft rocketed overhead, thundering north towards the city of Lubbock.

And that could only mean one thing, the Staff Sergeant realised.

The order had been given.

RAY WILSON WAS STILL ON THE ROOF OF THE SOUTH PLAINS Mall, huddled with the others between thick tubes of pipework that stretched the length of the building.

Below them, death continued to stalk the streets of Lubbock.

There were bodies everywhere, scattered across the roads and sidewalks. As the hours passed the gunfire had been relentless, rattling across the city, and then it had slowly petered out. To the south and west the freeway was lifeless and littered with abandoned vehicles. Sometime after midnight the power to the city had failed. Downtown went first, its bright cluster of streets and buildings suddenly plunged into darkness. The rest of the city had followed, then the suburbs, as far as the eye could see. It was as if someone had drawn a dark blanket across the whole of Texas, and the spectacle had frightened Ray. Artificial light represented life, order, civilisation. In its absence, something primordial lurked. Like the infected.

Ray saw hundreds, if not thousands of them, moving through the darkness in seemingly intelligent packs, reacting in unison to sights and sounds, selecting their targets, running them down, swarming over them. Ray saw people die, torn apart. He'd seen others pick themselves up in the wake of a passing herd and run to join its ranks. It was the most frightening spectacle Ray Wilson had ever seen.

The guys around him were equally terrified; Felipe, Leon, and two young men who wore kitchen scrubs. Their names were Kyle and Brian; Kyle hung on Felipe's every word, and Brian was a little more circumspect, but all of them huddled close as a cold wind whipped across the rooftop. None of them were dressed appropriately, and as the adrenaline wore off and the night wore on, body temperatures were dropping rapidly, Ray's included.

'We'll freeze to death if we stay here all night,' he said, shivering in the dark. 'I think we should get inside, find somewhere safe on the top floor.'

Leon hissed at him in the darkness. 'Are you crazy? Those things could be all over the place down there.'

'Take a look around,' Ray countered. 'There are half a dozen doors that lead to this roof, but no one else has been up here since it started.'

Felipe peered through a gap in the pipes. 'Man's got a point.'

'Fuck that,' Leon grumbled. 'I'm staying up here. When the sun comes up they'll send a rescue party or something.'

'Or maybe the infected will try to get up here. Their behaviour appears cognitive, as if they possess some form of rudimentary reasoning capability.'

Leon turned around and glared at Ray. 'Say what?'

'He's right,' Felipe said. 'They seem smart. Like they're working shit out.'

Leon sucked his teeth dismissively. Ray was still thinking about their next move when he saw Felipe frown.

'What the hell is that?'

Ray twisted his body around to the south. There was nothing to see, nothing except the dark, jagged outline of the Lubbock suburbs. Then he heard it.

'Aircraft,' Ray answered.

The rumble was building in intensity, like a storm approaching at five-hundred miles an hour. The thunder grew into a deafening roar and then a flight of dark shadows roared across the city a short distance away.

Downtown lit up in several blinding flashes and a sheet of fire engulfed the surrounding buildings and rolled up into the night sky. The shockwave gusted across the rooftop, whipping up a cloud of dust and dirt that made Ray blink and cough.

He got to his feet and Kyle tugged on his trouser leg, urging him to stay behind the pipes, but Ray was already stumbling towards the edge of the roof. He had to get a better look, to process what he was seeing, what his eyes told him was real but his mind refused to believe…

The United States Air Force had just bombed an American city.

And not just bombed. Whatever munitions they had used, it had caused the downtown area to burn like a Roman candle, the flames dancing across the glass of nearby buildings. The strike reminded Ray of old Vietnam footage, of napalm canisters tumbling through the air, of concussion waves and fireballs that consumed villages in their wake.

They were trying to stop the infection. Anyway they could.

A decision had been made. America had seen the horror and demanded action. It's the only thing that made sense to Ray. He hurried back to the pipes.

'We've got to get out of here, right now.'

Leon's eyes narrowed. 'Are you deaf? I ain't going nowhere.'

'They're going to level the city,' Ray told them. 'We won't be safe up here.'

'Why?' Brian asked. He looked scared, but there was strength in his voice. 'They can't do that. We're American citizens.'

'They can't allow the infection to spread,' Ray told him. 'If that means destroying the city, so be it.'

Felipe shook his head. 'No way, man. There are people out there, families and shit.'

'Wake up!' Ray snapped. 'They just dropped a ton of napalm on Main Street. The military are watching and they're taking no chances. I say we get the hell out of here, out of Lubbock.'

Ray could see Felipe struggling with the reality, just as Ray had. But Ray had an advantage; he was a cynical DC reporter who'd worked the swamp for decades. The guys around him were blue-collar types who lived sixteen-hundred miles away from their nation's capital. They were naïve in the ways of politics. Ray hoped they were fast learners.

'Does anyone have a car?'

Brian raised his hand. 'Yes, sir. I got a pickup. It's in the lot over yonder.'

'Show me,' Ray said.

He followed the kid to the other side of the roof. The

parking lot was a land of shadows. There were cars and bodies scattered everywhere, but no infected. Brian pointed to a Ford pickup truck sitting beneath a dead light pole. It was ten bays away from the rear entrance to the mall. Ray looked for the nearest stairwell and his hopes soared. A short distance away, along the edge of the roof, he spotted two curved steel rails. He jogged over and saw a caged, exterior ladder running down the side of the building, stopping maybe ten feet short of the ground. Good enough.

'Come on,' Ray whispered.

They scrambled back to the group, and Ray flinched as two large explosions rocked the city. The sound of aircraft rumbled across the horizon. It wasn't over, not by a long shot.

'I've got a plan,' Ray told them. He explained it briefly and waited for a response. Felipe was the first to speak.

'Count me in, man. How about you Leon?'

'You're fucking crazy,' Leon grumbled.

'Don't be stupid. You can't stay here.'

'Wanna bet?'

Felipe leaned in close. 'Then stay. When they find you you'll be charred to a goddamn cinder. Like one of your steaks,' he added.

Kyle and Brian grinned. Leon looked at each one of them, then caved.

'Fuck it. This better work,' he warned Ray, jabbing a finger at him.

Another flight of planes approached from the east. They all ducked as an incredible ripping sound filled the air before it was drowned out by the roar of the aircraft passing overhead.

'A-Tens,' Brian yelled over the noise, his wide eyes searching the sky. 'That's a thirty-millimetre cannon cutting loose. Oh, Jesus, they're using mini-guns now?'

Mini-guns. 'How do you know that?' Ray asked.

'I'm joining the Air Force. Got to pay my way through college first, hence the shitty job.'

'You two bitches on a date?' Leon hissed. 'If we're gonna move, move.'

They thrashed out the plan one more time and then they were moving across the rooftop towards the ladder.

SEVEN THOUSAND MILES AWAY IN SHANGHAI, MARION WAS enjoying a delicious Sea Bass lunch in the Ritz Carlton's Jin Xuan restaurant on the fifty-third floor. She occupied a table by the window, eating slowly as she enjoyed the spectacular views across the city. The weather was cooperating too, the sky clear and almost cloudless. Were it not for the mission in hand, Marion would've enjoyed spending more time getting to know the city.

She turned her wrist over to check the time. It was a subconscious move, because she'd deliberately left her watch in her room. Her smart phone was also tucked away in her handbag. Constant reminders of the time were proving unhelpful.

Thirty-one hours had passed since she'd received the text from Philip. She should've left Shanghai by now. She should be in Beijing, where the virus would also be deployed.

Something had gone wrong.

There had been no confirmation of that fact, but Marion was a professional of considerable experience. Her instincts had become finely tuned over many years, and those same instincts were telling her that the operation had run into problems.

There was nothing on the TV about Mumbai; it was Texas that dominated the global news cycle. Marion had been unaware of any operation on US soil. She was confused, and a little concerned. She'd been left out of the loop, and wondered if Philip had also been sidelined.

It wouldn't be the first time, of course. After all, both she and Philip were field operatives, and not always privy to operational decisions. But this was different. They no longer wore a uniform, were no longer links in a chain of command that stretched from the lowliest private to the highest levels of government. Their only master now was the person who wrote the largest cheque.

However, in this case, both Marion and Philip were committed to the cause itself. They longed for a single world government, for global order and discipline. Matt Sorensen was the key to that vision, and Marion, like her male counterpart, was a sworn disciple.

And she was worried about Philip. She thought about contacting Sorensen then decided against it. Maybe both of them had been compromised. If that were true, she might already be under surveillance, even at that very moment. She turned away from the window, her eyes conducting a slow sweep of the room. She could see nothing untoward, no quiet exodus of diners, the waiters replaced by square-jawed men wearing ill-fitting uniforms. The people around her were eating, conversing, enjoying themselves. There were children too, scattered around the room. It meant nothing, of course. If she was compromised, they would take her down anywhere.

So, the possibility existed that she was now on her own. She would have to —

The inside of her handbag glowed blue.

She put down her glass and plucked her smartphone from the Louis Vuitton. A message lingered on the screen and she swiped it away, slipping the phone back inside her handbag.

She finished her wine, her heart beating fast.

The message was the one she'd been expecting. She forced herself to relax, and rose slowly from her table, smiling at a passing waitress. She left the restaurant and took the elevator back down to her room. She locked the door and went to the wardrobe. She knelt down and prised off the panel where it met the carpet. The sealed plastic bag of H-1 infected wipes was still there.

Satisfied that everything was in order, Marion decided she would take a nap. Later she would shower and dress, and begin preparations for deployment. She kicked off her shoes and lay back on the bed. As she closed her eyes and waited for sleep to wrap her in its silent embrace, she was comforted by the images of chaos, death and destruction that filled her mind.

THE PLAN LASTED ALL THE WAY TO THE OTHER SIDE OF THE rooftop.

When they reached the ladder, Leon peered over the edge and said, 'Fuck that, man. I'm going second.'

'No, Ray goes second,' Felipe whispered. 'Come on, Leon. We got a plan, we stick to it.'

'Brian goes first, that's a given,' Ray told Leon. 'I'm fifteen years older than you and out of shape. It makes sense that I take the front seat. I don't want to slow things up trying to climb in the back of the truck.'

'Bullshit,' Leon snapped. 'I gotta risk *my* life because you're a fat, lazy fuck? No way. I'm riding shotgun, that's final.' He glared at all of them in turn, daring someone to challenge him. No one did. No one was stupid enough to start a fight in the middle of all this chaos.'

'Don't worry, Ray. I'll look out for you.' Felipe gave Ray a reassuring pat on his shoulder. 'Okay, let's do this. And be quiet. No talking, okay?'

Brian moved towards the curved rails and spun around, reaching behind him with his feet for the top rung of the ladder. He disappeared quickly from view and Leon followed behind him. Felipe went next, closely followed by Ray.

The steel was cold beneath his hands, and he moved gingerly, one rung at a time, ensuring both feet were on the same rung before dangling his foot into space and reaching for the rung below. He'd never been good with heights, and his hands clutched each rung with a death grip. He imagined dropping those last few feet, twisting his ankle, the pickup truck roaring into the darkness as he hopped after it. Then the silence, the footfalls in the darkness, the growls and breathing of the infected as they closed in all around him —

'Ray! Hold up!'

Below him, Felipe was whispering urgently. Ray froze. They were almost there. He saw Brian on the last rung, his head swivelling in all directions. That was the plan, to wait at the bottom, to watch and listen, to be sure. But as Mike Tyson once said, everyone has a plan until they get punched in the mouth.

'Hurry up, motherfucker!'

Leon again. The man was going to get them all killed. Or worse.

Ray watched Brian as he dangled his legs a few feet above the asphalt. Then he dropped to the ground.

Brian froze, watching and listening. The he stood up and walked towards his pickup. Ray admired the young man's courage. Given the circumstances, most people would've run, but Brian kept his cool, walking slowly, quietly, his head moving this way and that, the keys to his pickup in his hand. With poise like that, Ray was pretty sure the kid would make an exceptional pilot.

Then he was gone, swallowed by the darkness. It was the moment of truth.

Beep! beep!

Orange blinkers flashed in the darkness.

Ray heard a door open, then close. The pickup's engine roared into life. Brian hit the lights, and then the vehicle was moving, weaving carefully around abandoned cars, bumping gently over bodies until he'd cleared the line. Then he gunned

216

the engine and swung the vehicle round until the truck bed was close to the escape ladder.

'Let's go!' Kyle hissed above him.

Ray looked down, saw Leon drop to the ground. He flung open the passenger door and jumped in, slamming it for all the world to hear. Ray cursed him again as he clambered down, making sure his hands and feet made contact good contact, the vision of that broken ankle still front and centre.

Below him, Felipe was waving to Ray. 'Come on, man! Let's go!'

That's when Ray heard the sound, a stampede of running feet.

'Move, for Chrissakes!'

Ray couldn't see them, but he could definitely hear them. His shoes dangled in mid air and he let go of the ladder, hitting the asphalt and stumbling sideways. Felipe caught him, and next thing he knew Kyle was falling on top of him. Desperate hands bundled Ray into the back of the pickup. Felipe banged on the rear window.

'Go! Go!'

The truck lurched forward and Ray pulled himself up against the cab. That's when he saw them, dozens of figures, running behind the truck. Terrifyingly, they were gaining on them as the pickup negotiated the chaos of the parking lot, swerving this way and that, the tyres squealing. One of the pursuers, a young kid wearing a Texas Tech hoodie, was closing the gap, his arms pumping. Ray could see the whites of his eyes, and when Brian hit the brakes, he saw the others behind him, washed in a devilish red glow. Ray's skin crawled. They were in hell, and being pursued by demons.

He heard Leon in the cab behind him, shouting and swearing at Brian, threatening to commandeer the vehicle. The wheels bounced over bodies, over kerbs, weaving violently towards the main road. Ray held on tight as the pickup turned onto the street, fishtailing briefly before control was regained and Brian stamped on the gas.

The demons were still behind them. Men, women and, God forbid, children, screaming, clawing the air. Ray was thankful when the darkness swallowed them.

They'd made it, but only just. Still, the plan had worked, and Ray felt pretty pleased with himself. So far, so good. All they had to do now was get out of the city. The roads were empty, they had a decent vehicle, and a young but competent and level-headed driver.

How hard could it be?

FEET WET

COFFMAN MOVED QUICKLY BETWEEN THE DRESSING ROOM, THE bathroom and the main bedroom, snatching up several personal items and cramming them in her shoulder bag. She tugged on a black padded Moncler winter coat as her bag lady Sofia, and two White House domestic staff, busied themselves checking Coffman's luggage was ready for transport.

'Is there anything else, ma'am?'

'No, thank you, Sofia.'

Coffman watched her snap up the handle of the largest roller case and wheel it out into the hallway, her staff hurrying behind her like uniformed ducklings. As they left the room, Secret Service detail leader Tim McCarthy appeared in the doorway.

'Marine One is standing by, Madam President.'

'Thank you, Tim.'

She took a final look around then followed the detail leader out into the hallway, where another five agents formed a protective perimeter around her. They left the private residence via the West Colonnade and stepped out into the pre-dawn darkness. Coffman hurried across the South Lawn towards the waiting presidential helicopter, a VH-60 White

Hawk, its red lights blinking and rotors whipping up a cold storm. Two more helicopters circled overhead, a military escort that Coffman had publicly objected to, but privately welcomed. After witnessing the speed of infection across Lubbock, Coffman would take any level of security she could get right now. The plan had exceeded her expectations, so much so that she was beginning to doubt the decision to implement it. Right now though, Lubbock was the least of her problems. No, her problem was the man called Philip, now in US custody, a man who knew enough to get Coffman the needle.

She stepped aboard the helicopter and took her seat. There were six other people crammed inside the modified Black Hawk's plush and soundproofed interior; Erik, by her side of course, and Charlie Schultz who sat opposite. Also on board were Karen Baranski, Homeland Security Chief Diane Grady and her SecDef, Drew Clark. That meant she couldn't talk frankly, and she needed to talk, desperately. As the aircraft lifted off the South Lawn, Clark was the first to speak from the bench seat across the cabin.

'Ma'am, you need to make a decision,' she said, raising her voice above the rhythmic beat of the rotors. 'We simply can't afford to wait any longer.'

Coffman folded one leg over the other and leaned back in her chair. 'Given the circumstances I have no qualms with torture. God knows we'll all have to carry the burden of Lubbock with us for the rest of our lives.' She took pleasure in using the collective *we*, enjoyed watching the subtle squirming of her colleagues as the consequences of their decision to expend thermobaric and heavy calibre munitions onto the good people of Texas continued to play out on television. The sun would rise soon, and the cold light of day would trigger renewed horror as the world absorbed the scale of the destruction and the rising body count.

'Ma'am, I need a definitive order,' Clark pressed.

The President turned to Schultz. 'Thoughts, Charlie?'

The Admiral spread his hands. 'As I said before, Madam President, neither option is guaranteed to tell us what we need to know. Sure, the guys could get the pliers out and start pulling nails, but experience tells us that prisoners subjected to acute pain will say just about anything to make it stop.'

'So we go with the chemical option?'

'It does give us more control,' Schultz advised.

'Madam President, we may not that have long,' Clark insisted. 'The *Independence* is still some way from the fleet and it could take time before assets are in place to carry out a chemical interrogation. In the meantime this Marion person could be anywhere in the world, deploying the infection as we speak.'

Coffman gave her Secretary of Defence a long, hard look. 'And if we get it wrong, Drew? If we shout *Paris*, and Moscow goes to hell, what then? Do we shrug our shoulders and say, *sorry, guys, our bad*?'

'We have to do something!' Clark blurted. 'It could be New York next! Or right here, in DC!'

Coffman glared at her. 'Drew, we've just dropped fuel-air explosives on an American city. Thousands of infected people are dead, and thousands more will probably die, many of them unaffected by the virus. That will trouble my conscience for the rest of my life,' she lied, 'so don't think for one moment that I'm not aware of my responsibilities here.'

'Can't we do both?' Grady piped up. 'Couldn't they rough the prisoner up a little first, get him to talk?'

Coffman's eyes flicked to Schultz. She'd stalled long enough. 'It can't hurt, right Charlie?'

Schultz shrugged. He knew it too. 'It's risky, but what the hell. We might get lucky.'

Coffman dragged the moment out a little longer before nodding her head. 'Send word to the Task Force commander. Tell him the gloves are off.'

Clark got up and moved to the back of the aircraft. Coffman locked eyes with Charlie, with Karen Baranski. They'd done everything possible to delay Philip's interrogation without raising suspicion, but now events were out of their control. There was a very real possibility that Bob's people would be stopped, and if that happened, if they talked, Coffman's presidency would be over. And quite possibly her life.

Next to her, Erik was on his phone, scrolling through a Twitter feed that was jammed with videos from Lubbock, uploaded before the plug was pulled and the city went dark. There was no sound, but that was probably for the best. Much of what Erik was looking at was very graphic, but that didn't stop him from playing and rewinding constantly. Her Chief of Staff was troubled, that much was obvious. It wouldn't hurt to keep an eye on him, discreetly of course.

She'd speak to Bob about it as soon as they arrived at Snowcat.

'WHERE THE FUCK IS EVERYBODY?'

Leon had asked the question they all wanted an answer to. They were a mile south of the mall, driving steadily through the urban sprawl of south Lubbock. Felipe had pushed the freeway option, taking them south-west and away from the city. Leon had backed him, but Ray had talked them out of it. Did any of them want to be stuck on an elevated section of the freeway with the crazies on the loose? The freeway option was quickly abandoned. Now they were cruising through unlit suburban streets, and apart from the absence of electrical light, things looked pretty normal. There were cars parked on the street and in people's driveways. Ray saw a few curtains twitch as they passed. Behind them, the sky pulsed with white flashes, and heavy concussions rolled across the suburbs. The centre of Lubbock was being levelled. Ray wondered when the bombs would start raining on the suburbs.

'Where're the cops? The National Guard?'

'Fucking place is a ghost town,' Leon muttered. 'Leaving the poor folk to their fate. Motherfuckers.'

'There's probably a cordon somewhere,' Ray told them, though he didn't feel too hopeful. Everything to the south was cloaked in darkness for as far as the eye could see. Ray heard the same emergency message playing on the radio as Leon scrolled through the channels. People were being instructed to seek shelter, to stay in their homes and to lock the doors. They should've added, *don't make a sound.*

Brian drove with the lights off at less than twenty miles per hour. The streets around them were narrower now, the homes more densely packed, the cars a little older. Ray looked out over the cab; suburbia appeared to stretch for miles —

He rapped an urgent knuckle on the roof. The vehicle jerked to a stop. Kyle and Felipe stood up and leaned on the cab roof alongside Ray. There were people ahead, moving soundlessly across the intersection, more people crossing the intersection beyond that one. They moved in that strange way, their legs and arms thrown awkwardly, but they made no sound other than the collective shuffle of their feet and clothing. The numbers were difficult to estimate but Ray assumed there were at least several thousand people moving east to west through the southern suburbs of Lubbock.

Distant shouting carried on the night air. He heard glass breaking and several screams. New victims, Ray assumed, and then the relative silence returned, the crowd continuing their strange march west.

'Let's get the fuck outta here,' he heard Leon whisper.

No one argued. Ray held on tight as Brian swung the vehicle around. Ray took a squat and whispered through the cab window. 'What now?'

'We head east,' Leon told him, pointing through the windshield.

Brian shook his head. 'Not advisable. There's a lot of new construction out there, a lot of new roads that lead to nowhere. If we get jammed up we might not be able to get out.'

'Well, we can't go north, and those things are to the south and west of us, so what d'you suggest, college boy?'

Brian stopped the vehicle and jerked a thumb over his shoulder. 'I say we keep that group in sight. We stay north, drive parallel until we get ahead of them, then cut south, take Route Eighty-Two all the way to Brownfield. I've got a cousin there, a cop. He'll know what to do.'

'Sounds like a plan,' Ray said. He couldn't wait to get out of the city.

'I can't go.' It was Felipe. He was crouched down next to Ray, listening to the conversation. 'I got family in Melonie Park, a wife and son. I was gonna bail out as soon we got close. I can't leave them.'

Explosions rumbled in the distance. There was no time for arguments or persuasion.

'I understand,' Ray said. He reached for Felipe's hand. 'Thanks for everything. I doubt we would've made it without you.'

'If you're getting out, git,' Leon snapped through the hatch.

'Good luck,' Felipe whispered, and then he dropped over the side of the truck and scuttled into the shadows between two houses. Ray watched him go, admiring the man's bravery and hoping he'd make it.

Brian dropped the pickup into gear and headed north for a couple of blocks, before turning west. Ray leaned against the cab, his arms wrapped tightly around him. It was getting colder, and next to him, Kyle shivered too. After a few minutes, the kid pointed silently past Ray.

The reporter turned his head, saw the black mass of infected marching through the suburbs a couple of hundred yards to their south. Brian's pickup was blue or maybe black, Ray couldn't tell, but with the lights off they were about as stealthy as they could get.

Ray spoke to Brian through the window. 'We may not want to get too close,' he advised. 'If those planes come back we could be in the firing line.'

Leon stared up through the windshield into the night sky. 'He's right. Go north for another block or two.'

Brian kept his eyes on the road ahead, his hands resting on the wheel. The kid was calm beyond his years. 'I'm taking Frankford Avenue north until we hit Sixty-Sixth street, then we'll head west. That should put us on Route Eighty-Two in less than fifteen minutes, if we're lucky.'

'Fucking-A,' Leon said, sitting a little straighter. 'Sooner we get out of this rat's maze the better.'

'Hey Leon, any chance we could switch seats for a while? Me and the kid are freezing back here.'

Leon glared in the darkness. 'Get used to it. I ain't moving.'

'Appreciate it,' Ray snipped.

The wind whipped across the back of the pickup as it increased speed. Ray saw a road sign in the opposite direction and saw they were on Route 82, heading south west. Kyle scootched next to him, his arms folded tightly across his chest. Body warmth was about the best they could do right now. Neither of them spoke, the evening's events still fresh in their minds. Ray was already formulating the outline of a narrative, imagining the headline. Or a book cover.

The Life and Death of Lubbock, Texas. Not a bad title —

The pickup shuddered violently, tyres screeching as it slewed to a stop.

'Jesus Christ!'

'Move! Go, goddammit!'

It was Leon this time, screaming at Brian. The engine roared and rubber squealed. Ray was thrown against the side panel as the vehicle swung around violently and headed back towards Lubbock. He glimpsed bloodied, infected faces. A forest of hands reached for the tailgate, some slipping off the metal, others gripping hard. The pickup swerved danger-ously left and right, and the hands disappeared. Brian kept driving, doing forty, maybe fifty miles an hour.

'Slow down!' Ray shouted through the hatch.

'Shut the fuck up!' Leon barked.

After a couple of hundred yards or so the vehicle deceler-ated and turned left off the Eighty-Two. They were on a side road now, wide and quiet, and Ray watched the houses thin out, the outer suburbs giving way to scrubland and dry pasture. Ray felt a little safer knowing that they were finally out of the city. Before long they would be in Brownfield, where they could get warm and find out what the hell was going on. Ray's priority was to get back to Washington. Lubbock was a dead end. Literally.

The stars were bright overhead, and the temperature felt like it had dropped another degree or two. Then the pickup slowed and turned left. The smooth asphalt had been replaced by a dirt road.

Ray looked over the side. The road stretched into the distance towards a dark tree line, the fields either side of them flat, empty and endless. He settled back against the cab. The sky above Lubbock glowed orange. Kyle leaned into the window.

'What gives with the dirt road?'

Ray heard Leon's voice in the darkness.

'There was a whole bunch of them motherfuckers on Eighty-Two, hundreds of 'em. They were just standing across the highway, blocking it. We nearly drove into them. College boy got us out of trouble.'

'Good work, Brian,' Ray said over his shoulder.

'Thank you, sir.'

Ray made a promise to himself there and then; if they got out of this alive, he'd help the kid through college, give him the financial support he deserved. It was the least he could do.

'We're heading cross-country,' Brian explained. 'Hopefully we can avoid any more trouble and approach Brownfield from the west. I'm guessing another hour, tops.'

Ray's stomach cramped, and he clutched his belly. It had been a long day, and as the adrenaline receded, Ray's body decided there were other priorities to take care of.

'Can we stop?' he asked Brian through the window. 'Call of nature.'

'Just piss over the side,' Leon told him, squinting ahead through the windshield.

Ray pulled a face. 'It's not that kind of call.'

Brian pointed up ahead. 'Hop out, then. We'll wait at the edge of the wood. Here.' Brian handed him a pack of tissues. 'Don't be long, okay? You see or hear anything, you holler.'

'Thanks.'

The pickup squealed to a stop. Ray climbed over the side and waited for Brian to drive a little way down the road. He saw a ditch running along the verge. It was choked with weeds but relatively dry. As good a place as any. Ray unbuckled his trousers and squatted down amongst the vegetation, grunting as his bowels moved. The pickup was lost in the darkness somewhere up ahead. Ray turned around, saw the pale dirt road behind him, stretching back into the darkness. The wind moaned across the fields, stirring the weeds around him. Or maybe it was something else. Ray cursed his imagination, willing his body to get on with the job. A minute later, he was done. He cleaned himself and yanked up his trousers —

A blinding light lit up the road and Ray dropped back into the ditch. He squinted through the weeds, saw the pickup fifty yards away, bathed in a pool of blinding white light. A searchlight, Ray realised, and not just one. There were two of them. And then he saw the soldiers; well, he assumed they were soldiers because all he could see were silhouettes. They lingered at the edge of the light, their weapons held at the ready, and something about their posture made Ray think twice about breaking cover and racing down the road to gratefully shake their hands.

' — off the vehicle!'

' — just civilians — '

'Now! I won't repeat — '

Ray could only hear snatches of the exchange, but it sounded tense. He thought he heard Brian's voice, compliant, then Leon's angry tones. There were more shouts now, the voices angry and overlapping.

Then he heard feet running on the dirt, getting louder. A shadow sprinted towards him, backlit by the searchlights. Ray flinched as a volley of shots cracked overhead. He heard an awful, wet thump and the body fell close by.

Ray stared into Kyle's face. The kid lay on his belly, his mouth opening and closing like a beached fish, his eyelids fluttering. His fingers twitched, as if he was trying to tell Ray something, and then life left him and his whole body seemed to deflate.

Ray yelped as another, sustained barrage of gunfire ripped across the fields. He heard glass breaking and rounds hitting metal, like a storm of hailstones on a tin roof. It seemed to go on forever, but Ray figured it probably lasted no more than a few seconds. He inched his head up very slowly and risked a look.

Definitely soldiers. Their uniforms were clearly visible as they advanced on the eviscerated pickup. The bodywork and windows were shot full of holes and steaming water hissed from beneath the hood. One of the soldiers yanked open the passenger door and Leon's body flopped sideways, hitting the road. He stayed that way, a crumpled heap of soiled and bloody clothes.

'Two dead,' he heard a voice report in the darkness.

'They didn't stop, right? It was them or us.'

'Damn straight.'

'Call it in. And knock those lights off!'

Bile rose in Ray's throat. The searchlights blinked out and he got down on his belly. Slowly, and as quietly as he could manage, he began crawling across the field and away from the road. It took him thirty minutes to reach the trees, by which time his clothes were filthy and he was exhausted from the stress and effort.

He lay just inside the tree line, shivering, listening to the voices of the soldiers carried on the wind. They were faint, distant, so he pulled himself up behind a thick tree trunk. He watched and listened for several more minutes until he was sure he hadn't been detected. Then he turned around and headed through the trees, staggering faster as he got further away, desperate to put as much distance between himself, the dirt road, and the men who lay dead at its side.

MIKE SAVAGE HAD TO SHOUT TO MAKE HIMSELF HEARD.

'What?'

Tapper motioned to his ear and leaned in close as the USS Independence planed across the waves of the Arabian Sea. Both men held on tight to a bulkhead rail as the two-thousand tonne combat trimaran bucked and swayed as it headed west at thirty-seven knots.

'I said, we're running out of fingers to break,' Mike yelled above the roar of the wind and the ship's powerful turbines.

'He's a tough sonofabitch,' Tapper yelled back, his free hand cupped around his mouth.

'Guy's a player too. Those passports are clean, credit cards too. He managed to lose his phone and laptop before we breached, which means he was tipped off.'

'By who?'

'Someone on our end. There's no other explanation.'

Tapper shook his head in disgust. 'Well, they're sure buying this Marion broad a lot of time.'

'How long before we link up with the rest of the fleet?'

'An hour.'

Mike turned away and looked across the helipad towards the back of the ship. A thirty-foot rooster tail of water followed them as the ship powered towards the setting sun. Mike didn't like torture, sanctioned or otherwise, but it was an option in dire emergencies. Like now. Every minute lost interrogating Philip was a minute gained by Marion, and they all knew it.

Philip was on his knees at the edge of the helipad, his face white with shock and pain, his wrists and elbows bound behind his back with plastic ties. Ty Miller stood over him, his boots spread wide as he rocked with the motion of the ship. Miller had broken four of Philip's fingers, yet so far the violence hadn't worked. Mike grimaced. It was time to apply a little more.

He weaved across the moving deck and stood in front of Philip. The prisoner looked up, his eyes bloodshot and filled with painful tears, his face a chalk mask. Mike leaned forward, his hands on his knees, his dirty blond hair whipping in the wind.

'I can make all this go away, Philip. I can make the pain stop, get you fixed up. If you want to talk about a deal, we can do that too. You're not going to walk, but I can keep the needle out of your arm. I have that power.' Philip's chin dropped and Mike lifted it up. 'Where's Marion right now?'

The prisoner looked back at him, looked at the camera Tapper was holding. His bottom lip trembled. Mike gave Miller the nod and he reached down for the man's fingers.

The rear deck was a world of wind and noise. Mike never heard the break but he heard Philip's piercing scream. That's why they were doing this outside, away from the rest of the crew.

Mike grabbed the collar of Philip's shirt and shook him. 'Where's the next target? Give me the location!'

Philip sobbed in pain. 'Please, don't hurt me any more.'

Mike yelled in his ear. 'You knew we were coming! Who tipped you off?'

He shook him again and Philip heaved, vomiting down his shirt. It was bile, nothing more, probably a mixture of fear, pain and sea-sickness.

'Again,' he told Miller.

Another finger, another ear-splitting scream.

Mike yelled in Philip's face. 'Where's Marion? Tell me where she is, right now!'

A dark patch blossomed in the crotch of Philip's trousers. It spread down his leg, and Philip sobbed as he lost control of his bladder. And he mumbled something too, something Mike didn't catch.

He grabbed his shirt collar and pulled Philip close. 'Say that again!'

Tears rolled down Philip's face. His bottom lip trembled. And then he yelled, in pain, in frustration. And humiliation. '*He* knows where she is! Not me!'

Mike swapped a look with Tapper. 'Who knows? Give me a name!'

'I can't! He'll have me killed!'

It was a final act of defiance, a phenomenon Mike had witnessed many times. Subconsciously, the decision to talk had already been made, but the prisoner had to justify the betrayal to himself, even if it meant more agony. He gave Miller the nod and the big operator reached down for one of Philip's intact fingers.

'No! Please! I'm not lying — '

The scream cut off his words. Philip's eyes rolled up into his head and he folded sideways onto the deck. Mike crouched over him and checked his vitals. He pointed to a fire sign on the bulkhead.

'Run that hose out, wake him up.'

Miller turned and strode across the deck. Mike led Tapper out of Philip's earshot, unconscious or otherwise.

'So, there's someone on the inside, someone he's frightened of. Whoever it is must be juiced. We need that name and we need it fast.'

'I didn't think he'd break,' Tapper admitted. 'Tough bastard.'

'When he comes to, we'll take him inside — '

'Hey!'

Tapper barged Mike out of the way. He spun around and saw —

Philip sprinting across the helipad, his bare feet slapping the deck.

'Shit!' Mike went after him. Tapper was closing the gap and Miller wasn't far behind.

Philip veered to his left and leapt over the side like a high jumper.

Mike slammed against the rail behind the others. Wind and spray lashed his face. There was no sign of Philip. Mike ran to the back of the ship. The sea was a carpet of churning white foam. His hands gripped the rail as his eyes swept the water behind them, knowing only a miracle could save Philip now. And Philip wasn't interested in miracles, only in making sure his secrets went to the bottom with him.

Emergency sirens screeched and the rooster tail died as the ship slowed. Mike estimated that they were already half a mile from Philip's point of entry, maybe more. The rear deck swarmed with naval personnel as well-practised drills swung into action. Mike prayed they would find him, but his gut told him they wouldn't.

He'd been played by a master, and for that he'd take full responsibility. Yet it wasn't the terrible mistake he'd made that would cause him sleepless nights — it would be the lives lost because of it.

He turned for the bulkhead door, reaching for the sat phone in his pocket and dialling Lando's number.

CRY ME A RIVER

Marion left the Ritz Carlton hotel for the last time.

She didn't check out. Instead she strolled through the lobby and out onto the street, making her way to the Metro station a short distance away. It was a clear, crisp evening. Rush-hour crowds bustled along the busy sidewalks and the station was a frantic ants' nest of commuters. Marion wouldn't have looked out of place if she'd hurried, but she forced herself to relax, to act casually and be the tourist she was pretending to be.

The passports, cash and credit cards were in the security pouch around her waist. Her clothing was warm but light, and the Nikes on her feet would carry her swiftly to wherever she needed to be. Soon, that would be out of Shanghai.

She'd left her suitcase and other belongings in her hotel room. Somebody would eventually assume that the occupant had died during the outbreak, and by that time the world would be a completely different place.

After a short journey she squeezed her way off the Metro train and took the steps up to East Nanjing Road. The shopping Mecca was even busier than her first recon, and it took

234

some time to work her way through the multitude of shoppers that thronged the pedestrianised street. She allowed the human tide to carry her through the hub of brightly-lit shops to the Number One Department Store. Hundreds of people passed through its glass doors, all of them avoiding the small group of black-clad police officers standing outside the main entrance.

Marion cursed under her breath. As she passed them she made no eye contact, but she could see one of the male officers staring at her. Maybe he had little experience with Westerners, or perhaps it was because she wore sunglasses and the sun had already set, but Marion ignored the inquisitive stare and continued into the store.

She flipped her shades onto her head and took one of the glass elevators up to the ninth floor. The bookstore was crammed with browsers, the tables in the coffee shop overflowing. A line stretched away from the tills, and a short queue waited patiently for seats to be vacated. Marion felt a sudden stab of doubt. It felt much busier than her last visit, and making a clean getaway might be more difficult than she expected. Uncertainty bubbled deep in the pit of her stomach.

You have a plan. Stick to it.

She veered across the concourse towards the ladies toilet. Three of the four cubicles inside were busy, as were the sinks. Marion strolled to the far end of the room and waited for the last cubicle. She heard a flush, and a young girl left the convenience, averting Marion's smile as she hurried past.

Locking the door behind her, Marion realised why. The stench was ripe, and Marion tried to ignore it as she removed the clear, waterproof pouch from the pocket of her coat. She snapped on a pair of latex gloves. She was immune of course, but old habits died hard. Extracting an infected wipe from the pouch, Marion painted a generous film of liquid on the flushing handle and on the seat, paying particular attention to the edges, knowing the next occupant would have to lower it. She unlocked the door, wiping the rest of the solution all over the handle, and then she was outside and moving fast. She dumped the pouch and gloves in the waste bin and washed her hands quickly, passing a middle-aged woman on her way out. Marion stopped and turned. Two of the stalls were empty but the middle-aged woman made her way to the one that Marion had just vacated. She watched the door close, heard the latch click into place before a hand dryer blasted out the sound.

Marion waited.

The cubicle door shook.

Then she heard them, the familiar sounds she'd heard so many times at Scotton Manor; gagging, wheezing, then cursing and swearing as the virus swept through the woman's body and attacked her central nervous system.

The door shook again, then splintered.

Marion turned and headed for the exit. She was halfway across the concourse when she heard a scream behind her, and a couple of ladies stumbled from the toilet, clearly distressed.

There were at least twenty people waiting for elevators, so Marion headed for the staircase. It was nine levels to the ground floor and she took the steps two at a time. A few flights down she heard shouting above her. When she reached the ground floor she pulled a beanie over her hair and stashed her sunglasses in her pocket.

She wandered casually out into the main shopping hall, sensing a commotion far above her. As she neared the main entrance, police officers hurried into the building and Marion moved out of their path. The same officer glanced at her again, then continued into the store. Perhaps he would live to tell the tale of the Westerner he'd seen shortly before the outbreak, or perhaps he would join the ranks of the infected. Only fate could answer that question.

Now she headed south along Xizang Road towards the People's Square Metro Station. She crossed the road, weaving through the stationary traffic, grateful for the jam that would allow the infection to spread that much faster. She kept moving south until she saw the station entrance.

Inside, thousands of people criss-crossed the ticket hall. Marion felt for the pouch in her pocket. The bank of ticket machines was just ahead and Marion hesitated. People loitered outside the station, smoking and jabbering into mobile phones. There was no sense of urgency, no panic.

She went back out and joined them, looking north towards East Nanjing Street. It was difficult to see anything above the cars and crowds, but the situation looked normal. Why hasn't the chaos begun?

She slipped on a latex glove and walked back inside the station, removing an infected wipe from the pouch as she went. She stood in front of one of the larger ticket machines and pulled out her phone, pretending to be on a call as she wiped the liquid all over the buttons.

Someone barged past her, and the phone dropped from her hand. A suited man waved an apology over his shoulder and headed towards the barriers. Marion cursed him, but before she could pick up her phone a middle-aged cleaner picked it up and gave it to her. The man's smile faded as he noticed Marion's glove. He looked at his own hand, and then his face darkened, and he muttered something unintelligible, something angry. He spat on the ground, then looked at Marion with bloodshot eyes. He reached out and grabbed her arm, his fingers digging through her coat. Her heart raced. She had seconds to act.

She grabbed his wrist and drove her hand hard into his windpipe. The man tumbled backwards, arms flailing. He fell onto his backside and a couple of people went to his aid. She saw the man throw up, spraying bile over the good Samaritans. Marion took a couple of steps back, her path to the platform below now blocked. A whistle blew, and station staff ran towards the commotion as more people became embroiled in the melee.

Plan B, Marion decided.

She pushed her way out of the station, as more whistles shrilled and screams competed with the public address system. On the street, people were hurrying towards the Metro, many of them glancing back over their shoulders wearing troubled expressions. The traffic was at a standstill, and people climbed out of their vehicles, craning their necks to see what was happening up at East Nanjing Street.

It was spreading, Marion was relieved to see, but there was no time to admire her handiwork.

Plan B called for an immediate transit to the Metro station at Dasijie, eight-hundred yards to the south. There she would jump on a train to Yaohua Road, then change to Line Seven, which would take her to the Maglev station at Longyang. From there it was an eight-minute ride at one-hundred and fifty-five miles per hour to Pudong International Airport, where she would board a flight to Beijing.

She did the math as she ran south. Thirty minutes to the airport, another fifteen to check in and board. Her flight left in ninety minutes. She would make it, of that she had no doubt.

Mass public disturbances were rare in China, and the culture prided itself on order and obedience. Once the Shanghai authorities realised that a WMD attack had been carried out, they would defer to Beijing. That would take time, but the outbreak in Texas would concentrate minds at the very highest levels of government. The order would be given sooner than Marion had planned, and the city would be shut down. All transportation networks would cease to operate, every highway would be closed, every bridge across the Huangpu River sealed. The population would be ordered to stay at home or remain in places of safety. A curfew would be imposed, and transgressors would not be tolerated. Units of the People's Liberation Army would be issued live rounds and deployed across the whole of Shanghai. By that time, tens of thousands would be infected, possibly more. Each decision-making step would take time, and long before those orders went out, Marion would've laid a viral trap in Beijing airport and taken a flight to Mongolia, over twelve-hundred miles from ground zero on the East Nanjing Road.

She thought about Philip as she dodged the pedestrians and weaved between the stationary traffic. She dearly hoped he was okay, that he'd finally completed phase one of his mission and was en route to Istanbul to carry out phase two. She longed to see him again. Technically he should reach Norway before her, but right now things were uncertain.

She saw the red Metro sign ahead and side-stepped into the road to avoid a large cluster of commuters gathered outside, many of them with phones clamped to their ears. All of them were looking north to People's Square, chattering in tongues, to each other, to the people on the other end of the call. Word was spreading fast.

Marion looked up as a helicopter thundered overhead. She couldn't tell if it was civilian or military, but its low altitude and speed only served to ramp up the tension around her.

She headed into the Dasijie terminus and swiped through the ticket barrier, taking the stairs two at a time as she headed for the platform. She stood behind the glass wall, watching the information board on the platform. There was tension, but no panic. A warm wind whipped across the platform, signalling the imminent arrival of the train. People hurried down the stairs behind her, eager to leave the area. The train thundered into the station.

And kept going.

Marion watched it pass in a storm of wind and noise. She

heard groans of disappointment around her, and curses in several dialects. Amber warning lights pulsed along the platform. She hurried back up the stairs and out into the ticket hall. As she pushed her way through she saw a suited white man talking frantically on his phone as he struggled with a large roller case.

'What's happening?' she asked him.

'Station's closed. There's been an incident somewhere. They're shutting down the network.'

Marion swallowed. *Already?* 'I have to get across the river. To Pudong Airport.'

The man ended his call. 'Me too, but it looks like we're screwed.'

He was American, or maybe Canadian. He spoke the language, and could prove useful in other ways too. 'The Jinling ferry is less than a mile east of us,' she told him. 'We can cross to the other side and take the Maglev from Longyang Station.'

The man nodded. 'Sounds like a plan.'

'What's your name?' Marion asked him as they pushed their way through the crowd.

'Aaron Beatty. I'm with the Canadian Chamber of Commerce. You?'

'Jane,' she told him without elaborating.

People crammed the pavement outside the station, spilling onto the road. Emergency sirens wailed from all points of the compass. Order was starting to break down.

'This way,' puffed Beatty, taking Marion's arm. He was overweight, with saggy jowls and thinning hair, yet he moved fast. Fear was starting to infect everyone. Only Marion knew what was happening, but it wouldn't be long before the news broke.

They crossed the Xizang Road and headed east towards the river. The traffic was still moving, and Beatty managed to flag down a taxi. Marion climbed inside while Beatty crammed his suitcase into the trunk.

'Quickly!' Marion urged him.

Beatty squeezed in beside Marion. He spoke to the driver, who answered in the same vein. 'He says there's a ferry on the half-hour, but doubts he'll make it.'

'I'll give him two hundred dollars if he does.'

The journey was less than a mile, and the driver rose to the challenge, swerving in an out of the busy lanes, taking a couple of side roads that were more like alleyways, until Marion saw the bright lights of the Jinling East Ferry Terminal ahead. He dropped them right outside the ticket office and Marion slapped the cash in his grateful hand, wondering if he'd ever get the opportunity to spend it.

They boarded the small ferry with two minutes to spare, and Marion was grateful to see the water churning beneath them as the boat pulled away from the dock.

'Close shave,' said Beatty, leaning on the rail and mopping his brow with a handkerchief. Sirens screeched across the city, and an umbilical cord of emergency vehicles swept north along the road that ran parallel to the river.

'Jesus, it sounds bad.'

She turned away from the rail. 'What's that?'

'I just overheard those folks talking,' he told her, pointing at a small group of people heading inside the passenger cabin. 'There's some kind of riot going on in People's Square, a lot of folks attacked and killed. You think it's terrorists?'

Marion shrugged. She checked her watch; technically she could still make the flight, but it would depend on how quickly she could get to the Maglev station at Longyang.

'How about that Texas thing, huh? You see that?'

Marion nodded. 'Yes. Terrible. Do they know what happened?'

'Some kind of biological attack. You know what I'm thinking? I'm thinking this is the same thing.'

Marion studied his face as the ferry chugged across the

241

river. He was scared, that much was obvious, and the more she studied him, the more she realised he was right. If this fat, sweaty bureaucrat had made the connection then surely the Shanghai authorities would've done the same by now.

'I knew it,' Beatty said. 'They closed Pudong. All flights grounded.'

'What?'

Beatty showed her his phone. Everything was in Chinese but the flashing red box was bad news in any language.

'What hotel are you staying at?'

'The Ritz Carlton,' she told him.

'Great, that's this side of the river. I'd already checked out of my hotel.'

A deep, seismic boom travelled across the water. A moment later a ball of flame boiled up over the densely-packed buildings somewhere near People's Square. Marion thought she heard a collective roar of voices but she couldn't be sure.

'My God, this is getting bad,' Beatty said as other passengers crowded the rail around them.

But Marion wasn't listening. All she could think of was escaping the city. They could take a car, drive south, but the closest land border was Vietnam, almost twelve-hundred miles away. The chances of them making it that far unmolested were slim.

No, they would escape by boat, she decided. South Korea was only three-hundred miles across the East China Sea. When the ferry docked she would use Beatty's linguistic skills and her money, and they would find a vessel big enough to get them there. Beatty would have to be terminated on arrival, of course. She couldn't risk him talking about her to anybody.

So, Plan C then.

The ferry continued across the Huangpu River, leaving the west of the city in its steady wake, where the tentacles of bloodshed and disease were already snaking through the streets behind them.

'WHAT'S WRONG WITH HIM?'

Coffman had to shout to make herself heard above the roar of aircraft and the cold wind that gusted across Joint Base Andrews. A short distance away, a gaggle of dark coats were gathered around Mulholland's prone body, checking his vitals.

Coffman was confused. One moment Erik had been walking beside her as they hurried towards Air Force One, the next, he was clutching at her coat sleeve before sprawling onto the tarmac. She'd rushed to his side; McCarthy had tried to force her on to the plane but Coffman was having none of it.

As the rest of her party boarded the idling Boeing 747-8, the President stood a few yards away, watching her Chief of Staff being treated by the Secret Service detail. It wasn't the virus, she knew that much, but obviously she couldn't share that knowledge with anyone else.

'What's wrong with him?' Coffman yelled again, her words snatched away by the strengthening wind. There was a storm headed in from the Atlantic, one that was expected to dump snow as it reached landfall. Departure was a priority, but instead she was watching Erik convulse on the ground.

McCarthy broke away and marched towards her. 'Looks like Mr Mulholland has had some kind of seizure. He's conscious and breathing, but I wouldn't advise further travel, ma'am. There's a medical unit here at — '

'No,' Coffman shouted above the noise. 'I want him taken care of by the White House team at Bethesda. Use Marine One to get him there.'

McCarthy nodded. 'The base medic is inbound. I advise he travel with Mr Mulholland.'

'So, get him off the goddamn ground and into that heli-copter,' Coffman yelled, pointing at the idling Blackhawk.

McCarthy ran back to the huddle. A moment later Mulhol-land was being manhandled towards the helicopter. McCarthy ran back to Coffman's side. 'We should leave, ma'am. We have a very tight weather window and it's closing fast.'

She took another look at Erik, but all she could see were his shoes. She found it difficult to leave him like that, but McCarthy was insistent, so she hurried towards the aircraft as the first snow flurries began to swirl across the air base. The engines began to rise in pitch as she stepped inside. Schultz was waiting for her.

'How is he?'

'My office,' she pointed.

The Chief Master Sergeant briefed her as he escorted Coffman through the plane. 'The captain advises immediate take off, ma'am.'

'Tell him we're ready,' Coffman replied, handing him her coat. 'And bring coffee.' She sat behind her desk and Schultz took a seat opposite. Her private office was a warm, sound-proofed space decorated in beige with brown furniture. She glanced out of the window and saw they were already moving.

Schultz swung one leg over the other. He wore slacks and a roll-neck sweater, as if he were embarking on a winter vaca-tion. 'What's the prognosis?'

'Some kind of seizure, they think. He's not been himself lately. Have you noticed?'

'I'm sure he'll be fine.'

The room vibrated as the aircraft gathered speed along the runway. 'I saw him watching videos, the ones from Texas. He seems obsessed.'

A steward tapped on the door and entered with a tray of

coffee. Schultz waited until the man had left the room before speaking.

'Can I be frank, ma'am?'

Coffman settled back into her chair and waited.

'I think Erik has lost his nerve. It's no secret that the events in Baghdad spooked him, but now the stakes are much higher. As someone who has commanded men at every level, my gut is telling me Erik is cracking under the pressure. What we saw out there was some sort of nervous breakdown. He just isn't cut out for this.' Schultz held up his hands. 'Just my opinion, ma'am.'

Distracted by the conversation, Coffman hadn't even noticed they were off the ground and climbing. Below her, the lights of Washington DC stretched into the distance, and then they fell away as the wing tipped upwards and the plane banked towards the south.

'I've had my doubts too,' Coffman confessed. 'It's hard for me, Charlie. Erik's been by my side since the beginning. He also knows the decisions I've made to get to this point. He's a deep font of knowledge when it comes to Amy Coffman, more so than other person in my career. If anyone has got the goods on me, it's Erik.'

Schultz's eyes narrowed. 'Are you saying what I think you're saying?'

It took a moment for the implication to sink in. Coffman shook her head. 'Good God, no. I want him watched, that's all. Discreetly. Take care of it, would you Charlie?'

'Yes, ma'am.'

The phone on her desk warbled and Coffman picked it up. 'Put him through.' She listened for several moments then thanked the caller, setting the phone back in its cradle.

'That was Jim at Langley. Philip took a swan dive off the back of the *Independence*. The body is still missing.'

Schultz swallowed. 'Did he talk?'

Coffman shook her head. 'I'll say one thing, Bob's people are pros. So, how exposed are we?'

'Marion is the only link to Bob and Matt, and we have to assume she can prove it. The Brit is talking, but like all the other eco-nuts he thinks he was saving the world, which shores up the terrorist angle. Matt is on his way out, Bob we can flatter to deceive, which leaves you, me, Karen and Erik. Karen would kill for you, and I already have, so if you're asking me where our Achilles heels lies, my money's on Erik.'

Coffman leaned back in her chair and sipped her coffee. She knew deep down that she wouldn't give that order. Erik had become part of her DNA. Even thinking about green-lighting his murder made her feel nauseous.

'You're reluctant,' Schultz observed, 'I get that. Erik's as loyal as they come, but no one can predict how a mental health issue can affect a person's judgement. It can change them dramatically.'

Coffman stared over the rim of her coffee cup. 'Thank you, Charlie.'

Schultz took the hint and got to his feet. He closed the door behind him and Coffman was alone.

She glanced at the altitude indicator on the wall; thirty-one thousand feet and still bumping up through the clouds. Erik should be in the hospital by now, and Coffman would call for an update when they touched down in Denver. As soon as he was well enough he would join her at Snowcat. She would schedule a private dinner and they would sit and talk. She would express her concern for his health and then she would offer him the opportunity to disappear.

They would use a doppelgänger in the interim, someone who could pass muster for the long-lens shots. Karen would get the bump to temporary Chief of Staff, by which time Erik would be long gone; an extended sabbatical, a personal issue, something that wouldn't raise too many eyebrows. Then he could get on with his life. She would always be there for him, at the end of a phone, day or night, and when he was ready to come back, the door would be open.

Yes, she decided, *that is how the Erik issue would be resolved.* She had no doubt Schultz and Bob would feel a lot more comfortable if Erik slipped in the bath and broke his neck, but Coffman wouldn't allow that. Erik Mulholland had been her friend and confidant for a quarter of a century.

Nothing was going to change that.

DON'T TREAD ON ME

By THE TIME RAY WILSON REACHED THE FARM OUTSIDE OF Ropesville he was on the verge of collapse.

His shirt and trousers were filthy, his shoes caked in mud, and he stumbled through the dark with his arms wrapped around his body. He was hungry, and nauseous, and cold, and sweaty. His face and hands were lacerated in several places, the result of stumbling through black woods on a moonless night. He'd clambered over barbed wire fences and waded through freezing streams. He'd twisted an ankle, not badly enough to stop him, but the limp slowed him down. He'd been tempted to stop many times, to lie down on a grass verge or in the lee of an isolated barn, but he knew that if he did he may not open his eyes again. So he kept going.

And he had to be careful too. Knocking on the door of an isolated Texan farm in the dead of night was risky enough at the best of times, but that risk was multiplied a hundred fold in the grip of the current madness. People would be scared, and any notions of Christian charity would've disappeared the moment the United States government started bombing Lubbock. Outside of that unfortunate city, countryfolk wouldn't think twice about violently defending their home and hearth.

The first farm he came to was cloaked in darkness, and as he quietly skirted a nearby cattle pen he saw dozens of pickups parked outside the dilapidated main house. There were lights on behind drawn curtains, and Ray heard raucous laughter and gutter language. He imagined a wild bunch of good ol' boys s gathered around a kitchen table stacked with guns, sinking suds and discussing their post-apocalyptic strategy for survival. In Ray's case that probably meant shooting first and high-fiving each other afterwards. When a dog began barking he turned on his tail and scuttled back into the darkness.

He used roads where he could, both dirt and tarmac. He knew Route 82 was somewhere off to his right, and when he drifted closer he could see military vehicles moving along the highway. Ray had no intention of interacting with soldiers any time soon. The violent deaths of his former travelling companions were still fresh in his mind, and it was the fear of his own life ending in a cold Texas field that kept his feet moving.

The second farm he came across had a couple of police cruisers parked outside, so Ray avoided that one too, looping out towards the distant highway before heading south again. He must've trudged another three or four miles before he reached a dirt road that headed due west. This one had a post-and-wire fence running alongside side of it, and Ray decided it had to lead somewhere. He had no idea how long he followed that fence for, but he was staggering past the building before he noticed it. The ranch gate was a wide cattle-grid flanked by two huge granite boulders. The gate was open, and Ray weaved onto the property. He had nothing left. Either way, it was here he would drop.

There were three vehicles parked in front of a large ranch house. Ray couldn't see any lights, but his foggy mind registered neat grass verges and white woodwork. A Lone Star flag rustled atop a flagpole in front of the farmhouse, and below it, a yellow Gadsden flag, a coiled rattlesnake with the motto *Don't Tread On Me*.

He put his hand on the rail and pulled himself up onto the porch. His head swam. The voice behind him was calm and measured, and as cold as the Texas wind.

'That's far enough, friend.'

Ray held on to the rail, swaying on legs that felt hollow. He didn't turn around when he spoke. 'My name is Ray Wilson.'

All Ray could hear was the tapping of the flagpole in the breeze. Such a cold breeze too. He shivered.

'Have you come from Lubbock?'

Ray closed his eyes and braced himself for a bullet. 'Yes.'

'How did you get here? Government's got eyes on every road. Drones too, flying all over yonder.'

'Lucky, I guess.'

'Are you being smart with me, son?'

Ray opened his eyes again, but he didn't have the strength to lift his head. His fingers slipped from the rail and he folded to the porch. He lay there in a heap, unable to move anything but his lips. 'Just let me sleep, please. I'll be no trouble to you.'

He closed his eyes, and then he heard sharp voices. He felt himself lifted off the deck, heard the creak of the porch screen, felt a wondrous blanket of warmth envelop him as strong hands helped him inside. He glimpsed men, women and children, and mumbled another apology. He heard other voices, concerned, professional. They carried him into a room and laid him down on a large bed. His filthy clothes were removed and someone shone a bright light into his eyes. A t-shirt and shorts were pulled over his naked body. Ray had no control over what was happening to him, and neither did he care. All that mattered was the soft pillow he sank into and the warm duvet that covered him.

He finally gave in to the exhaustion that whispered his name. He took its offered hand and let it lead him into the void. Behind him, the voices grew fainter. The light dimmed. Before it went completely, he turned his head.

'Thank you,' he whispered.

And then the darkness was complete.

'My God, look at them. Jesus Christ.'

'This is awful. There must be something we can do.'

The video wall dominated the Situation Room, the high-definition feeds broadcast live from military helicopters and drones over Lubbock.

Dawn had revealed the aftermath of the previous night's outbreak in horrific detail. Downtown was a landscape of shattered buildings, some stripped naked of glass and concrete. The Wells Fargo and Metro Tower buildings stood burning as fires raged across several floors. Others had collapsed, forming mountains of rubble that blocked whole city streets. There were bodies everywhere, most dead, some moving, the infected, wounded and crippled, dragging themselves across roads and sidewalks. More fires raged across southern Lubbock, driven by a strengthening westerly wind, forcing survivors to flee their homes and hiding places. There were gasps from the assembled politicians as those people, those desperate families, were hunted down by large groups of infected through the smoke-filled suburbs. The elderly were abandoned first, and men with guns and other weapons fought savagely to buy time for their wives and children. None of them made it, Coffman saw.

There were other feeds too, Fox and MSNBC, CNN and all the other major networks, plus a couple of local affiliates, but the media were being kept outside of the containment zone.

All their viewers could see were distant smudges of smoke on the far horizon. Electrical power to Lubbock was still cut, and every conceivable communication channel had been shut down. The city was still a black hole, a decision justified by the need to prevent further national panic, and the scattered incidents of civil unrest already triggered by the crisis. That fear played beautifully into Coffman's hands.

She studied the drawn, frightened faces of her Security Council gathered around the granite conference table. Assistants and advisors shuttled between them and the surrounding shadows, relaying printouts and whispered messages. It was like a scene from a movie, the lair of a particularly audacious Bond villain, and Coffman thought that was appropriate, given what she was attempting to accomplish. And she felt safe here, far from any population centre, perched high above the surrounding, empty valleys. The Marine guard had been bolstered in number and further reinforced by four Apache gunships. In light of what was happening in Texas — and its potential to spread — temporarily relocating the Security Council to Colorado had been an easy sell. If things got out of hand the Cabinet would follow, and the 10th Mountain Division were on standby to deploy to Snowcat.

With every passing hour the infected were sucking more and more people into their ranks. Estimates put the figure at somewhere between forty and fifty-thousand. The Pentagon had also submitted their latest bomb damage assessments and casualty estimates via video link, and they didn't look too good either. Coffman was uninterested in the numbers, but she *was* interested in public opinion. This had to be played right.

She tapped her finger on the microphone stalk in front of her and her voice filled the cavern. 'Outside of Texas, how are the public reacting to the crisis?'

Attentions were refocused around the table. Homeland Security chief Grady was the first to speak.

'In a word, appalled,' she began. 'News of the bombing is not going down well at all, and conspiracy theorists are dominating the conversation. Much of it is anti-government talk, abuse of power, constitutional betrayal and suchlike, and in light of the information vacuum, the media are repeating it.'

'They're pissed because they've been denied access,' Karen Baranski countered. 'Nevertheless, it's hurting us.'

'Public opinion is not a priority,' SecDef Clark countered. 'What the country needs is reassurance. The terrorists are still out there.'

You're right, Coffman admitted silently. The faces around the table agreed with Clark. Individually they were safe here in the mountains, but their families were still in DC and elsewhere. They were scared, and Coffman couldn't blame them for that.

Her eyes were drawn back to the video wall. On the main screen she watched a huge river of infected pouring through a landscape of rubble and shattered buildings. On the periphery they snapped and lunged at each other like animals. And then there was the fucking, like gang rapes but with willing participants. Coffman's mind was pretty blown by it all, and again she speculated on the outcome of such a liaison. It was something to be considered seriously, and Coffman had no doubt that when academia eventually gained access to the material, they would certainly attempt to explore the phenomena further. To the point of birth, the President speculated. But that was for the future.

'Let's deal with the immediate situation in Texas. Admiral?'

Schultz drew rings on the tablet in front of him, which then appeared on the main video screen. 'There are three main groups of infected,' he told the room. 'The largest one is here in downtown Lubbock, about twenty-thousand strong, all circumventing a three-block area. There's a smaller one here to the south, tracking the fires and picking off survivors, and this one to the north, about fifteen-thousand strong. It's this group that concerns us most.'

'What're they doing?' Grady asked.

The admiral looked around the table and said, 'Reconnaissance.'

'You can't be serious.' It was Vernon Brown, Coffman's Vice President. The former Tennessee governor and hopeless party nominee had been plucked from obscurity by Coffman in return for his unquestionable loyalty and ability to say and do the right thing when required.

'The admiral is correct,' chipped in a Marine general. He used his own tablet to pull up the drone feed of the group in question. On the main screen, thousands of infected were moving beneath the freeway, while thousands more flanked the main group, spreading out through the streets in a loose formation. 'This main body of infected is heading north through the Guadalupe district, supported on either flank by these smaller groups. You can see they're moving carefully, as if they're scouting the terrain.'

'My God,' someone whispered.

'Why head north?' Coffman asked.

'We brought Curtis Stringer back in, ran the footage by him. He thinks they're drawn to the freeway. Some kind of collective memory phenomena. It's the only major road out of Lubbock, and he thinks they might've made that connection. The good news is, it's a hundred miles to Amarillo, which is the closest major city.'

'Does anyone else find that strange?' Brown asked.

There was silence around the room. Coffman waited for her VP to elaborate.

'What I mean is, why attack Lubbock? One of the remotest cities in the country?'

Not so dumb after all. 'Maybe this is a test,' Coffman said,

254

'or maybe the terrorists are drawing resources away from the real target. We can't know. All we can do is put the country on alert and deal with what's in front of us.'

There was a murmur of agreement around the table.

'What're we going to do about them, Madam President? The infected, I mean?'

It was Grady again, and Coffman was beginning to regret her appointment. It was all very well ticking the boxes and making sure she had enough women and minorities in her cabinet, but Grady's constant whining and obvious lack of moral fibre was beginning to grate on Coffman's nerves.

'I want you to go down there, Diane. Be my eyes and ears on the ground.'

Grady's own eyes widened. 'Excuse me, ma'am?'

'Let's get transport organised for Diane immediately,' she told a hovering aide, before refocusing on Grady. 'I think it's only right that the Secretary of Homeland Security be a prominent face during this crisis, so I want you set up at the Forward Operating Base. You'll brief us when you arrive, and Jim Magee will inform the media of your presence. Thank you, Diane, and godspeed.'

Grady was too shocked to argue. She got out of her chair and headed for the door. *Maybe we'll catch a break,* Coffman thought; nothing screams national crisis more than the Homeland Security chief getting gang raped on TV by a bunch of infected Texans. The mental image gave her a brief thrill before she concentrated on other matters.

'Talk to me about containment, Admiral Schultz.'

'Right now we have sixty-five thousand troops manning a perimeter over eighty miles long and covering five-hundred square miles. Thankfully, a vast bulk of the infected have not ventured beyond the greater Lubbock area, but as the general has pointed out, that could change very soon.'

'The infection cannot be allowed to spread, I think we're all agreed on that.'

There were more nods and murmurs around the table. Coffman got to her feet, waving everyone else back into their seats. She walked around the room until she stood in front of the video wall. All she saw was destruction and death. She'd expected that much, had prepared herself for it, but the others in the room were not so lucky, especially the civilians. They'd been shaken to the core and wanted it to stop.

'Our efforts to contain the initial spread have cost the lives of thousands of innocent Americans. It's clear those efforts have failed, which means the bombing option is back on the table. As we've discovered, the public is struggling with the reality of that decision, so I suggest we give them what they want; transparency. Enough to make them understand the danger we're all in.'

She turned and faced the room, her arms folder across her crisp white shirt.

'Tonight I will address the nation. We'll go public with the Baghdad videos, including the original footage of Jackson strapped to his bed. And I want some of the Lubbock footage out there too. The American people should know the threat that faces them, and the measures this administration must take to neutralise that threat. They have a right to know what's at stake and why we've been forced to take drastic measures. It's the right thing to do.'

Voices erupted around the table.

'This will terrify them — '

' — spark civil unrest.'

' — markets will fall through the floor.'

'Enough,' Coffman ordered. 'There will be trouble, that's for sure. And yes, the markets will take a hit, so anyone more concerned about their stock portfolio than the security of this country can leave the room now. And not return.'

No one moved. Coffman came back around the table and sat down.

'Once the American people understand the true horror of

this thing, they'll demand we carpet bomb the whole state in order to prevent it spreading. Obviously we won't do that, but the public will understand our choices are limited and the alternatives unthinkable.'

She studied the faces around the table and knew she'd won them over. They were desperate to assuage their own guilt too, that much was obvious. A supportive nation would go a long way in helping to achieve that.

'If we have to invoke emergency legislation then so be it, but we must pray it doesn't come to that. As for the infected in Lubbock, I think we've all seen enough bloodshed. We're not dropping any more bombs, not if we can help it. It's about containment and control now. We have a plan, is that correct Admiral Schultz?'

'Indeed we do, ma'am.'

She watched Charlie get to his feet, swiping his tablet as he projected maps up onto the video wall. 'We're going to physically block every road and track out of the city. We'll continue to deploy troops around the containment zone until the engineers arrive, and then they'll start to erect barricades and roll out the razor wire. At the same time, escape routes will be clearly marked for those survivors still able to make it out. We're working on identifying LZ's to get in closer to the city centre and get people out that way.'

'Save as many as you can, Admiral.' Coffman's eyes were drawn to the shadows behind Karen Baranski. A face emerged out of the gloom, whispered in her ear, then retreated. Baranski looked at Coffman, expectant.

'What is it, Karen?'

She leaned forward and spoke into her microphone, her voice echoing around the cavern. 'It's Shanghai, Madam President. There's been an event.'

'An event?' Coffman repeated, knowing what was coming.

'Yes, ma'am. An outbreak. In the city centre.'

'Shanghai?' the Director of National Intelligence stuttered. 'My God, that's a city of almost thirty million people.'

Forty-four, if you factor in the wider metropolitan area, Coffman corrected him silently.

She closed her eyes and hung her head in her hands. For anyone watching, it was a natural reaction to the news; the abject horror, the incomprehension, the fear of what lay ahead. They were wrong, naturally.

Because behind those expensively moisturised and manicured hands, the only emotions Coffman felt were relief.

And excitement.

THE NEED FOR SPEED

THE ARMY PHYSICIAN DEFLATED THE VELCRO CUFF AND REMOVED it from Mulholland's arm.

'Your heart rate is a little high.'

'I guess I'm excited by the prospect of getting out of here,' Mulholland quipped.

The White House doctor gave his chart another look. 'Physically you check out, but given the current crisis, I'd say you're suffering from mild exhaustion compounded by a little anxiety. I can prescribe a tranquilliser to smooth that out, a very mild dose, something that won't impair your judgement.'

Mulholland pulled on his jacket and overcoat. 'I guess it wouldn't hurt.'

'Well, you're good to go. Your meds will be waiting for you at the pharmacy. You can collect them on the way out.'

He left the room, and then a dark suited Latino appeared in the doorway. 'Mr Mulholland, my name is Agent Lopez. I'm here to escort you to Andrews. There's a plane waiting to take you to Denver, sir.'

Mulholland nodded and followed the Secret Service agent out of the room. Three of his colleagues waited out in the hallway. One of them had an ugly black shotgun clearly visible beneath his raincoat, and Mulholland was reminded of the tension the crisis had triggered, even here at the Walter Reed Military Medical Centre, where an atmosphere of quiet urgency permeated the air. They were preparing for the worst, and not even Mulholland knew where the next few weeks would take them.

Staff and patients stepped aside as Lopez and his detail cut a path through the hallway. They passed a busy TV lounge where people were watching the news. Texas had been replaced by Shanghai, but the footage from China was extremely limited; it was all shaky footage and a lot of running feet. Beijing had already pulled the media plug. Nothing was coming out of Shanghai anymore.

After collecting his medication, Mulholland continued outside. The sky was grey and a bitter wind whipped snow beneath the portico where two black SUVs idled, their red and blue grill lights pulsing. Mulholland climbed into the warmth of the rear vehicle and the convoy set off at a brisk pace. A couple of DC Metro cars met them at the gate and bracketed them front and rear, their own lights blazing a path through the morning traffic.

There were fewer cars and fewer people on the sidewalks, Mulholland observed. Panic buying was now a thing, and stores were rationing certain goods. That policy had caused a few mass brawls and a couple of shootings, and he wondered what would happen if the virus escaped from Lubbock and started to spread. Amy thought she could keep a lid on it, but Mulholland wasn't so sure. What would happen if the H-1 virus unexpectedly mutated? What then?

The end of life as we know it.

Mulholland swallowed a sudden rush of fear. The panic attacks had started not long after Baghdad. He'd woken in the middle of the night, used the bathroom and gone back to bed. As he lay in the dark, waiting for sleep to return and thinking

of nothing in particular, his heart rate had suddenly accelerated, and he was consumed by an inexplicable feeling of
dread that he'd struggled to control. That sunrise had brought
little relief.

The attacks had occurred regularly after that, and not
always in the dead of night. He didn't tell anyone, because he
had a pretty good idea what had triggered them — the
Baghdad footage, the unedited carnage, the violent deaths of
so many innocent people, and the subsequent cover up. The
attacks had worsened after he'd met the survivors, crushed
by the guilt of his part in the murder of their friends and
colleagues. He'd tried to block it all out, bury it, but the truth
was, it had psychologically scarred him.

And now it was eating him alive.

As the convoy headed towards the Beltway, Mulholland
reflected on how low he'd sunk. He'd been at Amy's side for
many years, and in that time he'd willingly participated in the
lying and cheating, the blackmail and bribery, and he'd
always chalked it up as the price of politics. Winning the
White House should've been the pinnacle of his career, and
yet it had turned out to be a nightmare. Amy wasn't content
with being President of the United States. No, she was moti-
vated by revenge on those who'd failed to welcome her into
their New World Order. Now she wanted to double down,
unleash H-1 across the globe and seize ultimate power, with
Mulholland by her side.

His hand wrapped round the pill container in his pocket,
knowing he wasn't going to medicate his way out of this one.
He was sickened by his complicity, by his inability to take a
stand against genocide. He was a coward. And for Erik
Mulholland, there could be only one cure.

They were travelling on the Beltway now, almost bumper
to bumper in the left lane. The traffic ahead was peeling to the
right, getting out of the way.

'Take me to Du Pont Circle,' Mulholland ordered.

Lopez swivelled around in his seat. 'Our orders are to escort you directly to Andrews, sir. The President is expecting you at Snowcat.'

'I need to stop at the house, pick up a few personal items. Don't worry, I'll call the President personally, make sure you guys don't get into any trouble.' He smiled, and the stony-faced Latino stared back at him. 'I'm not asking,' Mulholland added, his smile fading.

'Roger that, sir.'

Lopez spoke into his radio and a moment later the convoy was cutting across the road and exiting the Beltway at Forest Glen. It took another twenty-three minutes to reach Mulholland's townhouse on Newport Place, a leafy street in one of DC's better neighbourhoods. The convoy stopped outside, blocking the road, engines idling and lights flickering.

Mulholland climbed out of the vehicle and two agents followed him towards the house. He pulled out his keys and unlocked the security door, then the main one. 'I'll be five minutes,' he told the agents.

They didn't speak. Instead they turned to face the street, flanking the steps like bouncers outside a nightclub. Locals stopped and stared at the intimidating invasion of their quiet street. One or two held up their phones.

It was all about speed, now.

Mulholland closed the front door behind him and punched in the alarm code. The house was immaculate and expensively furnished, the front door thick and heavy. He turned around, and as quietly as he could manage, he dropped the top and bottom bolts. Then he checked his watch.

One minute.

He took the stairs two at a time. His heart pounded and his hands felt clammy as he ran into the bedroom and threw open the closet. He plucked a couple of hangers off the rail and changed quickly into jeans and a dark crewneck sweater. He went back to the closet, removed three of the shelves and pushed hard on the panel behind. It sprung out, revealing a small alcove. Mulholland removed thirty-thousand dollars in sealed packets, three pre-paid Visa cards, and a pre-paid smart phone. He also removed a USB thumb drive that was clipped to a black State Department lanyard. He looped it over his head and tucked it beneath his sweater.

Three minutes.

He hurried into the en-suite and flipped the shower on. He left a small gap in the door and ran downstairs in his socks, padding quietly through to the back of the house. He ducked into a walk-in closet, tied on a pair of Nike sneakers and tugged on a green Columbia padded jacket. From the shelf above he grabbed the black duffel bag he'd hoped never to use. It contained clothes, underwear, toiletries, a small first-aid kit, his usual pills and creams, and a brand-new Power-book. The military called it a bug-out bag, which was apt. Mulholland knocked off the light, closed the door and slung the bag over his back, tightening the straps.

Six minutes.

He unlocked the kitchen door, then hesitated — there was still time to turn around, to get back inside the SUV. For life to continue as normal, to remain tied to an administration as lethal as any twentieth-century dictatorship. For the panic attacks to continue, for the anxiety to worsen…

Mulholland twisted the handle and stepped out into the cold air. He crossed the small patio, opened the back gate and turned right into the alleyway beyond.

Seven minutes.

There were houses on either side, cars parked in bays, several dumpsters but no people. He walked briskly to the end of the alleyway and onto O Street. He hit the sidewalk and turned east towards New Hampshire Avenue, jogging casually, a guy late for something that wasn't that important.

He reached the intersection on 20th Street and checked his watch.

Nine minutes.

By now Lopez would be getting impatient. He would radio the guys on the porch and they would knock on the door, respectfully at first. That would last a minute, perhaps two. Then the knocking would become more urgent. Lopez would appear on the porch, and his first reaction would be one of concern; perhaps his charge had suffered another fit and was convulsing on the floor of his bathroom. They'd try to force the door but the bolts would hold them. Agents would be deployed to the rear of the property, and access gained via the unlocked kitchen door. Trouble would start the moment they saw the front door bolted from the inside.

The discarded clothes, the running shower, the ensuing search, they would all buy another few minutes perhaps, then reality would bite and the hunt would begin. Amy Coffman would be informed sooner rather than later. There would be doubt, hesitation, debate. More time banked. Then a decision would be made; find Erik Mulholland and bring him in.

By that time, Mulholland had to be far away.

Twelve minutes.

He boarded the Metro at Du Pont Circle and rode it for thirty minutes to Spring Hill station in Fairfax County. He walked three blocks to a multi-storey parking lot and collected a two-year-old Ford Taurus from long-term parking. The vehicle was registered to a college buddy who lived in Belgium. As long as Mulholland obeyed the rules of the road and didn't do anything stupid, the car would get him to where he needed to be.

He got behind the wheel, started the engine and let it settle. After another minute he pulled out onto the Leesburg Pike and turned south towards I-66, driving steadily. He glanced at the dashboard clock...

Sixty-three minutes.

She would know by now, and Mulholland wondered how she would react to the news that her Chief of Staff had executed a pre-planned escape? She would feel confused, angry, then betrayed. They'd always been close, climbing the greasy pole together all the way to the top. During Baghdad she'd expressed genuine concern for his well-being, had assuaged his doubts, convinced him that they were doing the right thing. He'd swallowed it too, because she'd told him everything was going to be okay.

But she was wrong.

Rain began to spatter the windshield as he passed the bright lights of Dulles airport to the north. It wasn't really Amy's fault. She was ambitious, yes, ruthless, absolutely, but ultimately she'd been manipulated into doing those terrible things. The person who should bear the brunt of the blame, for Baghdad, for everything that had happened since, was Bob fucking Blake.

He'd corrupted her. He'd handed her the power of life and death and convinced her she could rule the world. He was the devil on her shoulder, whispering in her rear, urging her to commit terrible acts. He remembered Rock Creek, remembered Blake laughing and pointing at the screen as people suffered terrible deaths. He was a sick individual, devoid of humanity, and Mulholland cursed the day he'd ingratiated himself with the vulgar industrialist, the day he'd introduced Robert Blake to Amy Coffman. Thanks to Blake, countless people had died, and his own life was now in ruins.

Mulholland gripped the wheel a little tighter and made a promise to himself, one he would fulfil, or die trying.

If Erik Mulholland was going down, he was taking Bob Blake with him.

'THAT GODDAMN FAGGOT! I *KNEW* HE COULDN'T BE TRUSTED!'

'Bob — '

'Cock sucker! What's he gonna do now, huh? What the fuck does he — '

'Bob!'

Coffman glared across the room. On the couches by the fire, Bob Blake lowered his head and grumbled into his drink.

She turned back to the glass wall and studied the plateau below her. The late afternoon had brought dark clouds and snow flurries, and the harsh landscape lay hidden beneath a thick blanket of snow that crowned the granite boulders and clung to the scotch pines. It was ruggedly beautiful, and Coffman had no intention of giving any of it up. No matter how many people had to die.

On the couches behind her, Schultz, Blake and Karen Baranski were debating the latest setback. Coffman was tired of setbacks. There had been too many of them, and they had introduced a significant element of uncertainty. None of it was her fault, of course. No, the man responsible was sitting by the fire, still full of bluster, his mood swinging between anger and humility. The anger she could relate to. Amy Coffman didn't do humility.

She took a last look at the calming vista and retook her seat on the couch. The others sat facing her, and the table between them was cluttered with variety of beverages; coffee, tea, juices and iced water. The working lunch had been a long one, and in the wake of Erik's vanishing act, no one had eaten much. Blake was drinking bourbon, his mood swinging back towards anger.

'Have a coffee, Bob.'

Blake looked up over his thick crystal tumbler and said, 'I'm fine, thank you ma'am.'

Coffman smiled sweetly. 'Have a fucking coffee.'

The industrialist put down his glass and reached for the coffeepot. Coffman upended the tumbler into the ice bucket.

'I understand your frustration,' Coffman soothed. 'We're all concerned. The question is, what's his next move?'

'Hard to say,' Schultz replied. 'The doctor at Bethesda said he seemed a little twitchy, but that wasn't born out by the Secret Service detail. The lead agent said Erik was acting perfectly normal.'

'Apart from disappearing into thin air,' Blake added. 'I had a bad feeling about that cock sucker from the get-go — '

Coffman grabbed a handful of ice and hurled it at Blake. Cubes bounced off him and skittered across the stone floor. It was Baranski who broke the uncomfortable silence.

'Erik *has* been acting strange for some time. We've all seen it, right? He's been off his game, a little subdued.'

'Everyone's a goddamn expert on human behaviour now.'

Coffman seethed. She knew Karen was right. If anyone should've seen this coming, it was the President, and the truth was she *did* know. She should've spoken to him, taken the appropriated steps, but it was too late. Erik had gone, his disappearance previously planned and well executed. Bob's people had taken his house apart and found the cavity behind his bedroom cupboard. Whatever secrets Erik had been hiding in there, he'd taken them with him. Coffman felt nauseous just thinking about what that could be.

'We need to find him.'

'Langley has him flagged,' Baranski told her, 'likewise the NSA. They're up on his passport, phones, credit cards, driving license, email accounts, VPNs, the works. If he goes anywhere with a facial recognition camera, they'll find him.'

'I don't want him hurt,' Coffman said. 'I want this done quietly. This might be nothing more than a cry for help.'

She saw Blake open his mouth to speak, then wilt beneath her icy glare. 'You're partly responsible for this, Bob.'

Blake frowned. 'Ma'am?'

'Let me spell it out for you. You set this whole thing up. You put it in a box, wrapped a big goddamn bow around it and sold it as a simple operation, a DIY pandemic kit that would save humanity from itself and put the United States at the top of the food chain in a few easy moves, right? Then I get my ass handed to me by that goddamn reporter, sniffing around Baghdad, asking questions — '

'I wonder what went through his mind before the virus got him?' Blake said. 'If he realised he'd been set up, I mean?'

Coffman stared at him. 'You're not helping.'

Blake sat a little straighter. 'My apologies.'

'All these complications, I think they added to Erik's stress. I think he wanted out but he just couldn't tell me. Not out,' she corrected herself. 'Erik would never abandon me, but he needed to get away, get his mind straight.'

Schultz ran a hand over his thinning white hair. 'It's a theory,' he conceded, 'but you know him best, ma'am. If you say that's all this is, then I guess we can all breath a little easier.'

'While maintaining the surveillance effort,' Baranski added.

The more Coffman thought about it, the more she was convinced by her reasoning. Erik's hands had blood on them too, all the way up to his armpits. He wouldn't talk, not unless he wanted to end his life strapped to a gurney, and he certainly wasn't cut out for a lifetime of running. No, this was a breakdown, and he'd made plans because he knew it was getting too much for him. That was the Erik she knew; the man who dotted the i's and crossed the t's, even under great pressure.

'He'll resurface when he's ready,' Coffman assured them, 'and the one thing that will bring him back into the fold is the end game.' She turned to Blake. 'So, where are we now, Bob? Mumbai and Istanbul are still standing. Granted, it looks like Shanghai is falling apart, but it's not going to be enough. The dominoes are not falling as we'd expected.'

Blake refilled his coffee and took a careful sip before continuing.

'Marion's next target is Beijing airport. That will take care of China. With Philip out of the picture, the secondary deployment team has been mobilised, all Europeans hand-picked by Philip with scrubbed backgrounds and cast iron legends. Right now they're at Matt's ranch, waiting to be briefed and issued the infected materials. Their targets are Istanbul, Cairo and Beirut. I've also rerouted a ship to Lagos. Nigeria's population is almost two hundred million people. We deploy there, there's no way to stop it. West Africa will fall within weeks, the whole continent in months. Any survivors will head north to Europe, and that'll trigger its own brand of chaos.'

'You make it sound so easy, Bob.'

'It will be, once the spread begins, but we need that momentum, that fear. Hell, once it's fully underway we can hit Mumbai with a drone loaded with H-1 and no one will notice. By that time the world will be in chaos. Except for the United States, of course. And that's when we come riding to the rescue with the antiviral. Everything is still on track, Madam President.'

Coffman leaned back in her chair, her eyes drawn to the fire and its flickering flames. Compartmentalisation was the key to keeping secrets; once global political power had been achieved, certain people would have to be removed, perma-nently. Bob's field teams for sure, Marion included. Bob would then supply the patsies, and they would be implicated in the biggest crime against humanity the world had ever seen. There would be show trials, and survivors across the world would bay for blood. By the time the guilty were executed, all traces of collusion would be gone and Coffman's global administration would be free to consolidate and rebuild. The vision sent a chill of excitement down her spine.

'What about the antiviral?' she asked.

'Kansas is working around the clock,' Blake told her. 'It's an automated facility, so when the world begs for help, we'll scale up, then step up.'

'The military roll-out is almost complete,' Schultz told her, 'and we're strategically stockpiling in every major city and beyond, for police and emergency services.'

'What about our people overseas?'

'Same deal. Protecting our troops is a priority. They'll be needed in the months to come.'

'And when every G20 country has fallen, we'll set about saving the rest of humanity,' Blake added. 'After all, we'll still need housekeepers and busboys, right?'

Coffman stared at him, but her earlier anger had receded. Bob was right; nothing would stop it.

'Just get it done, Bob. And find Erik. He should be here, with us. Understood?'

'Yes, ma'am.'

SHANGHAI SURPRISE

Marion stood at the window of her forty-eighth floor suite and looked down across the river to where it had all started.

Fires raged out of control through central Shanghai, and the low, dark clouds above throbbed with a devilish red glow, as if the gates of hell itself had been thrown open. Helicopters buzzed across the city, seen and unseen. One thundered right past her window, a huge black military aircraft that banked away towards the river. Marion wondered if they were plucking people from the roof of The Ritz Carlton, but even if they were it wouldn't help her. Not with those things roaming the corridors.

She took pride in the fact that her mission had been a success, the deployment phase at least. The East Nanjing Road had proved itself to be a well-chosen target, although the virus had spread much faster than Marion had anticipated. She'd been lucky to make the ferry across the river, and by the time she'd got back to the hotel, gunfire was already rippling across the city.

Finding a boat to take her out of Shanghai had proved impossible. With Beatty acting as interpreter, Marion had tried to bribe the ferry captain to take them upstream to the Yangpu Bridge where the commercial docks were located, but the captain had turned them down. They'd disembarked quickly, heading south along the river bank as tens of thousands of people had descended on the shoreline. Marion had hurried between marinas and pontoons, many with expensive day cruisers tied to them, but the owners were nowhere to be found. She had no experience with boats other than riding in them, and the Canadian businessman was equally useless in that regard, so she'd decided to head north. Worst case scenario, they would have to hike the three miles or so to the bridge, and the commercial docks beyond.

They'd already passed the ferry terminal when Marion had heard the screams and shouting behind them. She'd turned to see another ferry headed for the shore, but this one wasn't stopping. It had crunched into the dock in a cloud of dust and a terrible screech of twisted metal, and its cargo of infected passengers had spilled ashore. In that moment, Marion realised her choices were limited.

The arrival of the plague ship created a level of panic Marion had never witnessed before. As the crowds scattered she saw screaming women and young children trampled. She saw people scatter across the busy Fucheng Road, only to get mown down like skittles. She saw a car swerving wildly, a mangled body trapped beneath the front wheels, and then the vehicle had flipped onto its roof and slewed into the running crowds. It was at that point that Marion realised she wasn't going to make it to the Yangpu Bridge. All that mattered was finding sanctuary, and that meant heading back to the hotel. Leaving Shanghai was no longer an option.

The Canadian had almost made it. To her surprise he'd kept up with her along the causeway, energised by the screaming infected that were spilling out into the streets behind them. He'd made it across several chaotic roads before his luck ran out.

Marion saw the motorbike speeding towards her along the pavement and managed to duck out of the way. Beatty wasn't so lucky. The bike had hit him at speed, spinning him around like a top and spilling him into the road. Despite her better judgement Marion had tried to help, but it was clear his left leg was shattered. The infected were heading towards them, attacking cars, people. Policemen fired from behind the open doors of their cruisers, but nothing was going to stop the tide of death. Beatty had begged her, clutching the arm of her coat, his eyes filled with painful tears. She'd apologised, and whipped her arm away. She'd heard him screaming as she ran in the opposite direction, and then his voice was swallowed by the wild roar behind her.

She'd sprinted the five-hundred yards to the Ritz Carlton, ignoring the cries and screams around her, the gunshots, the crunch of colliding vehicles hitting each other. When she reached the hotel the glass doors were lined with staff and guests. They crowded the lobby, unaware of the approaching tsunami of death.

Marion pushed her way inside and took a lift to the restaurant on the fifty-second floor. More people were at the windows, and she headed straight for the kitchen where she'd helped herself to bowls of rice and other dishes as confused kitchen staff looked on. She'd loaded up two trays and taken them down to her room four floors below. Then she'd made two more trips to separate bars, buying as much bottled water and snacks as she could possibly carry. She'd laid it all out in her room, comforted by the fact she had enough to last her several days. She was standing in the fire escape stairwell, listening to screams drifting up from below when they'd cut the power.

She wedged a chair under the door and spent the rest of the night sitting by the window, watching the city go to hell and eating cold chicken and rice. She watched tracer rounds light up the night sky. She heard the rumble of low-flying jets and watched them as they thundered across the city, leaving a bright trail of explosions in their wake. Marion didn't sleep much that first night, and the grey light of dawn revealed a new ugliness.

Pillars of black smoke stretched across Shanghai all the way out to the airport at Hongqiao. Fires burned everywhere, out of control. As she surveyed the landscape, she felt pride in her achievements, but knew that getting out of the city was going to be a problem. She'd seen the Chinese navy on the river, their heavy guns blasting away at targets on either shoreline. In the streets below, thousands of infected swept back-and-forth, moving in huge packs, their visceral screams echoing through the steel and glass canyons around her. The sight had troubled Marion deeply; across the Huangpu, the Chinese had bombed the city without hesitation. There was no reason to believe they wouldn't bomb Pudong District. She knew she needed to leave, and leave soon.

As day turned to night, she'd heard screaming in the corridor outside her room. Someone was shouting in a coherent language, a man, his voice laced with urgency. She'd removed the chair and stood at the door, her ear pressed against the dark wood, her hand on the door knob. The shouting intensified, as had the sounds of fighting, of splintering timber, of pain-filled wails, and then there was silence. She'd stayed by the door, and then she'd heard the rustle of clothing directly outside. She'd backed away as something sniffed at her door. Marion had replaced the chair and lay motionless on the bed.

The second night came and went. A new dawn brought with it another tableau of death and destruction. The power was still out and there was no signal on her phone, but Marion had expected that. She doubted the world would know much about Shanghai, such was China's obsession with secrecy and its cultural need to save face. In Beijing the outbreak would be viewed as a national disaster, a complete loss of control, and that was something the authorities would not bear.

Day three became day four. Her supplies were holding out, but black smoke drifted past her window as fires broke out across Pudong. She saw other people in other buildings, waving sheets and hi-visibility garments. Many of the surrounding rooftops were crowded with people, all waving desperately at the helicopters that clattered overhead. Marion had yet to witness a rescue effort of any sort.

In the corridor outside she heard people moving around. They weren't people any more, but they shuffled to and fro, searching, sniffing the air, grunting. Sooner or later they would hear her, and then the assault on her door would begin. She was immune from the virus, but the thought of being torn to pieces filled her with dread. She'd tested the window, its thickness and strength, and accepted that she might not be able to break it in time in order to leap to her death. As the pale winter sun dipped towards the horizon, Marion began to accept that her situation was hopeless.

And then there were no more helicopters.

Their buzzing had been a constant feature of the crisis, the gunships that swept low over the city centre, mini-guns blazing, dropping munitions, criss-crossing the sky day and night. Now they were gone.

Marion stood against the window and searched the darkening sky. There were no more collision lights, no hovering aircraft backlit by towering fires, no clatter of rotor blades. For the first time in days, the sky was empty.

The river, too.

The gunboats had ceased their pounding of the shoreline. The flotilla of steel grey vessels that had churned the brown waters for days were no longer visible. The Huangpu River had settled. It was now calm, lifeless.

On the streets below the infected still funnelled between the buildings, tens of thousands of them, perhaps more, squeezed together by their sheer mass. Marion had witnessed the same phenomenon across the river, and the scene had frightened her. Shanghai was lost. Her options were non-existent.

Not just hers.

She placed her hands on the glass and looked out across the city. Night had fallen and fires still raged, huge pockets of red flame against a black landscape that stretched towards an unseen horizon. She craned her neck and looked up into the sky. She thought she saw something up there, far above her, the wink of a distant light, a disturbance in the clouds.

An object falling silently to earth —

The pulse of light was brighter than a thousand suns, and it blinded Marion instantly, scorching her eyeballs, melting the glass beneath her hands.

Then she felt nothing.

RAY WILSON SHUFFLED TO THE HUGE KITCHEN TABLE AND SAT down. He was dressed in jogging bottoms and a *Houston Texas* sweatshirt, and he wore slippers on his feet.

Around the table, most of the other thirteen chairs were occupied by a member of the Hayden family. Ray had learned that they were a hard-working bunch, horse and cattle breeders, and business had clearly been good over the years.

The ranch house was huge, constructed of stone and thick timber beams and decorated with a nostalgic mix of Tex-Mex furniture, rugs and artwork. It was a home in every sense, warm, comfortable and inviting. Ray couldn't remember the last time he'd been made to feel so welcome. He'd always been a little sniffy about the South, with their overt and often uncomfortable expressions of patriotism, their unyielding support for the Constitution, particularly the first two amendments, but the Hayden family had changed his mind. He decided his previously ingrained metro-liberal attitudes might just benefit from a little read-justment.

'Eat up now.'

Alice Hayden, the no-nonsense matriarch, smiled at him as she set down a plate of bacon and eggs. There was coffee and juice already on the table, and the other Hayden children and grandchildren — their ages ranging from teens to mid-forties — were at various stages of breakfast. People came and went around the table. A working ranch needed a working kitchen, he guessed.

'How're you feeling this morning?'

Joe Hayden sat down opposite Ray, nursing a mug of black coffee. His skin was deeply lined and permanently tanned by several decades of Texan sun, and his hair and neatly-trimmed beard were snow white. Ray figured he was seventy plus, but there was solid muscle beneath his check-ered shirt, and Ray felt a twinge of envy. He was out of shape, a condition that could've cost him his life.

'Much better, thank you,' Ray answered, lifting his own coffee mug in appreciation.

The youngsters drifted away from the table, some to school, some to the fields and pens in the surrounding acreage. Coats and cowboy hats were lifted off the pegs as people went about their business, and once again Ray was struck by the sense of family, of history. It made him a little jealous.

'The doc tells me you're okay,' Hayden said.

Ray nodded, swallowing a mouthful of eggs. 'Much better, thanks. And I'll be out of your way as soon as possible.'

'That's not what I meant, Ray. You're welcome to stay as long as you wish. We've got plenty of room and besides, it's not often we get a big-city reporter in these parts.' The smile faded. 'Though with this China thing happening now, you're probably itching to get back to DC.'

Ray took another sip of his coffee. 'What d'you mean?'

'They had a virus outbreak in Shanghai, same as here. Chinese government dropped a nuke on the city last night.'

'Those poor people,' Alice Hayden said as she plucked dirty dishes from the table.

It took several moments for Ray to recover. 'A nuke?'

Hayden stood up and cocked his head. 'Bring your coffee into the den.'

Ray followed him through into a log-walled room that had a lot of chairs and sofas arranged in front of a huge TV. Fox News was playing, the anchor sandwiched against a graphic of eastern China. He was talking about fallout and blast radius. And casualties. Ray watched the ticker at the bottom of the screen and his blood froze; four million estimated fatalities, another three million injured. Ray wondered if Coffman now had similar plans for Lubbock.

'Guess they felt they didn't have much choice,' Hayden reasoned. 'That's a big city, huge population. I guess the Lubbock thing spooked them.' He looked at Ray and said, 'I can't imagine how bad that must've been.'

Ray glanced down at his slippered feet, the memory still raw. 'I saw a little girl, couldn't have been more than three or four years old. She was naked, covered in blood, and quite clearly infected. One of her little legs was badly mangled, and she limped along the sidewalk, all alone, making this terrible screeching sound. It was heartbreaking.'

'Goddam,' Hayden muttered.

'When you see it up close, you realise it's got to be stopped.'

They watched TV in silence for a few minutes, then the rancher turned to Ray. 'Well, I've got business to attend to. You need anything, just ask Alice.'

'That's very kind, but I need to leave.'

Hayden hesitated. 'Doc says you should rest up a few more days.'

'I can't. I have to get back to DC.'

'Fair enough,' Hayden said, nodding. 'Your clothes were pretty torn up, so we threw them out. I'll get you some fresh ones.'

'Where's the nearest airport?'

'Abilene. That's about a hundred-and-fifty-miles to the south-east.'

'In Texas?'

Hayden frowned. 'Sure.'

'What the closest airport outside the state?'

The rancher thought about that one and said, 'Roswell, New Mexico. About the same distance due east. It won't get you direct to DC but they hook up to the hubs in Phoenix and Albuquerque.'

'I need to hire a car. What are my chances around here?'

Hayden smiled. 'Oh, I think we can do better than that.'

It took Ray almost three hours to drive to Roswell.

The Ford pickup was ten years old but clean and recently serviced by one of Hayden's boys. It ran smooth, and Ray saw little traffic as he headed west on Highway 380. He found a jazz station on the radio and the music helped to clear his mind, as did the empty road, the empty plains, and the huge Texas sky that was blue and clear and stretched all the way to the distant horizon.

He drove through small towns and past fields of nodding donkeys sucking oil from the ground. He crossed the state line a few miles west of the town of Plains and drove into the parking lot at Roswell Air Centre ninety minutes later, leaving the pickup in a long-term bay. One of Hayden's boys would collect it in a few days, but Ray paid for a week in advance anyway. It was the least he could do.

He waited two hours to board a feeder plane to Phoenix, and from there he connected to a United flight that got him into Dulles at just after nine p.m. Instead of going home he checked into the Intercontinental overlooking the Potomac River and charged it to the Times. He was exhausted, and although he'd slept on the plane a little, he felt bone tired. He took a shower, dressed in the complimentary robe and lay back on the bed. He scanned the room service menu, trying to decide what to eat.

It was still lying on his chest when the sun rose the next day.

BORN IN THE USA

The de Havilland turboprop came in low over the York River and touched down onto the runway at Camp Peary in Williamsburg, Virginia at a little after ten a.m. local time.

Mike Savage was already on his feet as the twin-engined aircraft taxied into a large, empty hangar. He waited until the wheels were chocked and the turboprops shut down before he cracked the forward passenger door and dropped the stairs. Outside, Stan Lando was waiting to greet Mike and his team. Two SUVs idled close by, doors and tailgates open, ready to transport them to the Special Activities Division building.

'Tough break,' Lando told him as they shook hands.

Mike began loading his gear and weapons into the back of one of the SUVs. 'I screwed up, Stan. Big time.'

Lando led him out of earshot. 'The guy played you, I get it. Your ego is bruised — '

'Fuck ego,' Mike snapped. He lowered his voice as heads turned in their direction. 'If I did my job properly we might've located Marion, stopped her.'

'We have no way of knowing if Philip knew her location.'

'He chose death over talking, Stan. He knew. Now millions are dead.'

'That was Beijing's call. Besides, given the timescales, I doubt even the Chinese would've been able to stop her. These people are professionals, Mike. More than that, they're fanatics, and you know how that goes. Folks like that can't be reasoned with. You did your best with the time and resources you had. Let it go.'

Mike folded his arms across his chest as he watched his team climb aboard the other SUV. Tapper lingered in the doorway and Mike waved him away. His XO nodded and climbed aboard, and the SUV drove out of the hangar.

'The guys know I screwed up. They've been good about it, but maybe you should consider reassigning me.'

'Tapper and Miller said the same.'

'You spoke to them?'

'That's my job, Mike.' Lando stepped a little closer. 'We've been doing this for some time, you and I, and right now I can't think of a single occasion when you didn't get something useful from an interrogation. Factor in the ripple effect, and you've saved a lot of lives.'

Mike didn't answer. All he could see was Philip leaping over that rail. 'Any luck with the prints?'

'Surgically acid-scarred, and no facial recognition hits either. Philip was a ghost. Same with this Marion broad, I'm guessing.

'Are we getting anything from the Chinese?'

Lando shook his head. 'The White House has offered assistance, but the bamboo curtains have been pulled tight. All borders closed, nothing in or out, and they've shut down their comms networks. China's a black hole.'

'What about Marion?'

Lando shrugged. 'She could be anywhere.'

'So where does that leave us? And more importantly, who's getting hit next?'

'Christ knows, but what I *do* know is this; I need all my top tier guys prepped and ready to deploy. SOCOM is running everything out of McDill now, and the DOD is mobilising every unit in the country. There's no time for navel gazing, Mike. I need you on your game and ready to move. Understood?'

Mike nodded. Stan was right, about everything. He knew he wouldn't make that same mistake ever again.

'Get your team turned around,' Lando told him. 'The call could come any time.'

'Roger that.'

The field supervisor held out his hand. 'Welcome home, Mike.'

Mike took it and shook it. 'It's good to be back.'

Tammy Lindberg had reserved a suite at the Hay Adams on 16th Street under the name of Fairbank. Ray Wilson arrived at one thirty and made his way to the beautifully-appointed room that overlooked a snowy Lafayette Park. The newspaper boss had ordered a light yet exquisite lunch, and Ray had to admit he was glad to be back in the bosom of a big city and all of its conveniences. He'd been gone from DC for less than a week. For Ray, it felt like a month.

He told Lindberg the whole story over scallops and steak frites, or his version of it at least. He left nothing out, not even the horror of Lubbock. The only detail he withheld was the name of the family that had taken him in.

Across the table, Lindberg listened without interruption. She took no notes or made any recordings. She didn't comment when Ray's recollections forced him to stop and compose himself, nor did she offer words of comfort. She simply listened. It was only after Ray had finished his tale of death and survival that he realised his boss had been shocked into silence. That kind of thing didn't happen often, and Ray knew why; there was simply too much blood in the water.

They waited until the table had been cleared and fresh coffee served before Lindberg attempted a cross-examination. It was her way of testing the veracity of a story, and she didn't any pull punches.

'So you think someone went to all the trouble of luring you to Lubbock — then release the virus — just to squash the Baghdad story? C'mon, Ray.'

'Baghdad is the key to all this, Tammy. It put Coffman in the Whitehouse, remember?'

'And you believe the White House is behind the outbreak in Lubbock?'

'I have no idea, but from a terrorism perspective, wouldn't DC have been a better target? Or New York? Chicago? Lubbock is literally in the middle of nowhere.'

Lindberg got to her feet and began pacing the room. 'Okay, let's back all the way up. The Delta guy you interviewed — '

'Kenny Chase.'

'Yes. You're saying his team was in Iraq to stop the dispersal of the Angola virus?'

'Correct. Angola was man-made, that's what they were told. The global outbreaks were field trials. Angola was designed to kill half the world's population.'

Lindberg stopped pacing. 'Excuse me?'

'You heard me correctly, Tammy. Right after the raid there was that avalanche in Switzerland, remember? The one that buried the hotel and killed a lot of very powerful and influential people? Then the arrests began, here at home; the President, half the Executive, military leaders, industrialists, all of whom are now being held without trial — '

'Yes, the so-called financial scandal. Get to the point.'

Ray set his coffee down. 'What if Coffman was part of the

Angola conspiracy but somehow slipped the net? What if she's finishing what they started?'

Lindberg bit her lower lip as she processed the theory. 'I don't buy it. Angola was a pretty benign disease. Flu-like symptoms, coma, then death. This H-1 thing is the exact opposite. I also have it on very good authority that Coffman was deeply troubled by the terror threats sent to the State Department.'

'So she's a good actor.'

'Maybe…'

'Get me back in the White House, Tammy. I can ask her about Lubbock, put her under a little pressure. You saw what happened last time.'

'I can't,' Lindberg told him. 'Coffman has relocated her Cabinet and National Security Council to a new facility in Denver.'

Ray sat back in his chair. 'Jesus, Tammy, what does that tell you?'

'It tells me they're scared.'

'Or they know what's coming. Maybe they're going to hit DC after all.'

'It's precautionary,' Lindberg explained. 'A prudent move, in the wake of Shanghai. And remember, the terrorists are still on the loose.'

'You don't sound convinced.'

Lindberg toyed with her wedding ring. 'I'm not sure what to think right now. And that's the problem, Ray; everything you have is circumstantial. We can't run with any of it.'

'We can publish my personal account. Why I was in Lubbock, what happened in that cinema, how I escaped, the deaths of those innocent men, all of it underpinned by Chase's testimony. No pointing fingers, just a timeline. It's explosive, Tammy, and I'll add a disclaimer. Legal won't have a problem with it.'

'The White House will.'

'So we shake a few trees, see what falls.'

Lindberg stood motionless, her tanned face devoid of expression. She was struggling with the decision, Ray knew. His boss had supported Coffman, the first female President, only to now discover she might be as corrupt as her predecessor.

'I'll sleep on it,' she told him.

'I can live with that.'

'Go home, get some rest.'

'I'm staying at the Intercontinental.'

Lindberg frowned. 'Why?'

'They tried to kill me, Tammy. Home doesn't feel very safe right now.'

'Use the suite,' she said, waving a hand around the room. 'I need you close by.' The newspaper boss picked up her coat and purse. 'Type it up anyway. We'll see how this looks tomorrow.' She paused by the door on her way out. 'There's a box by the bureau. It's your office mail, and a new Powerbook . Take care, Ray.'

Lindberg left the room, closing the door behind her. Ray locked it and slid the chain across, then he picked up the box and began going through the mail. A lot of it was junk. The padded envelope with the UPS stickers was not. It was addressed to Ray and had been signed for at the office the day before.

Ray set it down on the table, his heart beating fast. It was similar in size to the one the guy in Lubbock tried to pass him, the one Ray was now convinced had contained the virus. He turned it over in his hand, squeezing gently. There was something inside, something small and rigid, not angular. *Is this another assassination attempt?*

Ray sat and thought about his next move. He'd travelled from New Mexico using his driving licence, the tickets paid for on a company credit card. He hadn't been home since he'd landed, and he'd called Tammy from a coffee shop payphone.

Sure, his movements could be tracked, but was anyone *really* looking for him? The package was sent yesterday. Why bother if they thought Ray was already dead or trapped in Lubbock. They could send it to anyone and still spread the virus.

He got to his feet and crossed to the bureau. He wrote a note on Hay Adams stationary and left it on the carpet by the main door. Then he locked himself in the bathroom. He grabbed a towel off the rail and held it over his mouth and nose. He ripped the package open and emptied the contents into the sink. A mobile phone clattered onto the porcelain. No white powder or liquid, just a phone.

Ray stared at it. It was a Samsung Galaxy.

He unlocked the door and left the suite. Down the hallway he saw a maintenance cart. He gave the housekeeping maid a twenty-dollar bill in exchange for a few pairs of latex gloves. He went back to the room, pulled on the gloves and powered on the phone. The battery was fully charged and had a strong signal. There were no contacts in the address books, no text messages or call history. A virgin phone.

Ray scooped up the hotel stationary from the carpet, the one that said, *I am infected with the H-1 virus. I am locked in the bathroom. Do not open! Call the police!* He left the phone on the bureau and unpacked the Powerbook. He ordered more coffee and after it arrived he sat at the writing desk and began to type. At exactly three p.m., the Samsung rang, vibrating on the dark mahogany bureau.

Ray's heart rate began to climb. He got to his feet and picked up the phone. He swiped to answer it, then waited in silence as he looked out across the snowy expanse of Lafayette Park, and at the White House beyond.

'Ray Wilson?' asked the voice on the other end of the line.

'Who's this?'

The line hissed. 'Am I talking to Ray Wilson?' The voice was edgier now, more insistent.

'This is he.'

More silence, then what sounded like an exhale of breath. 'You made it out of Lubbock. I can't tell you how pleased I am.'

'Not as pleased as me,' Ray shot back.

'I saw the White House press conference. The President was very upset.'

'How would you know?'

'I was there,' the voice said.

The more he spoke, the more familiar the man sounded. Ray wracked his brain, trying to nail it down. 'We've met, right?'

'Not officially.'

More silence. Ray was getting impatient. 'Well, you have my attention, sir, and time is short. Who are you and what is it you want?'

At the other end of the phone Ray heard the man clear his throat. When he spoke again it was in a calm, measured tone.

'My name is Erik Mulholland, President Coffman's Chief of Staff. Along with several others, I'm responsible for the deaths of millions and before I hand myself in I'd like to go on the record.'

Ray's hand tightened around the phone. For the first time in many years, he found himself unable to speak.

BITCH SLAP

COFFMAN FELT AS IF SHE'D BEEN TRAPPED IN THE SITUATION Room forever.

The weight of the mountain was pressing down on her, and she saw that same pressure reflected on the faces of her Cabinet and National Security Council, their knotted brows and worried words, all of them squeezed by the tension between the granite walls.

Up on the video wall, satellite imagery from Shanghai was being fed onto several screens. It was recognisable only by its geography and the twists and turns of the Huangpu River. Everything else was gone, a city not just flattened but obliterated. The surface burst had left a crater two-hundred feet deep and four-hundred wide, and nothing stood for three miles in any direction. Far outside the city, firestorms raged around the horizon, sweeping through damaged and densely-populated districts. Shanghai had been effectively wiped off the map.

Understandably, the talk in the room was all about China. The Chinese premiere wasn't taking any calls, not even from the President of the United States, a snub that had infuriated Coffman. Quietly, she prayed the Beijing outbreak would begin soon. She was irritable and restless. The people around her grated on her nerves. The truth was, she was deeply troubled.

As Grady delivered yet another Homeland Security update to the room, Coffman's phone buzzed with an incoming message. She got to her feet, cutting Grady off in mid-sentence.

'Charlie, Karen, can I get a moment please?'

Schultz and Baranski followed Coffman out of the room. Her Secret Service detail formed a protective box around her as they hurried along the smooth stone hallway. China was now only the second country in history to have detonated a nuke in anger. Granted, it was in self-defence, but international tensions were high and Coffman was eager to calm them. There was no point inheriting an irradiated world.

Bob Blake waited for her in her private suite. He was standing by the huge windows overlooking the plateau below when she entered. He met her halfway across the room.

'Madam President, I hope I haven't — '

Coffman whipped back her hand and slapped Blake around the face. He staggered backwards, eyes wide, a hand nursing his glowing red cheek.

'Where is she?' Coffman yelled at him.

'Who?'

'Marion, you fucking retard. Where is she?'

Blake shook his head. 'She hasn't checked in.'

Coffman held up her phone. 'You told me that already. Do the Chinese have her?'

'There's no way of knowing.'

'So, she's probably talking.'

'Or she could be dead. The city shut down pretty fast, ma'am. Besides, the only person she can implicate is Matt, and he's barely conscious right now.'

'You mean Matt Sorenson? An American citizen closely tied to the US defence industry and the Coffman administration? Is *that* the Matt Sorenson you're referring to?' Coffman gave him a cold, hard stare. 'You made all this sound so fucking easy, Bob.'

Blake held up his hands. 'Everything is still on track, I can assure you.'

'Oh really? Philip is dead and Marion is missing, possibly captured. Four countries should be on the brink of collapse right now, but instead, three of them are business as usual and the fourth is an irradiated wasteland. How the fuck are things *still on track*, Bob?'

'Ma'am, the deployment team is waiting at the ranch as we speak. With Matt so sick, I'll need to get down there, brief them, assign targets, travel documents and infected materials, then send them on their way. It could take some time.'

Coffman took a step closer. She folded her arms and looked into Blake's eyes. She saw an eyelid flutter in anticipation of another slap, but Coffman had no intention of hitting him again. Not today at least.

'Where are the H-1 stockpiles?'

'We've got two one-hundred litre drums. One is at the ranch in Arizona, the other in a climate-controlled room at the house in Seattle.'

'Is the ranch secure?'

'Yes, ma'am. Fifty Northridge contractors are working external security, Peruvians mostly, and there's another dozen covering the main house and outbuildings. It's all very discreet, no uniforms, lots of CCTV, and way off the beaten path.'

Coffman chewed her lip, deep in thought. Finally she said, 'I need you to do two things for me, Bob.'

Blake stood a little straighter. 'Anything, Madam President.'

'Firstly, I need that deployment team on the move asap. I want to see those outbreaks all over the news. I want to see

Istanbul, Cairo and Beirut in flames and I want to see Nigeria become twice the hellhole it already is.'

Blake didn't argue. In fact, Coffman thought he looked relieved.

'And the other thing, ma'am?'

'I need you to take care of Matt. Unplug his respirator, squeeze an air bubble into his vein, whatever. Just make sure he expires before someone makes the connection. Can you do that for me, Bob?'

Blake tipped his large head. 'I'll be doing the poor bastard a favour.'

Coffman raised an eyebrow. 'So what're you waiting for?'

Blake took the hint and hurried from the room. Coffman invited Schultz and Baranski to join her at the dining table.

'Any word from Erik?' she asked. The looks on their faces told her all she needed to know. 'Me neither. No phone calls, no messages, no emails, nothing. So, we must assume the worst. Erik is talking, which means we're all going to prison for the rest of our lives. If we're lucky.'

Baranski's face had turned as white as the snow outside the window. 'I just can't see him betraying you, ma'am. He adores you, always has. He wouldn't do this.'

'Don't be naïve, Karen. Erik isn't coming back. This is a damage-limitation exercise now, so we need to undermine any testimony, discredit him personally.'

Schultz winced. 'Ma'am, with all due respect, this isn't going to be a wrongful termination lawsuit. Erik literally knows where the bodies are buried. When they come for us, it'll be with guns and leg irons. Like they did with your predecessor.'

'Oh my God,' Baranski whispered.

Coffman rapped her knuckles on the table. 'Focus, Karen. I want a file on Erik, as thick as you can make it. Drug use, sexual impropriety, dubious contacts with foreign nationals, anything you can think of. Oh, and his recent mental health issues of course. Depression, anxiety, suicidal thoughts, you know the drill. Go, get to work.'

Baranski left the room without another word. Coffman rested her elbows on the table and rubbed her face. The last week had taken a heavy toll, and it wasn't over by a long chalk. *This is what you wanted,* she reminded herself, but now there was nowhere she could run, no place to hide. If this blew back on her, there was only one way out.

'Are you okay, ma'am?'

Coffman opened her eyes and offered the admiral a weak smile. 'Not really, Charlie.' She took a deep breath and folded her arms on the table. 'So let's play this out. China first. Let's assume they have Marion, and that she's talking. She implicates Matt, and when she does, the Chinese will begin to suspect our involvement.'

'Sorenson won't be a factor at that point.'

'But his legacy will be. A proud American and patriot, that's how he portrayed himself. Beijing is paranoid at the best of times. So we drop it all in Matt's lap.'

'How?'

Coffman pinched her lip, deep in thought. 'The Brit. The one they captured in Vienna. He becomes our star witness.'

'But they've never met,' Schultz pointed out.

'Don't worry, we'll make sure he's coached. And when he's ready he'll make a statement, tell the world about Matt's cancer, of how the guilt began to eat him up.'

'Guilt?'

'Yes, Charlie. Kroll weapons have been dropped on America's enemies countless times. With death knocking on Matt's door, the guilt secretly ate him up, twisted his mind. The Brit will confirm his descent into madness and his determination to reshape the planet before he checked out. To punish us all.' Coffman shrugged. 'Something along those lines anyway. Start working the problem, Charlie.'

Schultz shook his head. 'Beijing won't buy it, ma'am. Accusations will be made. Tensions will rise — '

'Meanwhile Bob will get one or more of his people over their border and release the virus. Then it won't matter. Let's keep spitballing.'

Schultz drew his chair in a little closer. 'Okay, so Sorensen dies and the Chinese are thrown off the scent, but that still leaves Erik. His confession will be more devastating than that Shanghai nuke.'

'Agreed, and I know Erik better than anyone; he would've thought this through before he made his move, which means he's holding a get-out-of-jail card. Audio, video, something deeply incriminating and irrefutable.'

Schultz lowered his voice. 'Every conversation we had pertaining to H-1 was electronically scrambled. Audio equipment would not have worked.'

'I had many private conversations with Erik,' Coffman confessed, 'and I didn't always take precautions.' She saw the look on Schultz's face and shrugged. 'I never doubted Erik's loyalty for a second.'

'So, what do we do?'

'We need to find him before anyone else. If I can speak to him, we might have an opportunity to get this thing back on the rails.'

'That could prove difficult. If he's spilling his guts they'll have him buried somewhere deep.'

'Are you saying we can't find him, Charlie?'

Schultz leaned across the table. 'Ma'am, I'm saying that the Feds could be on their way here right now. Coming for us.'

Coffman pushed her chair back and stood. Charlie was right, the wheels for their arrest might already be in motion. *Might.* Because the chance still existed Erik had suffered some sort of breakdown and gone into hiding. The question was, could she take that chance? *No,* her inner voice told her.

'Then we go to plan B.' Coffman lowered her voice, even though she knew the room was clean. 'We stage another outbreak, here at home, in Los Angeles. The place is a cesspit anyway, and it'll ease pressure on the border if Lubbock hasn't made people think twice already. No containment this time, and when the infection spreads, we suspend the constitution, shutting down any potential investigation, and invoke martial law. And while attentions are diverted, we find Erik and make him disappear.'

Schultz's face paled. 'This is it, then? We go all in?'

'Or it's the perp walk, Charlie. In those leg irons you mentioned.'

'Fuck me,' he whispered.

Coffman smiled. 'Time to go all in.'

'We need to speak to Bob, work out the details.'

Coffman bit her lip. 'I shouldn't have hit him. He won't forget that.'

'He deserved it.'

'Maybe, but we need him more than ever now. We need his people on the move, we need China to fold and we need America to panic. LA has to make Lubbock look like an outbreak of head lice in a kindergarten.'

'That's a lot of spinning plates,' Schultz said, grimacing.

'It's nothing we can't handle. In the meantime, Karen will keep a discreet eye on the Judiciary and the FBI, see if she can pick up any whispers. Don't forget, we've got a lot of friends, Charlie. We need to reach out to them, discreetly, find out if there's anything in the wind.'

'Yes, ma'am.' Schultz got to his feet. Coffman came around the table and squeezed his arm. 'It's going to be okay. We keep our heads, and we keep our ears open. Bob will take care of the rest.'

'I hope you're right, ma'am.'

Coffman cocked her head. 'Go. Get to work.'

She heard the door hiss closed behind him. She crossed to

the drinks cabinet and poured herself a large glass of Argentinian Malbec. She dimmed the lights and sat by the fire, imagining a life without Erik Mulholland. The thought saddened her. The truth was, she felt alone without him. She'd assumed he'd always be with her, standing by her side as she became the world's first global leader, then later, as her companion. He'd always been there, in her plans, her thoughts, and sometimes her dreams. Yes, part of her was in love with him, despite his homosexuality. He was smart, warm, cultured, fiercely loyal, occasionally hilarious and pleasing to the eye. He was the reason she'd never taken a life partner. No other man could live up to the promise of Erik Mulholland.

Now he was gone, and Coffman couldn't shake her mounting loneliness. She thought about his murder, and it made her feel nauseous. There were other ways, of course. A private plane, a day or two under the knife of a plastic surgeon, a period of rehabilitation on a private island somewhere. She knew one or two people who had taken that path and wondered if Erik could be persuaded to do the same, because the truth was, his death would haunt her far more than the millions she'd already caused.

She sipped her wine, savouring its flavour as she stared into the flames. Everything was a gamble, including life itself. The world was filled with winners and losers, and Coffman had always worked the angles to ensure she remained on the winning side.

This time would be no different.

THE CITY OF CUMBERLAND IN THE STATE OF MARYLAND IS ONE OF the poorest cities in the United States. Located on a bend in the Potomac River close to the Appalachian mountains, the city once served as a major staging post for those travelling west across the country, where horses, wagons and supplies could be procured, and where hardy souls saddled up and headed out west, to the vast, untamed land beyond the wooded mountains.

Now Cumberland was in decline, abandoned by trade and industry for more strategically commercial locations on the east coast. But it was still a proud city, one steeped in history, and its inhabitants seemed pretty happy. At least that was the impression Mulholland got during his time as a new resident.

He'd blended in well too. He downgraded his wardrobe and rented a modest apartment in a former warehouse, with exposed-brick walls, metal-framed windows and off-street parking, which meant Mulholland could keep his friend's car hidden from passing eyes. The landlord had taken cash with a conspiratorial wink and no questions asked.

He'd settled in and waited, calling the burner twice a day, once at ten a.m. and again at three p.m. He hadn't expected an answer, assuming the man was dead, but he was top of Mulholland's list. He'd keep trying until his death was made official, then start moving down his list of trusted reporters.

But Ray Wilson had made it out of Lubbock and answered the phone. For that, Mulholland was grateful. Now it was in the lap of the gods.

The diner was called City Lights and was located downtown, right on Baltimore Street. It was pretty upmarket for Cumberland, and Mulholland had claimed a booth that offered an unrestricted view of the door. It was also close to the kitchen, just in case he had to make a fast exit.

It wasn't quite lunchtime but a few old folks drifted in, a lot of checked shirts, denim and baseball caps, accompanied by their overweight wives. Mulholland settled back and waited, nursing a coffee. He'd been there for less than fifteen minutes when the man walked in. Mulholland raised his hand and the man veered towards him. He saw him frown as he approached the booth.

Mulholland smiled. 'Did you think I'd be wearing my Tom Ford?'

He wasn't, of course. Instead he wore scruffy jeans and an old hoodie, a baseball cap and cheap glasses. The sophisticated urbanite was gone, replaced by poor white trash. Mulholland held out his hand and the man took it.

'Mister Wilson, thank you for coming.'

Wilson took off his cap and coat and sat opposite. Coffee was served. Mulholland took a sip and settled back in his seat.

'No one knows you're here, right? You've not discussed this meeting with anyone else, especially over the telephone or via the internet, correct?'

Wilson nodded. 'I've done this before.'

'Not at this level.' Mulholland glanced over Wilson's shoulder and watched a younger couple enter the premises. They smiled at the waitress and took a seat across the restaurant. Mulholland couldn't tell if they were genuine or not. He just didn't have that type of experience. He turned his attention back to Wilson.

'The NSA will find us in a heartbeat if you've screwed up, understand? And then we'll both be dead.' That got Wilson's attention, so he pushed on. 'I'm not asking for immunity, I want to make that clear from the get-go. I've committed federal crimes, terrible crimes. I want to go on the record, somewhere secure, far from DC, because if they find me, I'm a dead man. They have that kind of power.'

'You're talking about President Coffman?' Wilson asked. His sharp eyes never left Mulholland's. He could see determination there, and an obvious disgust. That was something he'd have to get used to.

'Yes, the President, and others.'

'You need to do this officially,' Wilson told him. 'Under oath. You need representation — '

'You need to act fast,' Mulholland cut in. 'The Shanghai

nuke won't stop them. Beijing was supposed to be next on the list, along with Mumbai and Istanbul.'

Wilson paled. 'What list?'

'A list of cities, where the virus was to be deployed.'

'Including Lubbock?'

'That was a pre-planned outbreak,' Mulholland told him. 'You were meant to be the first victim, in the multiplex. It was Bob's idea. He thought it would be ironic.'

'Bob who?'

'Bob Blake. Head of Kroll Industries.'

'*The* Robert Blake? Holy shit.' Wilson shook his head in disbelief. 'And you're telling me the White House is behind all of this?'

'To be specific, the Oval Office.'

'My God.'

The bell above the door chimed and a large group of seniors bustled into the diner, shuffling towards the booths and tables close by.

'We need to get out of here,' Mulholland said.

'I have a contact at the FBI Field Office in Pittsburg. It's a two hour drive, so we can be there by — '

'No, not yet. Before I hand myself in I need to tell my story, Mister Wilson. To you.'

The reporter looked confused. 'You'll be safe in federal custody.'

'Don't be naive. No, you need a record of names, dates, locations, everything. Then, in the event I have an accident — or I'm *suicided* — you can use it to bring the whole house down.'

'An insurance policy.'

'Correct. The Attorney General is clean, at least I'm pretty sure of it. After we're done I'll make the call. Then it's all in the lap of the gods.'

'Where shall we do this?'

'I have an apartment down the street. The camera is

already set up and I have a fast internet connection. I suggest you upload the files somewhere secure, a cloud-based service, something like that. And you need to make local copies too. Did you bring the hard drives?'

'I did.'

'Good. So let's go. And put your hat back on. We're just a couple of regular fellas going about our business, okay?'

Mulholland got up from the table and headed for the door. In the reflection of the glass he saw Wilson hurrying after him.

THE SUN HAD SET AND THE SKY WAS DARKENING FAST. IN THE surrounding woods, night birds called to each other in the gathering gloom. It was a peaceful setting, and unusual for a meeting of such critical importance, but the Attorney General was calling the shots now. The phrase *uncharted waters* didn't begin to cover what the country was going through right now.

The road stretched empty in both directions, and Ray used the moment to work the travel-stiffness from his legs. Lubbock had given him a new perspective on life, and in particular his health. He'd made it out, but only just. If — God forbid — he ever found himself in that position again, he was determined to be in better shape that he was right now.

He glanced over his shoulder, at the two Humvees parked in the deepening shadow of a disused ammunition storage bunker. Mulholland sat inside the rear vehicle, book-ended by a couple of stone-faced FBI minders from the Pittsburgh Field Office. The blindfold had been temporarily removed, but the peak of his baseball cap had been pulled low to protect his identity from the two Marine drivers who chatted quietly a short distance away. His hands were cuffed, a physical restriction that President Coffman's former Chief of Staff would have to get used to. Vanessa Holden, Pittsburgh's Special Agent in Charge and one of Ray's long-time law-enforcement contacts, paced up and down a short distance away, smoking a cigarette. She looked troubled because she was operating outside her normal chain of command and under the direct orders of the Attorney General, an unprecedented state of affairs for the FBI agent. As the executive jet had made its final approach into the Marine Corps Air Station in Beaufort, South Carolina, Holden declared that she was pissed at Ray for dumping Mulholland in her lap. Ray thought it was more than that; Holden was scared, the now-default reaction of anyone who learned of the enormity of the crimes committed by their Commander in Chief.

'Here they come,' Ray said, pointing at the distant lights heading towards them along the wooded road. Holden stamped on her cigarette, and they stood in silence as the approaching convoy drew closer. It was made up of three vehicles, two Chevy Impalas and a dark coloured Ford Explorer, all of them emblazoned with the Marine Corps Police livery. They rolled to a stop in the middle of the road, red lights flaring in the fading light. Engines idled as doors swung open. The men who climbed out were evenly split between business suits and combat uniforms. Ray didn't recognise any of the suits and the military men wore no rank or name tags. All he knew is that they'd been sent from McDill Air Force Base in Florida and they were operating at the highest authority, albeit without the knowledge of the Oval Office or anyone on Mulholland's list of known and suspected Coffman allies.

'Here we go,' Holden said under her breath.

Ray's heart rate climbed. He had a sudden vision of guns being drawn, of executions by the side of the road and his own body being tossed into the back of the Explorer on top of Holden's and her FBI minders. Mulholland's shocking and terrifying testimony had stoked Ray's paranoia. The grey-haired man in the dark overcoat who shook Holden's hand did little to allay those fears.

'Special Agent Holden, my name is David Parker from the Attorney General's office. My colleagues here are from the Legal Counsel's Office, and will bear witness to this exchange. The men in uniform are from Special Operations Command at McDill. They'll be taking custody of the witness.' He glanced over at the Humvees. 'Where is he?'

'Second vehicle,' Holden told him.

'We'll take it from here.'

A couple of uniforms marched across the road and manhandled Mulholland out of the vehicle, while a couple of the suits used compact cameras to record the exchange. The baseball cap was tossed to the ground and a black hood went over his head, secured in place by what Ray assumed were noise-cancelling headphones. The leg irons were clamped on next, and then Mulholland was perp-walked across the road and secured inside the SUV. He never made a sound, and Ray was puzzled by a sudden and irrational pang of sympathy for the man. For Mulholland, the road ahead would be a very dark one indeed.

'You must be Ray Wilson.'

Ray took Parker's offered hand. 'Yes sir.'

Parker looked at them both. 'So, this is as far as you guys go.'

Ray swallowed, the hairs on his neck standing on end as he imagined a gun barrel aimed at the back of his head. Holden brought him back to reality.

'Sir, with respect, I have to ask about jurisdiction here. This is a highly irregular situation — '

'Here,' Parker said, reaching into his coat pocket. He handed Holden a plain white envelope. 'Written authority from the Attorney General himself and countersigned by the Assistant AG. A copy will be made available to your Director in due course. You're legally covered, Special Agent Holden.'

She took it and nodded her thanks. Parker handed another envelope to Ray. 'This is for you,' Parker said. 'It's your security clearance.'

Ray turned the envelope over in his hands. 'But I didn't —'

'This is a national security matter, Mister Wilson. Everything you've heard and seen here today, including your videotaped interview with Erik Mulholland, is classified until further notice. That means you don't talk, period.'

Ray swallowed his protest. This went way beyond his First Amendment rights. 'I understand. So what happens now?'

'Now we leave,' Parker told him. 'Thank you for your assistance. Someone may contact you in the near future, Mister Wilson. Please make yourself available when they do.'

Parker and his team walked back to the waiting Chevys and climbed in. Ray followed him and Parker powered down the window. The men inside were silent, the Marine driver staring through the windshield. The radio spat bursts of garbled military traffic.

'Make it fast, Mister Wilson. We have a plane waiting.'

'One question; are we going to be okay? The country, I mean?'

Parker looked up at him in the darkness. 'JFK once said, *the only thing necessary for the triumph of evil is for good men to do nothing.* I can assure you right here and now that the forces of good are gathering as we speak. Have faith, Mister Wilson. Good night.'

Ray stood his ground as the vehicles swung around him in a squeal of tyres and headed back to the distant runway. Holden stood next to him, and together they watched the convoy's tail-lights until they disappeared.

'Strangest day of my career, no question,' the Special Agent told him.

303

Ray tapped the envelope in his hand. 'Worse thing is, I can't tell a soul. So, what now?'

'We fly back to Pittsburgh. I can make a stop at Dulles if that's where you need to be?'

'Much obliged,' Ray told her. He kept his voice low as they walked back towards the Humvees. 'You know, I'm still struggling with all of this. Our own president, for god's sake.'

'C'mon, Ray. It wouldn't be the first time a sitting president has ordered the murder of innocents. It's merely a question of scale. Must be a bitch for you, though, sitting on a scoop like this one.'

'Some stories are best left untold,' Ray told her. They climbed inside the leading Humvee and the driver pulled away, the other vehicle following behind.

'Back to the aircraft, ma'am?' the young buzzcut asked.

Holden nodded. 'As fast as you like.'

Ray turned to the Special Agent. 'What's the hurry?'

Holden's face was lost in shadow. 'I need to get home, make plans with Tommy and the kids. In case those *forces of good* that Parker spoke of are unsuccessful.'

Ray didn't respond. Instead he watched the passing woods, the shadows between the tress now dark and impenetrable. The scene reminded him of his escape from Lubbock, and that same fear and uncertainty returned once more. *Vanessa's being prudent*, he told himself, and he wondered if he should adopt a similar mindset, make his own plan. Perhaps he would. Perhaps he should, but the more he considered it, the more he preferred to hang his hat on Parker's words, the advice he'd shared before his car had pulled away.

Have faith…

It was pretty much all Ray had left.

THREE STRETCHERS OUTSIDE FLAGSTAFF

THEY COULDN'T USE THE ROADS BECAUSE THEY HAD NO IDEA whom they could trust.

The area was remote and sparsely populated, and the people who lived there might've been asked to watch for strangers, to write down license plate numbers and take photographs if they saw any out-of-state vehicles nosing around the area. To be a good neighbour and pick up the phone.

Some of those people would be civilians, recipients of the occasional gratuity, courtesy of the benevolent billionaire who lived on the secluded ranch in the Kaibab National Forest in northern Arizona. And then there were the park rangers, an organisation of more diligent observers, some of whom might've been duped into believing they were helping to protect the privacy of an American patriot.

So the roads were out.

The sky above the Kaibab National Forest was not.

The deployment involved four aircraft, two C-17 Globe-masters and two V-22 Ospreys. The C-17s had taken off from Fort Bragg in North Carolina, transporting a Joint Special Operations Task Force comprised of assaulters from SEAL

Team Six's Red Squadron and operators from Delta Force's D Squadron. After three hours and twenty-eight minutes, the C-17s landed at Kirtland Airforce base in New Mexico, where the JSOTF HQ and Delta Force recce troop elements disembarked. The HQ team was driven straight to the 58th Special Operations Wing where they would set up their Tactical Operations Centre, while the Delta operators boarded two waiting V-22 Ospreys. Shortly afterwards, all four aircraft lifted off into the night sky and headed west. After another hour of flight time — and taking slightly different courses — the C-17s levelled out at ten thousand feet above the Grand Canyon.

Inside each aircraft, the two-minute warning sounded and the Special Forces teams went to work, switching from the C-17s inline feeds to their portable oxygen bottles. They checked equipment, then each other for signs of hypoxia and decompression sickness. The High-Altitude-High-Opening jump was being performed much lower than usual, but these men never took anything for granted. Separated by eleven miles of freezing night air, assaulters and operators on both planes gathered near their respective ramps, their clothing and equipment buffeted by the wind, their experienced eyes searching the mountainous terrain, the distant clusters of city lights, and the bright, looping necklace of Highway 64 far below. Everything in between was a black void.

Hand signals were given and acknowledged. Final checks were made. Gloved fingers were flexed as all eyes turned to the Jumpmaster, to the amber light that glowed on the airframe above his head.

Green light on —

From the rear of both aircraft, a total of sixty-two SEALs, Green Berets and CIA paramilitaries stepped off their respective ramps and into the darkness. Chutes deployed within fifteen seconds and the teams formed up into high-altitude stacks, riding the gentle northern winds towards the Landing Zones thirteen miles away.

To the south, the SEAL element drifted down without incident, spiralling lower until the wide field below was visible to all. Six miles to the west, the Delta element had identified their own LZ, a narrow but elongated meadow surrounded by stunted spruce and Scotch pines. The HAHO stacks separated and the parachutists followed each other down. As the earth rushed to meet them, ram-air parachutes flared and booted feet hit the ground running. Harnesses were unbuckled and shrugged off, and canopies left to drift across field and meadow. Time was short, and there were several miles of ground to cover.

Further to the north, the Delta recce troops exited the V-22s and made their own cold and uneventful journey to earth. Their LZ was a vast, overgrown paddock located close to an abandoned ranger station, and they hit their target with silent, experienced accuracy.

Soon after, the encrypted calls went out to the TOC back at Kirtland; *three teams down and advancing to target.*

The assault was being monitored by two Gray Eagle UAVs, both of them mounted with the latest wide-area motion imaging cameras, giving the remote pilots at Creech AFB, Nevada, a crystal-clear, god-like view of the target and surrounding area. And there was a lot of information to process.

The target was a huge, sprawling ranch that nestled in a wide valley surrounded by low hills to the north and west, and open pasture to the south and east. As the UAVs flew high, lazy circles above the target's fifteen-thousand square acres, the Air Force pilots watched the three assault elements closing in on the main compound, a collection of barns, stables and equipment sheds, and thermal imaging revealed at least thirty armed hostiles within a hundred yards of the single-storey main ranch house. There were other patrols further out, moving on foot or driving along trails and tracks in open-backed pickups. There was no sense of urgency, no rapid, defensive deployments. For the private security force protecting the ranch, things were quiet, perhaps a little mundane.

Watching the Joint Special Operations Task Force converging on their target, the airmen at Creech knew all that was about to change.

THE SENIOR NURSE SWITCHED OFF THE MONITORING EQUIPMENT and the warning tone died.

Bob Blake stood in silence for a moment, gazing at the jaundiced husk of a man with whom he'd spent half his life with as they'd built a multi-billion dollar empire from the ground up. He felt a little sad, and also a little scared; cancer cared nothing for wealth or status. Matt had spared no expense, but in the end the disease was unstoppable. Blake briefly imagined the financial rewards of a one-stop cure for cancer, but it wasn't about money anymore; he'd need several lifetimes to spend what he'd already accumulated. Now, it was all about power, and once it had shifted to a single global throne, Amy Coffman would have to one day anoint a successor. Blake couldn't see any reason why it shouldn't be him, but recently he'd displeased her majesty. The grand plan had hit a couple of snags, and now it was time to get it back on track.

Matt's medical team stood around the room, half a dozen solemn-faced carers and nurses, two of whom were misty-eyed. They'd been paid handsomely for their services, and their confidentiality agreements locked them into a lifetime of absolute secrecy, but Blake wondered how long that would last now that Matt was dead. They would've heard Matt's drug-fuelled ramblings about depopulation, the H-1 virus, the garbled references to Mumbai and Shanghai. He wondered how many of them had joined the dots when Matt had clapped feebly at the TV as the news of Lubbock broke. Blake wanted to ask them, but it was pointless. They knew. Which was why they had to go.

'I want to thank you all for your kindness and dedication,' Blake told them. 'I know Matt and his family appreciated everything you did for him.'

'Would you like me to speak to Missus Sorenson?' the senior nurse asked. Her name was Estevez, a spare, fifty-something Mexican health professional.

'I'll take care of it,' Blake told her, and he would. Matt and his wife Beth had lived separate lives for many years, an arrangement that suited them both. 'In the meantime I want the body prepped for transport. And let's get rid of all this equipment, okay?' He lifted a radio to his mouth. 'Raul, meet me at the ranch house.'

Blake met him in the lobby by the main door. Raul Molina was a former commander of Peru's First Special Forces Brigade and the ranch's head of security. He wore jeans, a fur-lined denim jacket and an open-necked shirt. Strapped to his thigh was a large black pistol.

'Jefe?'

'Mister Sorenson is dead.'

Molina didn't blink. 'My condolences, Señor Blake.'

'I want you to take his body to the Medical Examiner's Office in Flagstaff tomorrow morning. They'll be expecting you.'

'Of course.'

Molina turned away as he answered a radio message. Blake caught a look on the Peruvian's pockmarked face.

'Everything okay?'

'The lookout post on the west ridge hasn't checked in. I'm going to take a drive up there.'

'Is there a problem?'

Molina shrugged. 'Probably a radio issue.'

309

'Keep me posted.'

The security chief left the building and Blake followed him a few moments later, pulling on a thick parka as he stepped out into the cold night air. He headed across the hard-packed dirt turnaround towards the single-storey prefabricated building that served as the ranch's security hub. Inside, two men sat in front of several monitors and a big chess-board screen of remote CCTV feeds, most of which were located within three hundred yards of the compound. There were a couple of others, covering the three-mile-long access road and the main gate out of the highway, and it pissed Blake off. He had more cameras in his Seattle home than here at the ranch.

'Hola,' Blake said, greeting the two Peruvians.

They smiled and nodded respectfully.

'Have we got a camera up on the west ridge?'

'No, señor.'

Blake swore quietly under his breath. He stood behind them for a few minutes, watching the low-light images. Aside from the occasional bug or a night bird, he didn't see anything that could —

'What's that?' Blake pointed to one of the feeds. 'Punch it up on the big screen.'

'Si, señor.'

The chessboard disappeared, replaced by a large, green-tinted image of the southern field. There was something in the long grass, a dark, moving shape that suddenly stopped. Blake couldn't make it out, the frozen form not quite revealing itself, its body made up of hues and shadows that blended perfectly with its background. Then it moved again, jumping once, twice, before bolting across the field.

A deer.

The Peruvians grinned.

Blake smirked too.

•   •   •

MIKE SAVAGE CRINGED AS THE BUCK LEAPT OVER HIM AND thundered away, its white tail bouncing wildly before disappearing into the darkness. He stayed perfectly still, crouched in the tall grass, surrounded by the dark forms of his SOG team. Red Squadron was spread further out across the field, silent, invisible to the naked eye, but through Mike's helmet-mounted QuadEye panoramic Night Vision Device, their thermal ID patches glowed in the dark.

They were two hundred yards short of the ranch's perimeter fence. Such was the stealthy nature of their approach that even the white-tail was oblivious to their presence until it had almost stumbled upon Mike. Now it was gone, and the peace of the wilderness returned.

A cold but gentle wind stirred the tall grass, providing cover for their silent approach. The night was moonless and clear, and stars dusted the sky. As Mike moved low and slow he listened to the comms traffic in his headset, the messages from TOC, from the UAV operators in Nevada, from the Delta teams to the north and west. Mike's brief was simple; allow the SEALs to clear a path to the compound and secure the target, alive. There was no room for screwups, not this time.

He watched the grass ahead of him stir as the Navy assaulters closed in on the perimeter fence. Billy Finch was just ahead of him, and he gestured for Mike to wait. Very, very slowly, Mike lifted his head until his optical tubes barely cleared the grass. He saw several security guards wandering back-and-forth, their chatter carried on the wind, along with the occasional whiff of cigarette smoke. They were well-armed, with pistols and M4 carbines, but they lacked the discipline, training and technical sophistication of the Americans watching them.

The SEALs on point would be much closer to the fence. Their weapons would be raised, their targets framed in their battle sights, their trigger fingers ready while they waited for the long guns in the hills to start whittling down the numbers.

. . .

THE DELTA SNIPERS OWNED THE HIGH GROUND.

There were sixteen operators, eight teams of two spread along the gentle rise of the wooded northern and western ridges that overlooked the main compound. Each team consisted of a spotter and a shooter armed with a Barrett MK 21 Advanced Sniper Rifle, and they had positioned themselves carefully to provide a clear view of the target area and an effective cross-fire envelope.

They had advanced to target quickly, covering almost three miles of wooded and open ground and killing six Peruvian guards in the process before reaching the foot of the low hills. They'd been warned about the lookout post on the western ridge, and two operators had moved in and killed two more sentries with suppressed weapons before calling the others up. Now they were spread out along two hundred and fifty yards of ridge line, expertly camouflaged and well-armed. One of the spotters, a Spanish-speaker, monitored a captured radio. The sudden and violent deaths of eight guards had yet to be discovered. They were still golden.

Below them, their Delta brothers from D Squadron had circled the rise and were now in position close to the perimeter fence. Four hundred and fifty yards away, the SEALs held position on the southern flank. Above them, the Gray Eagles fed live video back to the TOC. The task force was set and ready.

Down in the compound, halogen lights threw long shadows across the dirt. Guards wandered to and fro, unknowingly tracked through high-precision scopes. Cigarettes glowed. The wind lifted snatches of chatter up over the ridge line.

Final adjustments were made for range and windage. Breathing was regulated. Fingers curled around triggers as targets were centred.

The green light would come at any moment.

THE JEEP CHEROKEE WHINED TOWARDS THEM ALONG THE ACCESS road.

The four Delta operators were less than a mile from the compound, spread out in the grass, guns up. Headlights flared and NVGs were flipped up onto ballistic helmets. Four barrels tracked the driver, the engine block, the two passengers. The jeep cruised along the asphalt, biding its own sweet time. At fifty yards the operators opened fire. The driver's head snapped backwards as rounds punched through the windshield, and then through his left eye and throat. The jeep veered off the road and hit a power pole, its back wheels bouncing off the ground in a cloud of dust.

The Delta operators were already moving towards the disabled vehicle. The driver took another safety round through the skull. As the Delta semi-circle closed in, the survivors tumbled out. The rear seat passenger tried to bring a pistol to bear but he was dead before he could use it, his torso punctured by six high-velocity rounds. The front-seat passenger was on all fours, crawling away through the wash of headlights, a dark stain soaking the back of his sheepskin coat. Puffs of wool exploded as two more rounds put him down in the grass.

The jeep's engine was switched off and the lights were extinguished. Darkness closed in. The cooling engine ticked. The Delta team moved quickly. The jeep wasn't the target; it was the pole the vehicle had smashed into.

The power distribution box was mounted near the top, close to the drooping power lines, and they used the roof of the jeep to get to it. An explosive charge was attached and the operators took cover.

'Firing.'

The charge blew, the pole crowned with a sudden flash of

orange light. The detonation rumbled across the prairie. The electrical distribution box fizzed and popped and sparks showered to the ground.

Less than a mile away, the compound was suddenly plunged into darkness.

The call went out, heard by sixty-two assaulters, operators and CIA paramilitaries across the encrypted radio net.

'All call-signs, execute, execute, execute.'

THE DELTA SNIPERS OPENED UP FROM THE TOP OF THE RIDGE, dropping fourteen of their nineteen intended targets in the first volley of suppressed fire. They were some of the best sharpshooters in the world, and by the time the surviving guards registered the crack of a supersonic round fizzing by them, the operators had already reloaded and reacquired. None of the Peruvians heard the second shots that killed them.

'WHAT THE FUCK JUST HAPPENED!'

Torches snapped on inside the security portacabin, waving across the equipment. Everything was out; terminals, screens, light, everything.

'Go fire up the generator. Move!' One of the Peruvians sprang from his chair and Blake followed him outside, snatching the radio from his pocket. 'Raul! Come back!' Then Blake froze. Between the security hut and the ranch house, he saw a body lying on the ground.

'Go for Raul.'

'What the fuck is happening? I got a dead guy here and all the power just — '

The static nearly deafened him.

He heard Raul scream something in Spanish.

'Raul! Come in!' More static, then a flurry of garbled

messages all in Spanish. Across the compound he saw the bunk house door fly open and the Peruvian guards fan out across the property, guns waving in all directions. Bullets whizzed and cracked, and a couple of guys fell to the ground.

Blake snatched up the dead guy's M4 carbine and ran for the ranch house. It was a raid, had to be. FBI, military, whatever, and in that instant, Bob Blake knew it was all over. His heart raced. It was time to get out, time to implement his plan. After everything he'd done, it would've been stupid not to have one.

There was a back route off the property, a series of trails and wooded tracks that would take him out onto Highway 64 and then on to the Interstate. From there it was a three-hour drive to the executive terminal at McCarran Airport in Vegas where a private jet would transport him to Mexico City. He had money banked all over the world in dozens of secret accounts. No one would ever find him.

He burst through the door of the ranch house and headed to the suite of rooms on his right. He flung the door open and saw the Polish deployment team had taken cover behind the furniture. One of the windows had shattered, and the sound of gunfire rippled across the night air.

'What's happening?' one of them asked, a shaven-headed man with high-cheek bones and a broken nose.

Blake crouched down in the doorway. 'It's a police raid. Are you good to go?'

'We need the passports,' he told Blake.

'We're out of time. There's a Mercedes in the garage, fuelled and ready to go. The key's in the glove box. Take it, get out of here. Hit as many cities as you can.'

The Pole frowned. 'Here? In America?'

'Yes. Now go!'

The men, all former Polish military, scattered for their coats and rucks and bundled from the ranch house. Blake scuttled across the room and ducked into the kitchen. Outside he saw men running, falling. He didn't have much time.

The pantry was filled with shelves of canned and dried goods. There were four hooks on the rear wall, with aprons dangling from them. Blake pulled down hard on the two middle hooks and the door swung inward to reveal a metal ladder that disappeared into a black shaft. At the bottom, a tunnel ran beneath the prairie to a barn just over half a mile away. There was a pickup in the barn, and Blake would use it to navigate the trails and get away. Matt had the whole thing installed when he'd first bought the ranch, an emergency escape if ever one was needed. Blake felt like kissing his rapidly cooling corpse.

He pulled the door to and headed across the hallway into Sorenson's wing. There was business to take care of before he could make his own escape.

It was pitch black inside, and Blake cocked the M4. He could hear frightened whispers as he crept through the darkened kitchen. He barged the door open to Matt's private lounge and saw ghostly white figures in the gloom. The medical team, all cowering in the dark. *Excellent.*

'Everything's okay,' Blake assured them.

'Mister Blake!' a female voice cried. 'What's happening!' It was Estevez, and she sounded terrified.

'Who's shooting?' another voice gasped.

'Just stay still,' Blake ordered, his eyes squinting in the darkness. The figures were moving, some crouched beneath the windows, some hiding behind furniture. And then he remembered. He ran a hand along the M4's barrel and found the underslung torch. He flipped it on and swung the beam around the room.

'I need everybody against the wall, quickly.'

'Why?' someone whimpered.

Then someone else screamed, 'He's got a gun!'

Blake swept the barrel towards the voice, saw a male

nurse crouched behind a Lazy Boy. He opened fire, the sound deafening, the muzzle flash flickering off the walls, the chair disintegrating in a cloud of dust and stuffing. He swung the weapon around. The others were backing away into a corner, hands raised, pleading for mercy.

Sorry, muchachos, no can do.

Blake squeezed the trigger —

Click.

He squeezed again.

Click.

A male nurse roared, charging through the torch beam. He cannoned into Blake at speed, knocking him to the ground, the M4 skittering across the tiled floor. The nurse was a big guy, and his fists pounded into Blake's face. Blake tried to get up but the others swarmed on top of him, knocking the wind from his lungs. He felt more punches raining down and he tried to twist away —

'Hold him still!'

He recognised the voice. Estevez. No longer frightened.

'His head! Hold his head!'

Strong hands pushed down on his temple, clamped his jaw. He smelled bad breath and sweat. He winced as something pricked his neck, and then a warm sensation began to spread through his chest, through his arms and legs. The guy straddling him climbed off. His head was released. Blake smiled in the darkness.

'Hola,' he chuckled. He couldn't move his limbs, and neither did he care. He felt wonderfully woozy.

Estevez leaned over him, lifted an eyelid.

'Get him into the treatment room. Quickly.'

Such a sweet voice, Blake thought.

It was the last one he heard.

· · ·

MIKE WAS ON HIS FEET, MOVING FAST TOWARDS THE BOUNDARY fence. He vaulted it, leaping over the corpses of the dead guards. Ahead, a dozen thermal helmet patches glowed as the SEALs raced across the paddock, unhindered by heavy packs. Mike and his guys also travelled light, just personal rigs stuffed with spare magazines and explosive ordinance.

'Be advised, forty-plus hostiles in the compound, another thirteen, one-three, approaching from the east on foot.'

Friend and foe alike were converging on the compound, but the security force remained unaware or possibly ignorant of the fact that they were up against the very best the US military had to offer.

Zip.

Zip. Zip.

Incoming rounds cracked past them. Somewhere to his right Mike heard a grunt and a body fall to the ground.

A hundred yards to the inner fence.

He saw guards fanning out along its length, taking cover behind thick posts, opening fire with their assault weapons. A couple of them had NVGs and were laying down some accurate rounds. They were a problem, and the SEALs knew it too. The call went out, and up on the hill a couple of the Delta long guns switched targets and began dropping the guards with lethal efficiency. The SOG team made it to the fence. SEALs broke left and right and sprinted towards the compound. Mike turned to his guys who were crouched in the grass around him.

'Moving on three,' Mike told them. 'One, two — '

And then he was moving, looping towards the asphalt road to the east. They made it to the boundary fence and sprang over the top, landing on the grass verge that ran alongside the road. He keyed his radio.

'Sierra-Oscar-One moving north on access road.'

He watched another SEAL element leapfrog past them,

firing and manoeuvring. Then Mike was moving too. Rounds cracked off the tarmac in front of him.

'Contact left!'

He shouldered his weapon and returned fire at the targets behind the barn door up ahead. The guys behind him also engaged, their rounds splintering the timber frames. Both shooters were toes up in seconds. Mike raced to the edge of the barn. Tapper and the others were right behind him.

'Hornet Teams, friendlies in the compound. Clear targets only.'

Up on the ridge, the Delta snipers would now take clean shots only. Mike saw the SEALs racing into the compound from either side. The Delta operators would be closing in from the west, tightening the noose.

Mike led his men to the edge of the barn. A hundred yards to the north, the security team were falling back to the bunkhouse, a large single-story building with several doors and lots of windows. They fired wildly in all directions as they backed inside.

At Mike's ten o'clock there was a large, open-sided barn with a row of vehicles inside. It would serve as cover before they assaulted the main building, but to get there they had to cross fifty yards of open ground. Mike turned to Tapper and pointed.

'We're moving to that vehicle shed. Stay tight.'

'Roger.'

Mike did the count, and then he was sprinting across open ground towards the shed. Boots pounded behind him. Gunfire roared, but it was wild and ineffectual. The shed bobbed in his night vision —

Lights blinded him.

The Mercedes roared and drove right at them. Mike's team were caught in the open. There was no time to shoot, no time to do anything but leap out of the way —

Mike threw himself to the left, rolling across the dirt, his eyes

319

blinded by white fireworks. He felt a rush of wind as the vehicle missed him by inches. He heard a desperate cry and a sickening crunch. He came up on his knee, weapon shouldered, trying to focus. His eyesight returned and he flipped his QuadEyes down. He saw Boswell lying motionless on the floor, panting. Further away, he watched Miller and Flynn unloading everything they had into the escaping vehicle. High-velocity rounds and clouds of buckshot punched through glass and metal. The Mercedes fish-tailed towards the asphalt road in a cloud of dust.

It was going to make it.

Flynn dropped to his knee, dropped his aim and fired his M4 shotgun several times. The Mercedes' rear off-side tyre blew out, and the SUV careered off the road, crashing through the wooden boundary fence and coming to a stop a short distance away. He saw a group of SEALs converging on the shattered vehicle, firing as they went. He saw uniforms moving swiftly through the headlights, then more shots. Making sure.

A round kicked up dirt close by. Mike made it to the shed, took cover behind the cinderblock wall. Miller and Flynn dragged Boswell to safety.

'Where's Don?'

Miller shook his head. 'Didn't see him.'

Flynn waved to a group of SEALs taking cover behind the barn they'd just left. 'Need a corpsman here!' Three of them sprinted across and skidded to a stop behind the shed. They went to work on Boswell immediately. On the net, medevac choppers were confirmed inbound.

'Take care of him,' Mike told them, and then they were moving again, sprinting across another stretch of open ground for the ranch house. They made it to the side of the building. Another team of SEALs came up behind them, led by Billy Finch.

'Hostiles have fallen back into the bunk house,' the senior chief told him. 'They must have a shitload of ammunition because they're laying down some intense fire. Delta's moving into a blocking position, gonna choke 'em off.'

Mike slapped the wall of the ranch house. 'I need to get inside here, asap. Give me suppressing fire on that bunk house right now. '

Finch keyed his radio. A moment later the bunkhouse doors and windows were being shredded by incoming. Mike pulled a grenade from his kit. 'Popping smoke.'

He lobbed it out into the compound. Miller did the same, Finch's guys too. In seconds, the ground in front of the ranch house was wrapped in a chemical fog.

'Moving.'

Flash bangs went through the doors and windows. The ranch house shuddered with the force of the detonations, and then Mike was inside, weapon up, barrel sweeping the smoky darkness. Mike signalled to Finch who broke right with his team. Mike headed left.

They spread out, moving tactically through some kind of lounge area furnished with scattered couches and a large TV on a sideboard. There was blood on the wall and Miller motioned towards a pair of legs splayed out behind a shredded Lazy Boy. There was a body there, a Hispanic man with three large, bloody holes in his white tunic. His mouth was open and his sightless eyes stared up at Mike.

Shhh!

Gun barrels swivelled towards a partially open door. Mike took point, covered by Flynn and his Benelli, ready to discharge a cloud of killer buckshot. Miller stayed back and low, his trigger finger ready.

Mike heard a hushed conversation in Spanish, male and female voices followed by another urgent *shhh!* He was within touching distance of the door, his barrel pointed at the crack, the white phosphor imaging of his QuadEye's turning darkness into daylight. The door was open about three inches. As he reached out with his hand a moustachioed face filled the gap. The eyes widened and the face disappeared.

'Don't shoot, please!' pleaded a heavily-accented voice. 'We're nurses! Por favor!'

Mike backed away from the door. *'Policia,'* he lied. 'All of you, outside now, hands on your heads! *Movimiento!'*

The door opened and several men and women hurried out into the lounge, their hands clasped over their heads. They all wore white tunics, and Mike ordered them down on the floor. Miller and Flynn started binding their hands with plastic ties.

'Watch them,' Mike said, then he entered the room, gun up, ready to unload. The room was dominated by a high-tech patient bed and reeked of antiseptic. Tables stacked with boxes of medical equipment and drugs lined the walls. Someone was packing up, their services no longer required. That would explain the body bag on the trolley next to the bed. The window was closed, the blind lowered. Outside, the shooting sounded less intense.

Mike was more interested in the body on the floor, a man lying face down, his arms and legs tied with strips of torn sheet and a couple of trouser belts.

'Pat, get in here.' Flynn stepped into the room. 'ID the body.'

While Flynn checked the body bag, Mike knelt down next to the live one. His eyes were closed and he was breathing deeply, oblivious to his bonds. Mike grabbed his bearded jaw and twisted it towards him, comparing the face to the mugshot on his MX50 Tactical Tablet. They were one and the same. He called it in to Kirtland and received a confirmation.

'Talk to me, Pat.'

'It's Matthew Sorenson.'

'Get the lead nurse in here.'

A few moments later Flynn escorted a Hispanic medic into the room, her hands still bound behind her back, her eyes white and wide in the darkness. She must've been pretty intimidated by the heavily-armed men with the insect-like helmets surrounding her.

'What's your name?' Mike asked her.

'Rosa Estevez. I was Mister Sorenson's primary carer.'

'What happened here?'

Estevez told him and Mike nodded.

'I'm sorry about your friend.'

'Hector was a good man,' she sniffed.

Everyone flinched as several deep concussions shook the room. Mike led Estevez outside and eased her to the tiled floor. 'Stay down until I say so,' he told them all. Then he pointed at Flynn.

'Pat, you're with me. Ty, I'm sending Billy back here to provide security.' He called Finch on the radio, and a few moments later he met the SEAL in the lobby.

'Location is secure,' Finch reported.

Mike cocked a thumb over his shoulder. 'Need your team back there to watch over the HVT. He's sedated, so he'll need to be stretchered out. My guys will need help prepping him for transport. And get a corpsman to monitor him, make sure he stays alive.'

'Roger that.'

The shooting had almost stopped. Mike moved to the main door and took a quick look outside. There was smoke pouring from the windows of the bunkhouse. Guards were stumbling outside, coughing and hacking. Voices screamed in Spanish, telling them to get down. Most obeyed. Some came out blasting. It was the last thing they ever did.

After a few more minutes, the shooting had all but stopped. The radio net was filled with chatter as SEAL and Delta elements confirmed their objectives. Mike made his own call.

'Sierra-Oscar-One, what's the status on the medevac?'

'Birds inbound, ETA four minutes.'

With Flynn following, Mike ducked outside and ran across

the compound to the shed wall. Boswell was still there, surrounded by four SEAL corpsmen. The CIA operative's face was pale and twisted in pain.

'How's he looking?' Mike asked, kneeling down.

'Broken femur, broken humerus, busted ribs, probable punctured lung.'

'They h-h-hit Don,' Boswell gasped.

'Don't talk,' Mike told him. Definitely a punctured lung. 'Medevac is inbound. Hang in there.'

With mounting dread, Mike stood up and headed towards the shattered fence. The Mercedes was still in the field, its bodywork and passengers riddled with bullets, but Mike wasn't interested in that.

'Oh Jesus,' he heard Flynn whisper behind him.

Just beyond the broken fence, a body lay on the asphalt, covered with a ground sheet and weighed down with a rifle. The edges flapped and rustled in the wind as two SEAL corpsmen packed away their med bags.

Mike stood over the corpse. It was surrounded by bloody bandages and discarded med wrappers.

'He went under the hood of that Merc,' one of the corpsmen explained. 'Got trapped beneath the axle. There was nothing we could do.'

Tapper's left boot was missing, and his foot and leg were mangled to bloody pulp. Mike wasn't going to lift the sheet. He didn't want to remember his friend that way.

The radio net buzzed. The compound had been fully secured, and the clatter of approaching helicopters rose and fell across the prairie. LED landing beacons pulsed in nearby fields as wounded SEALs and D-Boys were helped to the LZ. A couple of SEALs headed over with a combat stretcher.

'We'll take it from here,' the corpsman said.

Mike shook his head. 'He's one of ours. I'd be obliged if you could secure him to the stretcher though.'

The SEALs didn't argue. 'Yes, sir.'

'Wait with him,' he told Flynn. 'I'll police up the HVT, then meet you back here. We all go together.'

Flynn's face was grim. 'Roger.'

Mike jogged back to the compound, where the fog of smoke and the acrid tang of cordite hung on the air. In front of the bunkhouse the surviving guards had been bound and hooded. The Gray Eagles were still overhead, still watching and reporting, but the assault phase was effectively over.

A Chinook cleared the ridge line and thundered overhead, dropping towards the LZ a short distance away. Dust swirled across the compound as more helicopters came in fast and low. When he got back to Sorenson's treatment room, Blake's unconscious body had been strapped to a stretcher while Estevez's medical team were gathered on the couches, watched over by Miller and the other SEALs. There were FBI agents on the inbound Chinooks who would process the civilians.

'Let's move him.'

Blake was lifted and carried outside. Surrounded by SEALs, his head and torso covered with body armour, the oblivious industrialist was stretchered down to the LZ where the helicopters waited, their massive rotors beating the grass. Mike watched a contingent of Chemical Corps troops and several FBI agents going the other way, heading into the compound. Blake was loaded onto the waiting Chinook and strapped down. Boswell was next, secured to another stretcher and tended to by the USAF medical team aboard the aircraft. Last to be loaded was Don Tapper, whose stretcher was secured to the hard points at Mike's feet. The SOG leader found it difficult to look down at his friend.

More SEALs and D-Boys climbed aboard. The powerful turboshaft engines cranked up, then the aircraft lifted off the ground, ramp down, skimming low across the prairie before starting to climb.

Mike looked back, saw the compound still blanketed in

darkness, the white smoke of the smouldering bunkhouse drifting across the ridge line, the pulsing lights of the helicopters and landing beacons in the surrounding fields. It was a lot of risk, a lot of effort and moving parts just to bag one guy, but they'd done it, with no small thanks to the Estevez woman and her team. Now it was about making sure Don's death, and the deaths of so many others, were not in vain. For the first time since Philip had slipped through his fingers, Mike felt a little better about himself. Not much, but it was still an improvement.

Then he looked down at his friend. The XO's star would be carved into the white marble wall at Langley, and his name entered into the Book of Honour, and that's where Don Tapper's story would officially end. For his brothers in the Special Operations Group, he would never be forgotten.

The Chinook banked to the southeast. The wilderness flashed beneath them as the aircraft continued its climb, heading at maximum speed towards the New Mexico border.

SAY HELLO, WAVE GOODBYE

'ARE YOU OKAY, MADAM PRESIDENT?'

Coffman nodded, a faint smile lingering on her lips. 'I'm fine, thank you Drew. It's just a headache. I can't seem to shake it.'

The Secretary of Defence stepped a little closer. 'Would you like me to call the doctor?'

'No, I'm sure it's nothing. I'm just tired, that's all.'

'Why don't you get some rest? It's pretty quiet right now.'

Clark offered her a sympathetic smile. Or was it patronising? Coffman couldn't tell which. She was losing her edge. No, not just her edge.

She got up from the conference table, and what remained of her National Security Council stood too. Up on the video wall, Shanghai and Lubbock were still the major focus of attention. Politically, the Chinese were starting to thaw, but their diplomatic silence had been replaced by a simmering anger. There was talk of retribution, of reparations. On whom, from whom, Beijing wasn't saying, but Coffman sensed trouble on the horizon.

In Texas, the city of Lubbock had been completely walled-in. People had been rescued, but not as many as Coffman had anticipated. Not that she cared of course, but perceptions were everything now.

She left the conference room and retired to her private suite, grateful for the opportunity to avoid human contact for a while. The headache had lingered at the back of her skull for the past twenty-four hours, and she certainly felt a little lethargic, but then again she'd been burning both ends of the candle for weeks now. She was entitled to a little down time, goddamit. After all, she was still the President of the United States.

She undressed in the master bedroom and took a long hot shower. She wrapped herself in a thick white bathrobe with the presidential seal embroidered above her left breast and poured herself a generous bourbon on ice. She popped two Tylenol, then curled up on a couch, watching the darkening sky outside the windows, the flurries of snow whipping past the thick glass. Christmas was approaching and the winter storms had finally arrived, driving snow across the Rockies and laying a thick white blanket across the plateau below. The skies above were leaden and ominous, a perfect metaphor for current events, Coffman reflected.

Erik was still missing.

Now Bob Blake was missing too.

She'd ordered Charlie Schultz to find him, and now *he'd* vanished. Only Karen Baranski remained by her side, although Coffman sensed a growing distance between them. Her phone had barely rang in the last four days. She felt like an outsider in her own Situation Room. Half her Security Council had left for Washington, citing urging departmental or personal issues, leaving behind nameless subordinates in their wake. Only her SecDef remained, and Coffman had sensed a growing assertiveness in Clark's speech and manner. The conclusion was inescapable and profoundly devastating. The walls were closing in.

The cordless phone trilled with an incoming call. Coffman reached over and plucked it off the table.

'This is the President.'

Silence. Then, 'Hello, Amy.'

Coffman bolted upright in her chair, her heart pounding. 'Erik?'

'How are you?'

'I've been better,' she confessed, but she smiled in spite of herself. 'It's good to hear your voice. I've missed you.'

'I've missed you too.'

Coffman leaned back in her chair, her legs curling beneath her. She sipped her drink, ice cubes singing off the glass of her crystal tumbler.

'It's a little early, isn't it?'

Coffman ignored the observation. 'Where are you, Erik? Can I see you?'

'I don't think so. Besides, you were right; orange doesn't look that great on me.'

Her body chilled. She took a mouthful of bourbon, the dark liquid burning its way down to her stomach. 'Are they recording this?'

'They don't need you on tape, Amy. I've given them everything. Bob is singing like a canary too, or so they tell me.'

Coffman closed her eyes. So, it really was over. Strangely, she didn't feel any sudden anger or fear, or even desperation. No, what hurt her most was the betrayal. 'Why, Erik?'

The scorn in his voice stung her. 'Is that a joke? After everything we've done, the countless lives we've destroyed? I hate clichés, but I couldn't live with myself. Worse than that, I couldn't bring myself to look at you anymore. You'd become someone else, someone I didn't recognise. A monster, I finally realised.' He sighed deeply. 'So I guess I did it for both of us.'

Now it was Coffman's turn to scoff. 'How very noble of you. I'm sure that defence will go down well with a jury.'

'I'm not interested in saving myself. Whatever happens to me, whatever hole they drop me into, I'll go willingly because I deserve everything that's coming. Besides, I'm not going out like Charlie.'

Coffman gripped the phone a little tighter. 'Schultz?'

'The very same. He knew it was over, so he shot his wife, then he turned the gun on himself. They're keeping it under wraps for now. She had breast cancer, did you know that?'

Coffman's voice was a whisper. 'I didn't.'

'They'll probably frame it as a suicide pact.'

The line hissed softly for several moments. When Erik spoke again there was a terrible sadness in his voice. No, more than that, Coffman realised. A finality.

'Every night I think of that moment, back at the house, when I told you about the outbreak in Baghdad, remember? I should've talked you out of it, threatened you, walked away, but I didn't. Instead, I went with you, willingly. I could've saved us both. Now millions are dead.'

Coffman's emotions threatened to choke her. She swallowed her drink and put the glass down. 'You mustn't blame yourself. This was all me, all my doing.' Coffman closed her eyes and said, 'You've been a good friend, Erik. My only friend, in fact. I wish I'd realised that sooner.'

She sat forward, bare feet on the granite floor, her knees pressed tightly together, her body lost inside the bathrobe. She felt so small now, so powerless and insignificant. There was nothing left but words.

'Is this the last time we'll ever speak?'

More silence. Then, 'Yes, ma'am.'

She blinked the tears away. 'I'm going to miss you.'

The line hissed and crackled.

'Goodbye, Amy.'

Coffman closed her eyes, almost choking on the words. 'Take care of yourself please, Erik.'

The call was terminated. Coffman put the phone down,

her thoughts and emotions swirling like the flurries beyond the glass. The door hissed open behind her and Coffman spun around in her chair. Four people were coming down the steps towards her. Three of them she recognised; Vernon Brown, her ineffectual Vice President, SecDef Clark and the White House doctor. The fourth man was in his forties, with short grey hair and a square jaw. He wore a thick black parka, camouflage trousers and boots. Military or Secret Service, Coffman could only guess.

She got to her feet, pulling the robe tightly around her. All four looked at her with cold, unsympathetic eyes.

This is the end.

And the beginning of a journey into the unknown.

Strangely, she wasn't afraid. She could feel her heart beating a little faster but her hands were steady. A weight had been lifted from her shoulders. She had no cause to feel relieved but for reasons she couldn't explain, she did.

The party stopped short. Coffman cleared her throat. Perhaps there was an opportunity for one last bluff.

'What's the problem? Has something happened?'

The unanswered question hung on the air. Bluffing was clearly off the table.

Her VP was the first to speak. He glared at her, his head moving slowly from side to side. 'This gives us no pleasure —'

Coffman waved a dismissive hand. 'Oh do be quiet, Vernon. Why don't you practice tying your shoes while the grownups talk?' As Brown stuttered, Coffman's attention switched to the man in the parka. Her instincts told her he was the real power in the room.

'What happens now?'

He pointed to the chair she'd just vacated. 'Take a seat and roll up your sleeve.'

Her defiance evaporated in an instant. 'My sleeve? Why?'

The man stepped towards her. His nostrils flared and his

jaw was set like concrete. He looked at her like he'd just discovered a dog turd on his boot.

'My name is Foley, and from this moment on you will do exactly as I say, when I say it. If you deviate in any way, from any instruction, you'll be immediately transported to a military facility in North Dakota where you will be detained below ground for the rest of your natural life. There will be no trial. No one will ever visit you, and you'll never see daylight again. Ever. This is your first and only warning. Have I made myself clear?'

Coffman had never been so frightened in all her life. She sat down and rolled up her sleeve. The White House doctor stepped forward. Patterson was almost seventy, balding, a favourite-uncle type of guy. Not this time. He put his bag on the table and went to work, assembling a fresh hypodermic and needle, filling it with a clear liquid. He squeezed the air from the needle and turned her wrist over with cold fingers.

'Keep still.' He wiped the skin of her forearm with an antiseptic wipe.

Coffman couldn't help herself. 'What is it?'

'Quiet,' Foley snapped.

Patterson jabbed her vein without ceremony, pushing the liquid into her bloodstream. Coffman's heart rate skyrocketed. She had no idea what to expect next; death perhaps, or some kind of crippling poison. Her mind was filled with images of pain and death, and then her heart rate began to slow. She tried to speak and mumbled something unintelligible. Her eyes drooped and her chin dropped towards her chest. She dragged her head upright in an effort to stay conscious, but that battle, like everything else, was already lost.

The faces watching her melted like wax. The room swam, and her head felt as heavy as a cannonball.

She closed her eyes and was swallowed by the darkness.

• • •

THE DARK CHEVY MINIVAN CLEARED THE LAST OF THE SECURITY checkpoints and turned north onto Highway 67. Alone in the rear seat, Ray Wilson watched the razor wire fencing and guard towers of ADX Florence fall away behind him, and felt a palpable sense of relief. There was something deeply unsettling about spending any amount of time inside America's most secure prison. It was a facility that housed the worst of the worst in the harshest of conditions, and the walls felt impregnated with all the hopelessness humanity had to offer. It was without doubt the most depressing institution Ray had ever visited. But at least he could leave.

Erik Mulholland could not.

Ray knew that for the former White House Chief of Staff and erstwhile sophisticated urbanite, each waking moment in his spartan, subterranean cell would feel like hell on earth. No one doubted he deserved it. Even Mulholland himself had stated many times that he should rot, but Ray still found it difficult to reconcile the man and the crimes he'd committed. Mulholland had spent the past several days laying bare those crimes and those of his co-conspirators in minute detail, and yet Ray was still struggling with their motivations.

Effectively, Coffman had continued the work of her criminal predecessor, although in this instance the H-1 virus proved to be far more devastating than the Angola variant. The President had been manipulated, tempted by the prospect of ultimate power, and in turn had manipulated her cabal and others in an attempt to castrate America's enemies, reduce the world's population and create a single world government. It was the stuff of movies and fiction novels, and yet the President and her inner circle had considered the plan to be a viable one.

Ray wasn't sure if he could trust another politician again, and he'd been a cynical DC journalist for decades. He remembered how dismissive he'd been of the Alt-media, how he'd sneered at conspiracy theorists, only to discover that it was *his* eyes that had been blinded by what could only be described as institutional programming. He wondered how the rest of the country would react if they ever found out that two of their presidents had conspired to kill American citizens. In Coffman's case she'd actually succeeded, a crime for which Ray could never forgive her. Like everyone else who knew, he wanted justice, but some things were just not possible.

He glanced over his shoulder. The prison was far behind him now, nothing more than a bright strip of bright lights in the distance. He was glad to be leaving Colorado. For the last three days he'd been driven from his motel to the supermax prison, where he'd been escorted to an empty wing and a windowless, soundproofed interview room. Every day, at the stroke of nine a.m., Mulholland had been escorted in by four of the biggest prison guards Ray had ever seen, and he'd barely recognised the former White House Chief of Staff shuffling in their towering midst. His head had been shaved, he'd lost weight, and he appeared almost frail inside a baggy orange jump suit. His wrists and ankles were shackled in chains and he moved like an old man, taking small steps, his shoulders hunched. A man who carried a significant burden, Ray believed.

Mulholland only came alive when he sat in the chair in the middle of the room and began to tell his story. He'd been grilled by a dozen individuals from various intelligence organisations, none of whom could find any inconsistencies in his testimony, and all of whom had been sickened by it. Ray was the only member of the media allowed to attend, a request made by Mulholland himself, and granted in the spirit of transparency. Ray wasn't sure how long that spirit would last.

As the Chevy headed north towards the airport at Colorado Springs, he reflected on his own journey and rewound to where it had all began, at Kelly Novak's funeral. He'd made a promise to her mother Barbara, a promise he would now keep, although he would only give her a watered down version of the truth. He would tell her that Kelly's work had resulted in several high-profile arrests for murder, one of whom was a man complicit in the death of her daughter. Novak senior would understand the need for confidentiality, and would be comforted by the fact that Kelly hadn't died in vain. He'd also tell her about the new program at the Washington Times, to be named *The Kelly Novak Journalism Scholarship*. He hoped it would go some way to assuaging the pain that Barbara Novak still lived with. Only time would tell.

He pulled the phone out of his jacket and made a call. 'Tammy, it's Ray.'

'How'd it go?'

Ray glanced at the back of the driver's head. 'Let's just say I'm glad it's over.'

'Any surprises?'

'None that I can talk about, though I imagine the other attendees will be busy for a while.'

'Maybe I can squeeze you for a snippet or two over dinner. Tomorrow evening.'

'Sounds good,' Ray told her. 'I want to talk to you about a project, a book in fact. About Texas.'

'Deal. I'll ask Moira to book a table at The Oval for nine. We can watch the President's speech beforehand.'

Ray frowned. 'What speech?'

'She's addressing the nation tomorrow evening. The White House isn't elaborating.'

'Interesting,' Ray said. 'See you then.'

He ended the call and settled back in his seat. He was tired, and not just physically. Emotionally it had been a turbulent time. He needed to get away, to take stock and make sense of everything that had happened. He'd find somewhere warm and quiet, a place by the ocean where he could take long walks along the shoreline, where he could think, or maybe not think at all. Later, when he was ready, he would sit down and revisit Lubbock in all of its harrowing detail. Then he would tell his story.

To the west, the sun had dipped behind the jagged peaks of the Rockies, dusting the bleak, frozen landscape in soft reds and pinks. He thought about Erik Mulholland, a man who might never see such a sight ever again. It was all he deserved, but Ray couldn't help but think he was a victim in some sense. There were many more victims out there too, millions of them, in Iraq and China, in England and right here in the United States. Ray had almost become a statistic himself, and whatever twinges of sympathy he'd felt over the last three days were tempered by his memories of Lubbock, and the plain fact that Mulholland could've prevented it all.

But the man had given something back too.

Ray had his confession on tape, recorded in Cumberland before he'd driven Mulholland to the FBI Field Office in Pittsburg. They knew about the interview, about the copies lodged with lawyers, but nobody was compelling Ray to hand them over, just not to make them public. They would serve as insurance policies, as bulwarks against future tyranny, and they would guarantee Ray could live a life without looking over his shoulder.

'Could we have a little music?' he asked the driver.

'Sure.'

As luck would have it, he tuned in to a smooth jazz station, and Ray stretched out in the back seat, hoping the world was headed towards a future that was as uplifting and chilled as the music he was listening to. Knowing humanity as he did, its dreams and desires, its greed and cruelty, he seriously doubted it.

But there was always hope.

IMPEACH THIS

SHE STARED INTO THE CAMERA, RESOLUTE.

'I wish I could tell you that the world is now a safer place. I wish I could tell you that the threat has receded and things will soon return to normal, but to do so would be disingenuous.'

Coffman paused for a moment, a thin smile twisting the corners of her mouth.

'I wish I could tell you the doctors are wrong, but they are not. And so in this, my last goodnight as your President, I thank you for the opportunities you have given me. To have served this great nation has been the ultimate honour, and in leaving this office, I do so with a prayer; may God's grace be with you all in the days ahead. Thank you, and goodnight.'

Coffman stared into the camera, her face expressionless, her hands resting on the antique wood. She remained frozen in place, both physically and mentally. She'd delivered the pre-prepared speech flawlessly, barely needing the autocue in front of her desk. *Not your desk,* she corrected herself.

'And we're out,' said a voice from beyond the camera lights.

Coffman blinked as they were switched off. The TV equipment was quickly dismantled and people began to file out of the Oval Office. No one asked for permission, there were no *thank yous* or *goodbyes,* no smiles or handshakes, just suits and uniforms heading out of the room in relative silence. The only people who *did* watch her were four secret service agents, two on either side of the desk, all of them armed and grim-faced. One of them stared at Coffman with obvious contempt, and the former president believed that if she sneezed suddenly, the woman might well pull her service weapon and shoot her dead.

Maybe that's your way out, Coffman mused. She could go for a gun, and then be shot down. A final gesture of defiance, her blood splashed across the carpet, lying dead at the feet of the stone-faced lesbian. It was an option. Not a favourable one, but she was fast running out of those.

Suicide was for the weak and selfish, she'd always believed that, but lately it too had become an option. And why not? Her hopes and dreams had crumbled. There would be no global collapse, no Infection Wars that would see the dawn of a New American Empire, ruled over by Amy Coffman. All that was gone now. What lay ahead was grim uncertainty.

The last of the TV crew rolled their flight cases out of the room. There were a dozen people left, all talking in a quiet huddle as they watched her. No one smiled. It was like facing a firing squad. Most of them were members of her Security Council, plus several judges from the Supreme Court, the Speaker of the House, Vice President Shit-for-Brains and President-in-Waiting Drew Clark. *A good choice,* Coffman had to agree. Her former SecDef was smart, tough and capable, and a more readily-acceptable transition for the American people to accept. Plus she had the brains to keep the VP in his box.

Clark was staring at her, and Coffman smiled awkwardly. Clark averted her eyes and continued her quiet counsel. Her pulse quickened as she watched Foley break away from the group. The parka and boots were gone, replaced by a dark suit with a US flag pinned to his lapel. He stood silently in front of the desk, his hands folded in front of him as the presidential entourage filed out of the room. The door closed behind them. Coffman felt her heart thumping in her chest.

'On your feet,' Foley told her.

Coffman stood. She glanced at the agent to her left, at his gun beneath his jacket, but the glance was fleeting. There would be no suicidal drama played out here today. The plain fact was, while she had taken the lives of many, the erstwhile Commander in Chief didn't have the stomach to end her own. She was now at the mercy of others, and she would have to steel herself for whatever that might bring.

One of the Secret Service agents stepped forward and handed her a hat and coat.

'Put those on,' Foley commanded.

Coffman did as she was told, tugging on the quilted winter coat and a plain blue baseball cap that was slightly too big for her. She felt like a child, standing in an older sibling's hand-me-downs. The grown-ups inspected her. Foley nodded. Then the lights went out in the room. Coffman made an involuntary sound, a nervous yelp that she swallowed as quickly as she'd made it. She'd never been to Dakota, and she didn't want to give Foley the excuse to take her there.

'Let's move.'

The Secret Service agents formed a tight box around her and escorted her out of the Oval Office. *For the last time,* she knew. Strong fingers pinched her arms as she was led through the darkened building to the west exit. Beneath the portico outside a dark Ford Transit van waited. The side door was open and Coffman climbed inside. There were two men in the back seat, and one of them pointed to the space in between them. She sat down and handcuffs were locked around her wrists. Coffman almost smiled; this was not the way she ever thought it would end, but it proved that one never knew what games fate decided to play. Foley and the agents climbed aboard and the door slammed closed. Then they were moving.

The van left the White House by the 17th Street exit and turned south. Coffman watched through tinted windows as people barely gave them a glance. There was no motorcade, no police outriders or flashing lights. They slowed for traffic and stopped for red lights. No one paid them any notice. She was nothing now, inconsequential to the people and the world around her. She was worthless.

Foley spoke into his radio and the gate at Joint Base Andrews was raised. They drove straight through without checks and boarded a US Navy Boeing 737. There were no flight attendants, and Foley marched her to the back of the plane where her legs were shackled to her seat. She swallowed a quip about in-flight safety.

Her armed escort sat in nearby seats, but never too close, as if she herself were infected. The doors were set to automatic and the cabin lights were dimmed for takeoff. She heard the engines run up to speed and then they were moving, bouncing across the apron and onto the taxiways. There were no waving servicemen and women outside the windows, no fighter jet escort waiting overhead; they were just another military flight about to depart, bound for who knew where.

The plane accelerated along the runway and lifted into the night sky. Coffman craned her neck as the aeroplane banked to the south. She looked down at the carpet of lights that stretched away into the distance, but she couldn't recognise any familiar landmarks. Washington DC was falling behind her, as was the life of power and privilege she'd so recently led.

She looked away from the window and saw Foley watching her from across the aisle. His face was expressionless but his jaw was still clenched with a simmering anger.

What is your goddamn problem? she wanted to ask. Did he not realise that her reason for being no longer existed? That the fire of ambition that had burned inside her for so long had been quenched? That she'd been unequivocally defeated? Or perhaps it was *his* desire that fuelled the hateful stare —

And then it struck her, a sudden realisation.

There was another game afoot here, some other agenda.

Coffman's political antenna quivered, and she thought back to those final minutes in the Oval Office, the furtive looks cast her way, the urgent whispers. It wasn't anger she'd witnessed, it was *frustration*. Foley was guilty of it too, which explained his belligerence, likewise the lesbian and her Secret Service colleagues. So, there was a final hand to be played.

Her spirits soared momentarily, but the cold steel of reality cut into her wrists. No, she had to appear cowed, vanquished, while keeping her eyes and ears open, because she couldn't shake the growing feeling that all was not lost.

The cabin lights remained dimmed. Foley snapped on his overhead and busied himself with a newspaper. The other agents did the same, settling in for the flight.

Coffman turned towards the window, not to admire the view, or to take one last look at the city they were leaving behind.

It was to hide the smile that crept across her mouth.

HE CHECKED HIS G-SHOCK AND WAITED FOR THE DIGITS TO ROLL over to midday. Then he waited another thirty seconds before speed-dialling the number. The man answered it almost immediately.

'Speak.'

'My name is Gary. I have intel for you that you may find useful.'

'I was expecting someone else.'

'He gave me your number. He's in DC right now, by the phone. He says hi. He hopes you're taking care of yourself.'

'Who are you?'

'A friend.'

'That so?'

'Uh-huh. And friends help each other out, right? Especially those who've been through OTC.'

More silence. 'When?'

'A while ago now. I've moved on since then. To Peary.'

The voice was still guarded. 'So, what have you got for me, *Gary*?'

'A number. I'm going to text it to you. You'll understand.'

'Okay.'

'And do yourself a favour. Memorise it, then ditch the burner.'

'Who says I'm using a burner?'

'Our mutual friend.'

He heard a truck pass by at speed, and imagined the man on the other end of the call standing by a highway somewhere. It would've been easy to trace, find out his location, but not this time. Not this man.

'Stand by for the text. And one more thing…'

'Yeah?'

'Good luck, brother.'

He ended the call, then sent the text message. He powered the phone off, popped the SIM out and snapped it in two. One half he dropped onto the floor of the bar and the other in a drain by the sidewalk two blocks away. The phone went into a trash can on the corner of Main and Cherry, then he walked to the Greyhound stop outside the Virginia State University. The bus arrived less than fifteen minutes later, and he climbed aboard.

'Where ya headed?' asked the driver.

'Williamsburg.'

'That's twelve bucks.'

He paid cash and moved to the back of the bus. He took off his coat, rolled it up and wedged it between his head and the window. Williamsburg wasn't far, just over an hour away, but it had been a long day.

A long few months, Mike Savage corrected himself.

As the bus rumbled through Richmond and headed south, his motivations still troubled him. He'd always worked within the law, had never questioned his chain of command, so today was a first for him. He wasn't a crusader, far from it, but sometimes it just came down to right and wrong. He knew the consequences of his actions too, but he doubted it would ever get that far. For those who knew, the news would come as a blessing. For Mike Savage, it would mean justice had been served.

At the end of the day, he could live with that.

When Felipe Gomez finally ran out of food, he'd started stealing from his neighbours.

He'd raided the Harrison's house first, because he hadn't heard a peep from the place since that first night. Felipe assumed that they'd been caught out somewhere and hadn't made it home, and he'd felt guilty as hell as he'd emptied their refrigerator and cupboards of food, but as the days turned into weeks, guilt stopped being an issue. It was all about survival, nothing more.

He'd seen helicopters loaded with civilians fly over his suburb. That had lasted for the first several days, and after that he didn't see any more rescue flights. He'd seen others ignore the emergency broadcasts, load up their cars and drive off, only to be swamped by hordes of fast-moving infected.

His wife Consuelo and twelve year old son Felix had held it together at first, but as the weeks passed, Consuelo had become increasingly desperate and tearful, and Felix had withdrawn into himself. When hundreds of infected passed right outside their house one night, trampling across his yard and thumping against his front door, it had taken all of Felipe's powers of reassurance to stop them both from screaming hysterically. Help was coming, he'd assured them. When it didn't, Consuelo turned on him and called him a liar. Felix withdrew further into himself. Felipe was losing his family.

Things got worse.

Felipe spent three careful days spelling out *HELP* on the roof of his home with torn sheets, only to have it buried by a snow storm. Without power, the cold December nights were black and terrifying, and they would huddle in the dark, listening to the infected crunching through the snow outside, snarling and barking. When he saw footprints around his doors and windows the next morning, Felipe knew they were running out of time.

He'd tried to persuade Consuelo to leave, but she'd seen the neighbours die too. The radio had convinced her that staying home was the safest option.

The snows thawed and the food ran out. Felipe started scavenging further afield. He broke into a house a block away and didn't see the infected senior dragging herself across the floor until she'd grabbed his ankle. He'd screamed, and that brought a couple more through the back door. Felipe had escaped through the bathroom window. He'd made it home, but only just.

They lost weight and Felipe had started feeling listless. Anything he could scavenge was given to little Felix, but even his son's face was starting to look hollow. Consuelo still wouldn't leave. Felipe started to lose hope.

Christmas came and went.

Felipe broke up some furniture and made a fire in the back yard under a clear blue January sky. He waited until the sun had set to light it, and then they watched it burn. When morning came Felipe fed it some more lumber, primarily the wood panelling from his lounge. When that was exhausted he broke up the dining room table and chairs and threw them on top. They had no food anyway, so what the hell.

It was Felix who saw the drone. He'd woken his father from an exhausted daytime slumber and pointed to the back yard. The drone was pretty big, a lot of rotors, but it was pretty quiet too. It dropped a box on the patio and then it flew away. Felipe thought he was dreaming. Consuelo told him to go get the box.

He snuck out of the house. The back yard was ringed with fencing but it wouldn't hold a sustained attack for long. He picked up the box, a green plastic container about two feet long and a foot wide. After the door was barricaded and the curtains drawn, Felipe snapped the latches and opened the box.

Consuelo cried. Felipe cried too, and so did Felix. That night they feasted on MRE's, bottled water and vitamin pills. The candy they gave to their son, who'd spoken for the first time in over a week. There was a radio in the box too, a walkie-talkie type deal. They huddled in the storage cupboard and Felipe switched it on. He pressed the transmit switch and asked if anyone was out there. When a voice answered and told them they were coming for them the next morning, they cried again.

They slept soundly that night, or as soundly as a family could with packs of killers roaming the neighbourhood. After the sun had risen, the voice on the radio told them to walk a hundred and fifty yards to the junction of Memphis Avenue and 63rd Street. Consuelo's fear returned and the voice worked hard to assure her that their short journey would be watched by an overhead drone. The voice also told her that her son would die if they didn't leave.

They stepped outside the house as a family for the first time in weeks. They crossed the yard to the back gate. Felipe checked the deserted alleyway beyond, and the voice told him to keep moving. The alleyway was long and dangerously exposed, and Felipe's heart hammered. He'd never owned a gun but he made a promise to himself that if they made it out, he'd never be without one again. He cringed at every creaking door, every shutter that swung back and forth in the wind. The voice in his ear told him when to move and when to stand very still.

They took cover between two cars at the junction of Memphis and 63rd. When Consuelo heard the sound of an approaching helicopter, she wanted to stand up and wave. Felipe did too, but the voice ordered them to stay low. The drone was watching.

The helicopter came in low and fast across the rooftops. The pilot hot-dogged it, flaring to a hover over the junction and almost touching the ground with his tail rotor. Then the skids hit the road and the voice was telling Felipe to run.

Felipe broke cover, swinging Felix into his arms and grabbing Consuelo's hand. The big grey helicopter sat in the middle of the intersection, its rotors hammering trees and bushes, the noise deafening. Uniforms waved from the open doorway, and a soldier behind a black visor sat behind a doorway mini-gun, sweeping the barrel left and right. The rotor-wind battered Felipe's body. Felix felt like a concrete weight in his arms, Consuelo like an anchor dragging behind him. Then he saw them, beyond the helicopter, a dozen infected, some clothed in rags, others naked, sprinting towards the intersection. Fear surged through his body, charging. The uniforms waved and yelled. One of them jumped down and ran to him, snatching Felix from his arms. Consuelo screamed.

Hands grabbed him, ripping at his clothes, at his flesh. Other hands dragged him inside the helicopter and then his stomach was left behind as the helicopter rose like an express elevator. Consuelo lay on top of him, sobbing, shaking. The soldiers made them sit and strapped them in. Consuelo wrapped her arms around Felix and cried. Felipe held his wife's hand and looked down. Hundreds of infected were converging on the intersection, their hands clawing the air, but they were too late. The aircraft dipped its nose and headed east.

As they climbed higher, Felipe saw for the first time the devastation caused by the outbreak. Downtown was gone, the heart of the city now a shattered, blackened pile of rubble. There were no lights anywhere, no vehicles, no life. Except for the infected. They were everywhere, moving in packs, large and small.

The helicopter passed over Highway 289 which resembled the aftermath of a murderous demolition derby, the lanes choked with blackened cars and corpses. Flocks of black-winged birds took to the air, their scavenging interrupted. Felipe knew how they felt.

The city fell behind them and the wall rose out of the early morning mist, a huge green barrier thirty feet high that stretched from north to south as far as the eye could see. They flew over shimmering fields of razor wire and then the wall was behind them.

The aircraft slowed and began to descend, sinking lower until another field came into view, one lost beneath a city of tents, portacabins and equipment parks, all systematically dissected by a network of muddy roads. And there were soldiers everywhere.

The helo settled onto one of a dozen landing pads and Felipe shook the hand of every crew member, including the hot-dog pilot who remained impassive behind his black visor. They boarded a humvee that drove them to a reception centre where they gave their names and other personal information. Then they were escorted to another huge, heated tent some distance away. There were other civilians there too, hundreds of them, sitting at tables, eating breakfast, talking quietly. People smiled at them as they passed, and children laughed and ran about, doing what children do best.

A big African-American soldier in a spotless camouflage uniform smiled as he approached them. He held a clipboard in his hand and he ruffled Felix's hair. His name tag said *SINCLAIR*.

'How's the little fella doing?'

Felipe shrugged. 'Okay,' he answered, shaking his head.

The soldier got the message. 'Don't worry, we've got a lot of medical support here. He's going to be fine. Be playing with the other kids real soon.'

'Lot of people here,' Felipe observed, looking around the room.

The soldier's smile faded. 'Not as many as we'd hoped. We've been bringing survivors out for weeks but then they pretty much dried up. You guys might be the last ones.' He gave Felipe a look that said, *you're a lucky sonofabitch.*

'How many?' Felipe asked quietly.

The soldier lowered his voice. 'A hundred-thousand, esti-mated. Another hundred-thousand infected. Where were you when it started?'

'South Plains Mall. I'm a restaurant manager. A few of us managed to escape in a pickup.' Felipe was reminded of that night, those men in that vehicle, and wondered if they'd made it too.

'South Plains? That's Ground Zero.' The soldier recali-brated and smiled. 'Go get yourselves something to eat while I arrange your accommodations. I'll assign you a family unit, afford you a little privacy.'

'How long will we be here?' Felipe asked.

The soldier shrugged. 'As long as it takes.'

Felipe sat his family down at the end of a long row of picnic tables. He got a couple of trays of food from the hotplate and they sat in silence for a long time, watching Felix eat, gently stroking his hair, all of them lost in their own thoughts.

There was a crash of metal and Felipe spun around. One of the cooks had dropped something behind the hotplates. He turned back again, trying to control his heart rate and stop his hands from shaking. He closed his eyes and forced himself to accept that they were safe now, all of them, for the first time in a very long time.

Consuelo reached across the table and took his hands in hers. She squeezed them and smiled. 'Thank you for saving us.'

Felipe was too overwhelmed to reply. Instead he held her hands as the tears rolled down the gaunt hollows of his bearded face.

PERMANENT VACATION

Amy Coffman stared up at the ceiling, at the brown stain above her bed.

Melting snow must've seeped beneath the shingle roof. Soon it would begin to drip and she would have to move her bed again. She wouldn't complain, nor would she expect them to do anything about it, but that's how things worked around here. It was better than being in a real prison.

She swung her legs off the bed and stood up, wrapping a thin grey blanket around her shoulders. Her accommodations were not just austere, they were *frontier,* yet she had become accustomed to the creaking wooden floors, the hard mattress on the single bed, the perpetual drafts. There were plus sides, however. She'd learned to master the art of fire building, and she made sure that one burned in the bedroom grate for most of the day. She stood at the window for a few moments, her eyes squinting at the bright field of snow that stretched away towards a distant forest. Sometimes she would pull up a chair and sit at that window for hours, watching a world that had passed her by, reminding herself that things could've worked out so much worse. But not today.

Today she had a visitor.

350

She stepped out into the hallway and shuffled into what passed as a bathroom. She sat down on the cold seat and peed, the blanket wrapped tightly around her. She ran the tap and washed her hands in icy water. She studied her face in the mirror, fingering the lines around her eyes that she was no longer keep at bay by expensive creams and serums. She ran a hand across her shaved head. Her hair was getting long, and soon one of her mute guards would sit her down and shave it again. She hoped.

Because they always came for her after a fresh clipping. They would crowd inside her cabin, strap her to a gurney and inject her. When she woke again she would be far from her wilderness prison. There would be central heating and thick carpets underfoot. There would be coffee served in china cups. There would be hot showers and soft toilet paper. She would dress in her own clothes and have make-up applied, and then she would tie an expensive silk scarf around her head. She would be given another sedative, one that slowed her speech and physical movements because they couldn't take the chance. Then they would escort her to a waiting limousine and whisk her to whatever ceremony they'd decided she would attend. There she would shake hands and smile weakly, but she wasn't allowed to have private conversations with anyone.

That was fine with Coffman. She cared nothing for the sympathetic smiles, the furtive whispers and the pitying glances. To ride in a limousine with a police escort, to dress in fine clothes and eat real food, to once again be called *Madam President*, was all she had left, and she was grateful. And once the cameras had captured the walking stick, the shaved head, the overlarge sunglasses and trembling hands, she would be transported back to the cabin at the edge of the world. It was a compromise she could live with, but the excursions were becoming less frequent, and it troubled her.

She dressed in thick corduroy trousers and a roll-neck

jumper, then jammed her feet into thick rubber boots. In the cramped lounge-cum-kitchenette, she made an instant coffee and sat down at the small table. She was hungry, but she was sick to her stomach of MRE's. She glanced up at the ticking clock on the log wall; almost ten a.m. Almost time.

She stood up and tipped the coffee dregs into the sink. She tugged on a quilted parka and pulled an orange beanie hat over her head. She opened the door and stepped out onto the porch, where the freezing air wrapped itself around her. It was cold, but she was getting used to it. It was summer she dreaded, where the air would be thick with insects, and where multi-legged abominations would lurk in every dark, dusty corner of the cabin. That's if she was still here, of course.

She slipped on a pair of cheap sunglasses as the bright sun reflected off the snow. She was convinced she was in Alaska. The valley was ringed by forests, and on clear days she could see jagged mountains the horizon. Big moose-like things often trotted across the valley, and she'd heard wolves too. Birds of prey drifted overhead, screeching and calling, or whatever it was that birds of prey did. There was an abundance of wildlife, but identifying them wasn't her strong suit. She'd thought about asking for a book on the subject because books were all she was allowed. There was no TV, no radio, just a dusty collection of American and European literary classics on a shelf in the lounge. Coffman had actually read a couple, and while she had never been a fiction fan, she appreciated good writing. At night, after she'd eaten her freeze-dried rations, she would sit at the table and read by the light of the lantern while the wind moaned across the cabin.

Other times she would sit for hours just watching the fire burn in the grate, imagining what life was like for those early pioneering families who'd made the trip out west. She imagined the hardships of building a home, of raising a family, the quiet desperation of the women as they'd waved their menfolk off to hunt and trade, the crushing loneliness that lasted for days, weeks, months on end, the dangerous challenges of weather and illness and a multitude of other threats that Coffman could barely comprehend. They'd fought to survive, to carve out a life. And often they died. How easily society had forgotten where they'd come from.

The crunch of snow brought her back to the present. Two men in white arctic gear and carrying automatic rifles stamped past her cabin.

'Good morning,' she waved from the porch.

They glanced in her direction before continuing their patrol. They were not allowed to speak to her, she knew that, but it was always worth a try. She hadn't had a proper conversation since her interrogation. During that time she hadn't stopped talking, eager to carve out some sort of deal, but once it had been struck, no one spoke to her anymore, not unless they were giving her orders. Her captors lived in the modern, heated modular buildings that surrounded her dilapidated cabin. She'd thought about setting fire to her accommodations in the hope that they might trade her up, but the ruse would be discovered, of that, she had no doubt. The cabin was damp and draughty, but it was better than any prison.

That's where Erik was. A deep, dark hole, Foley had told her, from which he would never return. The news had broken her heart. She'd demanded fairer treatment for the man, only to be told to keep her mouth shut or find herself in a deeper, darker hole than her erstwhile Chief of Staff. She'd considered calling their bluff, but as she'd shivered beneath her blankets in the darkness before the dawn, her instinct for self-preservation prevailed. She would say nothing more and live instead with her memories. And when she thought of Erik in his own private hell, she would banish those thoughts immediately.

'Coffman.'

Her head snapped around and she saw Foley approaching. He wore ski trousers and a dark parka with a US flag patch on his shoulder. His hair was a little longer and the beard suited him, she decided. She might've lost a lot of things but not her eye for a good looking man. The *only* man who would speak to her too. Her smile was wide and genuine.

'Hi, Foley.'

'Let's walk.'

She had to stretch her legs to catch him up, and they walked side-by-side as they headed towards the tree line, their breath fogging on the crisp air. Foley's arrival meant something was afoot. A new trip she imagined. Foley always travelled with her, always made sure she played her part. He was also a reminder of what awaited her in North Dakota; an abandoned nuclear missile silo, two hundred feet deep and as cold, dark and damp as any grave. Foley was life and death rolled into one. Coffman was still terrified of him.

She never initiated conversation or made small talk. That was still *verboten* in Foley's rulebook, so she trudged across the field in silence, focussing instead on lifting one knee after the other. They were approaching the tree line when he eventually spoke.

'You're going on another trip.'

Her heart leapt. 'Where?'

'DC. Arlington, in fact. One of the Joint Chiefs died. The funeral's on Wednesday. You're going to show your face.'

'What day is it today?'

'Monday. We're leaving after lunch. There's some weather coming in. We need to get ahead of it.'

Coffman could've wrapped her arms around him. Instead, she said nothing and kept walking.

'You'll be going to Texas in a few weeks,' he continued. 'They're holding an open-air memorial service outside Lubbock. The president will be in attendance, as will the world's media. You'll be there too, for a few days.'

'Okay.' She tried to keep her voice neutral. What she really wanted to do was scream with joy.

The world darkened as they entered the forest, the snowy path meandering through ancient pines. As they moved deeper inside, the frozen air became heavy and oppressive, the silence like a thick blanket. Foley's voice broke it.

'You'll be expected to say something at the service, just a few words. There'll be a Chinese delegation there too, and they'll be watching carefully. They may even want to meet you. That's something we'll try to avoid but neither will we run the risk of offending them. This is a big deal, Coffman, so you'd better start preparing yourself.'

'I won't let you down,' she assured him. Foley said nothing, and she decided to push her luck. 'I know I can't have a TV or a newspaper or anything, but I was wondering how things were? Politically, I mean.'

'Not going the way you planned,' Foley told her.

'And the Chinese?'

'You mean, are they still pissed about killing millions of their own people to stop a virus that you unleashed? Yeah, pretty much.'

'That wasn't really — '

'Things aren't so rosy for the people of Lubbock either. That's a couple of hundred thousand American lives you've destroyed right there. They're eating each other now, the infected that are left. Cannibalism, tribal warfare, hunting in packs - it's horrific, and you're responsible for all of it. And don't get me started on the Baghdad embassy. I knew a lot of people in Iraq, many of them friends. You're lucky you're still breathing, Coffman, remember that.'

The words tumbled out before she could stop them. 'How could I forget? You remind me every time I — '

Foley grabbed the hood of her jacket and yanked her backwards. He spun her around and slammed her against a tree, knocking the breath from her lungs. Heavy clumps of snow tumbled from the branches above. Foley shook her violently.

'Don't you *ever* talk back to me again. Ever. Do you understand?'

'I'm sorry,' Coffman panted. 'It's frustration, that's all. I never get to speak to anyone.'

'Boo-fucking-hoo,' Foley sneered. He jabbed a finger in her face. 'Remember this; the only reason you're alive is to keep this country together and the Chinese off the scent. They'll never stop looking for the people responsible for Shanghai, and if they somehow discover that the President of the United States was involved, two things would happen; first, they would nuke us, and secondly, the resulting conflict would tear this planet apart, so they keep you alive and visible, and for that you'd better be goddamn grateful. Your opinions are worth shit to me so keep them to yourself, understood?'

'Understood,' Coffman echoed breathlessly.

Foley took a step back. His eyes narrowed as he studied her face. 'Don't get complacent, Coffman. Situations can change, remember that.'

Coffman dropped her eyes. Foley was right, the fake illness and fragile public appearances could only last so long. Either way, her usefulness was finite. Sooner rather than later her *cancer* would end her. Then a thought struck her — *they'd do it after Lubbock.*

The timing would work, she reasoned. She would attend the ceremony, exchange a few slurred pleasantries with the Chinese delegation, and Beijing would be placated. The event would mark a turning point, and the world would finally move on. In its wake, Amy Coffman's health would deteriorate. She would disappear from public life, and then, sometime later, the news would be broadcast around the world…

Former President Amelia Coffman passed away this morning…

She was running out of time. She wasn't ready to die.

'May I ask a question?'

'What is it?'

'Bob Blake cut a deal, right? The man who was *really* behind this whole thing. He managed to walk. Why?'

Foley shook his head. 'Blake's dead. You're right, he cut a deal, at least that's what we let him believe. He gave us everything in return for a period of house arrest and assessment. He had some great footage of you, by the way. At Rock Creek? That meeting with Aswad?'

Coffman smiled. 'I knew he had something. Men like Bob Blake cover all the angles. What happened to him?'

'He was forced to step down from Kroll, and we kept him under surveillance twenty-four-seven. We had to be sure there was no one else out there, no one else who knew. Your girl Baranski corroborated a lot of it too.'

'I told you everything,' Coffman insisted.

'Your word doesn't count for shit anymore. Blake was similarly self-absorbed, which is why he didn't see it coming. Once we'd squeezed him dry we gave him a heart attack. He was dead before he hit the floor of his own bathroom.'

Coffman smiled without humour. 'Poor Bob. What about Karen?'

'She's still assisting us. She thinks she's going to cut a deal too. She's dead wrong about that.'

Coffman brushed the snow from the front of her jacket. 'Is that how it'll go for me, Foley? A heart attack? I grant you, it's quick and clean, and you won't have to go to the trouble of —'

The blow knocked her on her backside. Her head swam and a cloud of tiny feathers drifted on the air. Foley was dancing around her like a boxer, a blurry figure that yelled at her unintelligibly. The air sang and Foley danced away.

She held onto the tree and stood up, swaying like a newborn foal on watery legs. Then something hit her in the back and she fell against the trunk. She wrapped her arms around it, but her legs failed her as wooden splinters exploded just above her head. She dropped to her knees. Her head swam and she held on as tightly as she could, trying to catch her breath. An insect buzzed in her ear and tree bark exploded in her face. She blinked and looked up. The treetops swayed and hissed in the wind. In the sky above them, a bird circled, screeching. Foley was screeching too. Coffman decided that listening was too much effort.

She leaned her forehead against the rough bark. It was getting hard to breathe and she could taste blood in her mouth. Something had happened to her, something serious. They would have to take her to the hospital. That was an opportunity, wasn't it? An angle, another card to be played? *Yes,* she decided.

She would endure like she had her whole life. Because Amy Coffman was a survivor.

She never felt the bullet that blew her head apart.

HE SLUNG THE G28 RIFLE OVER HIS SHOULDER AND HEADED UP through the trees towards the ridgeline, lumbering through the snow, ducking beneath branches, weaving left and right. The drifts were much thicker up here, and he had to work hard to put distance between him and his kill.

It had been a tough shot too, a downhill trajectory of over two hundred yards through densely packed trees and gusting winds, but not impossible. He'd taken harder shots in his time and still made the kill. The easy shot would've been down at the cabin, but that would've meant taking on the cameras and the passive sensors, so he'd stayed high up on the ridge. Besides, the trajectory was much flatter lower down and that increased the possibility of hitting one of the security team, and he wasn't going to risk that. Enough good men had died already, most of them at Coffman's hand. He wasn't going to add to that body count. So he'd watched and waited. She came walking towards him on day three.

He didn't know who the guy was, CIA or military he assumed, so one of the good guys. He tracked them from above, saw the path they were taking and got into position ahead of them. As he'd watched them through his scope, Coffman had said something and the guy had reacted, slamming her against a tree. His G28 wedged in the crook of a tree branch, he'd taken a snapshot and registered the hit. True, he'd missed a couple of times but only just. The orange beanie had been a mistake, for her at least, and the kill shot had been a clean one.

There was no return fire, and by the time help arrived, he'd be long gone.

He had a tough hike ahead of him, about eighteen miles of forest, hills and valleys to where his kayak was hidden close to the Lamar River. There was also a storm coming, and the sky to the north was already darkening, but it would also hamper any search and cover most of his tracks. Once in the kayak, he would paddle south, stopping a few miles short of Route 212 where his Toyota Land Cruiser was parked off-road and well camouflaged. Then he would drive east before turning south.

The mission was over.

And for the first time in his life, Kenny Chase had no idea what lay ahead.

He wasn't sure if there'd be roadblocks somewhere ahead, and he pondered what he would do if it came to that. Put his hands up, probably. Get his day in court. Tell the world what had happened in Baghdad.

If he lasted that long.

Or keep his mouth shut, stay off the grid and keep moving because the world was still an uncertain place. But he had friends now, he knew that much. Ray Wilson for one, and the guy who'd called him, who'd sent him the grid reference of

Coffman's location. Maybe one day he'd get to buy that guy a beer. He hoped so because he didn't want to hide in the shadows forever. Sooner or later he'd have to step out into the light, face his own destiny. But not yet. For now, he'd just keep moving.

As the wind gusted and the first flakes of snow began to fall, Chase crested the ridge and headed down into the valley beyond, almost invisible in his arctic-white tactical suit. He moved fast, his energy boundless, the burden that he'd carried for so long suddenly lifted. He felt free. And to stay free he had to keep moving.

Twenty-four hours and five hundred miles later he'd be able to rest. He would find a decent motel and then he'd sleep, knowing that the nightmares that had plagued him for so long were finally banished.

Instead, Kenny Chase would dream.

And in that dream, he would stand with his Delta brothers and smile once more.

END

HAVE YOUR SAY

Did you enjoy *End Zone*?

I hope you did.

If you could spare a moment to rate the book on Amazon, or leave a review, I would be very much obliged.

Many thanks for your time.

Printed in Great Britain
by Amazon